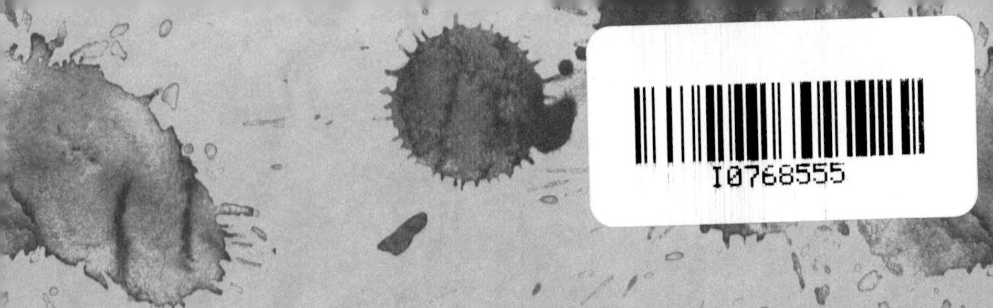

THE BLUE ROSE

FATAL FLORALS DUET:
BOOK 1

K. CARDELLA

Editing by Inked Edits Developmental
Cover Design & Interior Formatting by Disturbed Valkyrie Designs

NOT CROSS
POLICE LINE DO NO

CONTENT WARNING

THIS IS AN ADULT ONLY DARK ROMANCE, THE CONTENT IS INTENDED FOR PEOPLE OVER THE AGE OF 18. THIS BOOK HAS CONTENT WARNINGS THAT ARE, BUT NOT LIMITED TO.

- Torture
- Knife Play
- Blood Play
- Dub-Con
- Eating Disorder
- Body Shaming
- Stalking
- Primal Play
- Death Of A Parent
- Bullying
- Finger Breaking
- Burning Alive
- Dismemberment
- Disordered Weight And Body Thoughts
- Masterbation
- Cutting Up Body
- Anal
- Use Of A Chainsaw
- Mental Health
- Emotional Abuse
- Violence

- Blood And Gore
- Murder
- Terminal Illness
- Sexually Explicit Scenes
- Slut-Shaming
- Knife Violence
- Anxiety And Depression
- Grief And Loss Depiction
- Edging

PLAYLIST

Don't You Want Me Baby - The Human League
I Will Survive - Gloria Gaynor
Nightmare - Avenged Sevenfold
Undead - Hollywood Undead
Shackles - Steven Rodriguez
The Drug In Me Is You - Falling In Reverse
Bad Feeling - Jagwar Twin
Zombified - Falling In Reverse
Bad Things - iPrevail
The Summoning - Sleep Token
Popular Monster - Falling in Reverse
Disguise - Motionless In White
Freaky - Bryce Savage
My Friends - Black Veil Brides
Fuckin' Perfect - Pink
Trust Is A Cruel Friend - Tessa Jackson
I'm Your Fool - Katie Hargrove
Gravedigger - Livingston
True Friends - Bring Me The Horizon
Devil Knows - Armen Paul
Can't Get Enough - Jaxson Gamble

Can You Feel My Heart - Bring Me The Horizon
Iconic - Jason Gamble
Stockholm Syndrome - Chris Caulfield
Victim - Halflives
Like You Mean It - Steven Rodriguez
Hips To Be Scared - Ice Nine Kills
Fix Me - 10 Years
In The Shadows You'll hear my Voice - Kirra47
Monster - Lady Gaga

To everyone who becomes who they
were always meant to be in the darkness.

ONE
ASTER

When you're a serial killer, it's so easy to get caught. One wrong move, and you're in jail for the rest of your life. Well, when you grow up with serial killers as your parents, you learn not to make the same mistakes.

I'm sitting in my foldable chair, one leg over the other, holding the newspaper of my last kill. Singing in my brown leather apron, "Don't You Want Me Baby" to my newest victim who fell privy into my web of lies.

Not taking my eyes off of the page, "She looks so beautiful laid under the tree, for all to see." I turn the paper over so my newest lamb can see, "This will be you soon enough, gaining the attention you would never get alive." My newest lamb starts wiggling her body trying to get out of her restraints. I ignore her and go back to my paper. When the papers write an article of my latest kill, I always make sure to grab a copy. Never reading it until a new lamb is on my table. I like to reminisce while I get ready to slaughter my next lamb.

My cool down period is between two to three months, before I start hunting again. The newspaper sits in its special spot with the rest of them. In the bottom drawer of my dresser in my bedroom. When I know it is the night to prepare my lambs, I take the paper out and place it on the workbench in my shed, ready for when I strap my lambs down. It's a pre-kill ritual of mine, one that I must do, ensuring nothing will go wrong, during and after.

The room we're in is dimly lit with a light hanging directly above the stainless steel table. I cover the walls in plastic when bringing my lambs in for the slaughter.

Doing this assures for an easy clean up.

I started building this workplace when I was given the home. I tore down the barn where my first victim was rescued, I didn't want any reminders of that night, or my parents. It is half a mile down the dirt road leading past my house. Looking like a normal shed from the outside, just a little bigger. When you walk inside there are tools lined up, for when I get to work. Any normal person would use these tools for handy work, or a project to build something. I also use these tools for my side hobbies, but they're mostly used for my little lambs.

After my parents were caught and I was of age I was given a letter telling me instructions only I would understand, revealing to me where they hid it all. The letter read:

Our Little Fox,

The time has come, where you are finally ready to finish what we tried to start on your tenth birth-day. Oh how we wish we could've seen you grow, be there to help shape you into the man we hope you have become. We know you were always watching us work when you were supposed to be sleeping. Even though you never got to have a lamb for yourself, we hope all the watching paid off. We left you the house you grew up in and all the pelt from the lambs. There should be enough pelt that you won't *have to ever worry about anything ever again. Take the pelt to the local trapper and get the money in cash. Remember what we taught you about using cash over credit cards. We never meant to leave you, your birthday gift is what ultimately got us caught. Please don't blame yourself, it is not your fault and we hope you know that. We love you dearly and just remember we are always with you.*

Love, Mom and Dad

I BROUGHT EVERYTHING I COULD TO A PAWN SHOP PER THEIR instructions and turned it to cash. I took what they said to heart, and blamed my birthday gift. The first lamb that got away, the one that got my parents caught is how I chose my lambs after that.

You never forget your first.

I look down at my newest victim, stroking my fingers across her face.

With her mouth taped and tears streaming from her blood-shot eyes, she had never looked more beautiful. Blood is leaking through her clothes where I have made my cuts. Her dark hair is draped over the edge of the table where she lays strapped to. Her arms are bound on either side of her head above her. Her feet are spread apart and fastened down as well. There is one last buckle going over her stomach securing her nice and tight for the slaughter.

My god she is beautiful, struggling for her life.

With my radio playing in the background, I can barely hear her muffled cries through the tape that covers her pretty mouth. *It really is a pity I can't hear her screams.* I turn off the radio and stalk back over to the table, looking over her fear struck face. I reach down and rip the tape off and immediately she spews profanities at me.

"You're a fucking psycho, I trusted you."

"Ah now, that was your first mistake, trusting this fox in sheep's clothing"

It's not hard to trust a pretty face like mine. Most people use their looks to their advantage in life, I'm no different. I use mine to lure my victims to me, promising them a night they're never going to forget and one I never will as well.

"Please, please". She begs "My family…" She chokes on a sob as she struggles to finish her sentence. "They'll be looking for me."

"Now, Sasha, why would you lie to me? I know that isn't true; you're an orphan just like me". I lift my knife up, looking at my warped reflection in the blade, then point it directly at her. "I hate liars."

I choose my victims wisely, just as I was taught. Target women who won't be missed when they go missing. They have to have no one. The prey I prefer to hunt are the curvy, thick girls, mostly because their insecurities feed the beast in me.

Bigger girls usually have this preconception that a man who looks like me would never even look their way. With the way the media in this world portrays and sells beauty, they believe it. So, this makes the bigger girls easier to capture. All of their defenses are down, the moment I give them any type of attention, whether it be a look or even a simple hello. Complimenting and talking to them makes it easier to bring them back to my shed to enjoy the slaughter.

I usually meet them at a run down bar, where there are no cameras. Give them the number to my burner phone, take them out on another date to secure their trust in me. I Invite them back to my place, always being the one to drive, and never giving them my address. Once we get to my place, I park in front of my home and just as they're turning to get out of the car, I slip the needle full of ketamine into their neck. Then I drive to the shed and begin my work.

I have three rules when hunting and killing:

1. I never kill men.
2. I never kiss, touch, or fuck my lambs.
3. My lambs are never allowed into my home.

I will never break these rules.

Her eyes widen in fear, and she starts to ramble more lies.

"No! No, that isn't true, my family loves me, and-"

I take the knife and slice it slowly across her thigh, eliciting a bloodcurdling scream and making my point evident. I hate liars and I hate it even more when my lambs lie while I'm trying to do my work.

"Now I know I just told you not to lie to me, but here we go again. Another lie, I don't want to hurt you"

She spits in my face and laughs in a mocking way. "Ha! Now who's telling lies?"

I click my tongue several times, turning to grab the cloth from behind me off my workbench, wiping the spit off of my face. "No not a lie Sasha I don't want to hurt you, I *have* to hurt you, there is a difference" It was engraved in me at a young age, you could say I was groomed for this. Killing is like breathing for me, it keeps me alive.

While most serial killers start killing at a young age, and usually with animals, I did not. My mother would watch scary movies with me, pointing out everything that would prepare me for my first kill with them. Then, while they were slaughtering their victims, I would sneak out to the shed and watch through the hole I made. I never got to kill with my parents, but I eventually had my first and nothing has been the same. Nothing will ever quench my thirst for blood like my little lambs.

All the blood leaves her face, and she turns as white as a ghost. "I don't understand, why? Why me, what did I do?!" she screams, trying to hold back her cries. "I thought you liked me, I thought you wanted me?"

This is the best part, when they start to ask why me, and all I do is smile.

She looks absolutely petrified and stutters, "I know you're not whoever," she bobs her head up and down at me. "This is."

I brush her hair out of her face. "Oh but that is where you are wrong, I am everything you see before you, my dear lamb, and I do want you…" I bring my face towards her so she can feel my breath as I whisper, "On my table, under my knife."

She spews venom from her eyes. "Don't call me that, you fucking psycho, just let me go. I promise I won't tell anyone. Ever."

"Oh, my little lamb, I am never letting you go, that's why they call me The Morbid Monet."

Her eyes widen in fear, as she recognizes the name that the media has given me. The notorious Massachusetts killer, thirty-two victims, and still counting. "Nooo, please N-" she screams and I place the tape back over her mouth stifling her screams and continue singing my song to myself and slicing up her perfect little body.

I cut her with a hospital grade scapel, my movements precise and my slices just deep enough for my little lamb to feel the burn of pain. The way I cut makes the authorities and media think I must be a doctor or at least have medical training. Their ignorance makes it easier for me. I am not a doctor, nor do I have any ties to one. I learned restraint and control with practice, eventually becoming as good as a surgeon.

Perhaps I missed my calling, though I'd argue I have more fun.

I climb on top of her and watch her eyes widen in fear. She tries, and fails to buck me off of her. Little that will do when I'm straddling her and she's tied down with no escape.

"Shhh, hush now, it's okay" I caress her head, trying to

soothe her. "You will soon meet your maker, and never have to worry about this fox ever again."

I bring my knife up, look her in the eyes, savoring the fear in them. I take a deep breath and whisper, "Goodnight Sasha".

I bring my knife down into her heart, ending her life. I always end my lambs lives by plunging a knife into their heart to show I do not have one. The meaning behind it is just for me.

When her body goes limp beneath me, I get off.

I turn back on the radio, "I Will Survive" comes on and I chuckle at the irony.

I cut her out of the pink crop top with the words "ironically hot" on them. Her breasts are bare for me to see. At least she wore a fitting shirt for her last time with me, she was anything but hot.

Cutting off her booty shorts next, I see she wore a red G-string just for me. A lamb falling perfectly into this fox's trap. A date she was expecting but would never get, when she arrived hours earlier. Poor thing, probably thought she was finally going to get laid, little did she know I would lay her down forever.

I smirk, slipping them off and putting those on my desk next to her rose.

All of my lambs get their own roses. I take a white rose before every kill and place the petals into blue dyed water. I place it onto my work station and it sits there while I break them apart, and it watches as I put them back together. The slaughter, and the resurrection. The perfect circle of life and death.

After cutting off her clothing and cleaning off all the blood, it's time to sew her back up. All of my lambs must go out of this world the way they came in, and it's my job to lead them there. Grabbing my sutures, I start to stitch all the wounds I have inflicted. I cut them up to see the pain in their eyes, to revel in it, but I have to stitch them back and clean them up to paint them anew. Having open wounds ruins the integrity of my canvas.

It would be a shame to ruin my favorite part.

Starting with the face first, I close her eyes and repaint them on. Then, I add blush and contour with some highlights, turning my lambs into the person they wished they could be. Turning around to my work bench, I grab the bite block and place it in her mouth; the one a dentist uses to keep their patients mouth open. Next I take out every single tooth, placing them on the instrument tray next to me, then close her mouth.

Reaching backwards to my workbench, opening the small top drawer where I keep all the red lipstick, I select the color that is going to be the perfect finishing touch for my little lamb. I always use red on my lambs because it is the color whores wear. All of them are whores, wanting and pleading to have me, and never succeeding. So it is only fitting for their true selves to be revealed.

My mother taught me early that all women are evil. All have an agenda, a reason for batting their eyes and saying sweet words. She warned, to never give them the chance to entrap you in their smile, before that can happen, end them. She always wore a nude lip, that was her signature color. My mother was a woman of integrity, always loyal to one man. So giving my lambs the opposite color to what my mother wore, is a testament to her.

Next I start to paint her dress on, it is a dark green dress coming down to her knees, with lace sleeves. Bending down into the bottom drawer of my workbench, I pull out the foldable fans. Placing the fans around her body, so the paint hardens faster. As the paint dries, I take the rose out of the dye, placing it into a new empty vase to dry. Then, I start to gather her clothing and throw it onto the plastic on the floor. After all of the evidence is gathered on the floor, I wrap up the plastic. I open the door to my incinerator, throw it all in there, shut the door, and turn it on. By time the evidence is burning, the paint is all baked on, it is time to turn off the fans and flip her over.

Walking back I touch her skin to make sure the paint has fully dried and turn her over to finish the dress on the other side. I take my time, being mindful of each stroke I place along her skin, striving for the subtle imperfection of true clothing. When I'm done, my lamb truly looks as though she's ready to go out once more.

Turning the fans back on, I let her back dry. I walk to the sink to wash all the tools and dry them, then put them back where they belong. Once everything is back in its designated spot I go back to my lamb to check on the paint. I lightly tap around her body to assure it is all dried, then flip her back over.

Moving down to her feet I start painting on ivory flats to compliment the dress I just finished. Setting my paintbrush down, I admire the feminine quality I've given my little lamb. One she didn't possess in her desperation when she was alive.

Grabbing my handheld blowtorch that sits on the workbench behind me, I grab her hand, and burn off all of her fingerprints. I want my little lambs to forever be Jane Doe's, forgotten by everyone, but me.

The last thing I do to her, that I do to all my victims, is take three petals from the rose, and place them on my workbench. Then, I open the second drawer taking out super glue to take two petals and glue one petal to each eye. You could say this is my signature.

The eyes are the windows to the soul, and covering her eyes ensures that I was the last one to see her soul… Leave her body.

After I finish remaking her, I lay her to rest fully by taking her hands and have her hold them over her heart. Then I add glue onto the stem of the rose, placing it into her folded hands.

The authorities still haven't figured out why I do this. It's simple, the blue rose means unreachable love in some cultures, and in others it means devotion, trust, and love. Well my lambs give me just that, but I will never return it. My heart is just always out of reach, but they don't accept that, until my knife is plunged into theirs.

The leftover petal is then placed into a book with something I took from her and her name written underneath.

I place the book back in its hiding spot, in the vents under my workspace. I added the vents when I was reconstructing the space to be mine. Mom and dad may not have needed cool air to work, but I do. Before walking over to my little lamb, and gathering her into my arms, I whisper in her ear. "You look beautiful little lamb, now it is time for the world to see you"

Striding over to my 67' dark blue Chevelle, I place her body into the trunk of my car. Close the trunk, hop in the front, roll the windows down, blast the radio, place my hands around the wheel, and drive to one of my dump locations. Each location is always different from the last, so the cops can't stake it out to catch me. They will never know where I'll be dumping next, just that it is always secluded so I never get caught.

TWO

SERENA

Getting lost in my paintings is something that comes easy to me. Knowing exactly where the next stroke of my brush is going, to create what I see in my head, is like breathing. That's when I create a piece solely for me, my commissions, well that's a whole other story.

Sighing, I run my paint stained fingers through my coarse dark hair, place the end of the brush in my mouth, and just sit staring at the painting, waiting for inspiration to hit. When nothing comes, I pull my phone out from my apron and call my best friend, knowing she can help spark an idea.

She answers on the third ring, "Ugh" I sigh loudly tossing my paintbrush across the room "I just can't get it right"

Knowing exactly what I'm talking about she says, "chill babe, you'll get it, you always do."

Rocking back and forth, to calm myself, I take a deep breath and say, "you're right, I know you're right, but Jess I can't get this to look how I'm picturing it in my head"

"Well how are you picturing it?"

"Not like this!" I point at the canvas knowing she can't see it. "It's the colors, Jess. They're not right. They're not coming together how I need them to. It's all wrong," I let out a huff of frustration.

"First, uncross your arms; you're not a child."

I uncross my arms, glaring at my phone and silently cursing her for knowing me so damn well.

"Okay, now step away from the painting and try looking at it in a different perspective."

I step back, trying and failing to look at it differently. "It isn't working."

She sighs, "Babe, give it some time." She is silent on the other end letting me stew and stare at the painting, then says. "I think it is time for some hyping up"

I can hear her smile through the phone as she yells, "Who are you?"

I'm silent, in no mood for hype time. Anytime one of us is having a bad day, frustrated, or just done with life, the other hypes you up. A way to encourage and remind you it's not the end of the world. Today it is my turn to be hyped. I groan, stubbornly refusing to join in. I just want these fucking colors to do, what I want them to do.

Jessica blows out a breath and says even louder, "WHO ARE YOU?"

I laugh a little, finally giving in, and say, "Serena Raven!"

"I can't hear you!"

Closing my eyes, cupping my hands around my mouth, I yell. "Serena fucking Raven!"

She yells back, "And who is Serena fucking Raven?"

Doing a little dance, I holler back, "A badass bitch who can paint the hell out of everything!"

"That's right! And what is she going to do?"

Pointing at my canvas, I say, "Figure this shit out and create a masterpiece."

"Fuck, yeah!" Jessica says, with more vigor.

"Fuck, yeah!" We both start laughing, "Thanks, Jess, I really needed that."

"Of course, babe, that's what I'm here for; I'll always be here."

"I know, and I love you for that, but…"

"But you figured that shit out and are going to resume your painting." She says it as more of a statement than as a question.

I give a little smirk, "Exactly."

"I love you, babe; send me a picture when you're done, and call me if the colors start being assholes again."

"You know I will, I love you, too."

"Laters."

"Laters." I hang up and go pick up the brush I threw across the room. Sitting back on my stool, and resuming the music to center myself. "Don't You Want Me Baby" comes on, and I lose myself in my work.

Painting has been the one constant in my life for as long as I can remember. Everyone has left me in one way or another, aside from Jessica; I know she will *always* be there. But painting, painting is my everything. It is how I pay my bills,- It's my hobby, and my way to decompress. I usually know exactly what I am going to paint the moment the brush is in my hands, but sometimes, only with my commissions, I feel lost. I don't connect with the piece in the way I need to. This piece especially, at least, not until Jess hyped me up, and now I know exactly what I want to do with it.

My phone dings, alerting me of a new article on 'The Morbid Monet.' I have my phone settings set to a certain ringtone when he strikes again. That little ding lets me know a newspaper will be coming out tomorrow for me to add to my collection.

This will make thirty two. I can't believe they still haven't caught him.

Ever since he started his killings, even before he was named Salem's notorious serial killer, I always felt drawn to him. The way he lays his victims to rest, how he poses them always outside, there is just something beautiful about it. He never touches them, the article says, just tortures them and removes their clothing, painting on a new set of clothes.

Most would be terrified, especially since all of his victims are thicker women. I should be scared to even leave the house, but I'm not. He fascinates me, and if I were to come face to face with him one day, I don't think I'd run.

I'm so lost in my painting I don't hear the doorbell ring. It's not until I hear the banging, that I'm finally pulled from my trance.

Who the hell is at my door? I know I'm not expecting anyone today. I didn't forget I was expecting a visitor… Did I? It dawns on me as I near the front door. "Fuck…" I look out the window, and, sure as shit, my dad is standing right there with a scowl on his face.

He is dressed to the nines in a black suit and shoes. His hair gelled back. Thomas Raven would never allow a hair to be out of place or anything, but freshly clean shaven. My stomach drops as I watch him look down impatiently at his watch.

I do *not* want to have to deal with him today. I completely forgot we made dinner plans with everything else I have going on.

I answer the door, and he looks me up and down with annoyance. "I see you forgot we had plans."

I stand up straighter, looking him in the eyes, the paint pallet still in my hands. "Nice to see you, too, Dad. How long has it been? Oh, that's right, five years. But, no, I didn't forget, I was busy working and lost track of time." I spit through clenched teeth, knowing damn well I did forget.

"Working," he scoffs. "Last I checked, painting is a hobby, not a real job."

I try to hold in my anger, but I am seething. "Well, Thomas."

My father's eyes shoot up at me using his first name.

"Not everyone has a practical, real job, as you put it. My paintings pay for this house," I wave my hands around at the house. "Pay for the clothes on my back, the food in my stomach." I take a deep breath, trying to gather myself. "And I love my job; it makes me happy, and if you ever cared to support my dreams, or care to even take a look at one of my paintings, you would see I'm damn good at what I do and that I deserve every cent to my name."

My father just grunts and pushes past me, completely ignoring what I just said. "Go clean that paint off your face, and if you're done with your little tantrum, we can go have a nice dinner."

I turn my back on him and start to walk away.

"I said nice, Serena, so definitely nothing like what you're wearing now." he says with disgust.

I turn around, flipping him the bird, and the anger in his face gives me the satisfaction I was looking for. Walking to my room, I close the door and get ready.

It's been five years since I last saw my father. We have only communicated through email and even that's been sparse at best. He messages me once a week, mainly criticizing my life choices, and sending me job listings that would be more appropriate for a woman with my background. I barely reply, I know I'll never be able to change his mind.

A couple weeks ago, my father told me he would be visiting Salem the first week of September, and would like to see me and have dinner. I replied it only took him five years, but sure I could make that work.

His only response was, he would pick me up at six o'clock.

I appear twenty minutes later with a "nice" baby blue dress on, my hair styled in a tight bun, and fresh face of makeup.

My father looks me up and down and gives me an approving smile. "See, now was that so hard? You look nice; now," he reaches his hand to mine. "Let's go."

I brush past him, ignoring his hand, and walk to his car. It is a black Lamborghini Gallardo; a visual representation of his soul to the world. I get in, looking at the interior and sitting in the leather seat. The steering wheel looks like it belongs in a race car, and the radio screen is as big as my laptop. *This is one way to show off you have money and flaunt it in everyone's face.* My dad is notorious for showcasing his wealth, only satisfied when he can feel others' jealousy.

Sitting with my arms crossed and slouched in the passenger seat, I wait impatiently. Getting in, he takes a loud, deep breath. Raking his fingers through his black hair in the same way I do, he looks over at me. Clenching my jaw, my fingers go white against my arms. I hate that I take after him in any way, especially his mannerisms. I don't want to be my fathers daughter.

"Look, Serena, I didn't come here to argue with you or look down on your life choices; I simply want to have a nice meal with my daughter and catch up."

Scoffing, I look out the window. "Sure, Dad, if that wasn't what you wanted to do," I look back into his steely blue eyes, "Then why do you have to berate my life choices every fucking chance you get?"

His eyes harden, "Watch your mouth; I raised you better than that"

I scoff, "You raised me? That's rich, coming from you! Mom raised me. You spent your life at the office bending your secretary over your desk every chance you got."

"How dare you; I loved your mother!"

Disgusted with his lies, I laugh. "Is that why you fucked every whore who opened their legs, while she laid in bed dying?" I'm so angry tears trickle down my face. "Is that why it took you five *fucking* years after she died to reach out to me and have this fucking dinner?"

He lowers his head, looking at me with sad eyes. "Serena, I..." He's at a loss for words. "I'm sorry, okay? I did love your mother, but she was already gone."

I'm appalled at the words that left his mouth, cutting him off and yelling, "She was already dead? No dad, she was still alive, fighting for life. Fighting for you." I reach for the door handle and look back. "She did until her last dying breath, but you were too busy between another whore's legs, to even care." I get out of the car and slam the door shut.

He speeds out of my driveway, and I'm left standing there, crying over the man, who once again failed me.

I walk towards the house and call Jess, who answers after the first ring. Hearing my cries, all she says is, "I'm on my way." Hanging up, I fall to the ground and let the grief of losing my father for good take over me.

THREE
SERENA

"Are you fucking kidding me?" Jess shouts while shoving another chocolate chip cookie in her mouth. "The audacity of that fucking piece of shit."

The crumbs fall onto her shirt, and I reach over and brush them away. She looks down, and gives me an appreciative smile. Cookies are her kryptonite. She is a health nut, but when it comes to her favorite cookies, she can't say no.

"I know," I sniffle. "I don't know what I was expecting, but-" I wipe away the tears streaking down my cheeks. "I just... I wasn't expecting this" I try to collect myself, failing until Jessica wraps me in her arms, and brushes her hand down my hair.

She takes a deep breath, "Shhh, I'm right here, he didn't deserve you when you lost your mom, and he sure as shit doesn't deserve you now."

My breathing becomes erratic, her words helping heal the reopened wound in my chest. "I know, I just thought... Shit I don't even know what I thought."

I thought that after being estranged for so long my father wanted to start to rebuild the bridge he tore down. That he wanted to be a family again. That I could be his little girl again. *That will never happen.*

She starts to rub my back, concern etched on her face, she says. "You thought that after five years of being absent this was his way of trying to rekindle what he broke."

I look up at her with a snot filled face. "I mean, after the email exchanges, and him degrading my career choice, I should have known better". Jessica hands me a tissue, and I attempt a watery smile before blowing into it. "I don't know Jess, I just wish that tonight would've gone better, instead of turning into this mess."

She wipes the blotched mascara running down my face and pushes the hair that came loose from my bun away from my eyes. "You know, the night isn't over yet." she says with a devilish smile. "In fact, the night is still young, and I say we do what we haven't done in awhile"

I smile a little, because I know exactly what she is thinking, it's the same thing Jess always suggests when one of us is having a bad day. Although I feel like it is always for me. I swear Jessica never has any bad days.

"We haven't done that for a hot minute because people always look at us weird, mostly me, when we go out." I whisper looking down at my hands. But it's true, everytime I go out with Jessica, the stares we get are looks of confusion or pity. Always directed at me, which makes me feel uncomfortable and even more insecure than I already feel standing next to her.

She pulls me to my feet, grabbing my shoulders and, placing me right in front of her, a wicked smile on her face. "Time to let the devil out".

"Speaking of the devil, did you see the Morbid Monet, struck again?"

She lets me go, "You seriously need to stop obsessing over that psycho."

"I know, but I can't there's just something about his work." I say with a dazed face.

"Work!? Serena, he kills women, who, no offense," she

motions up and down, "Have your body type. That isn't work, he needs to be locked up."

Ouch.

I sigh, knowing I need to pick my battles wisely with Jess. This is one battle I know I will lose, so I nod my head in defeat, and we head to my room so I can get ready all over again.

I look over at my best friend, her eyes a beautiful shade of honey brown, her blonde, wavy hair cascading all the way down to her lower back. She smiles at me, emphasizing her cute button nose and small lips. Lips that she makes look bigger using lip liner and lipstick. I force a smile back, trying to shrug off the jealousy I feel. Jess is who everyone, including me, wishes they looked like.

She riffles through my closet, pulling out a tight black dress that stretches to fit any body type. With wide eyes, I shake my head no, she frowns, but puts it away with a sigh. Jess has always said I need to own my curves, but that's hard to do, since I want to hide away from the world tonight. She goes back to rifling through my closet, and I turn and sit down at my little black vanity. Turning to face the mirror, I lean over the table, my breast pressing against it, I start putting on my fake cat eye eyelashes.

She screams, making me jump out of my skin, nearly poking my eyes out when she excitedly yells. "This is perfect, Serena you have," she says the words with extra enunciation, "-To wear this tonight."

Turning around, my eyebrows raise at the red dress that is dangling from her hand. "Yeah, no, I am not wearing that- it is skin tight, and I do not want to show off every roll I have."

She stalks towards me, raises her right hand and smacks me on the back of my head. Rubbing the now sore spot, I glare at her through the mirror. She ignores my glare and protest and says, "Bitch you are fucking beautiful, and this dress was made for those curves- at least try it on before you say no." She sticks out her bottom lip, makes her already big eyes bigger, and shoves the dress towards me.

I look at the dress, then her pleading face, roll my eyes, and reluctantly grab it from her. "Fine, but if I look like a beached whale, I'm just going to wear what I had on."

She starts clapping and jumping up and down, excited that she won this round. Then eyes the baby blue dress lying on my bed in disgust, walks over and holds it with two fingers away from her body. "That does not scream 'let the devil out,' this-." She motions to the red dress I'm slipping over my head. "Screams Lucifers play thing, and the world needs to bow at your feet, in reverence."

She walks over to me and zips me up. I eye myself in the mirror, stunned at the person staring back at me. "I guess, I could be worshiped for one night."

Jessica smacks my ass, making me jump, "That's the spirit!"

She slides her hands around my waist, and resting her head on my shoulder, "See I told you, this is the one" she kisses my cheek, leaving a pink lip print, and saunters away.

I stare breathless at my own reflection. My inky hair is braided to one side, draping over my shoulder and caressing my skin through a cutout in the dress. My dark blue eyes shine brightly, highlighted by my smoky eye, making them look more vibrant. Like the waves Poseidon rides. Applying a bright red lipstick to my plump lips, matching the red dress perfectly. I stare at my reflection admiring the curves in the dress, grateful for my new workout routine and meal plan. I started that a couple months ago. I'd bought this dress in hopes of one day being able to wear it, I guess today is that day thanks to Jess.

I turn, grab my black pumps just as Jess is putting on her red ones. We both look in the mirror one last time, and head out for a night destined to make the devil say, 'Fuck'.

THE BASS IS PUMPING IN THE CLUB WITH THE SONG "BABY DON'T Hurt Me" blasting through the sound system, the DJ adding some remix beats to it. Jess and I are drunk on the dance floor, dancing the night away, and releasing all our problems with each drink and sway of our hips. She is grinding her butt against my stomach, and I hold her hips, swaying them back and forth. We lose ourselves in the music, and as the song ends, we're both dragged down from our high, and I notice two overly eager drunk guys walking towards us.

One of them is much better looking than the other, his brown hair pulled back in the way I like. Wearing a loose fitted blue shirt and dark jeans. Holding a drink in each hand, clear intent in his eyes. He looks to be around six feet with a lean build, muscular arms, walking with his head held high and a cocky swagger, as if he owned the place.

His friend next to him is a little shorter, but still taller than us, wearing a green shirt with black skinny jeans. He's lean, but his arms are smaller, you can tell he skips arms day at the gym. He has black hair, bleached tips. He also carries himself in an overly arrogant way, that's immediately off putting.

They walk over to us, the taller one going straight to me. He lifts his drink, with a wink and says with a slur, "You look like you could use a drink after all that dancing you were doing."

Jessica looks at me with a silent look of 'I'll get rid of them'. She leans forward, her cleavage spilling out of the top of her dress, in a flattering way, receiving looks from both men. I watch the Adam's apple bob on the throat of the shorter one.

"How would you know if we were thirsty and needed a drink after dancing?" Jessica looks them up and down, "Unless you two pervs, were watching us all night like some type of stalkers?"

The hotter of the two sweeps his eyes over her body, slowly stopping to look into her eyes. "What if that was exactly what we were doing, and just waiting for the right moment to strike? " He says with a venomous smile.

Jessica rolls her eyes, and with the sweetest voice says, "Well then I'd say you wasted your night; thanks, but no thanks. We don't take drinks from strangers."

Just as she goes to walk away the guy steps in front of her and says, "My name is Garth, and this is Tim, now we're not strangers."

Jessica grabs my hand and pushes Garth out of the way. I feel a tug on my arm, looking back to see the one named Tim grabbed me to stop me from leaving. He gulps again, regaining some of his arrogant swagger, finally speaking up, "Are you sure you're not interested? You could have the best night of your life with the both of us." He turns his head towards Garth, and gives a serpentine smile.

Jessica steps in front of me, pushing me behind her, and placing her hands outwards, in a protective gesture. She glares at Tim, and says with the most menacing voice, "Touch her again, and I promise I will rip off your dick, and shove it so far up your friend's ass, you'll wish you never spoke to us. Don't make me repeat myself again, we are not interested, so kindly fuck off."

Stifling a laugh, the two men stand there pissed and stunned. Jessica takes my hand, "I think it's time for some new scenery."

Nodding my head in agreement, we take off running out of the club into the night. We're instantly hit with a cool breeze, and I rub my arms to elicit some heat in my goosebump covered arms. We stop running a few blocks away, breathless, and start laughing hysterically.

"Oh my god, Jess! I can't believe you just said that."

She places her hands on her knees to catch her breath, giggling, "It's girls night, and I didn't want those losers ruining it."

"Well I'm glad you did. I wasn't interested in either of them, and you probably saved us from being roofied."

"You're probably right." She sits on the curb of the sidewalk, pulling me down next to her, and laying her head on my shoulder. "So do you feel better now?" She nuzzles into my neck.

I smile and pat her head, "Yes I do, thank you for tonight." I feel my phone vibrate in my pocket, and another email apology from my sperm donor I call father flashing across the screen.

If he thinks a couple emails are going to fix what he said, he is sorely wrong. *How could he just drive away?* I know I'm not the daughter of the year, and we've been estranged since mom passed, but I never expected it to go that way. I'm hurt from his words, his absence in my life, the disappointment in his eyes from my life choices. I start to rub my cheek, and my eyes start to water.

I feel Jess's shoulder nudge mine, I look over and see the concern laced in her eyes. She starts to rub my back, trying to comfort me. "This night is for you, not Thomas." She pushes my phone down, "Ignore him, Let's go back to your house and we can get in our pajamas, watch horror movies, and eat to our hearts content. What do you say?" A small smile starts to spread across her face.

Turning my phone on silent, I tuck it into my bra and sigh. "Okay, you had me at horror movies and snacks, that sounds like a perfect way to end tonight"

She gleefully stands up, pulling me up with her, and linking our arms together, before pulling out her phone to order an Uber. I place my hand across her screen, stopping her. Jess looks at me, her brow furrowed.

"Actually, can we go get one more drink at a bar down the street? I've been wanting to check it out, and there is no way in hell I want to go home yet, since we look like this. I don't want to miss my chance to seduce Lucifer himself," I say with a wink. "Just a small nightcap, then we can go back to my house."

She puts her phone down and smiles. "Of course babe, this night is for you, show me the way and I will follow."

After a ten minute walk, we arrive at the bar. The 'Boozy Books' Neon sign, lighting up the night sky. "This is the place." I grab Jessica's arm, an excited smile spreads across my face and we walk in.

FOUR
SERENA

Boozy Books is everything I've been hearing about and more. The moment you walk in, the walls are coated in a deep green. A subtle forest hidden within the depths of color that seem to suck up all excess light and sound, creating a muted but welcoming space. Music straight out of a fantasy novel flows throughout the room, transporting every listener to their favorite far away place with a simple crescendo. There's a steampunk vibe, pulling the whole bar together. Random pieces of art decorate the walls, from genre bending paintings and steamy sculptures, even what looks like handmade crafts from local artists and writers. In the corner sits a little book nook with hundreds, if not thousands, of different books from every genre you could think of, a literal library in the heart of the bar. There are two three-piece couches placed in an L-shape away from the bookshelves, and five bean bags on the floor. There is a little coffee table in the shape of a map in the middle, with several papasan chairs scattered about. Nearly every seat is taken, several people, unashamed in their reading preference, drape themselves throughout and take up the space. Lost in whatever story they have fallen into.

There's no dress code, but it's obvious Jess and I missed the memo for tonight. Readers wearing jewelry and accessories of their favorite characters cosplay in the various nooks around the bar. Acting out their favorite scenes in the safety of a space that welcomes everyone. The bar itself is towards the back of the building, offering drinks based on traditionally and indie published books from the past decade. There are several high top tables, giving people a place to rest between chapters, and a few open seats surrounding the high-top bar.

"Wow…" Jessica says, startling me from my admiration. "I can see why you wanted to come here. Where should we start first? Books or booze?"

We look at each other saying, "Booze-" at the same time, laughing as we head towards the open seats around the bar.

The bartender notices us right away and addresses me, "What can I get you tonight?"

Jess grabs my arm "We will have two moscow mules, please."

Giving me a funny look, he looks at the space around me, and he shrugs, "Right away," he says walking away, showing us the full extent of his Fae costume. Coming back a few minutes later, placing both drinks in front of me.

I grab one for myself, pushing the other towards Jessica, and earning another weird look from the bartender. *What is this dude's issue? Why does he keep giving me weird looks?*

Ignoring him completely, I sit back in the chair and start sipping my drink. Looking around at the patrons around me, I start to feel the hairs on the back of my neck rise, my arms breaking out in goosebumps. I feel a set of eyes searing through me, making me rub the back of my neck. I subtly crack my neck, searching for the eyes watching me and they zero in on a guy in the corner. From the shadows I see a smirk forming on his lips. He stands up, the low light of the bar still giving him a menacing look as he stalks towards me, knocking the breath from my lungs.

He stands well above six feet, sandy blond hair styled, in an intentionally messy way. His eyes are piercing green in the lazily strobing lights around us, but there is a darkness in them that he hides behind well. Too bad I'm familiar with hiding, I know where to look to see through the bullshit. His darkness draws me to him like a moth to a flame. He has a build like one I imagine Hades would have, and if he wanted to he could destroy me and break me in half, without breaking a sweat, and I would gladly let him. He is wearing a white shirt with a black leather jacket over it, long dark fitted jeans and black laced boots. He is dripping in sin and fuck, do I want to do sinful things with this man. I imagine him bending me over, plowing into me, stealing my very life with his cock. I want to sit on that perfect face and watch him feast.

He stands behind the chair next to mine, and as he takes off his jacket the first thing I notice is the orca jumping out of the blue waves on his right forearm. My eyes zero in on it, and I speak without thinking. "You know killer whales are the most deadly animal in the ocean? They even hunt great whites."

He looks at me with a quizzical face, making me look away. He doesn't speak, instead places both arms on the back of his chair, giving me a better view of all the ink he has.

There's a black and white grim reaper holding a scythe in a cloak on his left bicep that morphs into blue roses leading all the way to his wrist. The roses remind me of my paintings, dark, but different shades of blue. *Something we already have in common it seems.* The reaper speaks for itself, a messenger of death, or death itself. *I wonder which one it means to him?* On the bottom of his wrist, there are the roman numerals MMII, but I'm not sure what those numbers mean.

My body isn't connecting with my brain, because I find myself reaching out to touch the roses. Before my fingers land on his skin he speaks, voice low and husky. "The deadliest you say?"

I look up to see him with an amused smirk watching my hand almost touch him, and snatch it back, placing it in my lap, embarrassment rising to my cheeks. I nod my head too mortified with myself to look at him. I know he's looking at me. I can feel his stare burning into the side of my head. *Why would you do that, Serena? You don't just go touching hot men because you feel like it.*

"You know if you wanted to touch it all you had to do was ask."

My head snaps to meet his eyes, eyes I'm just now noticing are a piercing green, and when the light hits them the right way, spots of blue show, making them look almost teal. "Beautiful." I whisper.

"Sorry," I shake my head, not able to tear myself away from his piercing gaze.

"There's nothing to be sorry about, and to answer your question from earlier, yes I did know."

Confused, I ask, "Know what?"

"The whale," he chuckles.

If I wasn't horrified before, I am now. This poor man probably thinks I'm crazy, trying to touch him, then forgetting what we were even talking about because I'm literally getting lost in his eyes. I take a long sip of my Moscow mule, making myself shut up.

"You know you have beautiful eyes, too." Straw still in my mouth, I turn to look at him, mouth slightly parted. "They remind me of the north sea, alluring, but dangerous."

I've heard stories of the north sea, only the bravest go out there. After seeing the movie *Frozen 2*, the north sea became big on TikTok, and videos kept popping up on my feed. I went down the rabbit hole, and it is in fact dangerous, terrifying, but so beautiful. So many have lost their lives treading those waters.

He clears his throat, "I have more tattoos, then just the ones on my arms."

My eyes light up. "Really? Can I see?"

"They're covered right now, but I'll show them to you, one day."

"One day?"

"I promise," there is something sinister, but tempting behind that promise. It has me wanting to ask more, but something tells me to leave it at that.

"I don't have any tattoos, I want one, but I just don't know what I'd get." I create art all day long, making beautiful pieces for myself and clients. Getting to hang them up and take them down is different then choosing one piece and it being on your body forever.

He finally takes the seat next to me, "Why not?"

"What if one day you wake up and hate the art on your body, or you're not the same person you were five years ago? Sure there's coverups, or lasering it off, but the same problem, what if you hate it, and lasering, I've been told hurts more then the tattoo itself."

His head rests on his hand as he stares and listens to me ramble on. *Shut up Serena.* "Plus the pain of the tattoo itself, I don't know if I can endure that torture."

He lifts off his hand, "If you add pleasure to the mix, then the sting of the tattoo is drowned out by the pleasure."

"So you want me to either fuck the artist, or fuck myself while I get tattooed?" Something in his eyes sparkles at that.

"I can give you the tattoo." That makes me spit out my drink, completely taken back from his words. Full on spray lands all over the bar top, creating a mess, making the bartender come over and grumble at me while cleaning it up. *Does he want to please me or watch me touch myself?*

"Sorry," I whisper. He walks away, without sparing me another glance. "That was rude." I turn back to the sinful man sitting next to me and see he's glaring daggers at the bartender and his knuckles are starting to turn white. I do the only thing I can think of and place my hand gently over his fists, startling him. He pulls back, which makes me do the same and this time I'm apologizing to him. "Sorry, I didn't mean to touch you without permission, you just looked so angry, so I was trying to help."

"Don't apologize ever, to me or anyone else." He says in a threatening voice.

"I'm sorry?" I ask, turning my head, "That wasn't an apology, that was me asking what you mean."

At that he chuckles and leans in, the sound coming from his voice has me clenching my thighs. "Never apologize for being who you are, that asshole will be the one sorry when karma gets him later." He glances back at the bar keep and then back to me, "and don't apologize for touching me, I was just shocked, quite literally when your skin met mine."

Then I think about it, I didn't realize it at first but when I touched him I did feel a spark. A small one, that I brushed off because I was more concerned with how he was feeling at the moment then feeling at all. "I felt it too." I breathe.

His eyes pierce straight through me, to my very soul it feels like. I want to look away, but I can't. I feel magnetized to him, and I don't even know his name. "What's your name?" I ask robotically.

"Aster, and yours?" He asks back in that same hypnotized voice.

"Serena."

"Serena," He says my name, like he's tasting every letter. I watch as his lips plump out at the beginning and open slightly at the end. Now my eyes won't leave his lips, and I find myself wanting to lean in and kiss him. He must have the same idea, because he's staring at my lips, and leaning in too. The music and voices around us drowned out, like time itself has stopped, and it's just us, here in this moment.

When he's a breath away from tasting me, he clears his throat, leans back and taps the bar, gaining the bartender's attention. *Ouch.* Guess we weren't thinking the same thing. "Another mule for this beautiful woman."

Beautiful, but won't kiss me, got it.

The bartender looks at me and says, "Her?"

If looks could kill, the bartender would've dropped dead in

an instant. He shuts up, immediately spinning on his heel to get me another glass.

Just one look and this man has this asshole of a bartender just about pissing his pants. *I want to be in his pants later. What is wrong with me?* Maybe it is the fact that I haven't been with anyone since my mothers passing five years ago. I haven't even thought about having sex with anyone, but this man, just by breathing, he awoke the parts of me that have been sleeping for so long.

Stirring me from my thoughts by tapping the bar he asks, changing the subject. "So, Serena, come here often?"

That elicits a laugh from Jess who is sitting behind me, causing him to look at her as if finally noticing I'm not alone. He stares daggers at her, his eyes looking like a black pit of death, making the laughing cease, bringing his attention back to me.

I can't believe he just glanced at her, men are usually falling at her feet. *Am I dreaming?* If I am, this is a dream I never want to wake up from. "Smooth transition to change the subject," I tease.

My boldness has his eyebrows raising, and then a small grin crosses his beautiful face. "Are you talking about me giving you a tattoo, and distracting you from the pain?"

Didn't think he would admit to that so quickly, honestly thought he would try to change the subject again. Girls got to shoot her shot, so I played into it, laying my hand on the bartop and leaving my fingers inches from him. If he wanted to, which I hope he does, he could touch my hand lightly and even interlock our fingers. "How would you distract me from the pain?"

He looks down at my palm, bringing his fingers closer, almost as if he can't stop himself. His fingers are centimeters from mine, making me hold my breath waiting for the moment they touch, but that moment doesn't come. Leaning in he whispers, "I make my little lambs scream, are you going to scream for me little lamb?

Yes, God yes. His confession has my mouth going dry, and my panties soaking wet. "If I'm a little lamb, does that make you a fox?"

Shock registers on his face, but it's so quick if I wasn't staring so hard at him I would have missed it, then he grins sinfully and says "We have all of tonight to find out."`

I shift in my seat trying to get some release off of the pressure building low. A blush starts heating up my face, and I know he sees it because he looks at me and smirks. I probably look like a tomato, anytime I blush or get embarrassed, my whole face turns red, not just my cheeks. You can never tell which emotion I'm feeling, but I have a suspicion Aster knows exactly what I'm feeling. I blame my mother, I got her pale complexion making me burn, instead of tan in the summer. I usually stay in doors anyway, I prefer the cold to the heat, always have.

Jess clears her throat behind me, reminding me we're not alone.

I turn around, "I'm so sorry, Jess, I forgot to introduce you." I point to her, "Jessica, Aster, Aster, Jessica."

He looks at her with confusion pinching his eyes. He's probably confused with why a girl like her would hang out with a girl like me. The way he's looking at her, is like he's looking through her. Looking back at me with curious eyes, he tilts his head, not giving her the time of day.

I should be upset that he's ignoring my best friend, but I'm not. She's the one who always attracts all the attention, while I'm just in the background. For once I feel like the star, the one in the spotlight, so my caring has gone out the window.

Jess scoffs and whispers in my ear, "I'm going to head over to the books. It seems Aster here is very much interested in you. Don't do anything I wouldn't do, and for once get your dick wet." She winks and walks away, leaving us alone and me praying he didn't hear the end of that.

I love the girl, but she can be a little too forward at times, especially for me, and I honestly hate it.

My phone lights up a minute later. I go to check it, but Aster touches my hand bringing my full attention back to him.

"When you're with me, I want all of your attention on only me."

I nod my head aimlessly and put my phone into my bag. He's demanding, and I usually hate men like that, but with him I find myself wanting to do exactly what he says. If he told me to open up, I'd ask how wide? If he wanted to spit in my mouth, as gross as that is, I'd swallow every drop. He's like a drill sergeant, a sexy one, and I'm his lieutenant following every order given.

"Good girl," *Oh fuck me, please fuck me.* I have been dreaming of a man to say those words to me ever since I started reading romance novels. Those two words have me wanting to drop to my knees right now, just to hear him say them again.

My eyes drop to his crotch, seeing the outline in his jeans of his hard on. Making me smile, knowing the feelings I'm having are the same as his. He speaks, making my eyes snap back up to his. *I hope he didn't see me ogling his dick.* "Now, do you want to tell me why you look like you're trying to forget the world tonight, little lamb?"

That takes me by surprise, we go from flirty, to serious. *Talk about whiplash.* I did just have that whole fiasco with my dad, but there is no way in hell I want to unravel my burdens on him. The look in his eyes tells me he isn't taking no for an answer.

I take a deep breath and let out a nervous laugh,"Did I look like I wanted to forget my problems?" I thought I was doing a good job at masking my pain like I usually do, but he saw right through me. The only one who can see through my bullshit is Jessica, no one else has, until him.

His eyes soften, making them look more blue, then green. "You looked like you had the weight of the world on your shoulders tonight, and I would like to help lift some of it. If you'll let me?"

This man just keeps surprising me. Not only are his tattoos amazing; I definitely want to see the hidden ones. I might even take him up on his offer and let him do one on me. He's hot, tall, has a way with words, and now considerate. No way he's real, someone has to be pranking me. I start looking around, trying to see if there are any cameras. Nothing, okay, so I pinch myself next, definitely not dreaming. *Where did he come from?*

I stare at him, curiosity, and disbelief weighing my mind. "I appreciate that, but I don't want to bore you with my trivial life problems." Plus, I don't want to tell some hot stranger my issues, and scare him away when he actually seems to be interested in me. Maybe he is more interested in getting into my pants? Especially with all the earlier comments, I wouldn't be surprised or opposed to. After all this time, I could go find an empty stall in the bathroom and let him have his way with me.

"What if I want to be bothered by them?"

I sit stunned and unsure what to think about him. *Should I tell him about my daddy problems or just table it for another night?* He's looking at me with the same face, so I slam down the rest of my drink, take a deep breath, and tell him the events of today.

Fuck it, maybe telling him will help me lift the weights off my shoulders.

He sits back, listening to me ramble on and complain about my father, and he's so attentive, responding with head nods and small noises to let me know he's listening, but letting me talk and get it all out. When I'm all done, breathing heavy and taking another sip of my third drink, he finally speaks.

"Thank you for telling me, I don't blame you for getting out of the car and walking away, I think it was the right decision." He places his hand under my chin and lifts it up so I'm looking at him, my eyes glassy. "You have nothing to be ashamed of or apologize for, it sounds like your father needs to come back begging on his knees for your forgiveness."

I laugh through the sniffling. "Thanks Aster, that really does mean a lot"

He swipes the tear, that I didn't even realize had fallen. "Now, don't you feel better getting that all off of your chest?"

"Yeah, actually, I do. I guess unloading your heart to a stranger really does help."

He puts his hand on his chest, sitting back as if I hurt him. "Serena, I thought we were friends, not strangers, especially after such a deep conversation," he jokes.

I laugh a little, "Well, it takes a little longer than that, to reach friend status. I say you're getting close to acquaintance status. Maybe a few more dates and you can call yourself a friend."

He smirks, "Oh is this a date? I thought this was just two strangers getting to know each other and having a drink. One telling the other about the horrible day she was having."

"Well, I didn't necessarily mean it was a date. Shit! Sorry, I meant like-"

He grabs my hand, and I feel a stronger shock throughout my whole body that surprises us both. Our hands shoot back, both of us startled from the power behind it. He stares at me with curious eyes, bringing his hand back to lay back on mine. "Relax, Serena, I was just fucking with you, but if you wanted to go on a date all you had to do was ask."

"Shit, yeah. I mean do you want to go on a date with me?" I lean forward, eager for his answer. Getting butterflies from the rubbing of his thumb on my hand.

He leans in so close I can smell the sandalwood on his skin, and mint on his breath. He's inches from my lips, my body alighting at his nearness. *Is he actually going to kiss me this time?* He whispers, "I would love to go on a date with you."

I light up, thrilled he actually said yes. "Really? You actually want to go on a real date with me, someone you just met, who just minutes ago ranted about her entire shitty day?"

"Yes, I do, and if you give me your number, we can plan our date."

A smile lifts my lips. "Wow, that was a pretty sly way of asking for my number."

"Had to get it sometime tonight," he says, holding out his hand for my phone.

"Didn't you ask for my number and not the other way around?" I ask accusingly, handing him my phone anyway. Instead of answering he takes out his ancient flip phone, one I didn't think a man like him would have. Not that I'm judging, it's weird for anyone besides older people to not have a smartphone. I take his phone, typing in my name and number, close it and then hand it back,

He hands me mine back, and I see he put his name in as Fox. I look up at him, eyebrows pinched together. "Why did you put fox and not your name?"

He gives me a sinister smile, "Little lamb, you will find out soon enough."

Getting sucked into his stare once again, I'm shaken from the spell, when I feel my stomach and legs wet. I hear the chair scrape across the floor and Aster looking like he's about ready to jump over the bar and strangle the person responsible for my wet dress.

Wide eyed, and mortified, tears starting to form. I look up at the smirking bartender. "Oops, my bad, that was an accident, and we're closed, so leave."

It was no accident, he knows that, I know that, everyone left here knows that. He could've been nice, told us it was closing time, instead he had to pour a drink on me embarrassing me. *What did I do to deserve this?*

The feeling of embarrassment is gone as I feel it drip down my leg onto my shoes. My hands start to flex, my eyes starting to twitch, and my teeth grinding together.

Before I can even stop myself, my body reacts out of peer rage and I'm out of my chair, "Hey asshole."

"Excuse me?-" He turns around and I punch him right in the face, hoping to leave a black eye.

"What the fuck?" He screams, holding his eye.

He rears his hand back, and I close my eyes, bracing myself for impact, but the sting never comes. I open my eyes and see Aster has caught the bartender's wrist, rolls of something terrifying coming off of him in waves, it's anger, sinister, pure hatred. His reaction is pulling at my heartstrings.

The bartender tries to pull his grip out of Aster's hold, but he won't let go, he won't speak, he just looks like he's going to kill him any second. It isn't until I place my hand on Aster's shoulder that he's jolted from his trance releasing his hand. Placing his arm around my shoulder, he throws his leather jacket around me.

I look up at him and whisper, "Thank you." Hugging his jacket tighter around me.

He looks forward, eyes still glossed over in anger, "He'll be meeting the Grim reaper soon," he says menacingly.

Something about his promise should scare me, but with how he was acting towards me the whole night, it doesn't. I only wish I could be there when the messenger of death comes for him.

Stepping outside, I see Jessica sitting on the curb, shivering, waiting by the Uber, she must have ordered for us inside. Why she didn't get in I don't understand. She stands up, and opens the door to the Uber, not saying a word and getting in. *She's pissed.*

I can't believe I forgot about Jessica, it's only September, but it's a colder night. Both being in dresses, I know she has to be turning into a popsicle. I feel bad, but not enough to want to stop talking. If it wasn't for this place closing and the bartender, I would stay here all night, probably until the next morning.

Now I'll never come back.

Before he walks away he grabs my hand and kisses it. "Until next time, little lamb." The butterflies that were fluttering earlier are now in a full on frenzy.

I stand staring after him, completely in a trance until I feel Jessica pull me towards the Uber.

We get in the car, and I glance back hoping to catch one final look of Aster before he leaves. He's standing on the sidewalk, watching as our Uber pulls out. Jessica tugs my arm, turning to me with excited expectancy on her face, waiting for all the details.

I tell her everything that transpired, hardly believing the words coming out of my mouth. The Uber driver looks at me with a weird face through the rearview mirror. I look at him with the same face and give him my address.

He shakes his head and mumbles, "crazy bitch."

I ignore his crude words and go back to telling Jessica about my night. The driver navigates through the city to my house, occasionally looking back at me, but he doesn't say anything else. The Uber drops me off first, and I hug and kiss Jess good-night, telling her to text me when she gets home before making my way inside.

Heading straight to my room, I change into my pajamas and hear a ding from my phone. Looking at it, I see it's from Fox. I go into his contact, changing his name because I like Aster much better than Fox.

ASTER

Goodnight little lamb.

I don't bother to send a reply, instead I lay in bed holding my phone gleefully like a child and fall asleep thinking about Aster and the night we had. Hoping to see him again in my dreams.

Stirring from my sleep, already missing the smell of sandalwood and mint, I rush to my canvas compelled to add yet another blue rose to my forever growing painting of roses. I don't know what they mean, but after I have a nightmare, I feel compelled to paint a new one onto the canvas, never feeling like it's complete. After I paint the final petal, I get out a clean canvas and paint the nightmare I had, trying to shake off the hold it has on me, despite being awake. I place it with the other nightmare paintings I keep hidden from everyone, letting it dry with my secret paintings.

These are my favorite, so dark and twisted I'll never share them with another soul, not even Jess. These are parts of me that make me question my sanity and humanity for loving them so much. Every time I paint them, every part of me awakens, and I never want this feeling to go away.

Cleaning up, I head to the kitchen to pour myself a cup of coffee. There's nothing like a nice hot mug in the early morning. Looking out my kitchen window at the sunrise, the sky is full of life, yellows and oranges streaking across the sky like an abstract painting. *We should go to a haunted house, for our first date.* Graves, the best haunted house, opens up soon, and I think Aster would enjoy it as much as me, but tickets are impossible to get. I sigh, Thinking about Aster, and his magnetic eyes, and I can't help the eerie feeling that blankets me. I Brush it off, wishing the nightmare I just had would linger a little longer.

Remembering the text from last night, I grab my phone and shoot off a response to Aster.

SERENA

Good Morning Aster.

Setting my phone down I bask in the afterglow of my nightmare and stare off into the sunrise.

FIVE

ASTER

It's a nice autumn night, with a full moon illuminating the sky. I'm sitting on the hood of my Chevelle, watching my breath dance in the cool air and smelling my little lamb on my clothes, awaiting my next victim. I look down at my watch, tired, but itching to get my hands on him anyway. The time 4:15am is flashing across the screen, and I'm wondering when he's going to walk out the door.

Another minute ticks by in agonizing anticipation until I finally hear the back door open. Seeing him walking out into the alley where I'm waiting, a new wave of anger washes over me. He starts to walk to his car, reaching into his pocket to bring out a pack of cigarettes and a lighter. He takes one from the pack and places it in his mouth, covering the end from the wind so it doesn't go out as he lights it. Taking one puff, his eyes roll to the back of his head as he exhales the smoke.

I watch him, a moment longer, my fingers flexing as I wait for him to amble closer. He walks past the shadows I'm hidden within, not even hesitating a beat, clearly unaware of the predator hunting him. *This is almost too easy.* If I knew killing men would be this simple, I might have done it before now, but there is something about my lambs that make them my primary target.

I'm up behind him in a flash, a rag soaked in chloroform held over his mouth until his body goes limp in my arms. Hauling him over my shoulder like a sack of potatoes. *This worthless piece of shit weighs nothing.* I throw his body into the back of my trunk, closing it without a second thought. Turning around, I take a big breath and light up one of my own cigarettes to give me a minute to collect myself.

What am I doing? I never take males as my victims. Ever. I rap my knuckles against my car, the thrill of taking my first male victim making me nervous. I don't get nervous, ever, but this is different, this man could have people looking for him, as where my lambs don't have anyone. I made sure to check the street for hidden cameras, and that everyone was gone to cover my tracks, but I'm still buzzing with nervous energy.

Muted with the realization I'm breaking one of my rules. *All because he insulted my little lamb.*

It's not like she is anything special, aside from the sparks we felt touching each other, which never happens. None of my lambs have ever made me feel anything. I touch my hand, the memory of her soft hands in mine coming back to me. She has the softest, smoothest, tiny hands that fit perfectly in mine. I want to hold her hands again, next time properly. Her lips looked just as soft, I found myself leaning in more than once just wanting to feel them. I bring my hands to my lips, touching the bottom one, imagining what she would have felt like.

I shake my head from the thought, she's just my next lamb for slaughter, that's all. What is it about her that makes me want to kill anyone who looks at her wrong? I run my fingers through my hair, and take several puffs, letting the smoke fill my lungs, before I blow it out. The way this piece of shit was looking at her, like she was crazy, had me instantly seeing red. The same red I'm going to make pour out of him later.

I've never had this reaction to anyone, I couldn't care less honestly about anyone. The only woman I ever cared about was my mother, and now I don't even care about her. I always make my lambs think I care, when all I care about is their bodies on my table.

I'm always wearing a mask, hiding the devil inside that is fighting to get out at the most impromptu moments. Usually I'm pretty good at suppressing the beast until I'm home, in my space, doing my work.

Only my little lambs get to see the true me, but tonight he came out just a little. At that bartender and the girl laughing at my newest little lamb. I just felt something inside me start to crack. I needed to feel the bartender's life in my hands at that moment. As much as I want those girls who laughed at my little lamb on my table as well; I only ever have one victim at a time, so the bartender will do, for tonight.

He deserves it more anyway.

Letting my fingers fall from my hair, I let out an exasperated sigh, throwing my cigarette on the ground, and crushing it out with my shoe.

I get in my car and "Nightmare" by Avenged Sevenfold comes blaring through my speakers. I turn it down, trying not to draw attention, and make my way home.

I get home about twenty minutes later driving up the dirt road through the trees that lead to my home. I drive towards the house, passing it and driving five more minutes behind my house on a grassy path to my work space.

Pulling up, I exit and go to open the door to the work space. The light above my work table starts to flicker, and I make a mental note to go buy light bulbs later.

I grab a syringe and bottle of ketamine from my workbench, filling the needle with ease that only comes with years of practice. Placing the bottle back down, I walk back out to my car and open the trunk, seeing he's still asleep. Usually by now my lambs are awake, but he's not one of my lambs. He's dying in the same place, but he won't be as special as them. I look down at his ugly sleeping form smoothly inserting the needle into his neck. That should make sure he stays asleep while I get my work station prepped and his body ready for slaughter.

About an hour passes before he finally starts to stir, making my impatience grow. I've been waiting all night to torture him, but his sleeping is making me agitated. Blinking slowly as he shakes off the effects of the sedatives, looking confused he asks, "Where am I?" Without talking to anyone in particular.

I'm hiding in the shadows in the corner, enjoying the anticipation of what's to come now that he is finally awake.

He starts to move a little, trying and failing to sit up. His eye's bulge, panic setting in.

"Hello!" he starts to yell, "Is anyone there?" Now he's angry, jerking his body in every way in a fruitless attempt to get out of his restraints. "What the hell? This isn't funny, let me go or so help me I will-"

I step out of the darkness, remaining out of his sight, and in a menacing voice say, "You'll what?"

Fear leaving him frozen, slowly starting to look around to see where the voice came from. I do love seeing the fear in my victims eyes, it makes what's about to come next all the sweeter.

Stepping around so he can see my face, his eyes bulge in recognition. "*You*?!" He shrieks, rage forcing his voice to shake. "This isn't funny man. Why the fuck am I here?"

I get close to his face, hoping he can smell the cigarette I smoked earlier, and quietly say, "I didn't think it was very funny when you looked at my little lamb like she was crazy." He looks confused, trying to remember the events of the night, but coming up empty.

My body stiffens, eyes flaring, and my hands are begging to

grab the weapon to make him scream. I grab my knife from my instrument tray and slam it down into his hand so fast he doesn't have time to think.

He lets out a blood curdling scream, his voice echoing through the shed. "I'm going to fucking kill you, you think-"

Not letting him finish his sentence, I bring the knife up, and back into the same spot, increasing his pain. His hand starts to twitch, the pain I can only imagine starting to become too much. I contemplate taking the knife out and stabbing it into his other hand, but that would be showing mercy.

Mercy is not an option for this asshole.

I grab another knife, leaving the other one in his hand. Walking around to the other side of him, I push this knife in slowly, letting the skin hug the knife, the blood slowly coming up, and the pain all the more agonizing. "That was your punishment for making my little lamb feel crazy."

"I don't know what you're talking about. Little lamb? Fuck dude, there are so many people who come in the bar, I don't remember everyone." He says through clenched teeth.

"You don't remember my little lamb? Well, let me jog your memory." I twist the knife, I'm still holding, my patience wearing thin. "She was the one at the bar, in the red dress, that hugged her curves in all the right places." I feel a twitch, reaching down to adjust my growing erection, from thinking of her. *Now is not the time to get off.* Clearing my throat, I continue, "Drinking Moscow mules." Still nothing, like she didn't even exist in his tiny little world. I grind my teeth, "You almost made her cry."

His eyes light up, finally remembering my little lamb, and it pisses me off how long it took for him to remember. *He needs to be punished.* I walk over to my table, grabbing my needle-nose plier, with a sick smirk lifting my cheeks. I pull the knives out of his hands, intentionally dragging the blades through his skin, and absentmindedly click the end of the pliers together as I decide where to start.

His eyes widened in fear, "What are you doing with that man? Look, I'm sorry, I won't do it again. I promise!"

Placing the tool over his index finger, I look him in the eye. "This is your punishment for taking so long to answer me." I pull out the nail, and he screams even louder than when I stabbed him.

"P-please let me go. I swear I will never insult her ever again," he sobs, snot running down his face.

"I have nine fingernails left, by the last one, you wouldn't have even come close to learning your lesson."

This makes him cry harder, making it difficult for him to catch his breath. *Fucking pathetic. My lambs have more dignity than this worm.*

I grab his next finger, his wails grating on my nerves. "This is for looking at her like she was crazy".

His nail makes a sucking sound as I pull it from his finger.

Pull

"This is for giving her a disgusted look when I called her beautiful"

Pull

I grab his naked ring finger, bending it backwards, until I hear a *snap*. "That is for spilling a drink on her." He lets out a blood curdling scream.

Pull

His pinky is the last to go on this hand, "This is for trying to slap her back, after she punched you." I want him to really feel this one, so I take my time, slowly pulling it out.

One hand is completely drenched in blood, and the other is just starting to bleed. *Still not enough.* He's in so much pain, he is shaking. In a ragged voice, he pleads, "Please- please, no more. I can't take it. I'm begging you."

"I have one hand left, and you haven't even begun to feel a semblance of the pain you caused my little lamb."

He tries to move away again, his fight or flight instincts kick in, and he tries with all his might to free himself from the restraints. I continue dishing out his punishment, removing fingernail after fingernail until all that remains are bloody nubs.

He passes out after the last nail is taken, ruining my fun. Blood drips from his hands onto the floor, adding to my collection of invisible stains long since bleached away. I walk out of my kill room, into the cool morning, allowing the chill to help wake me. It's been a long night, and I wasn't expecting the sun to already be rising, but when it comes to torture, you lose all track of time. I stay out there staring at the rising sun, for what feels like hours.

Killing a man is so *different* from killing a woman. A man starts to beg instantly, and then tries to get away, while a woman is smart, trying to get away first, only begging for their lives once they give up. Most usually fight until their last dying breaths. The rest, they fight until the torture stops, and the knife comes out, holding it above their heart. They can always guess what's about to happen next, accepting their fate.

I don't enjoy this kill as much as I do my little lambs. This kill is insignificant to me, but I had to rid the earth of him. For what he did to my lamb, I'm giving her the justice she deserves. For some reason, one I don't even understand myself, I needed to kill him, for my little lamb.

When she punched him in the face, I was shocked. I felt a similar darkness to my own, seeping out of her. The anger matched mine. When I told her, he was going to meet the grim reaper, she didn't even react how a normal person would. Most would freak out that I was talking about his impending doom. She didn't, I saw her smile, the way her eyes danced with the idea. She wants his death as much as I do.

Being the gentleman that I am, I'm making her wish come true.

The sun is halfway in the sky and I turn back to the shed.

I need to finish what I started.

Walking over I slap the bartender awake. He startles, forgetting where he is for a second, then the fear starts to sink back in.

"You know," I say, cracking my knuckles, "I never got your name."

He glares at me, staying silent. The only form of rebellion he has left.

I chuckle. As if he could win this fight. "Oh, how naive you are. I'll ask again, this time I won't be so nice. Tell me your name." I demand.

Still, he stays silent, newfound bravado in his gaze.

Mindlessly, I pick up the dried bloody knife behind me and bring it down into his stomach. His body lurches forward, as much as it can tied down, as he lets out a bloody, gurgled cough. "Why do you want to know?"

Hand still wrapped around the handle, "I like to know the names of the people I kill."

"Gary," he wheezes, his eyes darting around in desperation.

I Laugh, "Of course your name is Gary. It's fitting, you're pathetic, but special."

"Wha-what makes me special?"

I smile cruelly at him "You're my first male victim, and you're pushing me to try something new. You don't deserve to die the way my lambs die."

He looks at me, his brows drawing together as sweat dots his forehead. "You keep calling that bitch-"

I pull the knife out, slamming it into his stomach again, twisting until I hit bone. Leaning in close in his face, I watch his pupils shrink in fear as I loom over him. "That was a mistake," I hissed. "Call my lamb any profanities again, and I won't end this fast."

Gary coughs up blood, having the audacity to smile at me. His body shakes from the pain and blood loss, but that doesn't stop him from saying in a raspy voice. "It sounds like you call your victims 'lambs', so she must be next." He pauses, his breath rattling his chest. "Does this make me one of your lambs, too?"

Yanking the knife up, I admire how his blood catches the low light in the shed. "No, Gary. You are not one of my little lambs. You are nothing."

I stab him again and again, blood flying everywhere, and tainting everything in my space with his filth, until I see his body go limp and my arm burns from overuse.

I'm breathing hard, looking around at the mess I created. *Why did I do this?* I never kill spontaneously like this, every kill is always planned meticulously so I don't get caught. I never kill men, I never break my rules. Breaking any of my rules could lead to my demise. I pace back and forth, running my bloody hands through my hair.

Tonight goes against every rule I've ever had, my breaths come faster and faster as I stare at the destruction around me. *What did my little lamb do to me? What did I do for her?*

I shake my head, forcing away the panic simmering just underneath the surface. I begin cleaning up, freezing for a moment not knowing where to start. There's blood everywhere, staining every surface around Gary. My lips curl in disgust, as I look at his prone body.

He doesn't deserve to be displayed like my lambs are. He needs to disappear, as if he was never here to begin with.

I wipe the blood dripping down my face, stopping it from getting into my eyes. Squelching through the puddles of blood to turn on my incinerator. Grabbing my saw, ignoring the ache in my shoulders as I begin cutting Gary into pieces. Sweat dripping down my back, I throw his body along with my clothes, into the flame without a second thought.

No one will ever find him.

I grab my burner phone, my body trembling in exhaustion, satisfaction, and anxiety, and send off a text.

ASTER

Good morning little lamb.

I got a response a few minutes later.

TORI

> Well good morning to you too. Do you miss me already?

I met Tori at a club a few weeks ago, she was alone, just like all my lambs are. I always take my time with my creations, usually spending a week or two getting to know them before luring them in. After I bide my time, I plan a date and bring them back to my place, making sure no one knows where they are going. Then I begin my fun. I usually hunt every two to three months, to give myself a break, but the anger and confusion I was feeling; I *needed* another lamb on my table. It may not be Serena, but her time will come. I want to play with her longer before I say goodbye. Tori has been on the hook long enough, and now, it is her time.

ASTER

> More than you know.

I cringe as I press send, getting a response right away.

TORI

> Well, can I see you tonight? The plans I did have backfired, so I'm free."

I copy the address of a bar to meet and click send.

ASTER

> See you at 8, little lamb.

TORI

> Can't wait, big bad wolf.

She is nothing like my newest lamb. Every single lamb I have captured has always called me their wolf, because that's what you think of when it comes to animals. Serena though, she instantly called me fox, taking me by surprise.

I smile at that thought, and place my burner back on my

work table. I kick off my work boots and slip on my regular boots. Making my way back towards my house, I let the morning light warm my skin. Slowly heading up the steps, I slip off my boots then head inside.

I glance between my bedroom and my bathroom, exhaustion slowly taking over the muted euphoria I feel from my kill. I battle for what seems to be minutes, if I want to shower or just knock out. Knowing I would regret it and eager to get rid of every trace of Gary, I grunt and begrudgingly make my way to the bathroom and turn on the shower.

Stepping into the hot spray, I let the water run over me, watching the blood go down the drain. I wash everything off, taking extra time to get the blood out from under my fingernails. I smirk as the water finally clears. *Good riddance, Gary.* Stepping out of the shower, I grab a towel and dry off, not even bothering to get dressed before collapsing in bed and succumbing to the dark.

SIX

ASTER

Waking up groggy a couple hours later, seeing it is already dark outside, I grab my phone and see it's 6pm. My stomach drops, my body is still exhausted from Gary. Normally I feel reenergized after a kill, practically bouncing around my property until the high wears off. I've never slept through preparing for my newest lamb.

Rushing to get up, still naked, I only have two hours until I meet Tori, and I need to prepare everything. Preparation usually takes me three hours, but I have to hurry since I slept through it. I throw on some clothes and head back to the shed, grabbing my burner phone. I have a missed call and text from Tori.

TORI

Hey I'm on my way, GPS says I'll be there a little before 8, hope that's okay! See you soon.

I curse and shoot a text back

ASTER

That's fine, that just gives us longer to be together.

Fuck. I scramble to get my kill space ready, rushing through my routine with shaky hands. After the table is set and my tools laid out ready and waiting, I grab her rose and place it in the vase, my nerves settling once I complete this step.. It's always the last thing I do to prepare for my slaughter. Before I leave, I grab the burner phone and a syringe prefilled with ketamine from my desk and make my way back home. As I'm buttoning up my shirt I see another text.

TORI

The Uber just dropped me off, where are you?

ASTER

I'll be there in twenty minutes, see you soon.

TORI

See you soon.

THE BAR IS DESERTED WHEN I GET THERE. I WALK IN AND SEE TORI sitting at the bar in a little black dress with her legs crossed and martini in hand.

I walk over to her, plastering my panty-dropping smile on my face. Giving her a hug before I sit down. She holds me longer than I'm comfortable with, letting my mind wander back to Serena, I release her. I ordered a Moscow mule, the same one Serena ordered, sipping on it slowly, imagining her lips around the straw.

We talk for twenty minutes about nothing remotely interesting. I see a flash of dark hair in my peripheral, heart pounding. *Serena?* When the woman turns towards the bar, my excitement shifts to rage. *It's not her.* I take a deep breath. *Relax. Focus.* I ask her if she wants to go back to my place, adding interest I don't feel into my gaze. She nods, quickly finishing her second martini, and we head out the door.

It's a ten minute drive from my house and she sits in silence the whole time. The silence pulls me back to thoughts of ocean blue eyes, red lips, in a sinfully red dress. I adjust myself, gaining a giggle from Tori. *Great, she thinks my boner is for her.* I ignore her reaction, focusing on the road ahead.

Pulling up, she stares at my house in admiration. "You sure do have a beautiful home, and a lot of property. I thought the road here was never going to end." She laughs, the noise grating and only causing impatience to rise.

"It was my parents home. They left everything to me, and I just can't seem to leave it. Too many memories."

"Oh, I'm so sorry, Aster," she says with a remorseful tone, gently resting her sweaty palm on my arm. She starts to say something else but I get lost in a memory of my mother, completely forgetting why I brought her here in the first place. I lay my hands over the steering wheel, and stare at the kitchen window.

"Aster." my mother calls out from the front porch of our farm style ranch home. "It's time for lunch, I made your favorite."

I drop my toy trucks and race towards the house, stopping at the door when Mama scolds me for forgetting to take off my shoes.

"Now, Aster, how many times do I have to remind you to take off your shoes before coming into the house? I don't want you tracking mud on my freshly mopped floors."

I bow my head, mumbling, "Sorry Mama," and take off my shoes, leaving them on the porch in a haphazard pile. I walk over to the round table next to the dining room window and sit down.

Mama walks over to me and places a plate filled with four hotdogs cooked in butter, on a bun drizzled with ketchup, fries, and an assortment of fruit on the side. My stomach grumbles in anticipation, my mouth watering as I wait for her to sit and begin eating before I dig in. She places a tall cup of iced tea down next to me, condensation already dripping down the side.

"To wash it all down with," She smiles, kissing my forehead and walking to the other side of the table to join me for lunch. She takes a bite of her hot dog, a spot of ketchup clinging to her lip, and takes a sip of her tea. She sets her glass down with a soft clack on the worn table. "Daddy and I have a lamb to slaughter tonight, so we need you to be a good boy and stay in the house and watch your show." She gives me a stern look, resting her chin in her hand. "It'll be after dinner, but I will make you some chocolate chip cookies if you're a good boy like last time."

I slink into my chair and cross my arms. "Why can't I help you slaughter those lambs? Mama, I swear I won't get in the way!" I whine. Mama and Daddy always go to the shed without me, it's not fair.

"Now, Aster, you know you're not old enough yet."

I huff, grunting without caring about my manners. "Can't I just watch? I want to learn, Mama, Please! Just this once."

She smiles sweetly at me. "How about on your next birthday, when you're ten. We will let you join in and teach you everything there is to know about the slaughter. Plus you're learning without watching, with the movies I show you, and lessons we have."

"But my birthday isn't for another 3 months, and it isn't the same," I grumble.

"Patience, my little fox. I promise you the wait will be well worth it. Your father and I will pick a perfect little lamb just for you. A special gift, for our special boy."

With a nod of my head, and the promise of my birthday in my mind, I finish the rest of my hot dog. Stuff the fries in my mouth, gulp down my tea and start to leave the table when Mama stops me. "Aster you didn't even touch your fruit. Have a couple pieces, and then you can go back to playing."

Grabbing my fork, I shovel all my fruit into my mouth, looking like a chipmunk with bulging cheeks.

She smiles at me, her eyes twinkling, "Thank you."

After dinner my parents leave me in the living room, with a bowl of popcorn and Courage The Cowardly Dog playing on the TV. They each kiss my forehead with a warning to stay inside, promising fresh baked cookies after they're done.

After about an hour of waiting, I decided I can't wait any longer. I could watch cartoons all night, but I really want to see Mama and Daddy in action, learn by watching. I put on my shoes and walk to the shed where my parents are. Walking up, I hear screaming, I panic, worrying about Mama, sprinting to the shed and peeping through the little hole in time to see my parents slaughtering a girl strapped to the middle of a table.

I gasp, stumbling back in shock. Tripping over my feet, I sprawled out on the ground, scared they might hear me. Quickly using my hands to cover my mouth, I silently pant, unable to take a full breath. The girl screamed again and I considered myself lucky. They couldn't hear me over her screaming. Slowly, I crawl back to the shed, unable to shake my curiosity. Peeking through the wall once more I watch, mesmerized, as my parents turn this girl into a work of art. Taking her heart, and placing it in a jar, to be stored with the rest of their victims organs. Each victim they take, they always choose a different organ. Each caress of their blade a delicate dance with her skin. Each drop of blood a new addition to the collection scattered around the barn.

Once they start cleaning up, I run back to the house and pretend to be asleep on the couch. When they walk in, I feel my Mama kiss my forehead, lifting me up to carry me to my room. She lays me in my bed and brushes the hair out of my face, her fingers gentle against my skin. I feel her sitting there, staring at me, before finally getting up and shutting the door, leaving me in the dark with flashes of steel and stained red filtering through my mind.

That was the first time I saw my parents slaughter a little lamb.

Since that night, I would sneak to the barn and watch them work every time they had a new lamb. The bright red against the barn floor burned in my memory, causing my heart to race. It was all I saw when I closed my eyes every night until the day of my birthday.

The day I've been waiting for.

My parents woke me by singing happy birthday. I open my eyes to a small angel food cake with a knife through the middle of it stretching out to me. "Aster, this is your knife. Your father and I picked out just for you and all your little lambs."

Gleefully, I take the knife out of the cake, enjoying the weight of it in my hand. It's a curved blade with a wooden handle that's difficult for my fingers to wrap all the way around. I start to jab the air practicing the stabs Daddy taught me during one of our many lessons, before my lamb is laid before me.

Daddy holds out the case it came in. "Let's keep it in here for safe keeping until you're ready to use it tonight." He ruffles my hair with a soft smile on his face.

I place the knife back in its box, and we all walk to the kitchen to enjoy my birthday breakfast. Mama made my favorite, chocolate chip pancakes with a side of scrambled eggs and bacon.

In the middle of having breakfast, we start to hear cars driving up our gravel road. I look out the window and see cops and F.B.I. pull into the grass surrounding our home. My parents show no movement to run or hide. Instead, they continue eating breakfast, as if it was any other morning.

I, on the other hand, was panicking knowing I'll never get to slaughter my first lamb with my parents.

The door gets kicked open. Chaos erupting in our kitchen. My father is tackled to the floor. My mother is dragged out of her chair. Neither make a single noise as they're both handcuffed and walked out of the house.

The little lamb my parents picked just for me was being carried to the ambulance by a pissed off looking man in a uniform I didn't recognize. She looked like an adult around my parents age, bigger build, with dark hair. Tears of frustration pool in my eyes, I will never get to see her beneath my blade. A young woman, with blonde hair flowing around her face, introduces herself as the social worker and takes me the opposite direction of my parents.

I'm kicking and screaming, desperate to get to them, when I hear my mother say, "Please, let me just say goodbye to my boy."

The cop sighs and nods towards the social worker who is holding me by my shoulders. She walks me over, and I hug my Mama for dear life. I didn't fully understand what was happening, but I'd seen enough on TV to know it wasn't good.

Mama whispers in my ear "Your birthday gift is in your secret hiding spot, when you're eighteen go back and get it. You can use it on your little lambs." She kisses my cheek, resting her forehead against mine. "I love you, little fox."

I wipe the tears from my eyes. "I love you, Mama."

The social worker takes me away, shepherding me into the back of an idling squad car. The cop shuts the door and drives away, taking me from them forever. I was so stunned, I didn't say a word for eight months after my birthday. They thought it was because of what my parents did.

But it wasn't.

They took me from my parents, and stole my chance to slaughter my first lamb. They took everything from me in an instant, all I wanted to do was the same in return.

I eventually did speak again. I was never adopted from the foster homes the blonde woman constantly bounced me between. No one wanted to take on the burden of the boy with the notorious serial killers as parents. Who could blame them? They all whispered about me being just like my parents. It's not like I stopped them or tried to prove them wrong. When I turned eighteen, I got the fuck out of there, changed my last name, and started my own legacy of killing, finally putting my birthday present to use for the first time.

Mama and Daddy would be so proud.

I'M PULLED FROM MY THOUGHTS WHEN I HEAR MY NAME BEING SAID over and over again in a voice that sounds like nails on a chalkboard.

"Aster, are you okay? I've been trying to get your attention for five minutes now," Tori whispered.

I shake my head, forcing my lips into a small smile I hope looks apologetic. "Sorry, little lamb. I'm okay. I was just remembering something," I say with a sad smile.

"Oh yeah? Wanna share?" She smiles, fluttering her lashes as she nudges me, taking advantage of the opportunity to stay pressed to my side.

I don't answer her, instead I get out of the car and she follows suit. I start to shepherd her away from the house.

Her eyebrows draw together as she looks back at the house. "Where are we going?"

Grabbing her hand, I pull her another step away from my parents house. "I have something special just for you, it's out back" I look down and see she is wearing stilettos, my lips thinning at the realization. "It's about a ten minute walk from here. We can walk, or I can drive us over."

She smiles shyly, "I would rather drive, I'm not wearing the right shoes for a hike." She gestures to her outfit, flexing her core as a way to make her seem smaller. Less significant. Less important.

Tugging her over to my other vehicle I open the door and allow her to climb into the green Dodge Ram before jogging around the hood and jumping in.

"Nice truck." She looks down, an impish look in her eyes. "I hope you're not compensating."

All I do is smirk as we make our drive out to my shed.

We pull up to the shed a few minutes later, and I help her

down, before escorting her to my work space. She hesitates, looking at me as if I was going to kill her. *If only she knew.*

"What's so special about... this?" She motions at the little house, clearly not impressed.

Reaching over her head, I open the door and smile down at her, ushering her in. "This is where all the lambs go for slaughter."

She looks up with confusion in her eyes, but before she has time to process what I just said I slide the needle into her neck, quickly injecting the ketamine. Her eyes roll into the back of her head, and she falls into my arms without so much as a scream.

I shut the door behind me and begin to play.

IT'S WELL INTO THE NIGHT BY THE TIME I'M THROUGH. INSTEAD OF my normal routine, preparing my lambs to be displayed, frustration won over. I burned her. Every piece was set to flames.

Presenting her just didn't feel right when I already had a new lamb lined up. I need to see her, but she's bringing feelings out in me that I don't understand.

I pull out my phone, searching for her name, even though I don't know her last name, yet. I find her pretty easily. She posts her whole life on social media.

Not the smartest, we're going to have to change that. Looks like she's staying in tonight. I click the video she just posted, smiling as I watch her.

She's in overalls, paint is smeared on her cheek, she looks completely enamored by the piece she's working on. *She paints, just like me.* Loving that we have that in common, I do a deep dive into all of her accounts I can find.

I need to see her again.

Hopping back in my truck, I speed towards the house, ready

to find out where she lives. I come to an abrupt stop. *What am I doing?* Completely dumbfounded by my actions, I close my phone, and decide I can't see her anymore. No matter how badly I want to lay her on my table, I can't.

Walking back into my house, I lay down in bed. Closing my eyes, I dream of the northern sea, and red waves.

SEVEN

SERENA

It's been two weeks since I met Aster at the bar, and still no word from him since the goodnight and good morning texts he sent. I texted him back each time, but he never responded after he first reached out. After the amazing conversation we shared and his hero act, although I'd call his heroic act more of a villian protecting the one he loves. Like in one of my books. Hero's never kill for anyone, but villains would kill everyone to save the one they love. Those are the vibes that Aster was giving me. I thought he would ask me on a proper date, but the question never came. I stopped texting, not wanting to seem needy.

Even though I've had commissions to keep me busy, my mind can't stop thinking about those teal green eyes. I even went to a candleshop to find a candle that smells like sandalwood and mint, very hard to find by the way. I did find it and bought three. I've been burning it nonstop just to be reminded of him.

It's crazy, we met once, I shouldn't be this obsessed with a guy who won't even text me back. That spark we both felt, that's what keeps that line of hope still open. The reason why I can't forget about him, among other things. He felt it, too. He was the one to mention it first, but now he's ghosting me.

I'm going to be pissed and petty if he reaches out again. Who am I kidding? I know I'm going to fall at his feet the moment he smiles at me.

I'm hopeless.

I place my paintbrush down, after putting the finishing touches on my latest commission piece.

It's a portrait piece of my client, her family, and their golden retriever. She requested an outside setting. So I painted them in a field with wildflowers, of blues, pinks, and purples surrounding them. There is a tree off to the right, a swing coming from it, and her children are playing together on the swing, both of them laughing with smiles on their faces. Makes me wonder what it would have been like to have a brother or sister growing up. Being an only child can be lonely, no one to tease, talk to, or share secrets with. Makes me envious of those who do have someone to share a life like that with. Someone by your side, who will never leave.

Their dog is running through the field, sprinting across the meadow chasing a butterfly. My client and her husband are standing behind their children, his arm around her waist. You can see the love in their eyes as they watch their children play. Their family carefree and enjoying the sun. I start to picture me and my future husband with our children, enjoying life so freely like that. I smile, staring at the painting for a few more minutes, when Aster's face starts to take the face of the husband, I shake my head, clearing it of the idea.

He won't even text you back, there's no way he's going to marry you.

I stand up to grab my phone, snap a picture, and send it to my client to see if she wants anything added. I get a response immediately.

KELSEY

It's perfect, better than I could have imagined!
Thank you so much!

I'm so glad you like it! I will get it wrapped up and shipped out first thing Monday morning.

That quickly? Wow! Thank you, truly, I can't wait to show my family.

I put my phone in my pocket and take off my paint apron. I make my way to my kitchen and grab a bottle of water from the fridge. I used to keep some by my easel, but I kept drinking my paint water and putting my brush into my glass on accident. I've gone without ever since, often forgetting how thirsty I am, too busy focusing on my art to remember to drink anything.

My phone buzzes in my pocket, and I see I have a new match on some random dating website Jess put on my phone, so I would stop obsessing about Aster not texting me back.

There have been losers and perverts, one after another, on this thing. After all the random dick pics coming my way, I'm ready to throw my phone across the room and give up entirely. Seriously, why do guys think girls like getting pictures of their tiny dicks. Let me just open my phone, oh look that's a nice dick, I'm totally going to message this guy back. Oh wow the way this one curves, I'm going to ask how that feels, no! Like ew, I wish they would just realize with how many blocks I'm sure they get, that they would stop. It's like blocking them makes them try harder.

I see my match is from a guy named Tyler. Looking at his profile, he has a skater boy look to him, with baggy jeans light brown, shaggy hair. It's messy, like he's run his fingers through it a few too many times, but still looks presentable. He has friendly blue eyes and a killer smile. Looking at the rest of his photos, he looks very outgoing and active. Something I am not, I'm more of a homebody, preferring the company of a good book, rather than going to a huge party where I'm running into people I don't even know.

Being forced to attend my parties when I was younger was more than enough for me. Dad wanted his friends to meet me and their kids to have someone to talk to. The other girls my age played Barbies, where I would rather play with my Living Dead Dolls. Needless to say, no one wanted to play with me. So when dad was distracted, mom would tell me I could leave and I'd run back to my room and watch my favorite shows on cartoon network, my favorite being *Courage The Cowardly Dog*. The show was so creepy, and I loved everything about it. I still watch it as an adult, when I'm feeling nostalgic.

His profile says he's outgoing, and loves to go on hikes, has a killer sense of humor, and is looking for the right girl to join him on his next adventure.

Even though we seem to be total opposites, he is cute, and I do need the distraction. I bite my lower lip, debating on if I should write to him or give up and hope Aster calls. The hopeful side of me loses, and I go to write a message to him, but as I am typing one pops up from him instead.

TYLER

What's a beautiful girl like you doing on an app like this?

SERENA

I could ask you the same thing?

TYLER

Looking for someone to share my next adventure with, but you know that already, if you read my profile.

SERENA

I did, and though you are cute, I don't know if you could convince me to go hiking. I am not really an outdoorsy type of girl.

TYLER

Aww, you think I'm cute? If I can't convince you
to come hiking, could I convince you to come
to dinner with me?

I sit on my bed, knees up to my chest, feeling giddy, that he's
actually flirting with me. Did I kiss a leprechaun in my sleep, or
did a dragonfly land on me? Where are all these hot guys
coming from all of a sudden? I glance at the mirror and stare at
my reflection. Grabbing a piece of my hair to examine, nothing
looks different, sure, I've lost a couple pounds, but I still look as I
always have.

SERENA

Someone's a little forward.

TYLER

I don't like to waste my time, and when I see
something I want, I go for it, worst you could
say is no.

I want to say yes, but I can't stop thinking of those green
eyes. I start twirling my hair around my finger, bringing the
piece up to my mouth, reminding myself of the blue eyes who is
shooting his shot.

TYLER

But please don't say no.

His message made me giggle, reaching up to touch my smile,
I decided, what's the worst that could happen?

SERENA

If I say yes, when would we be having this
dinner and where?

TYLER

How about tonight at 8? We can meet
downtown, there's a great little Italian place I
would love to take you to.

SERENA

Wow, you like to work fast, hopefully not in all things. I like how bold you are, so why not. What's the place called?

TYLER

Bold is the best way to live! Life is too boring otherwise. It's called Giovanna's Italiana. It's not a super fancy place, but most people usually dress nice.

SERENA

Is that your way of telling me to dress nice for our date?

I look towards my closet, seeing mostly black, with a few spots of colors.

TYLER

Only if you want to, no pressure.

SERENA

Guess you'll be surprised when I show up.

TYLER

I'll see you at 8, mia caro.

SERENA

Be honest, you totally looked that Italian word up?

TYLER

Guilty as charged, I wanted to impress you.

SERENA

Just be yourself.

TYLER

Noted, see you soon, Serena.

SERENA

That's better, see you soon, Tyler.

I close the app and shoot off a text to Jessica.

SERENA

Come over, and help me get ready for my date tonight?

She replies almost instantly.

JESSICA

Bitch, ordering an Uber now. Tell me everything when I get there!

I put my phone down and head to the bathroom, to wash off the paint. This is my first real date in forever, and I want to look presentable. My first real date was supposed to be with Aster, but you win some and you lose some. It's his loss for not texting me back. I'm going to go on this date and have the best time.

Thirty minutes later, I hear Jessica slam open the door and yells, "Bitch! Get your ass to your room. I need all the details, and we need to figure out hair, makeup, and what you're wearing."

Wrapping the towel around me, I make my way to my room, finding Jessica already in my closet looking through my clothes. I sigh, walking in and throwing on a pair of red laced panties.

"First, where are you going?" she says pushing dresses to the side.

I laugh, "Nice to see you, too. He's taking me to an Italian place downtown."

She turns her head, eyes wide, hands frozen over the clothes. "Giovanna's Italiana?" I nod. She turns back around. "I know the perfect thing for you to wear." A couple minutes later she pulls out my floor length forest green dress. A dress I forgot about, it was a dress I bought when my mom was still alive. We were going to get all dressed up, and go to our favorite Italian place, and just have a night together. She was getting worse, but told me to buy the dress anyway, her way of manifesting she'd be better and I could wear it. Mom passed before we ever got to have that date, but I couldn't bring myself to get rid of it.

I looked at her with hesitation, tears starting to glisten in my eyes. "I don't think I can, that seems a little fancy and too many memories connected to it."

She scoffs "Absolutely. Trust me, I've been there. This is what people wear when they go to Giovanna's. When I went there, I wore something even fancier. This is perfect." She thrusts the dress towards me.

Turning my head, I push the dress away, "Jess, you don't understand I was supposed to wear-"

"You're supposed to wear this dress now." She slips the hanger off, tossing it over my shoulders, "You know I'm right, your choice in clothing isn't the best. You said so yourself. You were going to wear this at one point, so live a little and put it on."

I squeeze my hands hard, to calm my anger towards her, that my fingernails leave behind half moon prints on my palm. I take a deep breath, closing my eyes and counting to ten. I open them and throw the dress over my mirror, and head over to my vanity to start putting my makeup on, ignoring her.

Jessica sits on my bed, looking at me through the mirror, picking at her nails, waiting for me to give her the details she's craving. I don't want to talk to her at the moment, so I toss my phone to her to look at Tylers profile, messages already pulled up. She excitedly scrambles to my phone and begins to read.

She places my phone next to her and says. "Well he is very flirty and more my type then yours, it's a shame he's already asked you out." She lays on the end of the bed, resting her head on her hands, "He is really cute. If things don't work out, I might send him a message myself."

I turn around to face her, mouth open, eyes squinting. *Did she really just say that?* "Such a shame that someone would notice me before you, way to be a bitch. Jessica." Saying her full name makes her mad, so I say it with a smile on my face and turn back around to start applying mascara.

Jessica comes up behind me and wraps her arms around my

neck, making me flinch from her touch. "I'm sorry, but you know it's true. I don't want to lie to you, Serena. Plus, if things don't work out then you have me to thank for not getting too attached."

Ever since I met Aster and he didn't even give her the time of day, it's like Jessica's become a completely different person. She used to be so nice, the one person I could call on always and she'd be there. Lately though, she's been mean, in a nice way. Like how Regina George, from *Mean Girls* is to her friends, the fake nice, and I don't like it.

"Thanks, Jess," I say sarcastically.

She kisses my cheek, like she didn't just insult me and stands up. I take a makeup wipe and wipe off her lipstick stain. *Great, now I have to redo my foundation.*

I finished getting my makeup ready for tonight. I opted for muted green eyeshadow, to compliment the dress I'm wearing, and nude lipstick.

Walking over to my mirror, I put my dress on, the fabric caressing my skin as it flows to the floor. *It really is beautiful. I hate that Jessica was right.* The dress is a high neck halter, and a cut out going down to the chest revealing an appropriate amount of cleavage. It is skin tight, hugging all the right places to show off my curves. There is a slit at the bottom, making it look more sexy than classy. My hair is half up, and half down, the loose curls falling at my breasts and emphasizing the delicate column of my neck.

Jessica whistles her approval from behind me, "I'd fuck you."
There's the best friend I know and love.

I laugh. "Shut up! I'm not planning on spreading my legs tonight."

"Looking like that will have Tyler frothing at the mouth, and begging on his knees for a chance to see that dress on the floor."

I look back at my reflection and smile, "Yeah, you're right I do look pretty fucking hot."

She leaps off the bed, walking over, smacking me in the ass, "Yeah you do!"

She looks at my reflection and whispers. "You are beautiful, Serena. I'm sorry I don't say it enough." Her voice is the most honest, and serene I've ever heard it. Tears fill my eyes, and I quickly blink them away to keep most of my makeup intact. "There's one thing you're missing."

I look back at her confused, as she walks over to my vanity, returning holding up two sparkly silver dangling earrings. "No outfit is complete without earrings to finish it off." Something I taught her and live by.

I smile, taking the earrings from her, and putting them in.

Looking over at my clock on my nightstand, I notice it is time to leave for my date. She notices and says "Guess that's my cue to leave." She kisses me on the cheek one last time and walks towards the door stopping, to turn and say. "Have a great time tonight! Be safe, have fun, and tell me all about it tomorrow." She leaves, with one final smile, and I put on my silver heels before heading out the door.

EIGHT

SERENA

Pulling up to the restaurant twenty minutes later, and I park my car on the ramp. I lock my car behind me, and walk towards the restaurant. Checking my hair and makeup in the restaurant window one more time before heading in. I'm fixing the lipstick on the corner of my mouth, when I see a person standing on the other side of the street. My movement stops as I try to look closer, in the reflection I see sandy blonde hair, and even in the dark, I can make out those teal green eyes. *Aster?* I whip around, heart racing, to see if I'm imagining things. A box truck passes by, blocking my view. When it has finally passes, the person has disappeared.

A sad smile crosses my lips. *Was it just my imagination?* Mindlessly opening the door, I see Tyler already waiting inside. I put on a fake smile, and walk towards him. He turns, seeing me, and what looks like a real smile stretches his lips, he reaches out his hand for me to take, I hesitate for a moment, but take it. His hand is soft for a guy, most men have rough calloused hands, like Aster, but his are kind of small.

He walks us to our table and pulls out my chair like a gentleman, then takes the seat across from mine. I look around at the people around us. All the women are way more dressed up than me, and that helps me relax a little bit. The fear of being over-dressed washes away.

He's wearing a green shirt, with a black long sleeve sweater vest over it, and white jeans. He looks better in person than the pictures. His hair is freshly cut, shaved on the sides and styled back on the top. Makes him look more preppy than punk, and I have to admit I like the change.

Pulling me from my thoughts of admiring him, he says, "You look even more beautiful in person, and I love what you chose to wear." He looks me up and down, eliciting a blush from me.

"Thank you, I was thinking the same thing." I say with a shy smile, "Looks like we are matching each other already." I motion towards his shirt.

He looks down and smiles, "To think, I almost didn't wear this. Must be fate" He says with a playful smile crossing his lips, and one eyebrow lifted.

I look at him, biting my lip to keep from smiling. "Oh yeah? What is it you almost wore?"

He gives me a playful smirk. "I almost decided to wear a bright blue Hawaiian shirt with orange flowers on it with khaki shorts, of course I opted for this instead," He says, pulling the top of his shirt out.

"I would have loved to see you in that," I say with a laugh.

To think if he actually did show up dressed in a Hawaiian shirt, in a place as fancy as this. Wonder if they would actually let him in, or make him change. This place is nice, but it's the kind of nice place that has rules, and you have to have connections to get in. A place I would usually never be caught dead in, but I'm throwing caution to the wind tonight.

He lowers his gaze. "Maybe on our next date, I'll wear that just for you."

His comment has me shifting uncomfortably, "Already talking about a second date? You really do move fast. How about we see how this one goes first."

"Like I said," He leans in and I can smell the cigar on his

breath, making me lean back. "When I know what I want, I take my shot, and I want you, Serena."

"Oh. Well." The words freeze on my tongue when I feel eyes on me, the same eyes I felt at the bar two weeks ago. A shiver runs down my spine and my heart starts pounding. I start to look around, looking for him, hopeful that the person outside was him. My body aches to look around the restaurant properly, but I don't want to insult Tyler. *Forget Him. He'd have reached out if he wanted to.*

I feel a hand touch mine, snapping me out of my thoughts. "Hey, everything okay? You look anxious," Tyler says, concern heavy in his voice.

It takes a few breaths to calm my breathing, but when I do I place my hand over his, "Yeah, I'm fine I just got a chill." He starts to remove his vest to hand to me, and I stop him, reaching across the table. "I'm okay now, thanks though."

He nods, bringing the vest back down, as the waiter comes over to take our order.

"What can I get you both this evening?"

I go to answer, but Tyler answers for me. "We will both have water and the chefs' special." The waiter looks at me, waiting for approval, but before I can speak Tyler says. "That will be all." The waiter bows his head and walks away.

Is this the fifties when a woman isn't allowed to speak her mind? Who is he to order for me? I place my hands in my lap, making little crescent moons on my palm again, to calm the anger starting to rise. He seemed so fun. So playful, when I first got here, but as soon as there's another person in front of us, it's like his whole personality flipped a switch. Rude and obnoxious and that is a major turn off.

Tyler turns back to me, and before he can speak, I interrupt him this time. "I could have ordered for myself, plus, what if I don't like whatever the chef's special is?"

"Trust me, you'll like it. Everyone does."

My leg starts to bounce uncontrollably. "Oh, everyone? Do you take everyone here?" I ask, annoyed.

"That's not what I meant." He pauses, rubbing the back of his neck. "Look, I'm sorry, we can call him back and change your order to something different if you want?"

"No, it's fine, I'll try it," I say curtly.

Asshole.

With a satisfied smile he sits back and he starts to talk about himself. I don't even listen to what he is saying, I'm too busy thinking about Aster. If he was here, he'd probably be giving him the same death glare he gave to that asshole bartender. If I didn't punch him, I'm sure Aster would have. If he was here, I wouldn't have to sit here smelling cigars and bourbon, instead I'd be smelling sandalwood and mint, and be staring at green eyes, instead of blue.

What if he really is here? I wonder if he would save me from this dreadful date? It was going well, until he ordered for me. That was a douche move. Who does that? I thought assholes only did that in movies.

When our food arrives, Tyler finally shuts up. At Least he's letting me eat in peace. Another minute of hearing his whiney voice, and I swear I was going to plunge my fork into the side of his neck.

The waiter places down a plate of tortellini, covered in a creamy sauce, with tomatoes and spinach surrounding it.

Tyler watches me, excitement sparkling in his eyes, as I go to take a bite. I pause to look at him, and he ushers me to eat it, with a wave of his hand. I hesitantly bite it, immediately annoyed at how good it is and how right he was.

He smiles smugly, "It's good, isn't it? I knew you would like it, it's never not worked."

I look up at him mid chew, wanting so badly to plunge my fork in his neck, and walk out of the restaurant, but I don't want to waste this delicious meal.

Instead I smile, gripping my fork, and nod at him, taking

another bite as Tyler launches into another story about his frat brother.

Can someone please kill him?

After we are done, he goes to pay the bill and walks me outside. "Where did you park?" He asks, looking both ways as we exit the building.

I nod my head in the direction of the parking garage. He looks towards it "I parked the other way, so this is where we part. I had a lovely evening, until our next date." He takes out his phone, and starts typing, smiles, then puts it back into his pocket. "I'll text you tomorrow and we can get something set up."

First, he's going to order for me, tell me other people like it. Then not walk me to the car, and is probably texting another girl right in front of me. If that smile was any indication, I'm right on the money. Guess the gentleman who pulled out my chair was just a front.

I roll my eyes, turning to go, without giving him a response, but Tyler grabs my arm and stops me from leaving. "Don't I deserve a goodnight kiss?"

I snatch my hand away, utterly pissed, but before I can lay into him, I see Tyler being grabbed by the throat, and slammed against the wall by a very pissed off guy. "Touch her again and I will break every single one of your fingers." The mystery man says in a threatening voice.

Recognizing the voice, I see Aster, pinning Tyler to the wall as if he weighed nothing at all.

I knew it was him standing across the street. I knew he was watching me. I want to be mad, yell and scream at him for ghosting me. Then showing up like the villain he is, to break Tyler's neck, but I'm not. I am over the moon to see him. The butterflies in my stomach are going crazy, I feel like my heart is about to jump out of my chest. The way Aster is squeezing Tyler's neck, makes me softly touch mine, wishing his hands were around my neck instead.

Remembering he pretty much ghosted me, I go to walk away, shocked by the sheer audacity of him, when his voice stops me dead in my tracks. "Don't you dare go anywhere, little lamb, this douche," he tightens his grip around Tylers throat. "Owes you an apology for how he treated you tonight. Then I'm going to walk you to your car and make sure you're safe."

I cross my arms, the only defiant way I can show I'm pissed, but still listen and stay put. Aster thrusts Tyler towards me forcing him to his knees, and whispers in his ear, "Now beg for her forgiveness, or you'll be begging me for your life."

Tyler looks up at me, fire blazing in his blue eyes with fear. He grates his teeth and grinds, "I'm sorry, Serena."

By the way he's saying it, I can tell he doesn't really mean it. Plus, he's being forced to. He looks pissed that he's being submitted to do what he's told, when he's the one usually bossing people around. You can tell who a person is based on how they treat their mother, and wait staff. The way he spoke to the waiter, you could tell it was a power play he thought I'd be impressed by. Being controlled right now has to be killing him, and I'm enjoying every minute of it.

Aster grips his hair, knuckles turning white in the low light, "For what?"

Tyler says through his teeth, "For being a douche at dinner."

Aster pulls his head back, making Tyler look him in the eyes. "If you are not sincere, and say *specifically* what you're sorry for, your life ends tonight."

I'm shocked and a little turned on at the sincerity in his voice. Never in my life did I think I would be okay with anyone harming someone else in any way, but here I am watching it all unfold before my eyes. Unable to look away, I stand captivated at the sight of Aster making Tyler beg for my forgiveness.

What he is doing is wrong on so many levels; I know, but how can something so wrong, look so right? He is awakening something in me and I don't even feel sorry for Tyler.

The thoughts I had back at the table, about the fork, and now feeling immense joy in his pain. Literal pain I'm watching him go through. Since meeting Aster I thought Jessica was the only one changing, but I am too.

I have a sadistic side, and I kind of like her.

He thrusts Tyler's head back towards me, his head flopping around like a puppet. Tyler looks at me with watery eyes, desperation in his gaze.

The motion alone starts to make me wet.

I clench my legs and shimmy uncomfortably, shocked at how horny Aster's dominance is making me. This is the kind of dominance I like, I need, I crave. Feeling eyes on me. I look up and see Asters staring at me with a dark and hungry look in his eyes.

His stare has my breathing erratic and making me even wetter.

I imagine his hands sliding down my stomach, into my panties, sticking his fingers into my soaked pussy.

Tyler starts to speak, reminding me that Aster and I aren't as alone as I wish we were. "I'm sorry, Serena, for ordering for you, and talking about myself the whole time." Aster shakes his head around, a low rumble coming from him. "And! And trying to force you to kiss me and not walking you to your car."

Aster throws Tyler onto the ground, stepping on his hand, and making Tyler scream. He leans over, getting in his face, "Lose her number."

I wish it was my heel crushing his hand.

He stands, his eyes burning into mine, and walks over to me, taking my hand and starts walking us to the parking garage.

I look back and see Tyler clutching his hand and crying. I stifle a laugh, I don't know why, but seeing him in so much pain brings me so much joy. I look up at Aster and see he's smirking in satisfaction.

NINE

SERENA

When we get to my car, Aster pushes me up against it, making me gasp with the force. He leans against me, fusing our bodies together, and his growing erection pressing against my thigh. "I've been dying to kiss you, since we met, it's all I've been thinking about for two weeks."

Got a funny way of showing a girl you miss her.

Before I can respond, he crashes his lips against mine. His kiss is as powerful and intense as the man himself, leaving me breathless.

I don't care that he hasn't spoken to me in two weeks. I don't care what his reason is. After that act he just pulled, I lost all senses. All I can think about is being lost in him. His lips are as soft as I imagined and they fit perfectly against mine.

Clutching his head, I pull him closer into me, deepening the kiss.

He groans against my mouth and effortlessly lifts me off the ground. He rips the slit in my dress higher, so it's easier for me to wrap my legs around him.

He pulls away and starts to kiss down my neck, making me moan softly, I feel him chuckle against my neck, the vibration flowing through me and making me throb.

I tip my head back to allow more room and feel his teeth penetrate my skin, I let out a small yelp. *What is he a fucking vampire?* He sucks down hard, my head falls against the window, and my eyes roll to the back of my head, lost in the sensation his mouth is bringing. His tongue replaces his mouth, and I feel him lick from the bite, all the way to the back of my ear, making me shiver, in the most delicious way.

He growls against my neck, "I want you so fucking bad, little lamb. I need to have you."

"Take me," I whisper breathlessly, looking into his hungry green eyes. He grabs the keys from my hands, unlocking the door, and pushing me into the back. My car has three row seating, the middle and back row are always down, easier to put my art supplies into. I parked away from all the other cars, scared that mine could get dented, and right now I'm happy I did. There is no one around to see the sinful act happening in this dimly lit parking garage.

He follows me down, kissing me fiercely, before slowly starting to nip down my body. He bites through the fabric of the dress, intentions clear in his eyes.

He lifts up my dress to kiss my thigh, looking up at me, and says "This dress was meant for me and me alone. I don't want you dressing up for anyone like this ever again."

I whimper and nod, too lost in the moment to realize what he's claimed.

He bunches my dress up, and I place my hand over his, stopping him. He tilts his head, "Why did you stop me?"

I whisper, turning my head away, "I don't want you seeing my stomach. I have stretch marks, and they're not attractive." Even though I've been working my ass off to get into shape, the marks stay, and I am most insecure about them. I've tried tightening exercises, creams, lotions, everything you can think of, but they stay plastered to my stomach, refusing to go away.

Keeping my eyes from meeting his eyes, I feel his hands grip my waist, tightening with each word, "Serena, look at me." I slowly turn my head, meeting blazing eyes. "Your body is a work of art." The rip he made earlier at the slit, he grabs, and tears the rest of the way off, in one swift movement and I'm left bare beneath him, in nothing but my red laced bra and panties. *Thank God I decided to match today.* He kisses each mark, "These marks are perfect brushstrokes, of the masterpiece that was made just for me. If you ever talk about yourself in a negative way again." He bites my stomach, making me twitch, "I will punish you. Stop me again and you will regret it."

His words make my eyes water, no one has ever made me feel so seen before, so beautiful. He looks at me like I'm a work of art, one he wants to explore. *How did I get so lucky?*

He kisses up my thigh, and I can feel his smile against my skin, "You're so soft." His hands squeeze the side of my thighs.

He reaches my waiting pussy, his nose brushing against my clit through the thin piece of fabric separating us, and inhales, "You smell so fucking good. I bet you taste even better." Using his teeth, he takes off my panties.

I bring my hand over my pussy, covering the hairs, face turning red, and regret that I didn't shave my lady parts earlier, washing over me. "Little, lamb." He threatens, "What did I just say about stopping me from tasting you?"

I begin to ramble, "You don't understand, it's just I didn't shave... But I usually shave, just not the top, because it leaves razor bumps in its place, and those are more unattractive than the hair, not to mention really itchy and-"

His hands cover mine, removing them from my pussy and buries his head into it, hair and all. "Little lamb, I'm not scared of a little hair, I want to suffocate in you, and if this is the way I go out, then fuck, I'd come back just to taste you one more time and die all over again."

The sight of this man below me, and his words have my pussy aching for him to make good on his threat.

He looks up at me through dark lashes, my breath hitching in my throat when I feel his finger slide into me without warning, instantly hitting my G-spot. There's something insanely intimate about a man staring at you, as if he could read your every thought, his fingers wetly sliding in and out of my most intimate place. I let out a soft moan and tip my head back. His fingers feel great, but I really want his mouth on me, devouring me, suffocating in me. His fingers are like magic, pumping in and out, making my legs shake. All the toys I have, all the men I've been with, which isn't many, none of that compares to Aster. If this is what he's doing with just his finger, then I can only imagine the sorcery his dick can perform.

He looks up at me with hungry eyes, "Do you want to know what you taste like, little lamb?"

I bite my lip, nodding, unable to form words. He curls his finger up even more, "Use your words."

"Yes!" I scream, as he pushes deeper and higher.

He takes his fingers out of me, sliding a trail of arousal up my body before sticking them slowly into my mouth, tasting the sweetness of my pleasure. *All that pineapple paid off.* I suck on them, flicking my tongue around the tip, and sucking my cheeks in to get off every last drop. Imagining it was his dick I was licking clean. He watches me suck his fingers clean, his eyes never leaving my lips.

"Fuck," he groans, and in an instant he's back between, my legs, devouring me as if I was his last meal.

I feel the swipe of his tongue on my sensitive bud, tangling my fingers through his hair as I move my hips against his face, finding that perfect rhythm. His fingers slide back into me, quickening their pace and making me see stars. I feel myself climbing closer and closer to the edge, toes curling, legs shaking, walls beginning to clench. Aster pushes another finger in, pressing against my walls and filling me.

He feels me clenching around his fingers, looking at me, a savage smirk on his face. I miss his mouth the instant it leaves my core. "You're not full of me yet, just wait until this cock is inside you," He growls darkly before dropping his head and devouring me once more. In seconds, I am shaking underneath him, screaming out his name in euphoria.

He keeps licking me, ignoring my pleas to stop or slow down. The pressure is too much, but he doesn't let up until he takes every last drop of his reward. After he sucks me dry, I am left lifeless and shaking. He kisses and nips up my body, coming up and kissing me softly on the lips.

I go to return the favor, eagerly reaching for his belt, but he grabs my hand and shakes his head. Tilting my head in a silent question he says, "We're going to be naked, in your bed, while I worship every part of you before I let you taste a drop of me, and consider this your punishment."

Cruel man, punishing me in a cruel way. He won't let me taste him, all I can think about is my lips around his cock, gagging me, until tears fall. I want him to feel the same release he just gave me.

He's looking out the window, confusion in his eyes. He looks lost in a world I wish I could see. He's tense and looks to be almost in pain. I reach my hand up to place it on his cheek, but he captures it in his, "Don't." He says, eyes never meeting mine.

I drop my hand and nod my head in understanding, eyes starting to water. He can eat me out, but I can't touch him? He was so possessive mere minutes ago when another man was trying to lay claim to me, and now he won't even look at me. What changed? My heart hurts at the thought of him pulling away. I bring my shredded dress up over me, hugging it to my chest, afraid if I move a muscle, he'll be gone and I'll never see him again.

Aster turns to leave, tears threatening to break free, my hand twitches, wanting to reach out to stop him.

Please don't go.

He turns around, and lifts my chin with a delicate touch, swiping the tear I didn't even realize has fallen away, "I promise I won't make you wait so long to hear from me. I won't put you through that again." His eyes search mine before he kisses me softly once more. "Until next time, little lamb."

He shuts the door, leaving me alone once more and walks away. I lie down and just stare up at the car roof lost in the tangle of my thoughts.

Did I really just let Aster devour me in a parking garage? I have really lost my mind, but damn does losing my mind feel fucking good.

The sweat on my brow was starting to dry, and not having the windows down was beginning to make me feel suffocated. I put my panties back on, and crawl into my front seat, draping my dress over me to keep me covered on the drive home. Turning on the car, "Like A Virgin" comes through the radio. I smile, reveling in the feeling and memory Aster left me, hardly paying attention as I make my way home.

I pull into my house, collapse into my bed, and shoot a text to Jessica, when I see a missed text from Aster. My heart starts racing at the thought that he kept to his word, he really isn't going to ghost me again.

ASTER

I hope you made it home safely, little lamb. I can't wait to see you again.

SERENA

I did thank you, and thank you for defending my honor tonight… and spending time with me.

ASTER

He deserves way more than what he got. I was more than happy to make sure he respected what was mine.

My eyes stare at the word mine, not comprehending anything else. He called me that several times tonight, what does that mean exactly? Is he calling me his girlfriend? Are we dating? I hold the phone to my chest watching the blades of the fan go round and round. Why was he even there? How did he know I was going to be there?

SERENA

It's funny that you were there, were you there on a date as well?

ASTER

No, I was there having a drink, You're the only girl I want to be taking on any dates.

SERENA

I'm glad you were having a drink

ASTER

Me too, get some rest, little lamb, I'll talk to you in the morning.

SERENA

Goodnight, Aster.

ASTER

Goodnight, little lamb.

I put my phone down and drift to sleep, waking from yet another nightmare a few hours later.

I sprint to my art room, desperate to get this feeling trapped on a canvas, painting another secret piece meant for my eyes only.

This one makes me feel more satisfied and brings me more joy than any of my previous ones, my body feeling satisfied in a way I've never experienced before.

I finish the painting by adding a blue rose and setting my brushes down.

Remembering the first conversation I had with Aster, I grab my phone and look up the meaning of his name, something I forgot to do two weeks ago, since he ghosted me.

When it finally loads, I smile. "Star; Flower?" That's fitting for him somehow.

I put my phone away, grab the painting and place it to dry with my other ones.

This one feels less like a secret, and more like a reward.

I head back to my room and lay down hoping to see the red sprayed everywhere on the plastic, and hear the screams of terror. The faces I can never see in a dream, always blurred, but I can feel the euphoria it brings the person, tearing the screams from the other faceless person's throat. Almost like I was the person doing it.

TEN

ASTER

What am I doing?

I haven't made it this far by not sticking to my rules. I made them for a reason. The moon is hanging low in the sky, and voices from the restaurant can be heard from the street. Inside I see a little family, a mother and father with their son and younger daughter. I stop to watch them through the window, wondering what my life would have been like if I had a sibling to play with growing up. Would I still be the person I am today? Would my siblings be like me? Would they have rules if they did?

After my parents got caught, I made the rules for myself that they didn't follow. They loved to play with their lambs before the slaughter, touch, suck, fuck, all of it. They even brought some of their victims into the house before taking them to the barn. The barn that I had torn down, and built my shed in its place. After the first night I saw them kill that girl, they started to bring more victims around, men and women. Into the house for dinner and then to the barn for dessert. Every single thing they did, eventually got them caught. I don't know the real reason behind how they were found, their files are locked tight, but I do know that I was never going to kill like them. Hence my rules, and it's worked in my favor so far.

So why am I following a victim around? Defending her? Killing for her? Breaking not only one, but two rules for her. Allowing a man to taint my lamb slaughterhouse, and allowing myself to taste her. There is only one rule left to break, and I won't break that one, she will never step foot into my home. She will never know about my rules, but I can't help myself, there is something about her and when the time finally comes, I can't wait to lay her on my table.

She is the first woman I have allowed myself to be with in a long time. I'm no virgin, but I don't ever take my victims to bed. I've allowed myself the pleasures of being with a woman, but I prefer the pleasure of killing over sex. I have always felt that way, that was until I got a taste of my little lamb. She tasted like the fires of hell themselves, sinfully sweet and tempting, pulling me into the abyss of her forbidden cunt, drowning in flames I never want to escape. The very reason why she needs to die, I'll treat her like I treat my other lambs, giving her what she desires after a night out, then I fulfill my own fantasies, putting her to sleep forever.

That image sends a pang to my chest, one I haven't felt before. *Weird.* I reach up, placing a hand over my heart, and I light up a cigarette. Happy to see that while I had my dessert, Tyler was still in his car waiting, giving me the opportunity to keep my earlier promise.

I never break my promises.

I stand in front of my car, several cars back from Tylers, in total darkness, the only light from the bud of my cigarette.

When I see Tyler exit his car, with a short, lithe redhead. She looks drunk, swaying back and forth, in her sky high heels and black mini dress, too short for this weather. It's still warm during the day, but at night it's cooler and most have a coat on. She's wearing next to nothing, her intentions clear in her outfit. She laughs at something Tyler said to her, while he holds her up.

How can this fuck face go on another date? Although, this looks more like a booty call than a date. The person he was texting outside, must have been her, already lining up another date, because of his failed one. I'm happy his date ended horribly, but my jaw ticks as I step into my car, thinking that he could just discard my little lamb so easily.

My fingers tap on the steering wheel to the beat of "Undead" by Hollywood Undead. Breaking my first rule yet again has me drumming harder with every beat. This kill is more deserving than Gary. Tyler touched and tried to force himself on what's *mine*, and for that, I will make his death slow and painful.

The stars start to become brighter, as the surrounding businesses, aside from a few, start to close and turn off their light. I pull out a pack of spearmint gum and start chewing, waiting for Tyler and his date to drive away. After what seems like forever, my gum having lost its flavor, I throw it out the window. A dark smile lighting my lips, as Tyler speeds out of the parking spot, onto the street, and I pursue, keeping my distance so he doesn't catch onto being followed.

We drive for fifteen minutes before he pulls into a neighborhood, pulling in front of a house leaving the engine running. I kill the lights on my car and park it far enough where he can't see me, but close enough I can see him.

Five minutes pass before the redhead gets out running into the house and then back down her driveway into his car. They speed off, and I follow them to a bar, in the more shady side of town, my favorite hunting ground. No lights, cameras, or witnesses. If people happen to see me leave with my victim they keep their mouths shut, they know the cardinal rule. *Snitches get stitches.* The things that happen here, even have the authorities avoiding it like the plague. So to see Tyler take the red head here, makes me wonder what nefarious things he has in store for her, not that I care.

I stay outside in my car, and wait for them to come out. When minutes turn to hours I grow bored, and take out the word search I keep in my middle console. When I'm watching my little lambs, learning their schedules, and seeing if they have any family or friends who would miss them. I spend that time in my car solving my word searches when I can't be near them. They help calm me, help me clear my head and get into the right headspace to hunt. Finishing five pages, I look up and see them leaving the bar. I kept a tail on him, and now here we are at his house.

They walk up the driveway, and I see the girl curling over herself, hand over her mouth, looking like she's about to throw up. A second later, her hand leaves her mouth and she vomits all over Tyler. He yells something, I'm too far away to hear, or read his lips, parked across the street, a couple houses down, hidden under the hanging branches of a tree. He pushes her down, and stomps into his house leaving her there sick and crying on the cold cement.

"Fucking douche," I mutter. While waiting, I pull out my phone and text Serena good night and put it back in the cup holder and wait for the redhead to leave.

Ten minutes pass and a car pulls up; probably an Uber. The red head gets in, she leaves crying and covered in vomit. I wait another ten minutes for good measure, making sure there are no cameras anywhere. If there's one thing I will take from my parents training, is always being vigilant when hunting and making sure there are never any cameras, and if there are, avoid them.

I don't know this neighborhood, or if his neighbors have any cameras. I place a hat on my head, hoodie up, and bring the ski mask up hiding my identity. Jumping over his locked fence, I find the backdoor is unlocked, quietly I open it and step inside, hearing the shower running.

Lucky me.

I find a pantry in the kitchen and slip inside and wait for him to go to his room. The slits through the door let me see when the door to the bathroom opens, steam billowing around him. He's got a towel wrapped around his waist. *Thank God.* He walks to his bedroom and shuts the door. I hear the bed creak, waiting another ten or so minutes to be on the safe side, then I make my way to his room; stealthily. Under the door, I see that the lights are off, I crack open his door, and find him sleeping soundly.

This really is too easy.

I stand over his body, watching him, waiting for his senses to kick in and wake him up.

Counting the breaths he takes, I stand behind him, and his breathing starts to become faster. He jolts up, chest heaving, eyes tired and wild, searching in the dark for what woke him. He catches his breath, shaking his head, thinking there is no threat until he turns over, and sees me staring down at him.

Before he has time to scream, the syringe I keep in my car is in his neck, ketamine flooding his system and knocking him out once again. I smirk knowing this time he'll be out much longer.

Tyler lives in a nice neighborhood, so I need to be extra careful getting him to my car. I sling his arm over my shoulder making it look like I'm helping a drunk friend to my car if anybody sees us. Not that they would. It is three in the morning and most people are inside asleep.

We make it to my car unnoticed, and I lay him in the backseat before heading home.

It takes an hour to get home, I avoid all cameras, and take the scenic route home to ensure I'm not followed and I don't follow any predictable patterns. When we get to the road that leads to my house, I drive past my home, heading straight to my work space. I park and get out of the car. A cool breeze hits me instantly and I inhale the humid air.

I never did well in the heat, the sun has always been my

enemy. I thrive in the cooler weather, especially with how I dress, always in pants.

I walk back to my car and drag Tyler's body from the back seat. He is still knocked out which makes it easier to get his body in and on my table.

While he sleeps, I strap him down and get all my tools ready. This kill was spontaneous and unlike me, nothing is prepped. My space doesn't have any plastic laid down, my tools aren't laid out, and my incinerator isn't turned on.

What is my little lamb doing to me?

I pace around the room, not sure where to start. Everything is messed up. My mind is in shambles. Part of me doesn't care, I so badly just want to end his life for touching what is mine. The other part of me knows if I don't get prepped, the clean up after what I have planned will take longer.

Here I am living in chaos, killing another man, all for my little lamb. Slipping on my overalls, I start laying down plastic, and start to prep, letting the meticulous side of me win.

Finishing the set up, he is still asleep. I look down at his face, my knuckles turning white, thinking about how he was on a date with *my* little lamb. I crack my neck, trying to loosen the tension building there.

Seeing him laying there, thinking back to how he tried to kiss what's mine, my anger wins over and I grab his hand and break his pointer finger.

There is a satisfying pop sound, making me smirk, I let his finger go, he tries to jolt up, screaming in agony. Flailing and failing to grab his hand with the other. I step into his line of sight, look down and with a smile say "Finally! You're awake."

He looks up realization instantly hitting him and pisses himself. The pee dribbles onto the floor, making me jump out of the way before it hits my work boots. After he's done soiling himself, I walk over and break another finger, eliciting a shrill that has me twitching from the sound.

"Look, man, I'm sorry," he says, already sobbing. I look down at him with pure disgust, anger bubbling through me.

"You almost pissed on me. None of my lambs have ever done that."

"You broke my fucking finger, and earlier tonight you had me by the throat! What the fuck did you expect?" He seethes through sniffled tears.

"I didn't break one." I grab his hand, making my intent clear in my eyes. I break three more fingers, making him scream louder. "I broke five." I release his hand, depraved satisfaction buzzing in my veins, and get in his face. "I made a promise that I would break all of your fingers if you didn't apologize."

Wheezing he says "I did apologize, I was on my fucking knees apologizing!"

"It wasn't fast enough, I had to *make* you apologize. You should have done so without a second thought." I step back, my hand shaking as I wrestle for control. "Then you had the audacity to go pick up another girl because *mine* wouldn't kiss you."

His eyes widened in shock. "You were following me?!"

I looked down at him with a snarl. "How else was I supposed to make good on my promise? Luckily for me you were still there when I got back to my car. From there it was like a cat chasing a mouse."

He starts crying again, begging me to let him go. "Please, man, I deleted her number after I left. I swear I was never going to contact her again."

I pulled his phone from his pocket, "What's the code?"

He stays silent, causing my anger to flare, grabbing a knife from the table and jamming it into his hand. He cries out, sobbing "six, nine, six, nine."

I roll my eyes, mumbling. "Pathetic," under my breath and type the numbers. The phone unlocks with a faint click and I go to the messages. I see a conversation with 'BITCH', and click it, opening to see it is the conversation between him and my little lamb.

My hand tightens around the phone and I shove it in his face, pissed off that he lied, and named her as bitch. "I hate being lied to, Tyler. You'll be punished for that." I break the phone and sim card, chucking it across the room, uncaring where it ends up.

Ripping the knife out of his hand, I walk to the other side of the table, his eyes following my every move. I grab his hand, making his eyes widen, and start slicing off each finger. His nails on a chalkboard scream, has me cutting faster.

"Please" he begs, "I can't take anymore."

"The night is still young, Tyler and I'm not even close to being done with you."

Walking over to my tools, I pick up my sharpest scalpel, then walk over to turn on my speaker. His screams are making my ears bleed, and I need music to drown it out. I turn on Spotify and "September" by Earth Wind and Fire blares through the speakers.

I walk back over and wave the scalpel in front of his face. "Do you know what this is used for?" He's crying, his words incomprehensible gibberish as he begs for mercy I no longer have. Instead of waiting for an answer, I grab his face, pressing my fingers into his cheeks, making his lips puff out like a fish. "Let me show you." I get close to his face. "This is for trying to kiss my little lamb."

I take the scalpel and cut off his bottom lip, blood pouring from it. I cut his top lip, finishing the punishment towards my little lamb, which caused him to lose consciousness. Pissed he was knocked out from the pain, I grab a kettle, fill it with water, and grab the bolt tongs to place the pot into my incinerator. After a few minutes I hear that satisfying sizzle letting me know it is hot enough to take out.

Carefully, I walk back over and tip the kettle letting a few drops hit his skin. When he starts to stir from the heat, I pour the rest onto him, making his skin blister instantly under it. He's trying and failing to thrash around, screaming from the pain, spitting blood down his chest.

The music drowns out his screams, and I walk over to my work table placing my scalpel down, grabbing my bayonet. I make my way back over to Tyler and start stabbing, uncaring of the mess I'm making; his blood flies everywhere, getting all over me and my work space.

I get lost in killing him and I lose count of how many times I've stabbed him even after his body goes limp. I watch the life leave his eyes, stopping as my chest heaves and blood drips down my face. Grabbing my electric-reciprocating saw to cut his body into pieces small enough to fit into the incinerator.

After I throw him and his belongings into the fire, I clean up my workspace, discard my boots and make my way back home. The sun is starting to rise as I walk back.

Once inside, I take a quick shower and when I get out, I notice it is already six in the morning. I collapse onto the bed naked, thoughts of my little lamb coming to mind, before I knock out.

ELEVEN

ASTER

When I wake up the sun is starting to set, I roll over, grabbing my phone and seeing it's six already. Squinting, I hardly believe I managed to sleep for twelve hours. Normally, I sleep that well after a slaughter, not after an avenge killing for my little lamb, but nothing about the past twenty-four hours has been normal. I have two texts from Serena.

My little lamb must be thinking about me as much as I'm thinking about her.

I type back cursing myself for missing her text. *She probably thinks I'm ghosting her again.*

Not promising a specific time, I place my phone down and start to get ready.

I opt for a long black sleeve sweater, dark blue jeans, and my black boots. I style my hair back where it is out of my face, but still falling at the sides. I go over to my watch collection and opt for my black one with a teal band.

My father used to collect watches, never wearing them, unless he was taking my mother on a date. I remember him always picking a band to match what my mother was wearing.

Before I clasp the watch I send Serena another text.

ASTER

What are you wearing?

I mindlessly run my hand over each band, waiting for a reply.

SERENA

A black top and blue jeans. Why?

The thought of her matching me without realizing it brings a small smile to my face. I place the teal band back in the case, grabbing for the plain black one, but stop myself. These are my fathers quirks that I picked up, he's dead to me, but his ways are still living deep inside.

ASTER

No reason, what color are your lips?

I hope they're red.

SERENA

Suspicious, but red

I knew it. I reach for the red band to match her lips, a small smile playing on my lips. Securing the band, my phone dings and I look down, disappointment falling over me.

SERENA

I'm here, I'm where all the books are

I was hoping for some flirty banter, not her telling me she is waiting for me. I type out my response, eager to see her.

ASTER

On my way, see you soon little lamb.

I place my phone in my pocket, grab a syringe from the kitchen drawer, grab my keys and head out the door. I put the syringe in the center console of my car, making it easier for me to grab later. I speed out of my driveway anxious to see my little lamb.

I PARK DOWN THE STREET WHERE THERE ARE NO CAMERAS, AND THE street lights are dim. My blood races as I stare at the door to the bar. I'm hoping she took an Uber here, so I can offer her a ride home.

I don't text her to let her know I'm here, I want to find her and watch her first.

Exiting the car, I make my way to the bar, when I walk in there is no sign of her. Not until I walk closer to where the books are and see her sitting on one of the bean bag chairs immersed in a paperback.

She is dressed in light blue skinny jeans that show off the supple of her legs and a black fringed crop top, exactly what she told me she was wearing. Her hair is pulled back into a high ponytail and looks to be straightened as well. She has subtle makeup on, only her bright red lipstick standing out in the dim light of the bar, and my cock twitches at the thought of those lips around it later.

I reach down to adjust myself, shaking my head from the thought. I may have broken two rules already, but sex is out of the question.

I stand there staring at her, and within seconds, as if sensing me, her eyes land on mine knocking the breath from me.

She closes her book and walks over. "Hey," she says in the sweetest of voices.

Her voice is like a siren calling the sailors to their death. If I was a sailor I would jump ship with just one word, letting her drag me down until the darkness enveloped us. Getting lost in the darkness together would be an easier death than I probably deserve.

Enveloping her in a hug, I surprised both of us and whisper, "You look beautiful." I see the blush creep up her neck as I place my hand on the small of her back, and walk us to a high top table.

I pull out her chair for her, earning an eyebatting and a "Thank you."

Pulling her chair out, I rest my cheek against her and whisper in her ear, "What can I get for you, little lamb?" My breath on her skin makes her shiver, which only excites me more. I trace my fingers along the goosebumps on her neck, mesmerized by the way they enlarge with every touch.

She turns, our faces so close I could kiss her. She's breathless staring at my lips, hers parting ever so slightly, and the rise and fall of her chest is quickening. "Moscow Mule," she whispers in a raspy voice.

The way her lips form an 'o' at the end of saying mule has me giving her exactly what we both want. My lips crash against hers, taking the breath from us both. Her mouth parts ever so slightly, allowing my tongue to slip in. I grab the back of her head, tipping her head back and a small moan escapes her. We break apart and I look down, noticing our kiss smudged her lipstick. Swiping my thumb across her bottom lip, I use the excuse of fixing it to brush my fingers against her soft skin. "I'll be back," I whisper against her lips, all she does is nod, looking dazed from our kiss. I walk away and head to the bar to order our drinks, a smirk stretching my lips.

She's playing right into my trap, everything is going according to my plan, with a couple hiccups of two rules broken. Now if only my dick would get with the program. *Why do I keep kissing her?* I can't seem to keep my damn hands off of her. No matter what, she'll be another one of my lambs for slaughter and I'll never have to think about her ever again. The hold she has on me will disappear when she does.

I get up to the bar, and see it's a female bartender this time, mumbling while cleaning up a spill about how Gary no showed again and pissed he's left all this on her. *If only she knew, he would never come in again.* She's blonde with her tits hanging out of the deep v cut black band t she made into a crop top so short her under breast can be seen, making all the guys at the bar look her way. Everyone, but me, I have eyes only for my little lamb. She notices me right away and struts over, making her breast bounce with her. When she gets to me, she places her elbows on the counter, and twirls her hair. "What can I get'cha, handsome?"

Looking back at Serena I say, "My girl would like a Moscow Mule, and I'll take a Manhattan." She looks over my shoulder at Serena and with an 'I'm better than her' smile says, "You should ditch the chubster, I can make it worth your while."

The fuck did this bitch just call my little lamb?

Lowering my gaze, squeezing my hands on the counter to keep from choking her, "She has more curves than your stick-self could ever dream of." She scoffs and turns away "Insult my girl again and that will be that last thing you ever do." Her eyes shoot into her hairline and she rushes off to make our drinks. She comes back a few minutes later and places the drinks down with shaky hands and walks swiftly away.

Not even going to apologize? I don't usually kill women who look like her, except on my birthday. I make that exception, but that isn't for another three months. The bitch can live another day, I don't want to hunt in the same place twice. They'll be looking for Gary soon, if fake tits were to disappear they'd shut the place down and question everyone. I'm careful, but my lamb has my mind swimming in chaos and I'm not risking getting caught to kill on her behalf again.

I grab our drinks and walk back to our table, setting Serena's in front of hers. I watch her take a drink, and she watches me over her glass.

"Do I have something on my face?" she says, swiping her finger across her lips.

Watching the movement, makes me have to adjust myself, "No, I'm just admiring your beauty."

Her eyes follow the action, squirming in her seat. "You must say that to all the girls to get in their pants."

"As I recall, I was already in yours, and plan to be again."

Her eyes meet mine, "Is that so? You'll have to try harder this time, I'm not so easy you know." She sits back and crosses her arms, a smug pout on her lips.

Crossing my arms, I lean over the table, "Guess that means I have to try harder then."

That earns me a playful smile. "I guess you do." Now she leans in closer, arms still crossed, her breasts laying on the table, and I can't help looking at them. "Like what you see?" I growl my approval. "As much as I'd love a repeat of last time, maybe in a bed this time, I think we should take a second to get to know one another better."

I never tell anyone any nitty gritty details of my life even if they ask, but with her I find myself wanting to tell her everything. Maybe it's because I know our time together will end soon, and I want her to know more about me than any of my previous lambs. Which is strange, but I'm ignoring the little voice in my head and start talking.

"What would you like to know, little lamb?"

She smiles, her cheeks heating with a hint of a blush. "First, why do you call me little lamb?

A chuckle escapes me, "You haven't earned that information yet, but you'll find out soon."

"Okay," She draws the word out. "What do you do for a living?"

"I'm an entrepreneur of sorts. What do you do?"

"That's an elusive answer, but I'll let you keep your secrets for now, we all have them. Promise you will elaborate later?" She has secrets, too? Everyone has secrets, but I'd bet she wouldn't take hers to the grave. They're probably nowhere near as dark as mine. "I'm an artist, I mostly take commissions, but have my own side projects and gallery pieces."

"All will be revealed in due time, little lamb, don't you worry." I sigh pretending to get emotional. "When my parents passed away," I say, knowing my parents are locked up tight in a cell they will never get out of. "They left me a rather large inheritance. I work mostly to keep my hands busy and not get bored with life. After all, idle hands are the devil's playground."

Her eyes bulged at my statement. "Wow, okay, I was not expecting that, but I understand. My dad comes from money, but the day I take anything from him, will be the day I die."

"You make an honest living, it sounds like."

"Yeah, I guess I do, and I am damn proud of how far I've come with my work. I never dreamed I'd be able to make enough from my art alone. I feel really lucky"

"Luck has nothing to do with it, talent gets you those orders." A small blush creeps up her cheeks making her blush look brighter. "You'll have to show me sometime, or maybe I could commission a piece from you?"

"I do have a long waiting list for my commissions, but I think I could *slip* you in," she says playfully.

"Is there any way I could convince you?" I ask, my chest rumbling with the desperation I feel for my little lamb.

The feelings she rouses in me are confusing, having me second guess my decision to take her life tonight. She was supposed to lay on my table, after I got to feel what my mouth tasted. She is making my chest tighten along with my jeans. I've already killed too many people recently. I need to take my time with her, savor her in every way, and then after my cool down period in a couple months I will give her a blue rose. Everything she's making me do and feel without even realizing it has me deciding that tonight I will kill her. These feelings need to stop, now.

She places her finger on her chin, tapping it and looking around the room. When her eyes land on me, she says in the most seductive voice, "I can think of a few ways."

The promise in her voice has me growing harder than I already was. I twist in my seat, trying to adjust myself with little success. Her eyes travel down, and she looks back up with heat in her gaze. "Looks like you're thinking of a way or two?"

"Oh, little lamb, I don't know if you could handle what I'm thinking."

I can't even handle what I'm thinking. *I want to fuck her instead of kill her? What has my little lamb done to me?* I've broken almost every rule for her, since spotting her in this very bar. I'm starting to learn that my rules don't apply to this little lamb.

She gets up and comes behind me, reaching her hands over my shoulders and down my chest, far enough she can almost reach my cock. She stretches her fingers across my lap, nipping playfully at my neck, my dick swelling even further. She brings her hands back up, locking them around my chest and surprising me when she says, "I want you to choke me, while you fuck me." She bites my ear lobe, pulling at the delicate skin with a gentle tug, and walks back to her seat leaving me dazed. "Now that I have your attention again, what do you say we get out of here?"

Nodding my head, we both get up to leave the bar. I take her hand, walking her to my car, when she stops me mid way. "I already called an Uber, I'll give you my address."

I grunt in frustration, my fingers tightening around hers. "Cancel it, I'll drive you back to my place."

She takes out her phone, a sultry smile on her face. "Done."

My heart races in my chest, an unfamiliar pang accompanying the usual surge of adrenaline as I continue to walk us to my car. Opening the door for her, I walk over to my side and get in. She looks over at me with her phone in her hands. "What's your address? I need to text Jessica where I'm going in case you're a murderer and I go missing." she says laughing.

Heart racing faster, and hand stopping to click in the seatbelt, I freeze. Is she being serious? Is she joking? Why would she joke about that? Does she know I'm planning on killing her eventually and is trying to get the truth out of me? A thousand thoughts race through my mind in that moment, unsure of what to do I click the seatbelt in place and start the car.

"I'm just kidding, I know you wouldn't kill me, but I do need to tell her your address."

She was joking, that's good. I lean in close, "Now how are you so sure I won't kill you?"

"Very funny, Aster, now please tell me your address." She says laughing, but I'm not laughing and the moment Serena realizes I'm serious, her face falls.

I turn away from her and ask, "What's your address? I'm taking you home."

"What? Why? Did I do something wrong?" Her voice shakes, and I can hear the tears in her eyes.

I take a deep breath. "No, but I'm not in the mood to play anymore, I want to save what I have planned for you for another night." I get in her face, "I want to have you screaming my name and begging for mercy, but tonight isn't that night."

She turns towards the window, mumbling me her address with a sad voice. I punch it into my GPS and drive her home in silence.

No one can have my address, there can't be a trace of me left behind on any electronic device. It's why I have a burner phone, why I pick my lambs up, and take them to my home. Her asking for my address startled me, making me rethink my plans for her tonight. I was going back and forth, should I kill her tonight or wait, having decided I needed to feel her blood between my fingers. Now it is all ruined.

The moon hangs dimly in the sky, and the clouds cover the stars, making for a gloomy and dark night. I have the windows down, letting the humid air hit my face and blow Serena's hair around, hoping the air will cool some of the tension that has built up. This was not how either of us were expecting tonight to go, with how Serena won't even look at me, and her eyes facing towards the sky, I know she is just as upset as me.

Once we get to the road to her house, I see it is a long road like mine, except it is all paved. Pulling up to the house it is a two story, it's teal all the way around and has wood pillars that compliment it outside. She has a two car garage and a little barn to the right side of her house. It's too dark to see what color it is, but my heart races at the sight. *This feels like home.* The barn reminds me of the one my parents used to have, but smaller. I park in her driveway, and she goes to leave, but I grab her arm, stopping her. With a defeated sigh, I say, "I'm sorry, Serena."

She looks at me with red rimmed eyes. *Fuck, shes been crying.* "Yeah… I'm sorry, too."

The car door shuts with a dull thud that seems to reverberate through my entire being. I watched her enter the house and shut the door without looking back. Causing me to second guess everything again tonight.

Slamming my fists down on my steering wheel, I rub my hands down my face. "Fuck it." I get out of the car and bang on her door, my fist unrelenting against the weathered wood. She opens the only barrier between us, just a crack door, tears spilling down her cheeks. Before she can say anything, I slam open the door and crash my mouth against hers, pushing her inside and kicking the door shut behind me.

She struggles out of my grip and punches my chest with glancing blows. "No. You don't get to come in here and kiss me like that after rejecting me. You lost your chance."

I growl frustrated, "I changed my mind."

She punches me again, harder this time. "You don't get to just change your mind!" She screams, crying harder and banging on my chest. "I've been rejected so many times, but being rejected by you, Aster, after what we already have done? Really fucking hurt."

I grab her hands and make her look at me. "I know, I'm sorry, but look I can't take you to my house, not yet; I'm not ready." My hands tighten around hers, as the confession I didn't mean to speak leaves my lips.

She freezes, looking at me confused. "Not ready for what?"

I sigh, "For telling you the reason why I call you little lamb."

This has never happened before, I have never second guessed who I choose as my little lambs. Never have I not wanted to kill a lamb, once chosen. Serena is making me lose my mind.

Her brow furrows. "That doesn't even make any sense, and even though I want to know why you call me that, why do I have to be told the reason at your home? Can't you just tell me now?"

"That is the only place it will make sense, and right now… I don't want to tell you. I can't tell you." I push into her, backing her close to the wall behind her "I want to be inside you." Her skin flushes and her breathing halts.

She yanks herself out of my grasp, crossing her arms like a child would when they don't get their way. "Yeah, well, right now I don't want that. You need to leave."

I scoff at her request. "That's not happening."

She turns to walk upstairs, "You can let yourself out." Before she makes it even one step, I grab her, spin her around, and pin her up against the wall. I run my nose along the graceful column of her neck, inhaling her scent. She smells like roses and lavender, reminding me of my home in the spring.

It's been so long since I've touched any woman, and her scent alone has all my senses going out the window. If she told me to get on my knees, I'd push her to hers, and shove my cock down her throat. The animalistic side of me needs to have her, ever since I got a taste I have wanted nothing more than to feel her wrapped around me.

"You smell so fucking good."

Pressing my hips against her, I feel her shaking beneath me, and I can't tell if it's from anger or if she's turned on. I opt for the latter and start to kiss her neck, eliciting a small moan. I chuckle into her skin and slowly move my lips up to her mouth. She turns her head, denying me the prize I crave. "Oh? You think, you can deny me what's mine?" I say pressing my fingers into her cheeks, making her look like an adorable pouty fish.

She turns to respond, her eyes flashing with the spark she hides deep within. "I know I can deny you what's *mine*."

Those words of her claiming herself are my undoing. Not giving her any more words to use against me, I grab her hands, pinning them above her head, and crushing my lips against hers. She struggles to move her head, fighting against my power, so I deepen the kiss. A small moan escapes, and my little lamb finally gives into what we both want.

Her hands separate from mine, and wrap around my neck, deepening the kiss. I nuzzle my face in her breast when I lift her up. She leans her head back, to give me easier access. "Aster," she rasps.

My hands tighten around her bottom, her legs wrap around my waist, "Hold on, little lamb." Her brows knit together and before she can answer, I'm running us up the stairs. She hugs herself into me, holding on for dear life, her body shaking from the fear or excitement, I'm unsure of, maybe both. "Where's your room?" I growl, impatience lacing every word. She nods her head in the direction of the room, lucky for me it is already open or I would have kicked it down.

The compulsion to consume her is fighting inside me with the fox who wants to run, who is frightened to take things further than I already have. I pushed the thoughts of running away, if I ran she would never speak to me again and I would lose my chance to play and lay her on my table.

I throw her on the bed, she bounces as she falls onto her back, her hair cascaded all around her, making her look like the siren she is. My chest heaves in and out, I feel my eyes darken, as I take in the woman laid before me. "Turn around and get on your knees." I demand, no room in my voice for argument. She doesn't respond, but obeys my command and turns over getting on her knees, ass high in the air, "Good girl." My hand lands a loud smack against it, echoing the sound in the room.

The sound that escapes her lips and the way her head hangs down, has me smacking it one more time, before I crawl onto the bed. My weight causes the bed to dip and I lean down to kiss her shoulder blade. Her skin is soft everywhere my lips touch. Making me greedy for more, I rip off her shirt from behind, tearing the fabric in half, her breast falling free, and landing right into my waiting hands. "No bra?" I question, massaging her ample breast. "Seems like your words tonight don't match your actions. You were always planning on being my subservient whore, weren't you, little lamb?"

She doesn't answer, I smirk and slip her jeans down a little just so I can see her supple ass. "Do you know what happens to bad girls, who don't answer when spoken to?" Silence is all I'm left with; this must be her way to defy me for rejecting her earlier tonight.

I will make her scream.

I raise my hand and bring it down hard, against her ass, leaving a bright red handprint behind. She whimpers but still stays silent. "Your stubbornness to respond, is going to be your undoing, little lamb."

I pinch her nipples and twist them, hard enough that her lips part and she moans her approval. "Feel that?" I say pressing my cock into her ass. She moans out yes, and I remove my hands from her. "Only good girls get to be pleasured. Are you going to be my good girl, Serena? Or are you going to be my bad girl and keep being punished?"

She turns her head, a small smile playing on her lips, "Bad girl."

She is going to wish she said, 'good girl'.

I flip her over in one smooth motion, she's on her back staring up at me with lust filled eyes, the defiance dimming as my hand wraps around her breast.

"You're perfect," I place my mouth over her taut nipple and bite down hard enough to make her cry out. "Perfect, but still going to be punished." Her back arches off the bed just slightly to show me the scream that left her lips, was one of pleasure, not pain.

That won't do.

Biting harder, her screams become louder, filling the room, I can taste the metallic of her blood, in my mouth. I can hear her cries echoing off the walls of my sanctuary back home, which makes my cock twitch, and beg for her heat. *Is this what she will sound like when she's screaming in my work space?*

"Fuck!" she moans out, arching into me.

I remove my mouth and hands from her nipples, kissing my way down her stomach. I reach for her jeans, sit back on my heels and take them off. I smile down at what I find, my mouth watering as her scent fills the room. "Wore these just for me, huh?" I say locking my fingers under her black lace thong. She looks down and nods her head, her skin flushing even more. I slide the delicate fabric off and inhale her once again. "Fuck, the things you're doing to me, Serena."

She bucks her hips up, her body begging for my touch. "Things you could be doing to me, but you're too busy talking."

I smirk up and chuckle "Oh, you are going to eat your words."

She smiles at me "Looks like you're the one whose about to eat"

"You're right." I plunge my face between her legs and begin meticulous licks which have her shaking in seconds. As a punishment for her smart mouth, I bite her clit making her yelp, and bow off the bed, pushing her sweet cunt harder against my tongue. Before she can scold me, I shove two fingers inside her and feast once more.

She's convulsing minutes later, I come back up and kiss her lips. "I'm not done with you just yet. It's my turn, little lamb."

I get off the bed and take my shirt off. She watches me, heat and desire pooling in her gaze as she grasps the sheets. I grab my wallet from my back pocket and take a condom out of it, tossing it across the room as I unzip my pants and slide them off. I watch her eyes travel down to the bulge coming through my black boxers, her tongue wetting her lips as she waits.

Smirking, I bare myself, my cock springing free as her eyes widen. "That thing is way too big, no way it's going to fit-." she says, scooting back on the bed away from me.

A dark chuckle escapes me, pinning her in place with my eyes. "We'll make it fit." I say placing the condom over my cock.

She shakes her head, her eyes panicked. "No, no, no, no… Don't you dare come near me with that, you are going to break me."

I grab her feet and pull her to the edge of the bed, her ass hanging off, throwing her legs over my shoulders. "Breaking you is exactly what I want to do." I plunge into her, making her scream as I slide against her slick heat. I thrust in and out, going faster and deeper with every snap of my hips. "Fuck, Serena, you're so fucking tight, I could stay buried inside you all night."

She lifts her hips allowing me deeper access, her eyes shuttering closed in bliss.

"I thought you said I'd break you?" I pull back and slam myself into her, enjoying every little flinch and gasp I pull from her body.

She winces. "I like a little pain with pleasure, no ones ever given it to me the way I needed it before."

Inflicting pain is my favorite hobby, I love to ring out the screams from my lambs, watching the fear in their eyes as they realize they're never going to escape me. Serena's screams are my favorite, when she's in pain, when she's releasing pleasure, all of it, music to my ears.

I'm beginning to think she's the fox, and I'm the lamb.

That thought has me spiraling as I squeeze her throat, my grip tightening with each thrust. Her eyes start to water, and I can see she's struggling to breathe. A tear escapes, and I watch as it falls down. I lean in and lick it, letting the saltines soak into my tongue. I moan my pleasure, "Even your tears taste addicting. I'm *never* letting you go, little lamb."

She is absolutely beautiful beneath me, my hands draining the life from her. I quicken my pace as she starts to gasp for air, her face starting to turn purple. I explode inside her, releasing her throat, her walls clenching around me. "Fuck, Serena." I say through clenched teeth, slowly pulling out of her.

She sits up and starts coughing while I discard the condom. I leave the room, heading downstairs to her kitchen and return a few minutes later with a glass of water. She takes it from me, a soft smile on her lips, and gulps it down.

"Thank you, at first I thought you just fucked the life out of me and then left."

My body tenses at her words, I contemplated leaving while filling up a glass of water. I decided against it when the thought of never seeing her again crossed my mind. If I left after that, she would never speak to me again and I would never get to hear her screams.

She takes notice, her brows pinching together, I lean down and kiss her lips softly. "I would never do that to my little lamb." Her eyes soften, trusting the words I say.

She gets under the covers and motions for me to come lay next to her, I hesitantly get into the bed and hold her in my arms.

She looks up at me running her hand across my chest, "Do you remember the conversation we had about your tattoos? When we first met?" She looks up at me through her lashes.

Does she want me to tattoo her now?

"Are you asking me to tattoo you, little lamb?"

She springs up, "No! I'm not ready for that yet." She bites her lip, "I wanted to know what each one meant, the ones I couldn't see."

My eyes lift, "Which ones would you like to know about?"

I watch as her eyes travel down my naked body, taking in all the ink. She touches the grim reaper tattoo, "Can I guess what this one means?"

Everyone who has seen this tattoo and makes remarks on what it means always gets it wrong. They usually guess the harbinger of death, anything among the lines of the dead. To normal people that is what it means, but I'm not normal.

She traces her fingers down my arms, stopping at the blue roses that morph into the reaper. Something like recognition in them for a moment until she shakes her head and brings her eyes back up to meet mine.

"I would say, harbinger of death."

I knew it.

She chews on her lip, "That would be too obvious though." *That's surprising.* "Everything about you, is anything, but obvious." I stay quiet letting her continue, curious as to what she thinks it means. "You have the roses morphing into the reaper." Her fingers leave goosebumps behind as she traces up my arm. "I think it means that there is beauty, even in death." My body stills, mouth parted slightly as she says exactly what this tattoo means to me. "If you look at it either way, the reaper turning into the roses, it means the same."

Her eyes meet mine and I'm captivated by how she looks, and how her brain thinks the same way as mine. "Aster?" She asks quietly, head slightly tilted.

I tuck her hair behind her ear, "You're right."

Her whole face lights up, "Are you serious? I actually got it right? I never get tattoo meanings right with anyone. I always think out of the box, and most people's reasoning are simple and boring." She sits up and throws the blanket off, "Let me see the one on your calf."

Before I can turn over for her, she grabs my leg and lifts it in the air. "A fox?" She taps her bottom lip, thinking. "I called you that the first time we met, and you looked shocked for a moment."

She noticed that?

She leans in closer, inspecting every inch of my tattoo. There's no way she will guess the reason for this one. Her hand holds firm around my ankle, her grip tightening the longer she stares. She drops my leg and sits back. "I'm not sure about this one. You call me little lamb, I'm assuming as a cute nickname." *If only she knew why I really call her that.* I smile, "I'm right aren't I?

If it's a nickname, then either you love foxes, or it was a nickname for you."

What the actual fuck? I stare gobsmacked at my little lamb, watching as she slightly bounces, waiting impatiently for my answer. "My parents used to call me, little fox."

She slaps my chest, "Shut the fuck up, I was right again?" The shock I was feeling, is replaced with admiration, for how cute and excited she is. "Do you have any more? This is a fun game and I'm actually winning."

I turn my head, letting her see the lighter with blue roses, wrapped behind a knife, behind my ear. "You really like blue roses, don't you?" I nod my head, "I like them too, they're my favorite flower, and the Morbid Monet uses them."

My world is spinning, my heart is racing, I can't breathe. Did she really just say my serial killer name? Does she know who I really am? I feel her breathing against my neck, her words bringing me back from my spiral. "I don't like them because of him, but I think it's cool I have a connection like that to him. Jessica thinks I'm crazy for how invested I am in him. He's a serial killer after all, one that seems to kill women who are plus sized. I don't know, I just feel drawn to him." She sits back and looks into my eyes, searching for my reaction.

She's right about my type for killing, that's why I approached her. The connection she feels between us, maybe that's why I haven't killed her yet. Not because of how delectable she tastes and feels, but because there is some unknown connection. This link might be the reason why I'm waiting so long to kill her, and I will. It might take longer than my other lambs did, but I will lay her on my table.

"It's weird, I know, maybe I should listen to Jess and stop this weird obsession with him."

"No!" I say gripping her arms, surprising us both with my reaction.

"No?" She tilts her head.

"Don't listen to your friend, you can like whatever you want, even if that is a serial killer who would kill you."

"You're right, normal is boring anyway. Back to the tattoo behind your ear."

She places her hand on the side of my head, and I lean into it, closing my eyes. "It's the first lighter I ever bought, I don't use it anymore, but I still have it."

Her hand leaves my head, taking away the comfort I was in. I open my eyes and see her bottom lips jutted out and her arms crossed. "That's not fair, I wanted to guess."

I uncross her arms and pull her into me. "It's okay I do have one more you missed."

She looks up with a pouty face, "Where?" I dip my head to my chest, her eyes follow my line of sight. "I can't believe I forgot this one! I was looking at it when you took your shirt off, but was quickly distracted."

"What do you think this means?"

She touches the blade that pierces my heart, trailing her finger down the blood. She looks at me with sad eyes, causing my heart to twinge. "I don't want to guess that one, my guess is sad." She looks back down at it.

I tilt her chin up to look at me, "Guess, Serena." My heart racing at what I fear she may guess correctly.

She takes a deep breath, "The blade is piercing your heart, with it placed there your heart can't beat… For anyone."

I knew she would get it right.

Instead of answering, I pull her into my arms and stroke her head. She doesn't ask if she was right, we both know she was. She nuzzles in closer and closes her eyes.

Once she is asleep, I sneak out of the bed, putting my clothes back on, and leave her room. I head to my car and sit there looking up at her house.

What the fuck am I doing?

I didn't kill her, instead I went back to her place and fucked her. She's still breathing, which wasn't what I had planned for tonight.

She's supposed to be dead.

Then she said she needed to text her friend my address, and I panicked. I can't have anyone knowing where I live. I can't have anyone finding my sanctuary. That's why I drove her home. That's why I didn't take her to my house. *That doesn't explain why I fucked her.* She did ask me to choke her and that excited me. The only way I could choke her was to fuck her. Yeah, that's why I did that.

I turn the music on, trying to drown out the thoughts plaguing my mind. "Shackles" by Steven Rodriguez starts to play through the speakers, as the lyrics drift through, I listen. Right before the second chorus plays I turn it off, thoughts of how true those words are, is frightening to me.

The moon is shining bright in the sky, the night so clear you can see every star shine, the complete opposite from what I'm feeling.

I roll all the windows down and I let the night air be my distraction on the way home.

THIRTEEN
SERENA

I wake up to an empty bed, Aster nowhere in sight. The warmth that his body gave me, now feels cold. Did he leave after I fell asleep? Did he fall asleep with me? I enjoyed having him next to me, his arms wrapped around me felt safe, he felt like home. A feeling I haven't felt since my mom was alive. A feeling I want to feel again.

Hoping he left after I fell asleep, I grab my phone to see if he texted me anything. When I look I see that I do have a message from Aster, I bite my lip to stop the giggle threatening to burst out of me.

I smile, the soreness I feel anytime I move, being a happy reminder.

Placing my phone on the nightstand, I stare at the blades spinning around and around.

We had a great time last night, learning a lot about one

another, but I still want to know more. I don't even know how old he is yet.

Is that even important?

Of course it is, I can't be dating someone twenty years older than me. That'd be like dating my dad, and the thought alone makes me gag. If he is way older than me; since I've already slept with him and started to catch feelings, I wouldn't mind as much. Plus once I know his age, I'll tell him mine. I think we're close, at least he looks to be around my age. When was he born? I wonder if his personality lines up with his zodiac sign. I hope our signs are compatible. Given last night I'd say we absolutely are.

My hands lay across my stomach as I wonder why he changed his mind about going to his place, why he decided to take me home. I was pissed and hurt at first, then he made it up to me, with his dick. I was not expecting that monster cock to be attached to him. I have to admit it felt amazing, and we fit perfectly together.

Thinking back on our conversation, my stomach drops, as a wave of nausea crashes over me. The realization of when he decided to take me home, when he went quiet and changed his mind, right after I asked for his address. I did joke about him being a serial killer, but there's no way. My joke must've upset him, and that's why he changed his mind.

I was too upset in the moment to even think about his reason, I was too hurt that he rejected me, changing his mind so quickly after agreeing in the first place. When we got to my house, I was sure he was going to leave, but he didn't. After I walked into the house and he didn't follow, I wanted to scream, cry, break things. Then the banging started happening and my heart started racing, and when he pushed his way in, I let him.

I was still pissed, trying to get him to leave, but hoping he would stay. Instead he claimed me and consequences be damned, I reveled in every moment.

What was I thinking? I wasn't, and that was the problem. I

wasn't thinking with my head, my vagina was running the show, and *fuck* I don't regret it.

Brushing off my fears as nothing more than self doubt at waking up alone, I begrudgingly get out of bed and head to the bathroom to shower and start my day.

After I get out of the shower, I swipe my hand over the steam in the mirror and my eyebrows raise at the damage on my neck. Erasing the fog, craning my neck, I push my hair back to see all the bruises not only from his mouth, but the mark his fingerprints left behind. Luckily, I'm not planning on seeing anyone in the near future or I'd need a lot of makeup to cover those up.

I put my overalls on and head to my art room, eager to start a personal piece for the first time.

Dipping my brush in the teal paint, trying to capture his eyes perfectly. There is something about his eyes. They're guarded and when you look into them, you know he's hiding something. We all have our skeletons in the closet, but I so badly want to know his.

I sit back and stare into the eyes I've captured with photo-like precision and smile.

How did a man who looks like this choose to be with a girl like me? He could have any girl he wanted, and he chose me. I'm not ugly by any means; no, I am rather beautiful. I know I'm no model, but both fireworks and flowers are beautiful despite looking nothing alike. *I'm Aster's firework.*

With the eyes finished, and knowing I have a list of clients waiting for their art, I stare at his portrait for a few moments more. Then, get up to put it with my secret paintings.

For some reason I feel like this belongs with them, and I don't want anyone, especially him, knowing I'm painting him. I've never felt so compelled to paint a man I was seeing, the way he looks at me, the way his eyes hide his secrets, I needed to get them onto my canvas. Capturing his photo would be creepy without permission, but painting it, knowing he won't know or needing his permission, isn't as creepy. *Who am I kidding?* I've gone full on stalker for this man.

I hear my phone ring and grab it off the windowsill by my easel, seeing it's an unknown number. I don't usually answer unknown numbers, but this one has called me twice. I was so lost in the portrait of Aster I didn't hear it ring the first time.

Thinking better of myself I answer, "Hello?"

The voice on the other end is silent for a beat and then responds, "Serena?"

"Yes, this is her," I say hesitantly. "May I ask who is calling?"

"Serena, it's me, your father."

My hand tightens around the phone, and my head starts spinning. The last time I saw him was when he was driving away after our screaming match in his car. *What does he want?* I've been ignoring him for a reason. I have nothing to say to him. If he wants a relationship with me, he needs to apologize, and accept all of me, not just the pieces he approves of.

"Serena?" he says again, worried I hung up on him and cleared his throat to gather my attention.

"What do you want? How did you get my number?" I say dropping my voice and lacing it with annoyance.

"You haven't been answering my emails, and I needed a way to contact you."

"You didn't answer my question, how did you get my number?"

After my mom passed away, our relationship turned sour fast. He started treating me differently, walking on eggshells around me, and not to mention, seeing another woman. I lost all contact with him, but he found my email, trying to reconnect. The hurt and pain I felt at his betrayal to my mother, his wife, hurt too much so I ignored his attempts.

Years passed and after my anger subsided some, he reached out again, and I told him about my life. I did miss my dad, no matter how upset I was with him and the whole situation, he was still my father. He seemed to be nicer, but then started insulting my way of living by saying he could get me a job at his company, I could make real money.

Anger coursed through me again, he tried to apologize but the match was lit. I agreed for him to come see me, and when everything happened, the fuse was blown.

"I have my ways."

"Meaning you throw money at something to get what you want, like always?"

"Serena, I didn't call to argue," he says in an exasperated voice. "I want a fresh start with you. I want to apologize for how last time went, and I want to see you."

Tears start to threaten, and my voice cracks "Why?"

"Sharon thinks-"

There it is, this wasn't his idea, it was this Sharon's. Fuck. That. They can both kick rocks.

"Oh, so you don't actually care, *Sharon* does. Who is she, Dad? Another one of your whores?"

"See, I told you this was a bad idea, she wants nothing to do with me." He says to someone in the background

A sickly sweet southern voice responds, "She's your daughter, Thomas, maybe you should tell her the truth. I want her at our wedding. I would like to meet my future daughter-in-law."

My dads tone is curt and serious, "She can never know the truth."

My stomach starts to gurgle and I feel like I'm about to be sick. *What truth are they talking about?* I start to lose my balance, my phone slipping from my hand. The last thing I remember is my dad's voice screaming my name before everything goes black.

"Serena!"

I feel strong hands gripping me by the shoulders as a voice that makes my heart pound in my chest yells my name. *What's going on?* I open my eyes slowly, the light stinging them, so I slam them shut with a groan. *My head hurts… Did I hit it?*

"Serena!" I hear the voice scream in a panicked tone.

"Dad?" My eyes flutter again.

I feel myself being guided into a sitting position, a hand caressing the back of my head, causing me to flinch.

"No, little lamb, not your dad."

My eyes flutter open at the realization that the person shouting my name, the same person holding me, is Aster. *When did he get here? How did he get inside?*

"Aster?" I say weakly

"Yes, little lamb, I'm here. You fell and hit your head. You're okay but there is going to be a nasty bump."

He wraps his arms around me and I touch the back of my head, wincing.

He grabs my hand and chuckles, "Yeah, that's the spot, how about we try not to touch it. Do you think you can stand up?"

Nodding weakly, I go to stand up, arm over his shoulder, and legs shaking. Aster's taller than me by at least a foot so he has to bend down to walk me over to my stool to sit down. I giggle at how awkward he looks.

He slowly lowers me to the stool, still holding my waist just in case I fall.

He brushes the hair out of my face, and I lean into his touch. "Do you want to stay here or go sit somewhere more comfortable?"

"My room, please."

He lifts me up, this time bridal style. As we're walking to my room, someone bangs hard on my front door, startling both me and Aster.

We look at each other, the banging continues, more frantic than before, faint yelling floating through the door. "This is the police, open up!"

Aster's grip on me tightens and I feel his body stiffen, freezing him in place. Something is off, he doesn't even hear me when I whisper, "Aster, the door." I pull on his shirt breaking whatever trance he was in and he makes his way to the front door, still carrying me, fingers digging into me with every step closer to the door.

He goes to open the door and the police are startled to find him holding me.

An older cop with a mustache that fills his face, says, "We got a call saying a father was on the phone with his daughter when he heard a thud, then silence. He thought something happened, so we came to check to make sure everything was okay."

The cops are staring at Aster, intimidated and on guard. The younger cop looks at how protectively Aster is holding me, and Aster is staring daggers at them both. The amount of hatred I feel coming from Aster, surprises me. To break the tension, I tap Aster's arm and tell him to let me down. I make a show of kissing his cheek to thank him and turn back to the authorities. "I'm fine, I just fell. Luckily, Aster was here to help me."

Mustache says, "Regardless, we are going to need to write a report. Mind if we come in?"

I nod, motioning for them both to come in, and lead them to my dining room, Aster holding my hand for dear life the whole time.

If I didn't know any better, I'd think he was scared. Aster isn't scared of anything though. So why are cops in my home, checking on me, making him come undone?

I sit at the head of the table, Aster on my left, Mustache to my right, and the younger one behind him.

The older cop gets out his notebook and pen, looking at me with concern shining in his gaze. "Alright, tell me what happened."

I glance at the younger cop, avoiding the watchful eyes of Mustache. He's short and lean, with a chip on his shoulder as he waits for a chance to prove himself, with black hair and blue eyes. He has some stubble growing back, making him look younger than he is, and his eyes are glued to Aster. On guard, but also with a look of recognition and opportunity, like he's trying to figure out how he knows him.

The way he is studying Aster makes me tighten my hold around his hand. My eyes lower and I want to tell him to back off, but the fear of the consequences has my lips shut and my face trying to relay my message.

The younger cop addresses Aster, cutting off Mustache with a youthful giddiness. "Do I know you from somewhere?"

I feel a slight shift in Aster, his hand gripping my hand with a bone breaking force. He looks at the cop, dead in the face, and says "No." his voice stern and ending any conversation before it begins.

"Are you sure? I swear you look familiar."

"Jason!" Mustache snaps to the younger cop. "He said you didn't. Now, don't interrupt me again." He turns his attention back to me, "Back to you, tell me what happened."

Grateful for his interruption, I answer. "I was on the phone with my father, and I heard a conversation between him and someone else. What was said shocked me and made me faint."

He's scribbling on his notepad, humming to himself. "What was said that made you faint?"

"He was getting remarried." The truth is worse, if I tell him it was because of a secret, I myself didn't know, they would ask more questions I couldn't answer. I want to get them out of here as fast as I can, if not to calm Aster down. The energy coming from him is buzzing, and it makes me nervous. If I don't get them out of here soon, Aster might hurt Jason, if the look in his eyes is any indication.

"Okay, why would that make you faint?"

I'm getting frustrated now, this cop has no business being in mine, and I don't want to explain myself to him.

Before I can respond, Aster is for me, "She is estranged from her father, her mother passed away not too long ago, and the news shocked her. That is all. So, if there is nothing else, officers it is time for you to go, so she can get some much needed rest".

I smile, grateful for Aster cutting in and telling the cops to leave.

Mustache clears his throat. "Yes, that is all. Sorry to disturb you, thank you for your time." He looks at me, "I'm happy to see you're okay."

We walk them to the door, the younger one standing there staring at Aster longer than necessary before finally leaving when Mustache yells for him to come. As he's walking away I hear him mumble "I swear, I know him."

I shut the door and turn into Aster's waiting arms. He holds me for a minute until I look up, "Everything okay? You seemed on edge since the cops showed up."

He looks down and smiles. "Yeah, I'm good, little lamb. Let's get you upstairs." His smile doesn't reach his eyes, his body is still tense, I can tell he's lying. Something tells me to leave it be, for now.

He helps me into bed, sitting on the edge next to me.

"So," he starts, brushing some hair behind my ear. "Want to tell me what really happened?" I tense and he levels his gaze with mine.

Did he see through my lie, like I did his?

"It's exactly as I told the police, I don't remember anything after everything went black." I jab him in the chest. "Want to tell me how you got into my house?"

He looks away, his cheeks heating with embarrassment. He schools his features before looking back at me. "I came over to pick you up for a surprise date, I saw your car in the driveway, so I knew you were home, but I kept ringing the doorbell and after ten minutes, with no answer..." He looks down and starts to fiddle with his hands. "I just had a feeling something was wrong, so I forced my way in."

"What do you mean you forced yourself in?" I squint my

eyes, and tilt my head, nervous to hear he broke my door or something.

"I picked the lock and came in."

Thank God my door is still intact.

Wait… What? I was not expecting that. My eyes take in everything that Aster is, trying to see past the man full of secrets in front of me. *What else can he do that he hasn't told me about yet?*

"Look." He runs his fingers through his sandy hair, "I didn't know if you were hurt and the feeling I had… I couldn't ignore it." He looks at me, taking my hands in his. "I had to make sure you were okay. I know I shouldn't have broken in, but I'm not sorry. You should get better locks."

"Aster, it's okay. I'm not upset, I'm actually grateful you were here, who knows what would have happened if you weren't. I was only quiet because I was thinking how much of a mystery you are to me."

He brings my hands to his mouth, kissing them with a smile. "I promise you will know everything in due time, little lamb."

He lets go of my hands, putting me into a lying position, and hovering over me, staring into my soul. I go breathless and my heart pounds in my chest.

He looks down at my lips, and I lick them without thinking about it. He looks back into my eyes with a predatory glint. I glance down, already see his growing erection, my core weeping in anticipation.

I go to grab it, and he grabs my arm stopping me with a soft grunt. I look up at him, sadness and confusion thrumming through me. All he does is shake his head at me.

Is he rejecting me again?

As if reading my mind, a smirk softens his face. He says, "I'm not rejecting you." I shake my head, eyes wide with shock, he's answering the question in my mind. "You just fell and hit your head and as much as I want to feel that sweet pussy again, you need rest."

I go to argue, but he places his finger over my mouth,

shushing me. "No arguing, Serena, I'm serious. Turn your cute little ass over and go to sleep. I promise next time we're together I will make you beg me to stop."

Feeling giddy about his promise, I nod my head, giving him a soft kiss before turning over.

I feel him get up, kissing my head and walking out the door. After I hear the front door shut and his car drive away, I find myself starting to slowly drift to sleep, flashes of teal and darkness swirling in my head.

FOURTEEN

ASTER

Well, there goes my plans again, this time ruined by an injury. Not caused by me. I punch the middle of my steering wheel, making the horn go off, hoping no one, especially my little lamb, heard it.

I so badly want to get my hands on my little lamb. I need to see her on my table. I need her screaming my name. *I need her.*

She would look so perfect, spread across my slaughter table. My most prized lamb. My most perfect doll.

Just imagining it makes my cock twitch.

She would look so perfect bent over-

No, what am I thinking? My breathing becomes accelerated thinking about her on my table begging for her life, not bent over.

Well… I push my head back into my seat, willing my cock to behave. *Maybe bent over before I stab her heart.*

Her blood would look so pretty all over my hands. Splattered against my skin. Staining the walls of my slaughterhouse.

My cock presses painfully against my jeans, the bite of pain pulling a visceral groan of pleasure from me. Glancing around I can't help myself. I use one hand to unbutton my pants, sliding them down a little. I keep my other hand firm on the steering wheel, so it doesn't swerve. I move my cock through the hole of my boxers, stifling a groan as it springs free.

Spitting in my hand to add some lubrication, I start to rub up and down, eliciting precum. I swipe my thumb over the tip, rubbing the precum around the top, then start to rub it up and down my shaft.

Thinking about the promise I made to Serena, what I will be doing to her once I finally make her mine, spurs me to rub harder and faster. My grip tightening with the thought of her black hair draped over the edge of the table, looking at me with those big blue eyes, begging for more.

My little lamb covered in blood, underneath me, at my mercy. I reach my breaking point. Tipping my head back, my eyes shuttered closed, and I explode all over my hand, a guttural roar escaping my throat at the same time.

I hear a horn blaring down on me, seeing an oncoming big rig hurtling towards me. For a moment, I embrace my imminent end, welcoming the pain sure to follow. My phone vibrates on my dash, my little lamb's name flashing across the screen. I swerve out of the truck's way just in time before I'm crushed. *It's not my time yet. I still need my little lamb.*

My breaths come fast and labored as I take a napkin from my glove box and wipe up my hand, glancing in the rearview mirror as the rig speeds down the road, and drive the rest of the way home.

The game of cat and mouse with death is a fun one, causing my adrenaline to spike even more, but when I saw my little lambs face, I needed to get out of the trap I created for myself. *I need to see her again. Soon.*

I never get off to my lambs blood, I always thought it to be sickening, especially when I saw my mother and father getting one another off in their victims blood. I didn't understand at the time what I was witnessing, but a little voice in my head told me to run when my dad tore my moms shirt off and she made a noise I never heard before. Only when I was older and understood what sex truly was, is when I vowed to never get off like that with my victims. Another reason why rule two was put in place.

My little lamb can turn that traumatizing memory into a good one with her spilled blood. Covered in blood, whether it be hers, or ours, what a beautiful sight that would be.

Time to plan our next date, and spill one of my secrets.

I PULL UP TO SERENA'S HOUSE, AND SHE'S ALREADY STANDING outside looking absolutely stunning. Wearing a black crop top that has a skull head with red roses around it and a deep vee she cut into the shirt to show off her perfect breasts. A red and black checkered skirt flutters around her hips with every step she takes. Her legs are covered by fishnets, and her shoes of choice are black combat boots. *Is she trying to match?*

She has her bangs half up, the rest of her hair wavy and falling past her shoulders. I want to wrap it around my fist and bend her to my will.

Her lips are painted red. Probably to match her outfit, which she looks sinfully delicious in.

The same red I would've chosen for her.

She runs over and gets in the car, kissing me on the lips, before sitting back in her seat. "Where are we going?" she asks excitedly.

I smirk, staring at the road. "It's a surprise," I say, glancing over at her before speeding out of her driveway, my blood thrumming in my veins.

The sun has already set in the sky, creating the perfect atmosphere for what I have planned for our date.

Tonight is the night. If all goes according to plan, this will be our last date, and I will finally get her on my table. *Finally.*

Looking over at her, I can feel the excitement rolling across her skin. *She wouldn't be so excited if she knew how the night was going to end.*

She reaches towards the radio, messing with dials as she flips through the stations. Her body freezes when she hears a song she likes come on. She mimics the drum intro, and bangs her head along with the beat, pretending she is part of the band, mouthing the intro. Paying attention to the road while she's being so cute is hard. I listen to the lyrics, realizing it is "Waking the Demon" by Bullet For My Valentine as soon as they say the title.

I didn't know she was into this type of music. Smirking, I turn the song all the way up. She starts to sing her heart out, never missing a lyric.

I wonder if she knows she has woken this demon?

The station plays several more songs she sings along to, dancing in her seat as she loses herself to the music. The way she just lets go, and is completely herself, has me tapping the steering wheel to the beat of the songs I know. *I hope she's only like this with me.*

Her whole face lights up as we pull into the abandoned parking lot, and she screams excitedly, "OH. MY. GOD! You are taking me to Graves Haunted Houses?!" She bounces in her seat, straining against the seatbelt. "Do you know how hard it is to get tickets? Me and Jess have been trying for *years*. Wait… they're not even open yet, don't they open next week?" She turns to me, her eyes bouncing between mine.

I get out of the car, and walk to her side, opening the door and grabbing her hand, suddenly craving the connection. "The owner and I are very close."

She gapes at me, leaning into me, my cock twitching at the sight. "You know the owner of Graves? The owner is one of the best kept mysteries of Salem. The only thing anyone knows is that the owner is a guy. No one, except a select few of his employees, know who he is." She steps closer and whispers. "I heard he makes his employees sign NDAs and those who break the rules become a part of one of the haunted houses…" Serena glances around, as if making sure no one was listening in. "Permanently."

This makes me belly laugh. "That is my favorite rumor."

She slaps me playfully. "I'm being serious, Aster. I'm desperate to know who owns Graves. Jess thinks I'm obsessed. She's okay with this obsession because it's not over The Morbid Monet."

If only she knew we are one and the same.

She looks around as we are walking up, nearly stumbling over the loose gravel, lost in amazement. "I wonder how he came up with the thirteen houses of horror. Each one is inspired by either an iconic horror movie or serial killers. He changes the movie houses every year so it doesn't get old. Since you know him, you have to know the reason why. What's the story behind the houses?"

When I first came up with the idea to use my inheritance towards opening Graves it took me sometime to come up with what I would do. There are so many haunted houses already, and I can't kill all the time, so I needed a distraction. I visited so many haunted houses, most of them were the same, and the owners of those had to use the same props every year, making it repetitive and boring. I wanted my attractions to be the opposite, and with the amount of money I had, I came up with the idea to change the houses every year. Bringing back the same people, new customers, far and wide. All the haunted house goers coming and going brought in more than enough money to keep changing it every year.

I have permanent staff, the ones who know the owner, who not only start building the new attractions after the season ends at the end of November, but who also love to be a part of the attraction. Dressing up and scaring everyone. It makes the transition period easier having the same staff, and that is their career, which they love and are grateful for.

I turn to her, getting in her face, backing her against a tree lining the path to the entrance, and whisper. "If I told you, then you might end up here." I lean in close, my breath brushing against her neck and leaving goosebumps behind. "Permanently."

She slaps me on the arm. "That's not funny Aster, but could you imagine working here? Oh, the fun I'd have tormenting everyone." Her eyes spark, something much darker lurking behind her excitement.

That's surprising. Her choice of words intrigues me, and I can't help but imagine what it would be like tormenting her in these houses.

Maybe I will.

When we get up to the entrance an employee is waiting to let us in. "Mr. Graves, we've been expecting you, we made tonight extra memorable as requested."

From the corner of my eye I see Serena gasp, pure shock on her face. "Thank you, Sam."

We walk past my employee, and Serena shrieks, "You're the owner of Graves?!" She shakes her head in disbelief. "Wait, so your name is Aster Graves? That actually fits really well."

I look at her, a small smile playing on my lips, heart racing. "Oh really? And why is that so fitting, little lamb?"

Serena lets go of my hands, skipping ahead with her hands behind her back. She glances over her shoulder and repeats the words I once said to her, "I promise I will tell you everything, all in due time."

She runs away laughing, but I'm faster, much faster then she is, and I catch her. Swooping her into my arms, she fights to get away, her body brushing against mine, fire flowing in its wake. "You will find out how fitting my name is to me, little lamb. Then you're going to wish you didn't."

She looks up at me, head tilted and shivers. I kiss her, my lips greedy against hers, and take her to the first house "The Dancing Clowns".

"I love clowns!" She looks at the entrance with fascination.

The entrance is an archway of everyone's favorite horror movie clown, with white faces, and red lines going through their eyes, wrapped around the mouths, stretched and their hands connecting at the sign that says "The Dancing Clowns".

One face he's smiling, wearing the mask he puts on to capture his victims.

The same mask I wear to capture mine.

The second is his true face, the one his victims see right before he devours them. His mask comes off, just as mine does, when our victims' lives are about to end. It's the only moment we can be our true selves.

I come up with the ideas for every house, give money to make my vision come to life every year, but it's the actors I hire that bring it all to life. They are the reason my haunted houses are the best. The reason people from all over the states come to experience it every year.

I see Serena running ahead of me, too excited to wait.

Watching her go, I slowly stalk after her, watching her chest rise and fall, her eyes wide as she takes everything in. The way her body is reacting to everything, how she touches the props that look a little too real with admiration, is making my cock strain against my jeans.

Most people are excited, with fear on the forefront when they enter the houses. Serena isn't showing an ounce of fear, she looks like a kid on christmas waiting to see all their presents. *I wonder if her fear will surface later?*

She goes up to the towering Pennywise standing in the corner of the first room and stares up at it. "It looks so real." she breathes. She rocks up onto her toes, reaching out to touch it, when the clown jumps at her, coming alive making her scream. Eliciting the fear I can't wait to make her experience again later. My chest heaves, my urges almost too desperate to control.

She closes her eyes, and runs right into my arms, which makes her scream again. She doesn't realize it's me at first. She tries to run away, but my hand wrapped around her wrist has her opening them and relaxing as soon as she sees it's me.

She grabs my hand, lacing our fingers together, and we walk through the rest of the houses together. Out one house into the next, each one scarier than the last, with more actors hiding and waiting to scare us. I don't even know where they're coming from, or how many there will be. Sam is the one who hires everyone who doesn't know my identity. All the actors have been told I'm an important customer, who knows the owner, and to put on a great act. I must admit, some of the makeup jobs and costumes are even making my adrenaline spike. Watching her look around, waiting for the next person to come after and scare her, makes my heart race in a way I've never experienced. The beating of my heart isn't from the fear that is creeping its way up, it is something else, a pang of joy from hers.

When we reach the end of the houses, she runs out, completely breathless, resting her hands on her knees trying to catch her breath.

Walking up beside her, I grab her hand, and start to lead us back to the beginning, heading to her favorite house, the clown smiling at us as we get closer.

"Are we doing it again?" she asks, looking around. "Wait, where is everyone?" She stops walking, and plants her feet into the ground, hesitant to continue.

"I told them to leave after we left each house."

"Why?" She asks, rubbing her thighs together.

Pulling her towards me, I whisper in her ear. "Because the things I plan to do to you tonight require no witnesses."

She shivers, her eyes going dark in anticipation, making my breath catch in my chest. The look she's giving me makes me reach down and adjust my growing erection.

FIFTEEN

ASTER

I walk her back into the first house, taking her to the center of the maze-like structure. Kissing her with hurried steps, shredding her clothes, throwing them to the sides, leaving just the stockings, as I back her into the rusty, bloody door.

Reaching into my back pocket, I take the blindfold I grabbed before our date, dangling it in front of her eyes. "Do you trust me?" Breathlessly she nods her head, her plump lip trapped between her teeth. My cock jumps at her submission, a smirk lifting my lip as I place the blindfold over her eyes, making her world go dark.

Her chest heaves as I grab both of her hands. One hand holding tight to her wrist, and the other undoing the belt on my pants, slipping it free and kicking off my jeans and black boxer briefs. I wrap the belt around her wrist, placing her arms above her head, securing the black leather on the hook nailed to the door.

Pressing her back into the door, my erection pressing into her stomach, I kiss her cheek, and reach up to grab the knife that is stabbed into the door. It looks like a prop to anyone who looks at it, but it is far from fake and will make you bleed. I like placing real weapons around the houses, not ones that I personally use.

It can cause chaos if one of the actors were to grab one of the real knives or axes, to chase their prey with it. No real damage has been done, yet. *A guy can dream.* The large clip point hunting knife catches the dim, red light in the house as I look at my reflection.

I place the flat part of the knife against her cheek, making her jump as I slide it down. "What is that?" She breathes, her body trembling.

"You'll find out soon enough, little lamb."

Her nipples are hard and taunt, from the cool breeze drifting through the door, tempting me to bend and take one in my mouth. Her moan makes me bite down hard enough, I taste crimson falling into my mouth. She isn't screaming, which is what I expect, no she's moaning even louder, arching into me as she silently begs for more. I remove my mouth from her bleeding nipple, kissing up her body until I reach her lips so she can taste herself on my tongue.

"Do you taste that, little lamb?"

"Yes," she says breathlessly

"Do you know what it is?"

"Yes."

"Tell me."

"Blood," she gasps.

Her answer has me backing up and removing my shirt, dropping it to the ground. "Are you scared?"

"No."

"Do you want me to keep going?"

"Yes," she begs, pulling against her restraints as she tries to get closer to me.

I kiss her stomach, sucking the spot just below her belly button as shivers tumble through her.

Bending down, I take the knife and slice a bigger hole into her stockings. My lips kiss her pussy, slipping my tongue through the folds, and lapping at her sensitive bud.

"Fuck. Aster!" She moans.

"Keep moaning my name, little lamb."

I spread her legs apart, throwing them over my shoulders, gaining easier access to suffocate in her folds.

My breath washing over her, I look up at her, "You taste even sweeter than last time."

A small smile forms on her lips. "Pineapple," she says, and I go back to lapping at her clit and drowning in her juices. I always thought the pineapple theory was a myth. Knowing it isn't, I'm going to be stocking up on that fruit.

She writhes above me, legs shaking, close to exploding. I shove two fingers inside her wet opening, she moans even more begging me for my cock. "Please, Aster. I need to feel you inside me. Fuck me."

Her core clenches around me as she teeters on the edge, about to erupt around my face, which makes me quicken my speed. I lick just below her swollen clit, pressing against her most sensitive spot, pushing her over the edge as she comes all over my face.

She gasps, coming down from her orgasm. I refuse to let her recover, shoving the handle of the knife into her, making her walls clench around it. My hand holds the blade, tightening with each thrust, making blood drip down my arm.

"That isn't your cock."

"No, it isn't." I move the handle slowly in and out of her, rubbing against her sensitive walls.

"What is it?" she says in labored breaths.

"Do you want to see?"

She nods her head, I stand, reaching behind her head with the hand not fucking her with the knife and untie her blindfold, letting it fall to the ground. Her eyes widen at the sight of my hand covered in blood, the knife going lazily in and out of her.

She doesn't scream. She doesn't look disgusted. *Oh, my naughty little lamb.* She looks intrigued by the sight, her arousal heightening as I feel her pussy grip the knife. Most people would be disgusted, or scared by the sight. My little lamb continues to surprise me with how she reacts to the things I do to her.

Watching her eyes darkening, I bring the knife up to my mouth sucking her juices off the handle, trailing my tongue up the blade, licking the blood off, my eyes never straying from hers. The taste of her mixed with my blood is a strange, but delicious mix, that has me moaning my approval. Her eyebrows shoot up, and tongue pokes out, mindlessly licking her bottom lip. "Untie me," She demands, and I find myself doing as she commands. She grabs my bloodied hand with hers, lowering the knife back down towards her entrance. My hand circles the blade once more, her grip forcing my fingers deeper onto the sharp metal. She watches as the handle penetrates her again. Her eyes flutter, fighting the control of wanting to watch, but the deeper the shaft of the blade pushes inside, the harder it becomes. Her breathing becomes more erratic, her eyes glazing over as she watches my blood drip down my arm.

"Beautiful," she whispers, her breath fanning over my face. I lose myself in the moment, getting lost in her awe as I continue to push in and out. "Can I try?" Her question has me stopping my movement, looking into her darkened eyes, I hand her the knife, she hisses from the sting of the blade as she grips it, watching the blood spill down her arm. Her eyes never leaving mine, she pumps faster, looking possessed, like she doesn't even realize what she is doing, and I can't seem to look away. The little moans she makes, the combination of her cum spilling down the blade, mixing with the blood from her hand, it's mesmerizing.

She grabs my hand, breaking the spell I was under, placing my hand over hers. "I. Need. More." She begs, placing her other hand and squeezing it over mine, making more of her blood drip down the knife and splatter on the floor.

I'm so turned on at our blood mixing together, at the darkness I see in her eyes, at the pain she inflicts upon us, my cock weeps for her. Desperate to feel her heat. I stop pumping our hands, she looks at me eyebrows drawn together, "Why did you stop?"

"This knife can't make you scream the way I can." I take the knife from her hand, grab the handle, and throw it across the room. I don't give her time to react, I slam into her, hard enough it throws her body back against the door and this time she screams, the beast inside of me growls with pleasure. "Those are the screams I've been dying to hear."

"Aster!"

"That's right, little lamb, scream my name." I place my hands around her ass, my blood leaving the perfect handprints, lifting her up to go deeper. In and out I thrust, the feeling of rightness, of home, settling over me. She grips my hair, getting her blood matted in it."So. Fucking. Tight." I growl into her ear. I pound into her over and over again, her walls clenching around me so tight I feel as though I'll never escape, until she comes for the second time tonight.

Her explosion triggers my own, and I settle deep inside her, not giving a fuck that I don't have a condom or caring that I didn't check if she was on birth control. None of that matters, she feels too fucking good to care.

I place her down in front of me, her legs shaking so hard she almost falls, but I catch her. She places her bloody hand in mine interlacing our fingers once more. She lifts our hands, her eyes blaze as she looks at them, mesmerized at the sight. *Me too, little lamb.* She brings our hands to her lips and kisses them. The sight goes straight to my groin, my dick swelling once more.

"You look so beautiful, covered in our blood."

I wish I could capture this moment forever.

She has a dark side to her, and I'm more curious than ever to let the devil in her out.

She lets our hands drop, and I bring my mouth to hers, tasting the blood on her lips. She opens her mouth and all I taste is our blood mixed together perfectly. It isn't copper I taste, no the way our blood mixes together is a sinful taste, one hard to describe. *It shouldn't taste this sweet,* but it does and we both find ourselves wanting more.

She bites my lip hard, making it bleed. I return the favor, savagely nipping at the lip that has been driving me wild all night. We pull back, breathless, lips bruised, and bleeding, wiry smiles mirrored on our faces. I tuck her hair behind her ear. "You're so fucking beautiful, Serena." She kisses my lips softly once more, her eyes holding an emotion I don't dare name. "You continue to surprise me."

"As do you, Aster."

"When you told me you were taking me on a date, I wasn't expecting the haunted house, you to be *the* owner, or you fucking me with a knife."

"Did I scare you?"

"No." She shakes her head. "You excite me. I want to know more. I need to know more about you, Aster Graves."

"I don't know why, Serena, but you're breathing life back to things in me I thought were long dead. You are special, and," I pause, hardly believing the tornado of emotions rushing through me. "I can't seem to get enough of you."

"I can't get enough of you either."

The emotions we are both feeling bring out a fear I never thought I would have. My little lamb made my heart, I didn't know I had, start beating. These feelings are unknown to me, scare me, and need to go away, but I don't want to lose this feeling, yet.

I grab her hand. "Let's get you back home and washed up."

She nods her head, her eyes clouding. I grab two drapes hanging over the windows, wrapping one around her shoulders and the other over mine. I rip two pieces of the fabric off, take her hand in mine, and wrap the cut. She grabs the one I'm about to wrap around mine, and repeats the action for me. I watch her finger trace the line the blade left behind, before securing the cloth around my hand and tying it. She brings my hand to her lips and I watch, my heart beating faster as she kisses it. "Kisses make everything better," She says with a small smile, "That's what my mom used to tell me." Her cheeks start to heat, which makes her drop our hands and turns away shyly.

"I know you're the owner, but don't they need these for next week?" She says fiddling with the wrap around her hand.

"Like you said, next week, which gives me a week to replace them." Her steps falter as we walk across the grounds, her eyes burning into me. "Don't worry, I'll give them back tomorrow."

She slaps me on the chest, leaving cakey blood in its place "Don't you dare give these back, they're covered in our blood."

"I promise I won't, I'll put them in a special place." I kiss her forehead, grabbing her hand and we walk to my car, unable to go more than a few moments without touching her.

The drive to her house is the exact opposite of the drive to the grounds, Serena stares out the window in silence, not even messing with the radio. We just had an amazing night, why does it look like she wants to forget what happened? I reach over and grab her hand startling her "Penny for your thoughts?" I ask, rubbing my thumb against her skin.

"Just wondering what you have done to me," she murmurs, still staring out the window.

"I corrupted you, little lamb."

"Yes, you have, but I don't regret a single thing."

I bring her hand to my lips, placing a delicate kiss on her knuckles. "Me either."

She rolls down the window, letting the cold air hit her face, her hair billowing around her. She looks enchanting with the moon shining on her, blood covering her face.

When we get to her house, we both walk in and up the stairs, fingers linked together. We go to her bathroom and I turn on her shower. It's a walk-in shower with dark blue distressed subway tiles. The floor is a simple white tile, the small hexagons contrasting nicely with the blue. She catches me looking at her and drops the cloth draped around her with a devilish smirk on her lips. Seeing her clearly in the light, no longer hidden by the darkness of "The Dancing Clowns," decorated in blood, makes my cock instantly grow. I drop my own, matching her bravado as we stare at each other's naked bodies.

One after the other, we step into the shower. I watch as the blood drips down the contours of her body, her eyes closed as she runs her fingers through her hair. I grab her, spinning her around, and press my cock in her waiting cunt. I bend her over, taking her once again, until we're both drained and satisfied.

Our limbs feel like jelly as we dry off and wrap ourselves in towels. Stepping out of the bathroom, she walks to her closet, and grabs an oversized t-shirt for herself and me.

"Sorry, this is all I have," she says, handing it to me.

"It's okay, it'll work for tonight." The shirt is a Slipknot concert tee. *She has good taste in music. I'll have to ask her about it later.* I slip the tee over my head, it fits tight, enhancing the muscles underneath and making my biceps bulge. The shirt she chose for herself sits like a dress on her 5'2 frame, making her look delectable.

"Good." She grabs my hand and pulls me into the bed, laying her head on my chest as she settles in my arms. She looks up at me, a question in her eyes.

I smile at her. "Is there something you want to ask me?" She nods her head.

"Okay." *Here we go.* She's probably going to ask about how I came to own the number one haunted house in the country.

"Why Graves? Why haunted houses?" she asks with such curious eyes, biting her lip, and I find myself wanting to tell her a little bit about my story. I never want to talk to or get close to anyone, unless absolutely needed. Not even my little lambs get to know me, they know the mask I put on and the killer who ends them. Serena, I want her to know it all, and that thought scares me.

I hum, realizing I was right. "The inheritance I told you about from my parents death..." She's quiet, not saying sorry for my loss like people usually say once they hear my parents are dead.

I am grateful, I can't handle the meaningless platitudes and the looks that come after. "Well, I used a small portion of it to create Graves." I pause, memories flashing through my mind as I think of how much I'm willing to tell the woman in my eyes. "When I was younger, my mother and I would watch scary movies. All of them." I smile. "The good ones, and the bad ones, every Friday night, that was our thing. I came to love scary movies, and learned a lot from them."

She remains silent, staring up with more care than I'm used to, taking it all in.

"Every Halloween, she would make my costume, fashioning hers and my fathers after whatever I chose. After they passed, I wanted to remember them in the best way I could. Bringing our love for horror to everyone, made sense to me. I knew they'd love it, so every year I create the most realistic haunted houses I can, each one different and new from the previous year. It's the reason tickets sell out as soon as they drop, people love to be scared, they're eager for it, and I love being the reason for their fear."

"Wow." she breathes, both of us falling into a comfortable silence.

"Well, now I know the mystery behind Graves. I wonder how much media outlets would give me if I tell them the inside scoop about the owner of Graves."

"Oh, really now?" I tickle her, forcing her under me until she begs me to stop,

"I'm about to pee! I can't take it anymore." I stop tickling her, laughing as I watch her waddle across the room.

When she comes back, she lays in my arms again, and looks up at me. "Aster, I want you to know I would never tell anyone any of your secrets."

I kiss her forehead, holding her close, we fall asleep in each other's arms. For some reason, I believe her. I believe she would never tell anyone any of my secrets.

I'm safe with her.

SIXTEEN
SERENA

Turning over with the intention to spoon Aster, I'm jolted awake when I pat the space around me and find him gone. *Where did he go?*

Slowly, I sit up, rubbing my eyes and hoarsely calling out his name. Silence greets me. I clear my throat and try again, but still nothing. Just silence. I get out of bed and start walking around the house looking for him, coming up empty.

Surely, he wouldn't leave in the middle of the night, without letting me know. After the night we had, the blood we spilled, the secrets we shared, he wouldn't just leave. He promised me he wouldn't ghost me again. He'd be stupid to do that to me a second time, especially since I know one of his secrets. He has other secrets, I know with the mask he tries to put on, but slowly both of our masks are slipping for each other.

I wouldn't dare dream of ever revealing his identity to anyone, but a woman's scorn can make even the most sane, conduct vengeful acts.

Going back to my room, I grab my phone, expecting to see a text from him, saying where he went. He's always been good about letting me know when something's come up, I'm sure today is no different. My heart falls, seeing it's a text from Jessica instead.

JESSICA

Hey babe, I forgot I had previous plans today, so I can't help out at the market, Sorry. Promise I'll make it up to you

Scratching my head, confused, I purse my lips, looking up, thinking about what she means.

Fuck

I go to the calendar on my phone and sure as shit in bold it says 'Flea Market Day.' Looking at the time, I let out a breath of relief. *I still have two hours until I have to set up, and three before it opens.*

Pissed she backed out, after she *promised* me she would be there to help, I just ignore the message. I love Jessica, but she is the biggest flake I know, and it drives me crazy. She has always been on her own time, but since my mom passed away, she only really shows up when I'm in a spiral. If I'm not on the verge of a mental breakdown, it's just crickets from her.

Chewing my lip, my fingers hover over the screen, I open my messages, and send a text to Aster before I lose my nerve.

SERENA

I had fun last night.

I place my phone back on the nightstand, and start to get ready for a busy day ahead.

I SIT IN THE LONG LINE OF CARS WAITING TO TAKE THEIR PLACE, ready to park and unload what I have brought to sell. Drumming my fingers on the steering wheel, I look down and grab my phone. The message I sent earlier to Aster was read over an hour ago, but no response.

My stomach bottoms out, my mouth forming a frown from being left on read. Waking up to him gone is one thing, being left on read is another. My insecurities from the first time come to the forefront. I bring my hands to my mouth and start mindlessly chewing my nails to the bed. His reasoning for making me feel unimportant, again, better be a damn good one.

Thinking better of myself, I type out another quick message, hoping this time I'll get an answer.

SERENA

Hey, I'll be at the flea market today, selling my paintings, it's on first street at 10am. This isn't an invitation, although if you want to come, you can. I'm letting you know, so if you try to contact me and I don't answer, that's why.

It's been five years since I've done one of these. I used to do them every Sunday when my mom was still alive, before she got really bad. She would come with me, so excited to be a part of something that meant so much to me. Little did she know, her being there is what made it so special. Jessica always said she would come, but never did. The things in her life were more important than me. Tears fill my eyes as I walk through the center to find my assigned spot. My mom was my biggest fan. She was my inspiration for my art. She was the one who would push me to sell it. I was always hesitant, convinced they weren't good enough, but when all but a couple paintings would sell, she would just sit there beaming, looking so proud and honored to have been a part of everything. I couldn't help but smile as well, her joy and confidence contagious.

After she passed, I stopped. I stopped painting. I stopped coming to the market. I stopped living. I just couldn't find myself wanting to do anything. I couldn't force myself to do the things I knew I needed to, especially the one thing I looked forward to most with her. *I am so upset that Jessica canceled on me. We made these plans so long ago. She knew how hard it was for me to come back here, for me to even start painting again. Sometimes, she's so selfish, but she's the only one I got, so I cut her some slack. She has a life outside of me.*

After everything is unloaded and set up just right, I snap a couple pictures to post on my Instagram, for my followers to see, and have a chance to come out to purchase. I didn't do a good job of promoting the market, too caught up in a certain someone who makes me see stars.

Once I am satisfied, everything is perfect, I sit down in the chair and wait for the market to open, my legs bouncing with nervous energy. The other vendors, those who have helpers, get the chance to walk around and get first choice, before the crowd starts to come through. I used to do that. My mom would watch, and we would take turns walking around. There's something special about wandering around the market before it's open. Something no one else gets to experience. It's hard to explain.

Not today though. Today I'm all by myself.

Scrolling mindlessly through TikTok while I wait for the market to open, my thoughts are interrupted when someone clearing their throat stands in front of my tent, to gain my attention.

I look up and see the most beautiful woman I ever laid eyes on. If I swung that way, I'd let her step on me, and say 'thank you,' with a smile. I can tell she's taller than me, without even needing to stand up. Her white blonde hair, that looks like Elsa's from *Frozen*, curls that falls over her breast, and down her back. I find myself swallowing, as my eyes travel down and up her body. She's wearing black leather pants, I know if she turned around they'd make her ass look amazing. She's wearing a black crop top, her flat stomach drawing my eyes to it, I squint my eyes and see a red jewel pierced on her belly button.

When I finally tear my eyes away from her body, I look at her face and the smirk playing on her lips, with her golden brown eyes, has me squirming in my seat. *Am I getting turned on by this woman?* I stand up to ask her if she needs any help, but when her eyes travel down my body, and she steps closer, making me step back, the words lodge in my throat. *Yep, totally getting turned on by her.*

I swallow past the lump, "Can I help you with something?"

She tilts her head as if she didn't understand my question. She reaches up and grabs a piece of my hair, lifting it to inspect it. "I like your hair, it's the color of a raven." I look at where she's looking, and she drops my hair, walking over to look at the paintings, as if she never touched me. I release the breath I didn't realize I was holding.

She skims her perfectly manicured fingers across a painting of a flock of ravens, titled 'Unkindness'. "Like this," she says. "Did you know ravens are associated with death and illness? They also never forget a pretty face." She walks back over to me, brushes her hand across my cheek. "If I were a raven, I'd never forget your face."

Is she flirting with me? I touch the spot she just touched, and stare in awe at how hypnotic she is. Here I am letting this goddess touch me, and instead of telling her to back off, or to keep her hands to herself, I stand frozen letting her do what she wants.

Walking back over to the paintings, she pulls the one I painted of a lone fox, with a bloody mouth and paws, sitting in the forest, an assortment of colors in the sky. "I'll take this one."

We walk over to the podium I have set up, she hands me her card, and I swipe it. "Thanks." She says and walks away with the painting tucked under her arm.

My brain starts working again, and I yell after her, "I forgot to wrap your painting!"

She turns her head, her pearly whites showing as a smile crests her face, "No need. I'm sure I'll see you again." With those parting words, I watch her walk away and stand in a daze.

What does seeing me again have to do with protecting her painting?

I see two friendly faces of the elderly couple Mr. and Mrs. Fredericks walking over to my table, breaking the spell I was put under.

What was that?

The Fredricks have been married for forty-seven years. They own Fredericks Flowers and come to the market every Sunday to sell their gorgeous bouquets. The last time I saw them was at my mother's funeral, they made a beautiful wreath to put over her grave. It was full of big and bright red roses, her favorite.

"Serena!" Mrs. Fredericks says gleefully with outstretched arms. I embrace her, and then her husband, the smile on my face feeling less forced than I expected.

"How are you, my dear? It's been, what?" She looks at her husband for an answer she can't seem to find.

"Five years," he says without missing a beat.

She looks back at me and grabs my hands, making me wince. "Five years, oh my, has it really been that long?"

I squeeze her hands, tears pricking at the edge of my eyes. "It has."

Her eyebrows raise to her hairline when she looks down at my hands, "Good heavens, what happened?" She asks, concern coating her voice.

I pull my hands away, the memory of last night coming to play like a movie in my mind. I rub at the cut, a small smile playing on my lips. I look up, meeting her worried eyes, "I accidentally cut it while cooking last night, trying to filet fish."

Her brows pinch together accusingly, "Be more careful. I'm glad you're okay." I nod in response.

She looks at me with sad, knowing eyes. Eyes that hold a lifetime of stories, ones she has told me and Mom many times over. She has lived a long fulfilling life. A pang of jealousy washes over me, that she is here, and my mother is not, but it's gone just as fast when I look into her blue wrinkled eyes.

"We're glad you're back, dear. Aren't we, Jerry?" She nudges him, he finally looks at me with pitiful eyes, eyes he knows I don't like to see.

"We have. We've missed your energy here."

We stare at one another for a while, unsure of what to say, until we hear Mrs. Fredericks squeal. We both jump and look. She stands holding a new piece I just finished a few weeks ago.

It's an autumn day, with the sun just setting painted in the background. There's a silhouette of a couple kissing next to a motorcycle. Leaves the color of fire and passion drift down from a tree falling over and around them.

She stands staring, captivated at the sight, a single tear falling from her eye. "Oh, Jerry, doesn't this take you back?"

He walks over to her, putting his arm around her, and looks down at the painting. You can see he, too, is getting lost in a shared memory, the two of them seeming to turn back time right in front of me. Looking up, he whispers, "How much?"

Smiling at the sight of them, I shake my head as he reaches into his back pocket and pulls out his wallet. I grab his hands gently pushing him away. He persists and tries to hand me a hundred-dollar bill. I close his hand around the bill, and say, "I'll take the story over this, whenever you have a chance, that is worth more than money to me."

He smiles, nodding his head with understanding, and puts the money back in his pocket. Looking at his wife, he pulls her close, and says. "I like the way you tell the story more, Alice."

Grabbing her hands, I squeeze them quickly before I sit her down in my chair. I walk over to my car and grab the other two I brought out of habit. Coming back, Jerry and I take a seat. With tearful eyes, ghosting her fingers across the painting, Alice begins her story.

"Back in the day, we used to ride as if we'd never have the chance again. We'd leave when the sun set, not returning until it rose again in the morning. We stopped riding fifteen years ago, when Jerry had his hip replaced. I could still ride, but it wasn't the same without my Jer beside me. So we put up our bikes." She looks down at the painting, running a hand over the bike. "Oh, how I miss the wind in my hair, the free flying feeling we used to get. We were birds, taking flight, everynight. Together."

I sit there in silence, letting her tell her story and listening to it as if the words would pull me from the darkness I felt falling for once more. Reliving the memory with her as she spoke her words.

"This painting brings me back to one night in particular. It was autumn in Salem, and the leaves had just changed their colors. The weather, oh, the weather was perfect." She looks up and stares at the sky and takes us into her memory. "It was close to Halloween, and we all know how it gets here around October, especially with the tourists. The town was littered with people."

I nod in understanding, cringing as I remember how it is about to become with October approaching.

"Back then, we all did more walking than driving." She grabs her husband's hand and places it on her lap, his eyes locked on Alice as she fights the smile lifting her cheeks. "After a long day of window shopping, we go home and Jerry says he has a surprise for me." She looks over to her husband with such loving eyes, the same excitement she'd felt all those years ago still in her voice. "We walk up the driveway, and he tells me to close my eyes, which, of course, I do, but I can't help myself. I peek as soon as I hear him walk away. Once the garage opened, I gasped and saw a motorcycle, sitting there with a giant red bow on the seat, the same one my daddy used to drive. The same one I'd told Jer about growing up, some of my favorite memories are of helping my daddy fix, and ride that bike until it was well and truly a part of the road. I cried so much at the sight of it, it was a red 1942 Indian Jr Scout."

I bite my lip, trying to hold my tears at bay. I'd hate to interrupt such a wonderful memory.

She looks over at me, still holding her husband's hand. "You probably don't know what that is, before your time, but look it up later. It was a classic, for good reason too. Anyways, that night he took me out. I held on, and he drove. We explored Salem all night, as if *we* were the tourists. We stopped in the middle of nowhere, and there was a tree with leaves falling just like in your painting. We stood under that tree and watched the sun come up, in each other's arms. He kissed me, and that was the beginning of our biker journey together."

Jerry brings his wife's wrinkled hand to his lips and kisses it. They stare at one another, so much love in their eyes. Love I hope to find one day.

The way their eyes shine while looking at one another, has me thinking of the green eyes that have given me the same look.

Alice breaks the stare and looks over at me. "Thank you for letting me relive this day."

I shake my head, fighting tears as my heart drums in my chest. "No, thank you."

We all get up, Jerry helping her, peaceful silence settling around us. *Absolutely worth so much more than what money could buy.*

"Want me to wrap that up for you?"

She hands me the painting with shaking hands. "Would you, dear? Thank you."

I grab the painting, carefully protecting it with specialty film, and offer to put it in their car. Jerry shakes his head and says he will do it, as they walk away hand in hand, lost in their own world of bikes and fiery bursts of color.

I stare at them as they leave, wondering what life they led to get to here.

I'm startled from my thoughts when I hear a male voice I don't recognize. "They're such a beautiful couple."

"They really are," I say, turning around annoyed to see who interrupted such a peaceful moment.

Looking up I see a beautiful man, with golden eyes. A smile that reaches the orbs, giving them a spark of life you don't often see, dimples popping out of each cheek. His hair a deep mahogany with slight curls framing his head. His face is covered in a darker beard, not long, but not stubble either. You can tell he takes his time with it, it is cut to perfection and looks more groomed than a show dog.

"You have beautiful paintings."

I walk back behind the table, shivers racking through me. "Thank you, if there is anything I can help you with, let me know please."

He nods his head and begins browsing.

He is good looking, and someone I would go for, the ruggedly handsome look has always been my weakness. He's attractive, yes, but there is something *off* about his energy. The longer I look at his eyes when he looks at me, the more crazed they become. *I hope he leaves fast. I wish Aster was here.*

I wonder where he went this morning. Did he leave last night after I fell asleep? He didn't even leave me a message, nothing. Did I do something wrong? After the night we shared, I thought we grew closer. Now I'm just sitting here, left on read, wondering what happened.

I jump when I feel a tap on my shoulder.

"Sorry, I didn't mean to scare you. I was saying miss for a while, and when you didn't hear me, I thought the next thing to do was to tap your shoulder."

"I'm so sorry, I was in my head. What can I help you with?"

"No problem, I get lost in my head, too."

My eyes soften, "Really?"

He smiles sweetly at me. "Really." He stares into my eyes longer than I'm comfortable with, forcing me to look away.

I don't know why, but another man staring at me with eyes of desire makes me feel guilty. I know Aster and I aren't together, but he is the only one I want. He is the only one I *need*. He makes me feel beautiful and wanted; when he isn't leaving me on read. Last night was like something out of one of my dark romance books, and every minute of it was perfect. Normal people would have been horrified being fucked with a knife, but I've never been a normal girl. When I saw him bleeding to bring me pleasure, something inside me cracked, and I found myself wanting to bleed for him too.

He clears his throat and points to one of my paintings. "How much for this one?"

The painting is of a wrinkled hand holding the hand of a young man. The background is a light blue blending into a sky blue with wisps of white clouds all around. It feels surreal and grounded at the same time. It's one of my favorites in my collection.

Walking over, I turn it over. "This one is sixty." He's leaning over my shoulder, trying to see where I'm looking, I point at the price, fighting the shiver from how close he is. "If you want to see any of the prices, you just turn it over, it is at the bottom."

Putting the painting back where it was, I turn around and bump right into him. Holding my breath, I back away, and move to the side. "Sorry, I wasn't watching where I was going." I mumble, avoiding his stare.

"No reason to be sorry."

He smiles down at me, and I feel all the hair on my arms raise. Remembering that feeling, I glance around, looking for the one person who elicits my goosebumps to rise. Looking around and not seeing him, I drop my head and walk over to the other side of my booth and start rearranging my paintings. Doing anything, but talking to my customer. Which is rude, I know, but I have a feeling he has other motivations for being here.

Tapping my shoulder once again, I refrain from rolling my eyes, already knowing who it is. I turn around and see Mr. Touchy holding the painting he was asking about.

"I'd like this one, please."

"Sounds great." I force a smile, grabbing the painting from him and begin wrapping it up. He hands me a hundred-dollar bill, and my blood freezes. Without touching him, I say, "It was only sixty, remember."

He grabs my hand, placing the bill in it "I remember, this is your tip."

I slowly pull my hand out of his "Thank you."

"It's for my mom, I hope this makes her smile. She has been going through it lately." My brows draw together, but I focus on finishing his purchase. Without responding, he continues. "You see, my brother went missing a couple weeks ago. Mom has a bad feeling something happened to him." He pauses to look me in the eyes. The dread I feel is unexplainable, but he takes my silence as permission to continue. "I think he's just gone on one of his excursions, turning off his phone and escaping reality. He does this all the time, but Mom is sure something has happened because he hasn't been gone this long before."

"Sorry, to hear that, I'm sure you're right, and he will be back before you know it." I hand him his now wrapped painting, "I hope she likes it," I respond in a half-hearted kind of way.

My smile wavers while he hesitates to take his painting. He's trying to tell me about his life when I didn't ask for it. All I can think about is Aster. *Why hasn't he replied? Is he really somewhere watching this interaction?* The touchy mama's boy seems nice, plus he's cute, in a creepy way, and is relatable. Being as close to his mom as I was to mine.

"She will." He smiles at himself, like he just made my day or something. Just as he starts to walk away, he turns around and heads back over to me.

Fuck.

I take a deep breath and prepare myself for whatever he is about to say.

"I know I'd kick myself if I didn't ask, but do you want to grab coffee sometime?"

There is such hope in his eyes, and after all the touching and bumping he did, I'm not surprised he's asking me out. Feeling goosebumps rise again, I look around and come up empty again. I think about Aster being somewhere lurking, watching, and my heart thunders in my chest as my core clenches around nothing.

These goosebumps are not for nothing, I know he's somewhere, and after leaving me on read. I feel a little vindictive.

I smile, batting my lashes at Mr. Touchy, reaching over to grab his arm, and I see his Adam's apple bob, and say in the sultriest voice I can muster, "I would love to have coffee with you."

He's shocked at my response, probably already gearing himself for rejection. "Wow, really? Based on your body language, I was sure you were going to say no. I mean, I'm glad you didn't." He reaches out a hand, a brilliant smile stretching his face. "I'm Bradley, thought you should know the name of the guy who just asked you out."

Taking his hand in mine, I shake it, saying, "I'm Serena."

Without releasing my hand, he stays holding it, scratching his thumb along my skin. "The market ends at three. Want to meet up at the coffee shop across the street then?"

I look over his shoulder, at the little coffee shop, then glance back at him. "I would love to." The words come out as a lie, as I look around once more for my green eyed man. *He is not going to be happy about this. Serves him right.*

With a huge smile, he finally releases my hand "Great! I'll see you soon." He walks away, looking back to wave goodbye. I wave back at him, a stiff smile on my face.

I walk back into the booth, plopping down into my chair and bury my face in my hands. "What did I just agree to?"

"Yes, what did you agree to, little lamb?"

My muscles lock, my entire body frozen as the timbre of a voice I'd recognize anywhere washed over me. I look up and see angry eyes staring back at me.

Double Fuck.

He barrels around the table, bracing his arms on either side of my chair, leaning in close and breathing in my ear. "You're *mine.*"

His breath tickles my neck as we hang suspended in the moment, neither of us knowing what to do next. He pushes away, nearly knocking my chair over and strides through the crowd without looking back. It takes me a second to gather my thoughts before I get up racing after him. *It's not like that! Let me explain.* Just as I reach him, I see a crowd of people forming at my booth. Groaning, I glance between the crowd and Aster before turning back around and losing sight of Aster completely.

I'll text him when I get a moment. He needs to let me explain.

The rest of the day goes by in a flash. Apparently, the town was waiting on bated breath for my return to the market. I'm still not sure how I feel about that. Finishing the day, and completely forgetting about my coffee date with Bradley, I'm cleaning up when I feel a tap on my shoulder.

"Hey, I thought we could walk over to the coffee shop together."

I turn around, already regretting my vindictive promise, especially after Aster showed up earlier. Debating on canceling, but seeing the excitement in his eyes I regrettably say, "Let me just put the rest of these paintings away, and we can go."

Closing the trunk of my car, I turn around, and before I can walk over to him, Aster is there between us. I can't see his face, but every muscle in his body is tight, his fists trembling at his sides as he gets in Bradley's face. He stands towering over him by a foot, and in a threatening voice says, "She's *mine.*"

Before Bradley can respond, or before I have time to process what is even happening, Aster turns around, grabs me forcefully by the arm and pulls me away. I feel a tug on my other arm, Bradley grabbing me trying to stop whatever is happening. "She didn't say she had a boyfriend."

Stopping dead in his tracks, Aster releases my arm, and stalks over to Bradley. In a blink of an eye, his hand is around his throat. Aster lifts him in the air with more ease than I thought possible, even despite his size. The veins in his arms bulge from holding Bradley up. Shaking him for good measure, Aster brings his head to Bradley's ear and says again "She. Is. *Mine.*" Venom flows through every word he spits, before he throws Bradley onto the ground. Silence falls across the market, everyone watching, but no one brave enough to take on Aster alone. Growling, Aster grabs my hand and pulls me away from a hurt and confused Bradley still sitting on the ground.

I stare up at Aster, anger rolling off of me. Not from hurting Bradley, but from the fact that he showed up after ghosting me, and is dragging me to God knows where. Pissed, but also a little turned on, I stay silent and plant my feet into the ground.

SEVENTEEN

ASTER

I feel myself being tugged, a growl building in my throat as I look behind to see Serena trying to plant her feet and hold me back. *That's cute.* With a chuckle, I pick her up, throw her over my shoulders, and walk us behind the bathrooms. She starts to bang on my back, pressing against me and trying to wriggle out of my hold.

"Put me down."

"If you don't stop moving, I'm going to place you over my knees and spank you." I'm thinking about spanking her for even entertaining a date with another man. She doesn't know what happened to the last man who took her out, and never will.

My hold tightens around her legs, as I think about how the one at the market kept touching her. He would die a slow and painful death, starting with both his hands being sawed off, *slowly*. The thought makes me grin. Maybe I'd wrap his hands in a nice little box, with a bright blue ribbon on it, *my signature color*, and gift them to Serena, since she allowed him to touch her.

She hits me harder, her little fists feeling like bb gun bullets pelting my back, throwing a tantrum like a damn child. I bring my hand around, spanking her ass with a solid hit of my palm, which makes her yelp. The little sound that comes from her has me picking up my speed, my pants feeling tighter by the minute. We get to the bathrooms, and I let her body slide down my stomach. She stands with her arms crossed, turning her head away from me with a huff.

Gripping her chin, I force her to look at me, but her eyes stubbornly look over my shoulder. "Look at me, little lamb," I demand, getting close to her ear and whispering a threat I know will get her attention. "If you don't look at me, I will fuck you in the ass with no lube. I will not be gentle. I will not stop with your tears. Do you want to bleed around my cock?"

"You wouldn't," she gasps, finally looking at me with fear hidden behind her defiant eyes.

I smirk, "You know I would."

"What do you want?" she spits, clinging to her anger despite everything.

"What I want is to know why you agreed to a date when you're *mine*."

She scoffs and stands taller, looking me dead in the eyes, "I. Am. *Not*. Yours."

So, this is how she is going to be? She looks away again and crosses her arms once more. Pushing her flush to the bathroom wall, I uncross her arms, and pin them above her head, as she starts to squirm against me. I whisper against her lips, "You are mine. This little act is going to get you punished." I look her up and down slowly, taking care to caress every inch of her with my eyes. "And not in the way you like."

She tries to twist her arms out of my hold, anger rising in her voice. "If I'm yours, then why did you ignore me, again?! Why did you make me feel like you were going to disappear for weeks?" She burst into tears, no longer fighting against my hold, and I feel a twinge in my heart. *What the fuck is this feeling?* "You promised you wouldn't do that to me again," she chokes out.

I pull her flush to my chest, her tears staining my shirt. Caressing her hair, I try to comfort her. "I'm sorry, little lamb, I was trying to figure some shit out." I take a deep breath, pulling her away from my body, and looking down at her. Her eyes are puffy, streaks of mascara running down her cheeks. Her cute little button nose is red at the tip, making her look like Rudolph. "Look, I'm here aren't I? I showed up," I soothingly say, rubbing her back.

She sniffs and nods her head. I run my fingers back through my hair, my thoughts chaotic "You're making me feel things, Serena. Things I don't understand. You make me crazy. You make me question everything. I am breaking all my rules for you."

She sniffs again, wiping her nose with the back of her hand, and looks up. "You are?"

I rub my thumb under her eye, wiping the tear and mascara away. "I am, and for the first time in my life, I'm scared." My breaths quicken, and my hands start to shake. *That's never happened before.* My hands form into fist, I close my eyes and take a deep breath to calm my breathing. When I open them again, Serena's eyes have softened and I feel her hands grab mine. "I'm scared of losing who I am. Who I have always been. I don't know how to be anyone else." I bring my lips to her forehead, and whisper, "I'm scared of losing you." The words leave my mouth before I can even register what I'm saying. *Am I really scared of losing her?*

Trusting people isn't a part of my nature. No one can truly know who I am, unless they're one of my victims about to take their last breath. Only then is the mask taken off and my true self revealed. But with Serena… My mask slips more and more. I find myself wanting to share more with her. When she's not with me, I actually miss her. She is changing me, and I can tell I'm changing her too.

She lets go of my hands, locking her arms around my neck, and kisses me. Reassuring me, telling me without telling me, she understands. Her kiss is filled with longing and passion, and I lean into her, slipping my tongue in, and making her moan. I groan into her, grinding my hardening erection against her.

She breaks the kiss, but leaving her lips a shadow away from mine, "I'm scared too."

With understanding in just those three words, I grab her hand and walk back to her car. The market is cleared out by the time we make it back, not a soul in sight. You can hear the voices and laughter from the shops across the street, but all the vendors and their vehicles are gone.

I help her in, leaning my hand over her head as I look down. My heart pounds in my chest as I realize what I'm about to do. She looks up at me, with hope in her eyes, and I can't help but tumble into that hope with her. I bend down to kiss her one more time, lingering a moment longer, savoring her taste.

"I have one last rule to break for you."

She tilts her head, confusion lacing her features.

"Follow me."

She nods. I shut her door and walk back to my car. The walk back seems to take an eternity. I'm dragging my feet across the pavement, hands in my pockets, trying to calm my breathing.

Never in my thirty-two years of living did I think I would ever fall for anyone, let alone one of my victims. The night at the haunted house when I saw a darkness hiding behind those blue eyes of hers, was when I knew she'd be mine forever. Today, I battled with myself about whether I should go or stay. When I finally decided to go, I found her right away. We're like magnets to one another, always able to find the other.

I showed up when that elderly woman was telling her love story, her hand in her husband's hands. As she took everyone back in time, all I could do was stare at Serena, and watch as her eyes started to tear up. All I could think about was, what a life would be like with her by my side. I was going to make my entrance when they left, then I noticed a man walking up.

My knuckles were turning white from how hard I gripped the tree I was hiding behind. Instead of intervening, I stayed back and watched. The tree camouflaged me well enough to not be seen, but I was close enough to hear every word they said.

Every time he touched her, I could tell she was uncomfortable and wanted him to leave. My teeth ground together so hard, my molars almost cracked. When he walked away and I saw her take a relieved breath, I took the same one with her. Then he turned around, and my body started to move on its own. Her body reacted to my presence first, her eyes searching for me.

When he asked her on a date, I was sure she was going to say no, then I saw her lips lift a little and those blue eyes of hers were forming a plan. When she said yes, I lost it. Once she was alone again, I needed her to know who she belonged to. *She was mine.*

I was so angry, I had to walk away, or else I don't know what would have happened. I would never hurt her, but I was going to hurt someone. The place was packed and the only way I wouldn't kill anyone, was going back to my car, waiting for the market to be over.

The drive back to my house is quiet. I keep the radio off, and the windows down to let the cool air hit me, hoping it will help break this trance. I wasn't expecting to react the way I did, but when I saw her tears, something in me broke. I really am terrified, I wasn't lying to her when I said that. I am scared and confused. I am feeling things for her I haven't felt for anyone ever. Maybe… maybe I don't have to kill her. Maybe she will be the one and only little lamb to make it out alive. Who knows maybe I can convince my little lamb to kill with me, she is obsessed with The Morbid Monet afterall.

We pull up to my house, and I look in the rearview mirror to see her right behind me. I get out of my car, and walk to hers, opening her door and helping her out. Taking her hand, I walk her up the steps and into my home.

The one place no one has ever been.

She is silent as she looks around, curiosity clear in her blue eyes as she tentatively steps ahead of me. My arm tugs at hers, and she glances back. I give her a tentative smile, squeezing her hand without thinking. Her cheeks lift as she lets go of my hand

and wanders around looking at everything. I follow silently behind her, watching her look. Her body language is almost reverent as she sees more of my life than anyone ever has. She picks up a fox figurine and examines it. I walk behind her, reaching around to cradle her hands with mine, dropping my chin on her shoulder.

"My mother gave me that one Christmas."

She looks over her shoulder at me. "Because your parents called you little fox?"

I nuzzle into her shoulder. "Yeah."

"Is that why you call me little lamb?" she asks, looking back down, and turning the fox over in our hands.

"You could say that."

She places the fox down and turns around her arms sliding around my waist. "You said you'd tell me why you call me little lamb."

"I will one day, but today isn't that day."

I do want to tell her, but I already decided she wouldn't be one of my victims. She is still my little lamb, just one I will keep. Forever. I'm not ready to show her who I truly am, I don't know if I ever will be.

She juts out her lower lip in a sensual pout, batting her dark lashes at me and making my cock twitch.

"Serena," I warn, my voice gravelly and full of promise.

She sucks her lip back in, biting it and making me groan. I yank her flush to my body, startling her, and making her yelp.

She wraps her arms around me, laying her head on my chest, as she looks up at me, and says, "If you don't tell me the reason, you don't get to fuck me."

I chuckle and my eyes darken. "I'm the one who makes the threats, you're the one who gets the punishments." I lift her up, too impatient to allow her to walk, and take her to my room. Throwing her on my bed, we both pant and stare hungrily into one another's eyes.

"Clothes off. Now," I demand, leaving no room for argument.

She does what I say and stands to take her clothes off. My eyes roam every part of her body as each piece of clothing comes off, my body humming in desperation to take her. Feel her. Fuck her.

I start removing my clothing, watching as her eyes trail every inch of my body.

"Kneel."

She does as she's told immediately getting on her knees beneath me.

"Crawl to me."

She slowly makes her way over to me, ass high in the air, swaying with every move closer. Gripping my already hard cock, I start to stroke it up and down. She watches me with hunger in her eyes. Smirking, I grant her wish, and place my cock on her lips.

"Open."

She parts her lips slowly, slipping out her tongue to trace the head of my cock. I groan at the pleasure her mouth brings me, desperate for more. She places her hand over mine and strokes up and down my long shaft, slow precise strokes, to match her sucking lips. I grip the back of her head, curling my hand in her hair, savoring the feeling she's giving me. She's a fucking succubus, sucking the life straight from my cock, and I am loving every second of it. She starts to quicken her pace, sucking faster, stroking deeper.

I lose control and ram my cock down her throat, making her gag. The sounds she makes has me pumping my hips faster, both hands wrapped around her head, shoving her as far as she can take me. Her eyes start to water, and she quickens her pace.

"Fuck, Serena," I hiss. "You cry so pretty for me," and swipe the tear that has fallen down her face.

I feel her smile around my cock, my head hung back, eyes closed, reeling in the pleasure her mouth gives me.

I feel myself about to explode, I wrap my hand into her hair, and yank her head back so she's staring at me. "Be a good girl and take all my cum," I demand.

She squeezes my balls, my nerves tingling at the extra sensation, and has me shooting my hot cum down her pretty little throat. She takes every last drop like it's the nectar of life.

I pull her from me, "Swallow," I command.

She swallows, her eyes never leaving mine, then takes her finger wiping the side of her mouth and sucking it clean.

"Naughty girl," I groan, lifting her off of her knees, and kissing her hard. I lay her on the bed and crawl on top of her body, leaving searing kisses in my wake. "We're not done yet."

I spread open her legs with mine and hover between her. I grab my cock, pumping it a few times to harden it, and tease her entrance. Feeling her wetness coat my head, I slowly move past her lips into her waiting cunt, making her moan in satisfaction.

"Aster!" she screams as I start to circle her clit, still pumping in and out of her as I suck up every bit of her pleasure. Quickening my pace, I watch her eyes roll to the back of her head. I start to feel her walls clench around me, my own thrusts stuttering.

"I'm about to come," she says in a breathless moan.

With one last pump, we explode together but I still keep my fingers rubbing her clit until she's a shaking mess beneath me. Grabbing my hand, she begs me to stop, but I can't. I love seeing her fall apart because of me, and my body is the next best thing to my blade.

"Please, Aster, it's too much."

Ignoring her pleas, I bring her to one more orgasm, making her whole body spasm. My cock still inside her, I start to grind my hips, as her walls start to contract around me once more, my dick springs back to life and I fuck her one more time, dragging one more orgasm from her. Third times the charm, they always say.

By the third orgasm, I slowly pull myself out of her, both

hissing from the loss of one another. I get up and go get a wash-cloth from the bathroom to clean her up.

Surprising myself, I lay back in bed, and pull her into my chest, as I look down at her. I stare at her for what seems like forever, simply admiring her beauty. *I can't believe she's in my house. In my bed.* She is the picture of pure seduction, laying naked with her hair falling over her breast, truly looking like the siren she is. The spell she has me under is one I don't ever intend to break.

She glances at me, and smiles sweetly. Leaning forward, she plants a soft kiss on my lips. I deepen the kiss, and she parts her lips, making it easier for me to slip my tongue in, and I growl in approval.

She pulls back breathless, and I say, "Careful, get me too excited and I might be up for round four."

"There is no way I could go again." she pants as she starts to get up.

"Never say never, Serena." I say with a chuckle.

She gets off the bed, and I grab her arm before I realize what I'm doing. She looks back at me, answering the question before I could even ask it. "I'm just going to shower."

With raised brows, I ask, "Without me?"

"Yes, without you. You're insatiable, and if we shower together, I'm worried you'll destroy my already sore pussy."

She's not wrong. I reluctantly release her arm and watch her head to my bathroom. I hear the shower turn on and slip out of the bed, making my way to the bathroom.

The door creaks, and I hear Serena warn, "Aster, I'm serious."

"I'm just getting you some towels."

With accusatory eyes she pulls back the curtain looking at me, then at the toilet where I laid the towels. "Thank you," she says in an unsure voice, as if she doesn't quite believe me. "You can leave now."

I throw my hands up in surrender. "I'm going, but you can bet your pretty ass I will have you again before the night is over." With that promise, I leave the bathroom, and go lay back in bed naked, waiting for my little lamb to emerge.

All my rules are broken now. She has made this dead heart start beating again, and all the fears I have with what's to come, are nothing compared to the excitement I feel just being with her. Everything has changed now, she is mine and I will never let her go. If she ever finds out the truth, or I go insane and tell her who I really am, I won't let her escape. Ever.

I hear the water shut off, and Serena emerges from the bathroom wrapped in a towel, her hair wrapped as well. She starts to put her discarded clothes on, leaning down to kiss me once more.

"Where are you going?" I ask with pinched brows.

"I have to get back home, Jessica texted me while I was driving. She's going to come over and spend the night. She's probably already there."

I grab her hand, pulling her towards me, "You don't want to cuddle?" *Who am I asking her to cuddle?* I should just let her leave. But I can't. I don't want her to go. Not yet.

She smiles sweetly at me, and with a defeated sigh, she crawls back into bed, into my arms. "Okay, but only for like ten minutes, then I really need to go."

Inhaling her scent, now mixed with mine, I pull her closer into me. We stay like that for thirty minutes, then she gets up, kisses me goodbye, and drives away. I let her leave. She's no longer one of my victims, but she is *mine*. Not Jessica's. She is getting in my way. Now that I finally know what I want, who I want, no one will get in my way. There's only one thing to do. Get rid of everyone who prevents me from having Serena completely.

EIGHTEEN

SERENA

It wasn't my intention to leave him like that, but after he said he could go one more time, I was scared. I take a deep breath, one hand on the steering wheel the other out the window. He already fucked me into oblivion, and the idea of not being able to walk straight for a week did not seem as fun as it does in the books. That, and he deserved a little pay back.

After all, revenge is best served cold.

He said he was sorry, but if he was truly sorry he wouldn't have made me feel insecure again. He says all these pretty words, but with the way he acted twice now, his actions aren't lining up. I wanted so badly to tell him to fuck off, to leave the market and go home. But when he was standing there, kissing me, leaving me breathless, clearly my pussy was doing all the thinking, because next thing I knew I was following behind him to his house.

Needy cunt… but damn, was it good.

He said he was breaking all the rules for me. *What does that even mean?* I keep meaning to ask him, but my curiosity for his little lamb pet name won over my curiosity for the rules.

Next thing I know, I'm on my knees, tears streaming down my face as I obey what he says. He just has a way about him that makes a girl get on her knees when he demands it. I chew on my lip, thinking about my lips around his cock. I'm not saying I didn't enjoy it, because *fuck* I did. The feel of his cock down my throat, cutting off my air supply, was orgasmic. But looking up at the pleasure it was bringing *him*, was what really took me over the edge.

Pulling into my house, I turn off the car, and stumble in. *Even without another round, I'm going to feel Aster between my thighs tomorrow.* Jessica is laying on the couch, feet dangling off the arm, with a bag of hot cheetos resting on her chest, stuffing her face.

"Hey, I got your text," she says through another fistful of chips.

I walk over, pick up her legs, and place them across my lap. Throwing my head back, I sigh as my body melts into the couch. Jess tenses, placing the bag on the table beside her as she sits up and scoots closer.

"What's got you so worked up?" she asks, rubbing my leg.

I look over at her, close my eyes, and sigh. "Aster," I turn and look into her honey eyes, my brows furrowing the longer I look at her. "How did you get here? Where is your car?"

"I took an Uber, the car is in the shop."

One eyebrow goes up as I eye her suspiciously. "You didn't drive here last time either, what's going on?"

"You're avoiding telling me what Aster did this time," she says, crossing her arms.

"You're avoiding telling me why you never drive here anymore," I snort, mimicking her, as I cross my arms too.

She looks at me, concern lacing her features. "Serena, you know why."

I stare at her, my head tilting to the side. *What does she mean?* A stabbing pain in my head stops everything. My ears ring. My vision blurs. My stomach roils.

My body lurches forward, my hands pressing into my temples. My eyes pinch shut, as if that would ease the burning, the agony within my mind. I scream, my throat already raw and brittle. It isn't until I feel Jess shake my body, shouting my name, that the pain evaporates.

Sitting up slowly, the room spinning as I look over to Jess whose eyes are wide with concern.

"Are you okay?" she asks in a quiet voice.

I rub the spot of my head banishing the final echoes of pain. "Yeah. I don't know what happened." My eyes meet hers, my breaths shallow. "Maybe I need to go lay down."

"Maybe you do." She gets up, offering me her hand, and walks me to my room. She lays me down in the bed, and gets in to snuggle up next to me.

"Want to watch a movie?" she asks, grabbing the remote from my nightstand.

"Sure," I say, laying my head on her shoulder.

She turns on one of our favorites, embracing the cult classic and admittedly unusual comfort movie, *It*. I prefer the new one to the original, but Jess loves Tim Curry. Don't get me wrong, he is a genius actor in everything he does, my favorite role being *Rocky Horror Picture Show*, but Bill Skarsgard is the very embodiment of Pennywise. No one can convince me otherwise.

The beginning of the movie starts to play and I get up, making Jess pause the movie.

"Where are you going?" she asks, the remote still suspended in the air.

I flip the covers over, a soft smile on my lips as I turn to look back at her. "To get some movie snacks, keep playing the movie, I'll be right back."

Handing her the snacks, I get back under the covers next to her. She passes me the Red Vines, one already hanging from her mouth, and presses play. We lay snuggled up, enjoying the comfort of one another. Halfway through the movie, I feel my eyes drift close, letting sleep take me.

The sky turned dark, as clouds roll in, the first sign of the impending storm. I stare out at the brewing chaos from my school desk, watching the first drops pelt my window. Watching two race to reach the bottom, a quiet calm settling over me. Just as I'm about to see which will win, a voice creepily whispers in my ear.

"Whatcha watching?"

Jumping up, I yelp, whirling around to glare at Jess, "I was watching to see which raindrop was going to win the race," I say, pointing at the window.

She looks at the window, shrugging her shoulders. "You're so weird, Serena," she quips, sliding onto my desk, and crossing her perfectly toned legs one over the other.

What I wouldn't give to have her legs, to have her body. *The boys just flock to her, following her every demand. She says sit, they sit. She says run, they run. Hell. I'm sure if she told them to jump off of a bridge, they would do it. She is a goddess, and they are her servants. At least, that is what she calls them. Classless, but if they choose to kiss the ground she walks on, who am I to object.*

She'll crush them eventually, like she does to everyone.

Leaning down, Jess whispers in my ear, "I heard Tony was going to ask you to prom."

Peeling my eyes from the rain, I look over at her, my pulse quickening, and my mouth hangs open in utter silence. There is no way the star quarterback is asking me to the prom. *He is obsessed with Jess, as are all men. I thought to him, to everyone, I was just her sidekick. The girl she is friends with just to make herself seem nicer than she is. That is what everyone snickers about anytime they see us together. It is all they have said since we were kids, and it's only gotten worse since highschool. Me gaining more weight, and less confidence. Jessica getting prettier, and more cruel. It has to be a lie. There is no way Tony is actually into me.*

Jess places two fingers under my chin, shutting my mouth, then turning around to jump off the desk. "I know, I was just as shocked as you." She looks back over her shoulder as she walks away. "I thought he was another one of my servants, turns out he has the hots for my best friend."

She turns around and slams her palms onto my desk, making me jump once again. "You know what that means, right?" She asks, jealousy dripping off her tongue. I shake my head slowly, confused at her anger. She clicks her tongue, leaning in close, and says, "I was wrong, and you know I'm never wrong. How could I be wrong about Tony, of all people?" She places her hands behind her back, and paces around looking at me up and down as if I'm nothing more than something to study under a lens.

"I'm pretty sure it's just a rumor, Jess," I say, digging my nails into my palms, making her pacing stop. "There is no way the star quarterback is into me." I hate having to comfort her when she already has the whole school at her mercy. If I don't show my indifference to such a big comment, she will make this whole situation worse. So, I bite my tongue and give her what she wants. My insecurities.

"You're probably right," she says, plopping into the seat next to me.

Ouch. That hurt. *I shift in my seat, feeling uncomfortable with her so worked up.*

She turns, a cocky smile lifting her cheeks. "But just in case you're wrong, which you usually are, we need to get you looking better than," she motions to my outfit, her lip curling. "Than that."

I look down at my clothes, pulling at my band tee, and my torn up blue jeans. They're comfy, and this was the concert we went to together last month.

"What's wrong with what I'm wearing?" I ask, leveling my eyes with hers.

"Only everything, if you're going to say yes to Tony asking you to prom, you can't look like, well, you."

I should be used to her insults, the words she claims aren't meant to hurt the way they do, by now, especially given how long we've been friends, but I'm not. Each word she throws my way is always laced in venom, and it stings just the same.

I turn my back on her, blinking back the tears I feel threatening to fall. I will not cry. *Her words are just that. Words, I have the power to let them hurt me or fall off me. I know from experience if I don't seem upset after she insults me, the next words leaving her lips will be even worse than the first, so I always make myself seem hurt and upset, even if I lie to myself and say they don't, which makes her back off. That is just how she is. She is the only friend I have, so I take it.*

I don't want to be alone.

I hear her mirror snap shut, the smacking of her lips as she checks her lipstick. She places a hand on my shoulder, and sighs, "Serena, you know I love you, and I don't want to upset you, but you know I'll never lie to you either."

Before turning around I sniffle and wipe my eyes. When our eyes lock, I see the glint in hers, the happiness my pain brings her, just for a second, before she pretends to be concerned.

"I know, Jess, I love you, too." I force myself to say the last three words. If I don't, things will get ugly fast.

She claps her hands and jumps out of her seat. "Great! Meet me at my house after school." She starts to walk away, but stops at the door and shouts so everyone else in the class can hear. "Bring your clothes! You know mine don't fit you. Don't worry, we will give you the makeover you need. Tootles." I shrink down into my seat, feeling all the eyes on me, and this time I do cry.

Walking up the steps to Jess's house, my hand tightens around the bag of clothes, I brace my knuckles against the door, and on the third knock I'm yanked inside by an over eager Jessica.

"Stop dragging your fat feet, Serena and move! We don't have much time, I have plans after this with Toby, but I made time for you," Jess says, dragging me to her room and slamming us inside.

Toby is Jess's flavor of the week. She can never stick with one guy, and after a week, a new one replaces the last. They are always in rotation, fully aware of Jess's pattern, and don't care in the slightest how she fucks and dumps them. She literally fucks them all week, every day, even at school, then come Friday, she's already fucking the next. She is the school's whore, but she somehow bears that title with her head held high.

She acts like it doesn't bother her, but I know it does. I see the way her face falls, and her knuckles turn white, from squeezing her fingers so hard, when other girls cough into their hands, calling her a slut everytime they walk by. I mean, they're not wrong since her legs open for literally anyone, but they could have more class about it and say it straight to her face. One of these days, I know she is going to snap, and when she does, I have a feeling it will be taken out on me.

Jess places me in the chair in front of her vanity and stands behind me, pulling my cheeks up and back.

"See how beautiful you would be if you lost a couple pounds?"

Staring at my reflection, I can't help but agree with her. I know she is insulting me, I know she's doing it because of what happened with Tony, but she isn't wrong. I've been a bigger girl my whole life, and I know if I put down the ice cream and picked up a salad, maybe I would be happier. At least I'd be skinny and beautiful just like Jessica.

She lets go and pulls my hair into a ponytail. Grabbing the bag of clothes I brought, she starts to lay everything out.

"All your clothes are hideous, but you can't fit into mine." She taps her chin, groaning as she prances back to the vanity. "I can work with what we have, but first we need to cover your face with makeup." She takes out her foundation, shaking it in my face. "Lucky for you, we're the same complexion."

The makeup all over my face feels foreign. Heavy. Do people really do this every day? I don't know why I am getting dressed up for a boy. Jessica says he's interested in me. Me of all people. Can I believe her? It's probably a rumor. No one ever turns their head to look at me. No one ever watches me or imagines doing anything with me. I'm the quiet big girl who likes art, who escapes in it, who just happens to be best friends with the school whore.

One time a boy did talk to me, and I remember being so excited. He saw me, he was actually flirting with me, and I went through my whole day feeling on top of the world. Until I heard him later with his friends saying if I'm friends with Jessica, then I must be a whore, too. He bragged about how he couldn't wait to get into the fat girl's pants.

Jessica overheard too, and as I was standing there, weeping, she went right over to him and slapped him across the face.

"No one speaks about my best friend that way," she hissed, spitting in his face. I was so shocked, I thought I was in the twilight zone. Until she walked back over, linked her arms in mine, and said,

"No one treats you like that and gets away with it, except me."

I slipped out of her arms and ran to the bathroom to cry. She didn't follow.

"There! All done."

I look up into the mirror and stare at my reflection. I don't know how she did it, but she made me look like a literal Disney Princess. She hid my double chin, and highlighted my chubby cheeks, accentuating them. I don't recognize the person staring back at me, she radiates the confidence I try so hard to wear.

"Oh my God, Serena, what's wrong?" Jess screams, gripping my shoulders.

I don't know what she means, until I feel wetness running down my cheeks.

Swiping the tears away, I whisper, "I'm beautiful."

"Oh, is that all?" Jess says as she sits herself on the bed. "Of course you are, I made you."

"My mom and dad made me, actually."

I regret saying it as soon as the words leave my mouth.

"You know what I mean, and if you're going to be a bitch," she sneers, walking back over and lifting my hair. "You can finish your hair and pick your own outfit."

"I'm sorry, I know what you meant." I look back at her. "You. Made. Me," I say, biting out every word, knowing the only way to salvage this is to apologize and tell her she's right.

I hate bowing down to her. I hate succumbing to her constant put downs and being a yes woman, but I know if I want to stay on her good side, hurting and vicious as she is, then I need to become one of her many slaves; sitting when she says sit, and doing her bidding when ordered.

Her eyes spark with triumph, thrilled she got me to bow so easily. Jess loves to remind me she chose me out of everyone, that I am special. Special my ass. I'm just insecure, and no one wanted to be my friend. She saw that, she took her chance and sunk her claws down deep.

I've been trapped ever since.

One day, I will escape this hell of a friendship. One day, I will no longer be her slave. One day, she will be the bitch at my feet begging me to stay as I walk away.

But that day isn't today, so I relent and apologize. She kisses my cheek, leaving behind her signature pink lips. I swipe the mark away with my thumb as she begins curling my hair.

Finally, after three hours, we are done, and she has me standing at her mirror, her hands over my eyes, my nerves buzzing, and relief washing over me that I can finally go home.

"One. Two. Three!" She says with a little too much enthusiasm, releasing her hands so I can look at myself.

Staring back at me is someone I don't recognize. That can't be me. That person is stunning. She is confident, her head held high, as she turns to admire herself. I reach up, cupping my cheek, admiring my own reflection. The long lashes glued to my eyes. The perfect cat eye eyeliner with a subtle smokey eye. The black dress Jess chose is hugging the upper part of my chest, showing off my breast. Squeezing the dip in my sides and flowing down past my knees, hiding the muffin top I hate so much.

My hands trace my curves as my eyes follow them all the way down to my waist. Turning around, my eyes bulge at how amazing my ass looks. My ass has never looked this good. I grab and shake it. No jiggle. I would describe my ass as round and big, but pitted, kind of like cottage cheese. My mom says I had her ass when she was my age, she says cellulite is normal and no matter what, I am beautiful. I turn back around to Jessica and, without thinking, hug her so tight, she gasps, thanking her for the magic she performed on me.

She pushes me away, claiming I'll ruin her energy by tainting her. I refuse to let her words bother me, choosing to let them brush off me. Not even Jessica can ruin this high I am feeling.

Jess pushes me out the door, eager to spend time with Toby, instructing me how to sleep tonight so I don't ruin what she created. I know I won't be able to replicate Jess' talent so I stay up all night for fear of smudging one perfect line on my face.

The next morning I find a note in my locker telling me to meet Tony behind the bleachers on the football field before school starts with a *heart at the end. I squeeze the letter to my chest, excitement washing down the nerves I feel.*

I make my way over, dressed and looking just as Jessica made me last night, excited and hopeful my luck might be changing. Maybe this is real. Maybe this wasn't a rumor. Maybe the star football player really is going to ask me, of all people, to prom.

Walking behind the bleachers, I stop dead in my tracks, dropping the note I clutched to my heart.

Standing a few feet away, I see Tony, gripping Jessica's ass, making out with her. Dropping my eyes lower, I can see his dick hardening. It's not even Friday. I grind my teeth so hard I feel like they're about to crack. The pain from the little half moon indents from pressing my nails into my palm starts to fade as the anger starts to bubble over. Jessica opens her eyes, looking dead into mine. I swear I can see her smile for a second. She pushes Tony away and acts surprised.

I know she isn't surprised.

As if noticing me for the first time, Tony glances at me, and scratches the back of his head, then tells me to leave as he suggestively pulls Jess into his chest. Like he didn't just invite me to meet him here.

Oh. My. God.

I stumble back and start running, tears streaming down my face. Jessica screams after me, telling me, no, demanding *me to stop. I don't listen. Instead, I run up to the roof, the one place I know Jessica won't follow.*

The janitor, who also happens to be my uncle, gave me a key to the roof. He knows how my relationship is with Jessica, and after begging and failing to dump her as a friend, he gave me a place to escape to, when it becomes too hard. No one knows about my secret place; it is solely mine. Jessica has tried to follow me once or twice, but I always lose her. She takes it out on me later, mad that I won't tell her where I go, but she will not taint the one place that I find solace.

How could she do this to me? *She told me he was going to ask me to prom. She gave me a makeover, making me look unrecognizable. She turned me into a version of* her. *She had this planned from the beginning. I am fuming, gripping my hair, ruining the curls she made. This goes way past making fun of me, way past giving me backhanded compliments and using me as her personal ego trampoline. She crossed the line. She lied to me. Got my hopes up. Wrote a fake note. For what? All to make me see her with a guy I thought actually wanted me? What the fuck is wrong with her? I'm pacing back and forth, my hands shaking. My heart hurts. I can't catch my breath.*

Kids are just now entering school, shuffling inside and I drop to my knees and let out a guttural scream. I release every single emotion I have been bottling up for so long, and silence descends on the parking lot.

Jessica will pay. She will not get away with this. This time, I will rain down hell. I am no longer her puppet, and she is going to rue the day she did this to me. I will end her.

Fuck. Her.

MY HEAD IS POUNDING WHEN I WAKE UP, THE SUN MAKING ME squint and groan as my head throbs harder. I reach over, patting to wake up Jessica, almost excited to tell her about the crazy dream I had. But when I turn my head, after feeling an empty bed, I realize she's gone.

Still half asleep, rubbing my eyes, I get out of bed and walk around the house calling her name. When I don't get an answer back, I head back to my room and grab my phone. Looking at my notifications, there is only one text, and it isn't from Jessica.

ASTER

Meet me at my house tonight. Making you dinner

SERENA

What time?

I need to call Jess. This isn't the most unusual thing she's done, but I hope she's okay. She just keeps disappearing and showing up randomly, and I'm starting to become concerned. The first ring sounds in my ear when I get another text from Aster, like he's been waiting for my response all morning.

ASTER

7 and don't be late, or I will punish you

I don't bother responding, still a little salty about him ghosting me, and I feel like being petty and leaving him on read is the only fair response. *Let's see how he feels when he doesn't get an answer.*

I don't bother finding out where Jessica went. She probably got an Uber home and will call me later. My head still pounds, and I can't worry about Jess. She's always done what she wants. I know she'll be okay. Instead, I take a couple Advil and go to my art room to paint.

What was that dream about? I don't remember Jessica ever treating me in such a cruel way, but something about it feels familiar. The way she acted, the things she said, all of it gives me deja vu. *Surely my mind must be playing a cruel joke on me.* There is no way Jessica would ever do and say such intentionally hurtful things. She's been my cheerleader, my rock, for as long as I can remember. Sure, she can be stuck up at times, and her overly confident ways can come off arrogant, but that girl in the dream wasn't *my* Jessica. No, it had to be a Jessica from an alternate universe or something.

Still not completely convinced the dream was just a dream, I throw on my paint apron and let the colors take all the fear, all the anxiety, all the hurt, and turn it into something beautiful.

Nothing. There is *nothing* anywhere about Serena's best friend. I've combed through her Instagram hoping for her to be following a Jessica, or have tagged her in or been tagged in something. But the only thing on her page is her artwork. I scroll mindlessly through her page, admiring the way she brings her pieces to life. She truly is a talent to this world, one we see once in a lifetime. Kind of like Picasso or Michelangelo, she makes work that stops you in your tracks and forces you to bear witness. It's no wonder she can make a living on her art alone. *Just another reason to add to the list of reasons why I spared her life and made her mine.*

She can't be mine fully until her pesky best friend disappears. I tried all social media outlets I could think of, Facebook, TikTok, even Linkedin, but Serena doesn't have an account of any of those. Without knowing what Jessica's last name is, it is impossible to find her. It is like she's a ghost, no presence on any social media at all.

Shutting my laptop and giving up on my search, I go to the kitchen and make myself a Moscow Mule, smiling to myself when it brings back the memory of first meeting Serena. Taking a fresh lime and squeezing it into my cup, I take a long sip, closing my eyes and basking in the memory. Adjusting my pants, I give my dick, hardening and pressing against my gray sweats, a small squeeze, taking some of the pressure away while the thought of Serena in her sinful red dress haunts me once more.

The hunting grounds I chose that night were new to me. I'd never be caught dead in a place like that, but switching it up is what keeps me from being caught. After a fresh kill, I usually wait a couple months to go out and hunt, but that night something was telling me to get off my ass. I feel like I was in that god forsaken book bar for hours before a flash of red caught my eye. When she walked in, all by herself, looking like a lost lamb in red, with lips to match. I knew she would be my next victim. It was like the flames of hell guided her straight into my arms. I didn't approach her right away, which is what I usually do, instead I watched her. The way her eyes lit up taking in the whole place, the way her lips moved when she was speaking to herself. The way she commanded attention without even trying, totally oblivious to the rapture she created.

My lips lifted at the corner, watching her excitement, like a kid in a candy store not knowing where to start first. My reaction of not being able to tear my eyes away, standing still in a trance when I first saw her, and smirking at her cuteness should have been my first indication she was more than just a lamb to slaughter.

She stumbled over to the bar after looking between the books and the drink trying to make up her mind on where to start. I watched her mouth the word 'booze' and the way her lips made an 'O' had me standing up straight and adjusting myself. The way her breasts bounced when she hopped onto the bar stool, gathering the attention from everyone but that piece of shit bartender, made me see red. More from everyone staring at my lamb. *She's mine.* The hold I had on the beer I was sipping could have shattered the bottle at any moment if I squeezed any tighter. Instead of helping my little lamb, the bartender was helping a group of girls behind her, the same group who mocked her later that night with their laughs. One look from the grim reaper shut them right up. I wanted each and every one of those bitches on my table that night, but I was already breaking one rule by going after the bartender. He deserved it more than those girls for his blatant disrespect, plus, they were in a group. No way was I risking my life to take theirs.

After she ordered her Moscow mule, she started to look around while sipping her drink through the little black straw that came with it, her spine straightened and I could just tell she was looking for me. When her piercing blue eyes met mine, I knew I couldn't wait any longer. I emerged from the darkness and made my move. A move, I didn't know at the time, would be my salvation.

MY PHONE BEEPS, ALERTING ME THAT SERENA IS DRIVING DOWN MY road. I had a system put in after being taken by surprise and my parents being arrested. I was never going to let the authorities take me by surprise, if they ever did catch me. No one was allowed on my property without my permission. I'm careful with what I do, so it is highly unlikely they ever would, but I am not taking any chances. I'm the only person who ever enters my property, and my victims are always with me when I do, but now Serena is a permanent part of my life, she will be welcome as well.

Opening the door to wait for her, with her drink in my hand, I watch as she gets out of her car and steals the breath from my lungs. The outfit she is wearing is wickedly beautiful and has me thanking whatever God is listening that she is mine. She's dressed to the nines, wearing a short and tight little black dress that hugs all of her delectable curves. One side of the dress is cut higher than the other, and if she bent over her plump ass would show, teasing me even more with a flash of soft skin. The dress is cut in a deep V, showing the sides of her breast, with a long necklace of an animal of some sort dangling just above the opening. She's wearing black heels, accentuating her legs, gracefully gliding down my driveway. My eyes travel back up her body in a slow perusal, stopping at her mischievous eyes staring back at me.

She knows what she's doing and the way her hips sway as she walks over to me makes a smile lift my lips.

"Aster," she says as she attempts to walk right past me.

Two can play your little game.

I shut the door with my foot and snatch her by the waist, still holding her drink in my other hand. Bending down I whisper in her ear, "Just because you're on time, doesn't mean I won't still punish you, especially if this is how you're going to greet me."

Without turning around, she says, "I'd like to see you try."

I growl into her ear, my breath teasing the strands of her hair. "Don't test me, Serena."

Flipping her hair right into my face, she bends over to take her shoes off, and I lower my eyes to see her exposed, glistening pussy. *She's not wearing any panties. Good.* Getting a whiff of her arousal, I bend over her, and whisper in her ear. "Tempting this fox with his dessert before dinner is a wicked thing to do."

She squirms against my hardening erection, moaning quietly. I close my eyes, relishing in her ass pressed up against my dick, groaning from the sensation.

Then, all too soon, I feel nothing. I hear the front door open and see Serena sprinting barefoot across the grass. The soft moonlight is illuminating her form, her dress riding up her waist as she runs, the wind whipping her hair in all directions.

I slip off my shoes, place the drink down, and take off after her, yelling, "When I catch you, little lamb, I am going to make you scream." My threat makes her look back, eyes widening when she sees how close I am. She picks up her pace, sprinting for a line of trees. I know this land like the back of my hand, there's nowhere she can go that I won't find her. Stopping in my tracks, I glance around before heading the direction I know exactly where she will end up.

If my little lamb wants to be chased, then this fox will hunt.

Hiding behind a thick tree, I hear Serena approaching, breathless and unaware of the danger she's in. Peering around my cover, I see her frantically looking around. After I make sure she sees no sign of me, watching as she walks behind a tree in my eye line, smiles, and sits down.

She thinks she lost me? A dark chuckle silently escapes me. *Oh little lamb, you can never escape me.*

Bending down to pick up a rock, I throw it in the direction she came. I smirk as I watch her spine straighten, her hands going over her mouth to quiet her breathing. I chuckle quietly to myself, silently making my way over to her from the other direction. I blend into the shadows around me, but my little lamb can sense me coming. She always knows when I'm near. I realized it the first time I met her, and at the market when she searched for me as I hid. The connection we have outstretches anything humanly possible. It's as if we're intimately connected by something unseen. Something fated. Although we can sense one another, she is looking in the other direction. *I need to train her senses better.* The second she is distracted, I pounce.

Coming around the tree, I crouch down silently, and brush the hair from her neck, making her freeze and goosebumps rise all over her body. The hairs on the back of her neck rise, and I blow a soft breath against them. Her shiver makes my cock jump, then I bite, hard, making her scream. Her voice echoes through the trees, heating my blood further. She turns around, fury and arousal lighting her eyes while one hand holds the back of her neck. Scooting back, she tries to rise, but my body hovers over hers, trapping her on the forest floor. Grabbing both arms, I pin them above her head in an instant. She grunts and glares at me.

"You thought you could escape me, little lamb?" I'm sitting above her exposed sex, her scent driving me wild, as she squirms underneath me.

"Let me go, Aster," she spits with venom.

I lean down so my lips brush hers. "Now, is that really what you want, Serena? For me to let you go without dishing out your punishment?"

"Fuck. You."

I smile against her lips. "No; my dear Serena, that is precisely what *I'm* going to do to *you*." I straighten, staring down at unforgiving eyes. "But in the way I promised you would learn to love."

Her brows pinch together, then her eyes shoot up, and the fear I love to see shines brightly. "Don't you *fucking* dare, Aster." She seethes and starts to buck up against me, but it is no use. She is pinned tight underneath me, the fox finally having caught his prey..

I let go of her hands and flip her onto her stomach in one swift motion.

"I swear to God-" she starts to say.

"Shh, shh." I brush my hand across her back, move her hair, and kiss her neck, silencing her idle threats. "Trust me, Serena, I would never hurt you. The pain you feel will only last a moment, then I will bring you bliss. I will send you to heaven and back. I will make you feel like you're flying high above the clouds, and when you start to come back down, I won't let you. I will send you soaring again and again and again, until you're begging me to stop. That is a promise, little lamb."

She starts to shiver from excitement below me, and a wicked grin lifts my cheeks. She can deny all she wants, but her body gives her away. I know she wants this as much as I do, and because she does want this, I'll play her little game of keep away.

I pick her up effortlessly, making her yelp in the process. Her breast pressed against my back as her little fists pummel it. "Let me go right now, Aster!"

One smack to her plump ass, perfectly in my line of sight, makes her heartbeat accelerate and a little moan escape her lips. A small smile plays on my lips, my desire to hear that noise again making me spank her once more. This time she squirms a little, and I can tell her lips have parted with the tiny little breaths escaping her perfect, defiant mouth. I can smell the arousal coming off of her and it makes me turn my head to inhale her sweet scent even more. Her body freezes at the intrusion of my nose gliding up her leg.

"Where are we going?" Serena asks breathlessly as she bounces on my shoulder while we walk.

Silence is all that greets her, and I can feel her cross her arms and huff out a puff. *Cute, now she's pouting, another reason for punishment later.* I know why she is being like this, it doesn't take a genius to figure out her petty, vindictive behavior. Even though she forgave me for leaving her on read, she hasn't forgotten it. Absentmindedly, I drum my fingers against her flesh. *No, my little Vixen.* My fingers still, digging in hard enough for her to release another moan.

Vixen, yes, that's what she is.

The way she didn't shy away from our blood. The way she loves to be punished. The way I crave her. The way she consumes every fiber of my being. The way she makes me question everything. She was never my little lamb, no, she was always my equal.

My little vixen.

We are both foxes who wear the face of sheep.

I stride back towards the house with purposeful steps and an angry little vixen over my shoulders.

"I thought you were going to fuck me?" Serena says in a mocking tone. I don't acknowledge her taunt, so she continues, "I guess the big bad fox doesn't hold true to his threats. I guess, like his promises, his threats are empty, too."

Not responding to her childish remark, I grip her tighter, so I don't bend her over, and dish out her punishment right here. I stride up to the door, throwing it open, and head straight to my bedroom. I throw Serena onto my bed, enraptured as she bounces across the mattress. I walk over to my bedside table and retrieve the lube I bought when I first made my promise, feeling Serena's eyes on me the entire time, her body frozen.

I wanted to fuck her in the woods, to claim her sweet ass with nothing but the moon as our witness, but I also want my vixen to enjoy what's to come, not be scared and never do it again. Hence why we are now in my room, and I will get her ready to take all of me. That and as an extra punishment, I won't be giving her exactly what she wanted. To be chased and then fucked in the woods. No, I'll save that for another time. *A reward for being a good girl.* The look in her eyes, the smile that splayed across her face, when she first took off. She was trying to push me into giving her exactly what she wanted. She has to try a lot harder to trick this fox.

I pop the cap open on the bottle, making eye contact with Serena, and I unbuckle my jeans. Squirting the lube into my hands, I free my cock, a sense of power I normally feel once my lambs are strapped to the table flowing through me. She licks her lips, and I stroke my painful length, relieving some of the pressure. She sits still, like the perfect doll she could have been, but I like her alive and begging for something more than her life.

"Turn around," I demand, and motion with my hands.

She obeys with no retort and turns around, back facing me. I crawl onto the bed, grabbing her feet, pulling them out from under her and pushing her legs up, so she is on her knees, ass up in the position I intended. The way she bends displays her ass perfectly, just begging to be bitten and that is exactly what I do. She lets out a guttural moan that has my hand stroking my cock faster. I shoot some lube around her forbidden opening, getting her ready for what she thinks she fears.

I circle my finger around her tight little hole, not giving her any indication when I will enter her. She shudders, her fingers curling into the sheets as she pushes her ass back, granting permission for entry. I slip one finger inside slowly, allowing her muscles to clench around my finger. She hisses, as I push further past the tight ring. "Relax, Serena, this will only be enjoyable if you relax." Like a puppet obeying their master, my words make her slowly relax.

Her moans grow louder as I stick another finger in, stretching her further, making her gasp.

"You're doing so good, little vixen." I say, slowly going in and out. After a few thrusts I pull my fingers out and line up my cock at her entrance, circling my head around her glistening hole. Not giving her a warning, I slowly push inside, making her clench around my tip, denying access as her whole body tenses. I reach my hand under her and start to rub her soaked pussy, making her body start to relax. "That's it, Serena, concentrate on my fingers, and breathe." Her body relaxes, her moans growing louder, as I push all the way in. "Fuck, little vixen." I moan, "Your ass is even sweeter than your pussy." One hand grabs one side of her hip, while the other circles her clit.

"Fuck," I groan as I start to go in and out, my speed increasing with every thrust. *She feels too good to slow down.*

"Aster! I'm about to come," she stutters, shaking below me.

"Come for me, Serena. Let go." With that, she comes undone, her ass tightening around my cock as I continue to tease her, not stopping until I fill her hole. As the last of her orgasm dies down, I grab both of her hips and thrust hard, coming undone inside. Both breathless, I pull out of her and lay beside her. Our breaths tangle as she turns over, the last of the lust leaves her eyes, replaced with something else. I'm not quite sure what. I don't know if I've ever seen that look before.

I look down, finally seeing the animal on her necklace. "A fox," I whisper, grabbing the animal to inspect it closer. It is in a sitting position, its head tilted looking up with big innocent eyes hiding so many secrets. The tail a big bush behind him, creating the perfect backdrop for the excited sparkle in his eyes. *How can such a small trinket hold so many questions?*

Eyes still locked onto the small critter, I feel Serena's hand wrap around mine. "Aster, are you okay?" she asks with concern, her hand tightening around my shaking one.

Shaking my head, I release the necklace watching it bounce and still across her chest. My eyes rise to meet hers, a million questions swirling in both of our eyes.

"When?" is all I can manage to say.

She looks away biting her lip, subconsciously grabbing the necklace, shocking me with her next words. "The night we met."

The truth in her words makes me sit up and look out into the room. The night we met she knew. *She knew* what I denied for so long. She knew we had a connection, one that made us both do crazy things. She bought a necklace when she called me by the name only my mother used. Fox. Seeing past the mask I wear, wanting to remove it to see the truth of what lays behind it. The truth of who I am.

"Aster?" she asks quietly, tapping my shoulder. I turn to face her, and stare, not saying anything, knowing a thousand thoughts are racing in her mind, just as they are mine.

"Why? You'd only just met me. A *stranger*, who could have intended to kill you, who ghosted you, even after all of that you kept this." I say pointing down at the little fox around her neck with trembling hands.

She grips both my hands in hers, calming the erratic beating of my heart. Taking a deep breath, her spine straightens and my eyes meet her determined ones.

"I trust you, I don't know why, but the night we met I knew you could never hurt me." Her hands tighten. "And as for you killing me? Don't make me laugh, if you wanted to kill me, you would have already done so, not fuck me, tell me your secrets, and take me to your home."

She's right. Her truth is what I refused to believe.

I broke rule one by killing the bartender.

I broke rule two by fucking her.

I showed her one of my closest guarded secrets, what the world is desperate to know, with who owns Graves Haunted Houses.

I broke rule three by bringing her here.

My eyes trace her face, my mind finally accepting the truth she always knew.

I interlace our fingers, and say, "You were mine, Serena, from the moment we met in that bar to right now. You were my greatest fear realized. I never expected that a guy like me could be more than what he was bred to be. More than what his parents made him to be." Her eyes glisten from the tears threatening to fall, silently allowing me to continue with a gentle squeeze of her hands. "I'm sorry it took so long for me to realize, you were never my little lamb." Her brows pinch together, and her shoulders drop, a single tear falling. I swipe it away with my thumb, my hands never leaving hers. "You knew you were never one of my little lambs, and now I know you, Serena, are in every way my equal. My twin flame. *My vixen*. My fear, my disbelief, kept me in the dark. Now you're here with me, and everything has aligned as it was supposed to."

She jumps into my arms, pushing me onto my back, and straddling me. Without hesitation she kisses me with so much force, so much passion, I'm breathless. Her kiss tells me her walls are crumbling and the secrets I know she hides will reveal themselves.

Our kiss is broken, a loud smoke alarm blaring through the house. Both of us still, our eyes locking, the moment broken.

"Shit! the lasagna."

She giggles and pulls back, "We can always order a pizza and pass the time waiting doing other things. It'd truly be a shame if we had to leave the comfort of your bed."

"I like the way you think, little vixen," I say with a smirk, lifting her off of me. "I'll go turn off that alarm and throw away the lasagna. Can you order a pizza? Then I'll come back for my dessert."

She gets out her phone, and I hand her my card before I leave the room.

"Oh!" she gasps. "What kind of pizza do you like?"

"Hawiian," I holler from the hall.

"Me too," she giggles, which makes me smile as I continue to the kitchen.

TWENTY

SERENA

Does that confession he just made mean he loves me? He didn't exactly say the words, but the words he did say meant something. *If not love, then what?* I lay across the tangled sheets, my heart racing in my chest while my body relaxes into Aster's arms.

Do I love him?

Of course I do. I loved him the moment he crushed Tyler's hand and stole me away. The pleasure I felt when Aster caused Tyler pain, the euphoria he later took me to in the back of my car sealed the deal for me, and is a memory I won't soon forget. I was grateful I didn't throw away the fox necklace I got after that night at Boozy Books. I didn't feel like wearing it until tonight. A little voice in the back of my mind kept telling me it wasn't time yet. To wait. Up until tonight that's what it told me every time I laid it across my neck. When I tried it on tonight, the little voice said it is time, and I clasped the necklace into place. Nervous and excited to see Aster's reaction.

I could have worn it the night he took me to Graves and revealed who he was, but that little voice screamed no. Later, I was grateful I trusted that voice since he left me on read, but after his apology later that day at the market, I did truly forgive him. I know it's childish reacting that way to being left on read, but after being rejected by him once, my father all but abandoning me after my mother died, and having no one but Jessica, I started to crack. My abandonment issues caused my insecurities to come full force to the surface. I have worked too hard to let any man make me go into a spiral, but I'm a vindictive bitch, and he needed to learn his lesson. He needed to prove to me his words matched his actions.

He proved it to me when he texted saying he wanted to have dinner. Then I saw him at his door, waiting for me with a drink in hand, and I knew I wanted to play a game. I've always read in my books the scene where the girl runs and the guy catches and fucks her, and my slutty self wanted to recreate that with my man and his constant talks of punishment.

Of course I wasn't expecting the punishment to be anal of all things, I bite my lip and smile, rubbing the spot on the bed where my fear vanished, replaced by immense pleasure. I was grateful when he picked me up and carried me back to the house, but I do admit I was disappointed, and that was where my snide remarks came into play. Luckily, he didn't call my bluff, working me up to his true punishment. I rub my thighs together, trying to ease some of the tension building. If he took me with no lube, completely dry, I think I would have fainted from the pain. Not that I've ever done anal before, but from all the horror stories I read online about it. It stung at first, but once I relaxed like he told me to, I felt a pleasure like no other with his cock fucking my ass and his finger rubbing my clit. I can still feel the ghost of his cock deep inside me, I massage my already hardening nipples through my dress, trying and failing to find the spot that makes my eyes flutter.

He really did take me to the clouds and back, and he was right there to catch me when I came down from the high.

Pulling my dress up, I reach my fingers into my wet pussy, close my eyes, spreading my legs, and throw my head back as I rub my finger back and forth slowly over my sensitive bud. With my other hand, I pull one side of my dress down, to pinch my nipple, making me move my fingers faster and faster. I start to moan, my hips bucking the closer I get to my release.

I feel the other side of my dress being ripped down, the cool air blissful against my heated skin. Looking down, I see Aster place his mouth around my other nipple and bite down hard, a moan escaping my lips from the pain. He replaces my fingers with his own, sticking the first two inside and circling my clit with his thumb. His fingers can reach places mine can't so I let him, further spreading my legs to hit that sweet spot.

"I leave for five minutes and come back to you touching what's mine." He snarls as he bites down harder, pulling a scream from deep within me. The pain I'm feeling is nothing compared to the pleasure he's giving me. He lifts his head, and says, "I thought I told you I was coming back for my dessert. Yet, here you are, sampling it before I even get a taste."

"I don't see you tasting anything," I say through gasping breaths.

The challenge in my voice makes him nip me once more, leaving a trail of heat to my waiting pussy. His eyes meet mine, darkening as he bends to devour me.

My legs close around his head, and my hands grip his sandy hair as he feasts. His hands grip my inner thighs pushing them apart further, his fingers no doubt leaving behind imprints.

"Aster," I moan as his hands slip under my butt, lifting me to suffocate in my folds.

"You taste so fucking sweet, Serena," he says when he looks up at me with lust filled eyes. "The most delectable sweet a man could ask for." I struggle against his hold, as he goes back in, tongue lapping at my greedy cunt and two fingers shoved deep inside making my back arch off the bed.

The magic he has with his tongue and fingers is a feeling I will never grow tired of. The way he makes me feel, both mentally and physically, is out of this world. He truly makes me feel so secure in everything. No man has made me feel the things

Aster makes me feel. *I want to show him my paintings.* The ones I don't show anyone, not even Jessica. The paintings I pour my truth into, the ones that hold every drip of my darkness.

He hits the right spot, and my body responds as if I was hooked to a livewire. My hips start bucking profusely, and he can tell I'm close.

"That's it, baby, come for me. Come all over my face, let me drown in your juices," he growls, his lips never leaving my pussy.

His words thrum through me, and I explode all around him. Darkness surrounds me, my body feels disconnected from my reality, and I want nothing more than to stay in this moment. Closing my eyes. I feel his hard length slide into me, startling me and causing me to soar once more. In and out he pushes, deeper and deeper with each thrust. Our grunts and sighs turn into a song that's all our own.

This time doesn't feel like the others. This time is different. So much better than I ever imagined. *This doesn't just feel like fucking. This feels like we're making love.* The confession he made makes everything clearer, and my thoughts untangle, aligning as if there was never any other way. His actions say more than his words ever will, and each thrust feels like a love bomb going off inside me.

"Fuck, Serena, you're so fucking wet," He says through clenched teeth, throwing his hands above my head against the headboard to hold himself up. I wrap my legs around him and squeeze. His body starts to tense beneath mine, and he lets out a roar that echoes in the air around us as he comes undone inside me.

He stays like that, eyes locked on mine, sweaty hair falling over his green eyes. His hands clutching the headboard, arms flexed, with veins protruding as he catches his breath. He leans down and captures my mouth with his, both of us breathless. Our lips part, and he falls to the side next to me, pulling me against his body. I splay one hand over his chest, feeling his heart racing. *His heart is beating as fast as mine, but I wonder if it's for the same reason?*

Looking up, I meet love filled eyes staring back at me, the sweetest smile I have ever seen him give stretched across his cheeks. Not one of his fake smiles, like the one he gave me at the bar when we first met. *No, this one is different.* A matching grin lifts my lips. *This smile is filled with love.*

Cupping his cheek, he leans into it, eyes closed. Lacing his fingers with mine, he places a gentle kiss to the back of my hand, holding his lips there for several seconds before he curls our hands to his chest. We sit like that, hand in hand, staring at each other while silent words pass through our eyes, both with a new found trust for one another. Although neither of us has said those three words, I know we both feel it.

Aster's phone dings, and he reaches over to look at it, leaving me cold from his sudden departure.

"Pizza is here." He takes my hand and pulls me out of bed. I resist, wanting to stay and cuddle a little longer, Pulling at his hand, tugging him back into bed. He looks down at me and smiles, his eyes playful in the low light.

"I would love to stay in this bed with you all night, little vixen, but I know we're both famished from our activities. We need some fuel to continue later," he says with a devilish grin, throwing on some gray sweats while I adjust my dress.

Reluctantly, I get up as the doorbell rings, my stomach growling in response. We both look down, laughter easily filling the air between us. Aster heads to the door to retrieve the pizza, and I head to the kitchen.

He comes back moments later with the biggest box of pizza I've ever seen.

My giggle fills the kitchen. "Are you trying to feed an army?" I ask sarcastically.

He laughs, placing the pizza in front of us, and swats my hand away when I reach for a piece. "This is for me, you get to eat the burnt lasagna."

"Very funny, Aster," I say, reaching for another slice, but he takes the box and turns away from me. *He can't be serious.* I look at him with my mouth parted, my eyebrows threatening to disappear into my hairline.

"I am serious." *Did he just read my mind?* "Only good girls get pizza, and if I recall, you ran out the house-"

"You can't be serious. You know I was just messing around, and I more than made up for it in the bedroom," I say crossing my arms over my chest.

He takes a piece out of the box, the cheese dripping and making my mouth water. He takes a bite and moans, never breaking eye contact. "While that may be true, my little vixen, you still need to be punished. Since you seemed to like what happened in the bedroom, I can't count that as your punishment." He takes another large bite of his pizza, a piece of pineapple falling off and landing on the island. Placing his hand on his heart after he finishes his first piece, his eyes flash. "It pains me, truly, to have you watch me eat this delicious pizza, but you have to learn your lesson."

"I'll show you 'little vixen'," I say as I leap over the island, tackling him and the pizza, to the ground.

We both turn and look at the box, silence weighing on us, and I kick him in the chest, jumping off him to grab a slice. He grabs one of my legs, forcing the air from my lungs and dragging me back to him before I can grab a slice. I thrash against him, but he is bigger and stronger than I am, easily flipping me onto my back. Straddling me, he leans over and reaches for a piece of pizza taking a large bite.

"Aster, I swear to God, if-"

"If what, my little vixen? What will you do if I don't share?" he says, pinning my arms above my head with one hand and waving the pizza in my face with the other.

If I lifted my head and opened my mouth, I could take a bite, but I know he will just pull it away. Groaning, I resist the urge and turn my head to the side, unashamedly pouting.

"I guess you don't want this?" he mocks, swiping the pizza across my cheek and leaving sauce in its place.

I don't budge, ignoring the shock of the warm liquid dripping down my cheek. I keep my head turned. *I'm not going to give him what he wants if he doesn't give me what I want.*

I feel his hands rip apart the top of my dress, and I whip my head around, staring daggers. The pizza hangs from his mouth as the fabric of my dress flutters to the floor. *First, he denies me food, and now he rips my dress? Oh, he's going to pay.* He takes a bite of the pizza and hovers it over my bare chest, both of us watching as the cheese and sauce drip onto my exposed breasts. I wince at the burn and he bends his head to lick the sauce off, looking up at my eyes while he does it.

I'm more turned on then I want to be, and by the feel of Aster's hardening erection against my stomach, I know he is, too. I sneak a glance, *It seems we're both insatiable for each other.*

"You're my dessert and main course tonight," he says as he dips his finger in the sauce, bringing it to my mouth. "Now suck."

I part my lips, reveling in the feel of his finger against my tongue. I tease the tip, savoring the taste of the sauce, making eye contact as I do. Right before he pulls his finger out of my mouth, I bite down. Not hard, but enough to elicit a reaction. He pulls his finger out, smirking at me, then he bends down and bites my nipple, making me yelp and moan in return. Satisfied with my reaction, he starts to suck and lick the rest of the sauce off my chest.

He releases my hands, dragging his fingers along my arm and starts to tease my other nipple, pinching it between his fingers. While he is busy pleasuring me, I start to scoot up towards my prize. I moan, refusing to let his touch distract me while I'm distracting him from seeing me slowly scoot up. My hands barely touch the box, a grunt of triumph escaping my lips. *I'm so close to finally grabbing a piece.* My head and hand are outstretched, my wrist resting against the edge of the box.

Then I don't feel his mouth or hands anymore.

I freeze and look down, seeing Aster staring up at me, a smile playing on his lips.

"You thought you could distract me with your moans so I wouldn't notice you going for the pizza?" he scoffs, reaching over my head and closing the lid. "Oh, little vixen, you have to be a lot sneakier than that to not get me to notice."

My bottom lip juts out, and I lower my head, starting to pout, as I cross my arms over my chest. This makes Aster chuckle, and he opens the lid and retrieves a slice of pizza from the box. I wiggle underneath him, excited I finally get to taste the cheesy goodness.

"Open up."

I do, and I'm met with the cheesy, salty goodness of my first piece of Hawaiian pizza. The best piece I've ever tasted, *victory truly is sweet*. I moan my pleasure, swallowing as I take another bite.

"If I knew you would be making these sounds below me, I would've given in sooner, but I do admit, I love watching you beg," he says, as he gives me another bite.

I glower at him, "You know, most people gag at the mention of Hawaiian pizza," I say with a mouth full of nirvana.

"Good thing I'm not like most people then," he breathes, a shadow from my lips, never breaking eye contact.

"No, no you are not." My eyes dance, locked with his.

He pushes off the floor and stares down at me. "Should I take that as a compliment?" He raises an eyebrow.

"You can take it however you want, compliment or insult." I go to take another bite, but he jerks it away.

"Now vixen, you want this pizza? Then it was a compliment, but if it was an insult, then…" He drags my pizza across his lips, slowly opening his mouth.

The words rush out of me. "Compliment! It was a compliment."

"Good girl," he smirks. "Open up."

I reluctantly open, and he places the pizza in my mouth, letting me finish it.

He gets off of me with a secret smile and helps me up, grabbing the box of pizza and placing it on the island. We both take a seat on the chairs and start devouring the cheesy goodness. By the time we're both finished, there are only three slices left.

"We really put a dent in that pizza," I say while sucking the sauce off each finger.

Aster grabs my hand, placing each finger into his mouth, cleaning off the rest, and I stare at him dumbfounded, lips slightly parted. His lips quirk as he leans in and licks the corner of my mouth before kissing me.

Did he really just do that? Do I like that? How am I turned on and not grossed out?

"There, all clean," He says and kisses my lips.

"Thank you," is all I say, still staring at him like he has three heads, adjusting in my seat to ease some pressure down below. *This man continues to surprise me and keep me on my toes.*

Aster's phone dings, and he grabs it quickly, his whole body freezing. My heart stalls in my chest. He actually looks scared.

"Aster?" I ask quietly, trying to find out what has him so shocked. "What's wrong?"

He doesn't say anything, silently flipping the phone in my direction, and I see a police car, driving up his road. My whole body tenses up, a thousand thoughts racing through my mind.

What are police doing on his road, and why is he reacting like that?

I grab the phone and place it down, holding his hands in mine. "It's probably nothing," I say, not believing the words coming out of my mouth. If my intuition is right, and it usually is, I have a bad feeling.

Three loud knocks shake the front door, and both our heads turn to look, neither of us moving. Another loud knock, more impatient this time, accompanied by a stern voice saying, "This is the police, open up."

Aster is frozen in place, I try to get him to move to go to the door, but he won't budge. So I do what any good girlfriend would and release his hands, walking to the door myself.

I open the door and see two cops standing there, one I don't recognize and the other is the cop who first questioned me after my accident. The one who kept thinking he knew Aster from somewhere.

Shit.

TWENTY-ONE

ASTER

My hands are shaking. Sweaty. My breaths shallow and way too fast. *Why are the cops here?* My vision goes black around the edges. *They can't know I'm the Morbid Monet, I'm always so careful.* That's right. They're not here to take me. I hear Serena talking to the cops at the door. They're trying to come in, but they aren't allowed in without permission. *I don't want them snooping around my property.*

I wipe my hands on my sweats and walk to the front door. Bracing my hand above Serena's head on the doorway, I look down at the two cops, recognizing one of them from Serena's house. My jaw tenses when our eyes connect.

"Gentleman, what can we do for you?"

Serena tucks herself into my chest and I wrap my free arm around her. She looks up at me with a small reassuring smile and squeezes my arm.

"Are you Aster Graves?" I nod my head, fingers digging into Serena's stomach from the nerves swirling around in mine. *How do they know my name? Is this about my parents? Was I too careless about breaking my rules?* "We would just like to ask you a couple questions about a missing person, Tyler Blackwell," the one with the sheriff badge says. He holds up a photo of the guy I killed for trying to kiss my girl when she clearly wasn't interested.

We both look at the photo, neither of us giving anything away, but I know they have to have *something* to show up at my door, so I don't lie, instead opting for a half truth.

"He went on a date with my girl, got handsy, I told him to back off, and that was the last either of us saw him." Serena's grip on my arm tightens, but she gives nothing away.

"Mind if we come in and get the details of that night?" the sheriff asks.

The younger cop, who thought he recognized me, is staring at Serena wrapped in a blanket. Only a blanket. I pull her behind me and level my glare on him. He clears his throat and looks away. The sheriff looks between us, then levels his own glare on his deputy.

"Give me and my woman a minute to get dressed, as you can see, you interrupted us."

The sheriff bows his head and apologies, and the deputy's face turns bright red as he turns around and looks off into the distance, embarrassed he was caught ogling my woman. *If he wasn't a deputy I'd lay his ass on my table and enjoy the screams I would rip from his throat.* But they're here, and they know who I am, kind of, so unfortunately can't kill Mr. Looky Look.

I shut the door, taking Serena's sweaty hand in mine, rubbing my thumb across her wrist. She's nervous, though she shouldn't be, I know exactly how to get them off of our trail and leave us alone. "Aster, what are we going to do?" she says, taking her hand from mine, fidgeting with them, and looking everywhere but at me.

I grab her twisting fingers, stopping her fidgeting and place my hand under her chin to look up at me. "Everything will be fine, my little vixen, you just tell them about your date, and I'll tell them how it ended."

She looks up at me, eyes wide, with her mouth parted in an

"o" shape. "You crushed his hand, and I stood there and watched, are we really going to tell them that?"

I pull her into me and rub her back, as I rest my chin on top of her head.

"If they're here, they already know what I did." Her head shoots up at me, fear laced in her blue eyes, the ocean is swirling within them. *Her eyes will always give her away. I need to teach her how to wear a mask.*

Kissing the top of her head, we walk over to my closet, and I hand her a pair of sweats and a shirt. She mindlessly puts it on, and I do the same. She bites her nails, and I stride over, taking her hands from her mouth.

"I'm scared, Aster, what if they take you away for hurting him?" she whispers.

"They won't do that," I say matter of factly.

"If they were going to arrest me, they would have done so when I came to the door." I feel her body relax a little as she takes a deep breath and nods like she's ready for battle.

"Okay, let's go tell the police what happened." She lifts her head, charging for the front door, pulling me right along with her. A chuckle releases from my throat as I watch my brave vixen walk towards the lion's den.

Opening the door, we only see the sheriff there, and every bone in my body freezes, fear of if the deputy started walking the property lacing through my brain. Scenario after scenario plays out in my head of what he could find. If it stumbles upon my shed, and starts asking questions or wanting to enter it. Scared their discovery could lead to Serena discovering the truth. Then everything relaxes as I see him jogging back to the house from his car with a pen and notebook. I open the door further to allow them inside my home, every instinct screaming at me for allowing them to taint it with their presence. We go into the kitchen, and the officers take a seat at one side of the island while I grab the two other chairs and pull them to the other.

"Ms. Raven–"

"You can call me Serena."

The sheriff clears his throat, pen on paper. "Serena, I am told the night the victim went missing, you were on a date with him?"

She steels her shoulders and places her hands crossed in front of her. "That is correct."

He scribbles some more on his notepad, and the deputy is just watching us. "Can you tell me how your night went? When did you last see Mr. Blackwell?" His bushy eyebrows relax as he waits for her to respond.

She takes a small breath and looks the sheriff right in the eye and repeats the events of the night. My girl is so smart, showing no signs of nervousness or signs she has something to hide. The sheriff is furiously writing everything down, and I feel eyes penetrating me. I look up and see the deputy staring at me, his eyebrows pinched together, not looking away from my gaze. He must still be trying to figure out who I am. I look like my mother and if this deputy knows who she is, he can put two and two together. My face was all over the news when they were taken, and after I started my venture into their hobbies, I made sure my face wasn't anywhere again. I look the same, just older. Even if he does connect the dots my files were sealed after I turned eighteen, I made sure of that myself.

Serena finishes her story with me showing up, then the sheriff places his hand up to silence her. I see her nails dig into her hands, my back tenses, and I crack my neck, pinning my glare on his hand. If he wasn't a sheriff, that hand would already be snapped and his head would be bashed into my island, blood dripping to the floor.

"Aster–"

I place my hand up to silence him the same way he did to Serena. "Call me Mr. Graves."

His eyes round and his fat head shakes a little. "I'm sorry?"

Is this guy dumb? I place my hands infront of me, the same way Serena had hers, and stare this dumb fucker right in his eyes, repeating slowly so he can understand. "I said, you can call me Mr. Graves. Don't call me by my name, only those I trust can call me my name, and you, and your deputy, aren't on the list of names I trust, so, again, call me Mr. Graves."

The look of shock on his face turns to anger quickly. He points his fat stubby finger at me. "Now you look here *boy*, I very well will call you whatever I please, so you better respect your elders and answer my questions," he cautioned.

I lean over the island to get closer to him. "You're in my house, and, by law, I can kick you out anytime I please." The sheriff's hand tightens around his pen, face turning red. "I'll answer your questions, but if you place your hand up to silence *my woman* again, the respect you want from me will be the same respect you showed to her." Leaning back and crossing my arms, I continue. "Apologize to Serena, and if she forgives you, we can continue this conversation. If she doesn't, then both of you can leave my home and take your questions with you."

The vein in the sheriff's forehead pulses, and his cheeks puff out. The deputy places a hand on his arm, making him take a deep breath. He looks at Serena and grits his teeth, like it's painful to have to apologize to her. "I'm sorry, miss, that was awfully rude of me to tell you to be quiet with my hand."

Serena looks up at me, then back at him, her eyes growing darker.

She's pissed.

She narrows her eyes on the sheriff. "While I find it was very rude for you to silence me when I was only answering the questions *you* asked, I'll forgive you only because I want to help you find Tyler, so let's continue."

That's my little vixen. I smirk.

They both clear their throats, and the sheriff turns to me. "When you got there what happened?"

"I punched him for trying to force himself on Serena and told him to lose her number, after that, he ran away, and I walked Serena to her car, before following her home to make sure she was safe."

"So, you assaulted the victim?" The deputy finally speaks, making me clench my jaw.

"No. I protected my woman from a *boy* trying to touch her without her permission."

"If she was your woman, why was she on another date with a different man?" the deputy asks.

He's really pissing me off and testing my patience by asking dumb questions. *I wish I could kill him.* "She wasn't officially mine at the time, but I saw him hurting her arm, so I took action."

"The action being, punching him in the face?"

"Yes," I grind out.

"We have footage of you doing something else after punching him." My fingers press slightly into my hands, my heart rate picking up. The deputy gets out his phone and shows me the footage of punching him in the face, but you can't see me crush his hand. My hands relax, and my pulse slows down as he points to the screen, "What is it you told him when he fell to the ground?"

"I already told you, I told him to lose her number and that was it, then we walked away." My hands start to open and close, my breathing becoming faster as my vision narrows. I'm about ten seconds away from laying this deputy on his ass, conse- quences be damned.

"Are you sure that is all? Because when he gets up." He points at the screen, "He's holding his hand. Did you do some- thing to his hand?" he questions, with an accusatory tone.

"No-"

"That's enough, deputy." the sheriff interrupts silencing his partner. The deputies face contorts from shock to anger and then annoyance. "I think we have enough information, thank you for your time." He gets off the chair and tips his hat. "And I'm sorry, again, for being so rude." Serena offers him a small smile and we walk both pigs to the door.

Before I can shut it the deputy says, "I remember you from last time, but I still don't know where I know you from."

"Don't know, don't care," is all I say, slamming the door in his face.

I grab Serena's hand and walk us back into my bedroom. My steps slow, and back tense as I lay down in the bed and pull her on top of me.

"Aster-"

I cut her off by smashing my lips against hers, our tongues dancing around each other and her hips start to grind against mine. I slide her off me and pull her into my arms. We lay there in silence, both saying so much, without saying anything at all, and after a few minutes, I feel Serena relax into me and hear her breaths become deeper.

She's asleep, I can tell by her tiny snores. She's exhausted, falling asleep almost instantly. After our fucksesh, and the cops interrupting our dinner, her body is shutting down to recharge. I don't blame her. I'm exhausted. I pull her closer, basking in her warmth. *I can't believe I was so stupid and got caught on camera.* I am usually so careful, but the anger I felt in that moment, when Tyler's hand was gripping her arm... I saw red. The red of his blood staining my hands, and I didn't care about the consequences. Yet... now I have cops sniffing around and asking questions. *If they think I did something to him, they could come back and search my property with a warrant.* I was careful. I cleaned up and disposed of his body, but after Serena leaves, I will go to my workspace and make sure everything is truly clean. I can never be too careful especially with the slip up of getting caught on camera.

Serena's body starts to fidget around me, and little whimpers escape her lips. I brush my hand on her head and shush her, pulling her tighter into me. Her body starts to relax, and the whimpering stops. Her breathing evens out, and whatever dream plaguing her has now ceased. I close my eyes, my breathing starting to match hers until eventually, sleep takes me too.

TWENTY-TWO
SERENA

It's been a week since the cops showed up at Aster's, and we have both been too busy to see each other. Me with some commissions for clients, and Aster brainstorming new ideas for next Halloween, so that hasn't given us much time to talk about Tyler's disappearance. I didn't even know he was missing, after Aster threatened him I figured I'd never hear from him again. Aster didn't seem all that surprised by the cops telling us he was missing, he didn't show a reaction at all, but I could feel he was nervous.

I have a feeling we haven't seen the last of those two cops, and when Aster kissed me goodbye the next morning. I watched him head not inside, but down a path further from his house. Something told me to run after him, to see where he was going, but the little voice in the back of my head screamed to drive away, so I did.

What he was doing is beyond me. *Maybe he was taking a walk on his property to clear his head?* Afterall, it was a very stressful night. I got home and took a long hot bath, threw in some bath bombs, and soaked to release the tension.

One day I'm going to ask him to show me more of his property, I still have a gut feeling he's hiding something from me.

We made plans to meet at a nice Italian restaurant, in a more secluded area of town. A place my mom and I used to frequent, but I haven't been back since her death, not wanting to relive the memories.

No matter how good they were.

Even after five years, I'm not ready to go anywhere with memories of us. We were regulars there. We got to know the owners pretty well, they even came to her funeral. I know as soon as I see them again, they'll look at me with eyes of pity. Eyes showing an ounce of condolence that make me want to take a knife and pluck them right out, then the look would be one of horror. *That I could deal with.* But I don't want to pluck Gene and Betty's eyes out, so I hope after five years all I get is a 'we missed you' and 'what can we get you'.

Aster suggested it, and with him by my side, I think I could face it. After all, I did go to the flea market again and that went well, who's to say this won't be the same. Plus, I was happy to break out of my little cocoon, pushing me deeper in my work.

When I'm working, I tend to block out the world. I forget how to be a human. If I have more than three paintings, I sometimes forget to eat, and I definitely don't have time to shower. Gross, I know, but I can't help it. When I get in the zone, the rest of the world fades into nothingness.

I wring out my hair as I step out of the shower, fresh and shaven, all ready for my date tonight. Contemplating on what to wear, I sift through the pile of perfume I own and spray a couple in the air, giving them a quick sniff test. I choose the more flowery scent, one that reminds me of my mom, and walk over to my closet to find tonight's look. Immediately overwhelmed and nervous, despite knowing Aster will love anything that ends up on his floor, I grab my phone to text Jessica and ask her opinion, filling her in on everything going on.

SERENA

SOS! I'm freaking out!

> Aster is taking me to the italian restaurant me and mom used to go to once a month. I haven't been since she died, but I think I'll be okay. Deep breaths right?

> I'm Serena Fucking Raven!

> Like you always tell me. I need help choosing a dress for tonight. I am thinking either the blue, green, or burgundy dress, you know the ones.

> Help!

I wait for a text back, but after five minutes of pacing back and forth in front of my closet, without an answer. I throw my phone on my bed, frustrated that she's ignoring me, I bite my nails and decide it's up to me to choose.

What does one wear to a place she hasn't been to in five years while trying to conquer her demons with a hot boyfriend on her arm? Shuffling through dress after dress and laying them out on my bed, I stand with my finger playing with my lip.

Fuck it, let's go with green. That means growth and new beginnings, and I'm getting both with Aster.

Since meeting him, Aster has shown me who I am. He's helped bring out the darkness I try so hard to hide, finally giving me permission to accept it. The first time it slipped was when I enjoyed watching him crush Tyler's hand. I saw the look in his eye when he realized I wasn't going to run scared from a little pain. Then again at the haunted house. *I think, no… A* smirk lifts my lips curling them into a sinister smile. *I know we both enjoyed fucking in each others blood.*

We are both starting to open up more about how we feel towards one another, and although it is scary and I'm terrified it could be over in the blink of an eye, I want to see where this leads. I'm diving headfirst into uncharted waters knowing even if I drown, he won't let me die. He would jump in after me to save me, that is just who he is.

I sit in front of my vanity, applying my red lipstick, smacking my lips together and grabbing my dangle gold leaf earrings.

It's getting cooler outside, but still warm enough, at least for me to be able to wear a long emerald green dress without a jacket. It has lace at the top, and hugs my waist to accentuate my curves. My black boots give me a few extra inches, bringing me closer to Aster's height and bringing the look together.

As I'm zipping up my boots, my phone dings, and I already know it's from Aster, probably telling me he's almost here.

ASTER

I'm here.

I knew it.

SERENA

Be right down, don't bother coming to the door

Aster is standing at his car, arms and legs crossed, staring at the ground. He looks amazing dressed in all black with the sleeves of his button down rolled up. *That man is a damn snack, and I can't wait to savor him later.* He looks up, a smile spreading across his face as I saunter towards him.

He lunges for me, grabbing me by the waist and smashes his lips against mine, leaving me breathless.

"I missed you, too." I giggle, pecking his lips one more time as he opens my door. Before I can step into the car, he spins me around and whistles low, the sound settling deep within me.

"You look ravishing tonight, I can't wait to rip this dress off of you," he murmurs while licking his lips.

"If you want to taste your dessert tonight, you better not rip this dress."

He helps me in the car and leans down, one arm above his head against the frame of the car and looking down with a devilish grin. "Your threats don't scare me, little vixen, I *always* get a taste." He stands up, about to close the door, his eyes sparkling in the waning light. "Besides, you know you can't resist me."

He's right, I can't.

THE PLACE IS JUST AS I REMEMBER. RIGHT WHEN YOU WALK IN THE doors, you get an instant smell of garlic and herbs that make your mouth water. We get seated as soon as we walk in, since the reservation is in Aster's name. I haven't seen Gene or Betty yet, but I know they're here. They're always here. They love to walk around and get to know their patrons, making sure everything is to their customers' liking.

That's why Mom and I loved coming here, they make you feel so welcome. Once you enter their doors, you're family, not just a dollar sign.

The waiter brings over a basket of fresh baked bread and a saucer of olive oil to dip them in. The smells immediately bring me back to the last time I was here with my mom, and I have to blink back the tears. *I don't want Aster to see me cry.*

I feel Aster grab my hand and tilt my chin, breaking me of my morose thoughts.

"Is everything okay?" His eyebrows pinch together, concern written all over his face. His thumb slowly rubs my hand, and I smile weakly at him, nodding my head. "Serena, I can tell something is bothering you. If you don't tell me what it is, I will bend you over my knee, lift your dress, and spank your ass for everyone to see."

A blush creeps up my neck and I look away. *That doesn't sound like a threat to me, sounds exactly like the distraction I need.* I know Aster's words aren't an empty threat, and as much as that excites me, I don't need to make my presence known. Not like that. I don't want my presence to be known in the first place.

I feel Aster's hand tighten around mine, making me look back up to meet his eyes. My lips tighten into a thin line, and I take a deep breath glancing around at the memory filled room.

"This used to be mine and my mom's place. We'd eat here once a month as an escape. We know the owners really well, and I haven't been back since her death."

Looking back up, his eyes soften, silently urging me to continue. My hand tightens around his, my breaths coming easier now he knows. "When you first mentioned this place as a date, I was nervous, but I thought I did so well at the flea market, I could do fine here too. Plus, you're here with me, so I'm taking this as a sign from my mom that this place will be ours now, like it was mine and hers."

He lifts my hand to his mouth, pressing his lips against my knuckles, never taking his eyes from mine.

"Thank you for telling me, I had no idea that this place was so special to you. Thank you for allowing me to bring you here and create new memories with you, making this our place now." He stands up and walks over to me, leaning down to kiss me softly. His lips feel like a promise filled with so much passion and love, I feel a tear slip down my cheek. He catches the tear, never lifting his lips from mine.

We hear someone clear their throat behind us, making his body tense as he reluctantly stands up. I look up seeing two familiar faces beaming down at me. *I knew they would come over to us at one point, but I was hoping I would have more time to prepare before seeing them again.*

Gene is dressed in his usual attire, black dress pants and a nice dress shirt, with a bow tie. Betty is in a blue polka dot dress, reminiscent of something you would see in the fifties. Her hair is styled like it, too, with tight waves and her bangs clipped back. They both look like they stepped out of a romcom, and I can't help the smile playing on my lips when I see them.

"Is that our beautiful Serena?" Gene says in his thick Italian accent, taking my hand and kissing it, making Aster tense, I pull my hand away, Aster's eyes still burning a hole through the side of Gene's head. "I thought we'd never get to see you again, what's it been? Five years, I think?" he says, scratching his scruff and looking down at his wife.

Betty looks at me, a small smile spreading across her lips. She doesn't say anything, just looks at me, her eyes starting to water.

"I'm sorry-" I start to say, but she lifts me out of my chair and pulls me into her arms, holding me tightly. We both burst into tears, and she rubs my back, reminding me even more of my mom.

"I'm so happy to see you," she whispers, voice hoarse. "I thought I never would again. You've been away a long time. Let me get a look at you." She pushes me away, looking me up and down. She takes a napkin from the table wiping my eyes then hers. "How have you been, dear? How is the painting coming along?" She looks to Aster. "And who might this strapping young man be?"

I sniff, in an effort to calm myself and walk over to Aster, standing beside him. "I've been really good. I've been painting a lot, especially lately. I actually just finished three new pieces and got them to my clients." I take Aster's hand in mine, my thumb rubbing against his knuckles now. "This is Aster. He's my boyfriend."

Aster, refusing to let go, shakes the hands of my old friends." Nice to meet you," he says, gripping Gene's hand a little too hard.

I squeeze his hand, glaring at him through my lashes, mouthing stop. He releases his hand, but still glares daggers.

Gene clears his throat and motions for all of us to sit. I go to take my seat across from Aster, but he tugs me into his seat, and grabs another chair for himself, sitting right next to me. I chuckle lightly to myself and shake my head. *I can't believe he's jealous over a sixty-year-old man,* it's not like he's flirting, that's just how he was raised. Gene pulls out the chair I was sitting in for his wife and grabs himself one. Snapping his fingers and motioning for our waiter, he says, "Get us a bottle of Chardonnay, and everything they order is on the house." The waiter nods his head and walks away.

"Gene, you don't have to do that, we can pay."

He places his hand in the air, and I feel Aster tense beside me, seeing his jaw tighten. I squeeze his leg letting him know it is okay and to calm down. My touch sizzles some of the anger from him, last time a man did that Aster looked like he wanted to kill him. The same look is being given to Gene.

"Nonsense, your money's no good here. I won't have you paying a dime. You're family. No matter how long you've been gone. We all grieve in different ways, and I'm simply glad you didn't stay away forever."

Feeling the tears start to threaten to spill over again, I grab my tissue, wiping at the corners of my eyes, and whisper, "Thank you."

He grabs my hands and nods his head. After a moment he releases them and sits back, placing his arm behind Betty's chair.

"Tell me how you two lovebirds met?" Betty asks, eagerly glancing between us.

Aster and I look at each other and smile, after a moment I break eye contact and look back at Betty. "We met at a book bar, he approached me and we got to talking, exchanged numbers, and after silence from him." I look over, giving a playful nudge, "he showed up at another date and stole me away. The rest is history."

Gene huffs and crosses his arms, narrowing his eyes on Aster. "What? Were you stalking her? How'd you know where she'd be?"

Aster is just silent and glares back at Gene.

I laugh nervously and answer, "It was clearly a coincidence, don't worry, Gene."

Gene grumbles something, but I can't quite hear him. "How long have you been seeing one another?" he finally asks loud enough for me to hear him, eyes never leaving Aster's.

Aster answers this time, not breaking the staring contest the men are having. "Two months."

"Not much of a talker I see," Gene grouses.

"If you boys are done with your pissing contest," Betty says, smacking Gene's chest, "I think we should leave these two to their meal and give them some alone time." Betty stands and drags her husband away, turning around, she says, "It was so wonderful seeing you again Serena, and Aster it was wonderful to meet you as well. Please take care of our girl, and don't be strangers. Enjoy the rest of your night." They walk away, and I go back to my seat.

"What was that all about?" I glare at him, crossing my arms.

He just crosses his arms and looks away. *He's acting like a child who's mad about having to share his favorite toy.* I know he can be territorial, but there is no reason for his behavior toward Gene. He barely said two words, and now he's pouting.

The waiter comes over with the bottle of wine, pouring it into my glass first. I pick it up and down it, hardly tasting the kind gift. The waiter's eyes shoot up, and he refills my glass, a look of judgment passing over his face. Aster notices and glares at the waiter. I take one more hearty gulp and place my glass down with a loud clack.

"Are you two ready to order?" the waiter asks, placing the bottle into the bucket of ice in the middle of the table.

I look at Aster, waiting for him to respond, but he doesn't answer, choosing to glare at the waiter instead. I kick him under the table, which makes his glare turn on me. I roll my eyes, looking up at the waiter, heat flooding my cheeks. "Yes, I'd like to order the seafood pasta please." Handing my menu to the waiter, he takes it and looks to Aster.

"And for you sir?"

Aster turns his glare back on the waiter. "What's your name?"

My lips tighten into a thin line, and hand tightening around the wine glass. *He keeps up this attitude, and the only thing he will be seeing tonight is my ass, walking out the door.*

Taken back by Aster's sudden question, he shakes his head. "I'm sorry?"

"We never got your name," Aster says with a raised brow.

"I apologize, sir, my name is Pierce." he responds, sweat dotting his forehead.

Aster breathes in the man's fear and smirks, finally settling back in his chair. "Pierce, I'll have what she's having."

He takes a cloth from his pocket and swipes his face, mumbling "Very good, sir," then walking away.

I kick Aster again, harder this time.

"If you kick me one more time, I'm going to make your ass raw later, and you won't like it." Our eyes narrow at one another and I smirk at him, breaking the standoff. "Go ahead and laugh now, you won't be later."

"Stop being an ass and I might stop kicking you." I sass, tapping my foot on his leg and pushing my luck. "Seriously, what's gotten into you? Tonight is already hard enough. I thought you being here would make it easier. Clearly, I was wrong."

His eyes soften, and he tries to take my hand but I pull it away. Son of a bitch's arms are longer, though, and he manages to grab me, not letting go despite my tugging. "I'm sorry. I just-" He pushes his hand through his hair, making the curls fall into his eyes. I hate seeing him like this, he looks so innocent when he's upset at himself that I can't stay mad at him.

I squeeze his hand, and he looks at me. "It's not okay what you did, but I opened up and talked to you. Now, it's your turn to do the same."

"You're right, I just... don't like seeing you with any other guys, and when he silenced you like that cop did, I just..." His jaw feathers, his eyes darkening. "I lost my anger. I'm sorry. You mean so much to me, and I got a little jealous."

"I understand, but I'm still pissed. Thank you for telling me, but you owe Gene an apology. You were glaring at him the whole time and were rude. He's one of the few connections I have left to my mom, and there is no reason to be jealous of him. He's a sixty-year-old married man who I think of as a fun uncle." The waiter brings our food over, and I release my hand from his, waiting until the waiter is gone before I continue. "You mean a lot to me, too, and to prove you are special to me. I want to show you something… tonight. After dinner. Something no one has ever seen before."

I take a bite of my food, Aster's eyebrows knitting together as his head tilts to the side, curiosity lacing his beautiful green gaze. "I would like that very much," he says finally, and we enjoy the rest of the meal in comfortable silence.

I'm going to show him my paintings. The secret ones. My nightmares no soul has ever seen. I pick at my food, moving it around my plate, butterflies flying around in my stomach. *I wonder how he will react, if he will see me differently.* The paintings are gruesome and bloody, not meant for anyone to see, but something has shifted in our relationship. *I think it's time.* Maybe if I share this with him, we will grow even closer, and he will finally drop the last bit of his wall he keeps up so strong.

We finish our meal, and I place everything in a pile on the table. "I'll be right back, I need to use the restroom." Aster nods his head and I leave the table after kissing his temple.

Heading back down the hall to our table, I hear a voice say my name, startling me and making me clutch at my chest. "Oh, Gene! It's just you," I say, seeing him standing there by himself.

He looks behind him and grabs my arm taking me further down the hall. "I didn't want to say this in front of your man or Betty, but there's something off about Aster."

"What do you mean?" I ask, confusion and anger lacing my voice. *How dare he ambush me to talk bad about Aster.* I know the two were glaring at each other all night, even after we got our food, but he has no right to do this.

"There's nothing wrong with Aster," I say, yanking my arm

out of his grip. "And I would appreciate it if you didn't judge him based on one interaction."

I walk away, but he grabs my hand, stopping me in my tracks. "I mean no harm, but it's just a gut feeling. There's something not right with him, you can see it in his eyes. He's hiding something, Serena. Something big"

Pulling my hand away once more, I level my glare at him, "Look, I understand your concern, but Aster would never hurt me. So please, mind your business."

I finally walk away, and he hollers after me, "Just be careful!"

Aster waits near the front, taking my arm in his, and we head back to my house. Nervous energy surrounds us. What's to come entirely up to him.

Painting relaxes me. It has always been my escape, which is why as soon as we got back to my house, I changed and took Aster straight to the one place that always eases my nerves. Aster does the same, when I'm nervous or scared, he knows exactly how to bring me back down. He can block out the rest of the world, just like painting does.

He walks around the room while I tie the apron around my back. Picking up a paintbrush from the easel, he stares at the tip stained red.

"You know, I paint myself."

I walk over and take a seat on the stool. "For your haunted house?" I ask, already knowing the answer.

"Among other things," he hums, wrapping his arms around me and leaning his head on my shoulder.

"Oh, yeah?" I turn my head to meet his curious green eyes, "What else do you paint?"

Standing up, he grabs another stool to sit beside me. "Maybe one day I'll show you."

"You know, secrets don't make friends," I tease, grabbing a brush and dipping it in water to wet the tip, then black before beginning my strokes.

"They may not make friends," he leans in, whispering against my ear. "But they make excellent lovers."

He nips my ear, making my eyes shut, and shivers rack my body. I turn my head, my lips inches from his, glancing at his sinful smirk as I whisper, "Does that mean you're keeping secrets from me, Aster?"

He licks his lips, looking at mine and whispers back, "Yes."

I lean back, taken back by his sudden confession, my brows shooting to my hairline. *He's keeping secrets? What kind of secrets?* I can't be mad, I'm keeping a big secret of my own. Well... not anymore, I'm actually going to tell him.

I start painting, the secret bleeding onto the canvas. I'm not ready to show him the nightmare pieces yet, but if he reacts well to what I'm about to create, then I know I can share my secret. Secrets can eat you alive. Keeping them can tug at you until there is nothing left. Until you're nothing but a shell of the person you once were. Keeping this secret, always wearing a mask to hide it, it's stolen almost everything left within me. I have never shown a soul my true paintings, the ones that bring me a sense of peace. I should be terrified. I know there are artists out there who paint nightmares, but that is what their work is labeled as. My so-called nightmares are anything but something I fear.

"You're not mad?" Aster asks, stirring me from my painting.

I shrug my shoulders. "Why would I be? We are all entitled to keep secrets."

He tilts his head, studying me, and crosses his arms, "What are you painting?"

The corner of my lip lifts, and this time, it's my turn to make him wonder. "It's a secret."

He tickles my side, and luckily I was dipping my brush back in the paint, making my grip tighten. "Oh?"

"Yeah," I say, dabbing the black paint on his nose.

His eyes cross as he looks down at the tip of his nose. "You're going to pay for that," he growls, with a smirk playing on his lips.

"I'm *so* scared," I say in a mocking tone.

"You will be," he says, dipping his finger in my red paint.

"Don't you dare!" I squeal, falling backwards out of my stool. He's on top of me before I can get up. "I'm sorry! I'm sorry! Aster, please don't get paint on my clothes, that's why I wear an apron!"

He tears the apron off. "What apron? I guess the clothes need to come off."

He swipes the red paint on my face, making sure every bit of it is off his finger. Heat courses through me at his wicked promise, and I start to feel his cock harden above me, desire pooling low in my belly.

He pulls my shirt over my head, a cool breeze hitting my breast making my nipples harden instantly.

I'm supposed to be sharing my secrets, not fucking him right now. "Aster, wait-"

I'm cut off, his mouth crashing against mine, his fingers pinching my nipples. *The secret can wait,* let's count this as foreplay, a fun distraction before I potentially change everything between us.

My back arches off the floor and a quiet moan escapes my lips, muffled by his mouth. He twists and pinches and nips, making me writhe beneath him, desperate to get some friction against my pussy.

He grinds against my core, giving me the friction I need.

But it isn't enough. I need more.

I try to rip his pants down, but he captures my wrist, stopping his teasing to secure both hands over my head. *Fucker loves putting me in this position.* I strain against his grip, solidly stuck in his grasp. *I love it too.*

He sticks his other hand down my pants. "You're soaked, my little vixen, never patient, are you? Always waiting and wanting and forcing my hand."

He circles my clit, his fingers relentless. "Aster," I moan, seeing stars. *He always knows exactly where to touch.*

"I love it when you moan my name," he whispers, circling faster. My hips buck, moving with the rhythm of his hand. He leans down to whisper against my lips, "Come for me. Soak my hand in your juices." He circles faster and faster, and just before I'm about to explode all over his fingers, he removes his hand.

I open my eyes to protest, my hips seeking the friction it lost, seeing Aster smiling down at me, hand raised in the air, his fingers dripping with red paint mixed with my juices. *When did he dip his fingers in more paint?* The son of a bitch distracted me with an orgasm that never came, just so he could get me back. *I'm screwed.* I wiggle underneath him, trying to scoot away from his hold, but my arms are still above my head, and my legs are immovable, his legs trapping them.

"Aster. Don't," I warn.

"Don't what?" he says as his fingers caress over my bare chest, marking me from my chin to my belly button.

Oh, it's on.

He lets go of my hands, standing up and removing his shirt. *I guess he's playing fair.* I dip my fingers in the same red paint and rush forward, marking his chest with painless scratches. He darts behind me, gathering more paint into his hands, this time green, and rubs it across my back making me jump from the chill and turn around.

He holds my pallet of paint above his head, well out of reach. *Time to fight dirty.* I reach down and take my pants off, slowly pulling my underwear down. His eyes trail every movement I make, going completely dark. I hold my panties to the side and drop them to the ground. He mimics my movements, taking off his pants and boxers, in a slow deliberate dance just for me. I watch as his already hard cock stands at attention. *He's always as ready for me as I am for him.*

He drops the pallet to the floor, causing me to flinch, and he walks over to me, reaching for me with paint covered fingers. I avoid his hands, jumping to the side and running behind him. He realizes what I'm doing too late and laughs as I snatch the pallet and the little paint that remains on it.

Now I hold the power but, turning around I see him grab the bottles of paint. *He one upped me, somehow always one step ahead.* I shake my head back and forth, stepping back slowly. *Fuck me. I fucked up.* I run just as he opens the bottle and squirts it at my back. I feel the paint dripping down my skin, hitting the curves of my ass.

I chuck the pallet at his head. He dodges it, and I lunge for the bottles of paint.

Two can play this game.

I grab four bottles of paint, quickly opening the tops and spinning around, to aim and squirt, but he's nowhere to be seen. *Where did he go?* I look around the room, ready for an ambush, but… nothing.

I don't trust this. I know he's waiting for me to lower my defenses, but he doesn't call me vixen for nothing. I turn to faking putting down the bottles, and just as they hit the table, I feel him on me. Spinning around, I close my eyes and squeeze. I feel paint land on me at the same time I hope it lands on him. We're both laughing like crazy, and being able to be this carefree with one another really helps solidify my choice in showing him my secret.

Once I hear the air from the bottles on his end, I slowly open my eyes. Seeing I did, in fact, hit my mark bringing a messy smile to my face. His chest, legs, and face are covered in red, blue, and green paint. I look down at my chest and see it's covered in red, orange, and black.

Silence blankets my studio.

We stare at one another, chests rising and falling rapidly, trying to catch our breaths. His eyes travel down my body, taking in every inch of my painted skin. I do the same, appreciating my blind handiwork. I look back up and he steps into me, looking down, his bright green eyes turning darker.

His lips crash against mine, my hands tangling in his hair, dragging the paint through it. His tongue greedily tangles with mine, neither of us giving an inch in this fight. *I love kissing him, our lips fit perfectly together, always doing a bone melting dance.*

He wraps his hand around my throat and slowly lowers us to the ground. He lays his body flush against mine, mixing the paints to create a rainbow of colors. His finger traces my belly, spelling a word I can't quite make out. *S.E.C.R.E.T.. Why would he spell that, does he want to know my secrets or is he finally going to tell me his?* My breaths become ragged from the thought of him finally fully letting me in.

I look down at him, kissing my inner thigh. "Did you just spell 'secret'?"

He stops kissing. "I did."

"Why?"

He bites my thigh, ignoring my question and making me hiss before kissing to ease the pain. He spreads my thighs further, dipping his head just a breath away from my entrance. "Enough talking." He dives in, distracting me from my thoughts with his tongue. He laps at my core as if he was starving for a taste. My fingers find his hair, and I push him deeper, slowly gyrating against his mouth, finding my perfect rhythm.

"Are you going to let me come this time?" I pant.

Instead of answering, he sticks a finger straight into my pussy, instantly finding my G-spot and making my legs shake. "That's it, little vixen. I want to drown in your juices." He licks and pumps faster, my eyes rolling back as my whole body convulses as I come undone into his mouth.

My legs close on instinct. It's too much. I try to push him away, but he forces my legs apart, his mouth never leaving my clit. "Aster, *please*, it's too much."

"This is your punishment for kicking me earlier."

My punishment for kicking him? He wants my body to go into shock from coming back-to-back. I wouldn't call that a punishment, but as my body bows even more, the pain of coming undone mixed with the unrelenting pleasure is too much. I agree, this is a punishment, but I love it.

After he sucks every last drop, he doesn't give me time to move before he thrusts his cock hard and deep, making me yelp from the sudden intrusion. I'm wet and sore, my muscles weak and numb, but him filling me is exactly what my body craves.

My pussy clenches around him, pulling him deeper with every thrust. My breath catches in my chest, my eyes shutting closed.

"Fuck! You're so tight and wet. I'm balls deep, and your pussy is so greedy it wants more," he groans.

His thrusts quicken, and I wrap my legs around him, grabbing his ass with both hands and pushing him further in. He palms my ass, lifting me slightly, and hitting a spot deep within me, making me see stars. I move my hips, matching his momentum. He leans down and bites my neck hard enough I know he's leaving his mark, and I do the same. Piercing his throat, he comes undone inside me, hitting just right, and I come for the third time.

He rolls off me, laying on his back and breathing hard. I turn to look at him trying to catch my breath as well. He rests his hand on his head, staring at me. "You look beautiful, especially with our paint mixed all over your body."

"You don't look so bad yourself. We made paint magic." I say, propping my head up on my hand. "How about we take a shower? Then I have something I want to show you."

"Oh, yeah?" he asks, wiggling his eyebrows at me?

"Not like that!" I playfully slap his chest.

"Are you going to tell me a secret, little vixen?"

I bite my lip and look away. "Actually... yeah."

He sits up. "Really?

I look back at him shyly. "Yeah, so let's take a quick shower before I chicken out."

He lifts me in his arms and takes us to my shower, turning it on and stepping in. I watch as the colors swirl down the drain, getting hypnotized by how they all blend seamlessly. The last color to disappear down the drain is the red, and it makes me think of my paintings and what I am about to show him. *I was going to paint him an example first, but he distracted me with his beautiful cock.* Guess I'm skipping right to showing him my nightmares.

Finally clean, we make our way back to my studio. I stop in front of the closet I keep my paintings in. Taking a deep breath, hand shaking as I turn the knob.

Aster stands behind me, his eyes showing no emotion, not even curiosity laces his features. I fidget with the paintings before I pull out a couple, making sure the image is turned towards me. "Turn around and close your eyes."

He obeys instantly, and I grab the rest of the paintings, even the blue rose one, and display them all side by side, on the floor, leaning against the wall. I take a deep breath, calming my nerves. "Okay, you can turn around."

I hold my breath as I watch him take in my paintings. He observes each of them, something like recognition crossing his features. He moves down the line, stopping to touch one painting. It's of a faceless man over a faceless woman, her body painted and holding a blue rose on her stomach. A lot of my paintings, not all, look like that one, each faceless woman has a different painted outfit on, all holding a blue rose. Some of the paintings are more gruesome, in some the faceless man is torturing the woman.

If anyone were to see these they would think of the Morbid Monet, if they knew who he was. How it is painted is how he lays his victims. Where they're painted isn't where they're found though, but still eerily similar. Since these paintings began, I always felt connected to the Morbid Monet. That's why I'm so obsessed with him and keep every news article about him. *There's no way I'm actually dreaming of his actual kills.*

He gets to the blue rose painting and starts counting every

rose in the lineup. He looks at me, his eyes blazing with shock and awe.

"These are my paintings I've never shown anyone, not even Jessica," I say, playing with my hands. He turns his head silently asking a question. "When I have a nightmare, well, I don't think of them as nightmares. I'm fascinated by them, a whole scene plays in my head, like I'm watching the scene play out in front of me. Every time I have a dream I feel compelled to bring it to life and paint it."

I can't look him in the eye, *he's not talking. Why isn't he talking?*

"I started painting these when I was fourteen years old, I don't know why, but part of me loves that they happen. Look," I say, walking over and pointing down at one of the girls. "Isn't she beautiful? You can't see her face but look how her body lays there. There is just something so *beautiful* about it." I point to her chest where her heart is. "Look here, you can see the red like she has a bleeding heart. Makes me wonder if her love for the faceless man is what made that happen…" I mumble more to myself than to him.

He grabs my hand gently, but firmly, tugging me through the house. "Come with me."

Is that seriously all he has to say? Why isn't he asking me any questions? Why has he been silent? He was staring and touching the paintings like he was transfixed by them, so he should say *something*.

"Where are we going?" I ask as he grabs my keys and walks us out the door.

"It's my turn to tell you a secret." he says, not looking at me, but ahead and walking with purpose.

I look up at him, mouth parted, and a shocked face. He places me in the passenger side of my car, then peels out of my drive to wherever his secret is.

What the actual fuck? I grip the steering wheel, reaching over and turning on the radio just for something to do with my hands. "The Drug In Me Is You" by Falling In Reverse comes on. *Well isn't that just the perfect song.*

She was fourteen when she started painting my kills which means I was eighteen. We have been connected without even knowing. Our meeting was fate. I didn't kill her because we were always meant to get to this point.

Our love is kismet.

I reach over and hold her hand in mine. She jumps, glancing at me instead of staring out the window, and gives me a small smile. I can tell she's nervous. I didn't say one word after seeing her paintings. *How was I supposed to react to her dreaming about me and my lambs?* I couldn't very well just say 'oh, hey, you're dreaming and painting about me, I'm the man killing those girls.' I don't think that would go over very well. Then again my little vixen may surprise me like she always does.

She has to see. She painted my workspace. Once I show her the shed… I'm hoping things will click into place. She's been dreaming of the same place for fourteen years, she's sure to recognize it.

She said she loves when she has those dreams, so she should react well, right?

We pull onto the road to my house, driving past it without slowing down.

Serena looks at me, eyes drawn together. "Where are we going?"

I squeeze her hand in mine. "Do you trust me?"

She nods. "With my life."

I smile at her, pulling up to the shed and throwing her car into park. I turn over and look at her. My fingers tapping the steering wheel, trying to calm the anxious feeling down. "I didn't know how to respond when I saw your paintings." She looks down and takes her hand from mine. I turn her head back, making her look me in the eye, taking both hands this time. "I didn't know what to say, but I told you it was my turn to share a secret. I hope this secret is answer enough."

"I don't understand? You don't say anything, then take me to a tiny house I didn't even know was on your property. You either think I'm crazy or not, why can't you just say something?!" She yells, throwing her hands in the air at the end, breathing hard.

Glaring at me in anger, making her blue eyes swirl darker, I sigh and get out of the car. Walking over to her side I open the door, holding my hand in front of Serena for her to grab, eyes pleading for her to understand. To trust me.

She crosses her arms, and turns her head away from me. "Serena, if you don't get your ass out of the car right now, I will throw you over my shoulder and spank your ass like the child you're behaving like."

Her head whips back to face me. "That's rich coming from the grown man who acted like a child at the restaurant."

Exasperated, I push my hair back. "I already apologized for

that. If you want to know how I feel about your paintings and your dreams, you will take my hand and come. With. Me."

She huffs, grabs my hand, but bows her head. "Fine, but only because I want to know your big secret since I told you mine."

"Thank you." I lead her to the front, she's looking around the property at everything, taking in her surroundings. Pulling up the metal door, I walk us in and flip on the light. As soon as the bulbs shine on, she winces, squinting her eyes against the bright lights.

Letting go of my hand, she walks around looking every-where, taking in everything. She walks over to the table in the middle and runs her hand along it. Turning around she starts opening the drawers seeing all the tools. I stand with my back against the wall, arms crossed watching her take in everything.

Recognition hasn't lit her features like they did mine. *Will I have to explain to her what this place is, or will looking around some more finally help her open her eyes?*

She turns to look at me, motioning around my domain. "You took me to your work shed? I'm assuming this is where you make the props for the haunted house. What does this place have to do with my dreams?"

"Look again, really look, Serena."

She pauses, looking around again, at the wall of tools, at the incinerator, then she looks at me and down at the table again. Her head tilts, and she steps back, her hands covering her mouth, eyes wide and whispers, "You're the faceless man?"

I smirk, "You can call me The Morbid Monet."

She stands frozen in time, her eyes shift to the door, and she slowly backs into the wall of tools. I smirk, a knowing smile at what she is planning lifting my lips. *My little vixen thinks she's clever.* "You're Salem's most notorious serial killer, killing thirty-two women. All who are curvy and have dark hair."

"The one and the same, and as the Morbid Monet."

Her arms are behind her back. "You haven't always been The Morbid Monet."

I shake my head, inching closer. "No."

Her breathing starts to pick up as she blindly grabs a hammer. "The paintings I started when I was fourteen up to the time The Morbid Monet was named, was that you too?

Another step closer. "Yes. It took me many years, and a couple… mistakes to become him."

"Are you going to kill me?" she breathes, as she rips the weapon off the wall, swinging it at me.

I grab the hammer and she pinches her eyes closed, backing further into the tool table. My hand caresses her cheek. "My little vixen, I could never hurt you. I wanted to show you my sanctuary. I wanted to show you we are connected." I drop my hand. "Look at me, Serena." She shakes her head, refusing to look at me. "Please?" I beg, my hands grabbing hers. She slowly opens her eyes, tears forming and clinging to her lashes. "You said you loved your dreams, you said they were beautiful."

Her hands shake and tears cascade down her cheeks. "That's when I thought they weren't real, that they were only dreams!"

I kiss the tear falling down her face, tasting the salty bitterness. "Can't you see you're like me? You've been dreaming about me long before we ever met. We were always supposed to meet at that bar. You and me are one in the same."

"I don't kill innocent people, Aster,"

How can she react like this? I don't understand. She was supposed to be happy. She was supposed to understand. *We are connected. Why doesn't she see that?* Anger bubbles up, but I shove it back down knowing I dropped a major bomb, and I need to be patient.

She whispers, "Was I going to be another one of your victims?" I look away, unable to look her in the eyes and tell her the truth. Anger rises in her voice, knowing my answer without me voicing it. "Is that why you called me little lamb at first?!" She shoves me, pushing me back into the table. "Answer me!"

"Yes!" I yell, regretting it the moment it leaves my lips. She stumbles back, tears streaming down her face. "You don't understand, my little vixen. At first, yes, you were my little lamb, destined to lay on my table." I motion behind me, a nearly indiscernible tremble in my fingers. *That's never happened before.* "But I couldn't do it. I didn't know why at first, then I started breaking all my rules for you!" I seethe pointing at her.

She jumps, startled by my voice echoing around the room. "Rules?" she whispers.

I don't want to scare her, but I need to make her understand. I need her to see I won't hurt her. I need my little vixen back. I can tell by the way she's hugging herself she is terrified, and that is not what I wanted.

I pace back and forth, pushing my hair back. "Yes. Rules, all of them." I start counting on my fingers. "One: killing a man, I've never killed a man before, but after I met you I killed every single one that looked at you wrong."

She lowers her trembling, her eyes still guarded. "What are you talking about? What men did you kill?"

"Only two, that bartender and Tyler."

She throws her hands in the air, anger making her body shake. "The Tyler that went missing? The one who the fucking police questioned us about?!"

Anger I can handle. I shrug my shoulders. "One and the same."

It's my vixen's turn to pace.

She stops once I start talking again. "When I saw you with another man, I was so enraged, I *needed* to kill your date. When I saw him trying to kiss you, I decided my lips would be the only ones to touch any part of your body. Something inside me snapped, and I needed to have you. So I broke the second rule: fucking my victims."

"Wow, I should feel so *special* I was the only victim you ever fucked. Fuck you, Aster!" She flips me off, anger rolling off her in waves.

This went a lot better in my head.

"Can I continue?" I ask, trying to be patient.

"Can you continue telling me why you didn't kill me? Sure, why the fuck not." She waves her hand in front of her, her body tense. She went from scared little lamb, to pissed off vixen fast. Her anger and spark to stand up to a serial killer has me smirking.

"Rule three: bring you back to my house, but by then I knew I was never going to kill you." I walk closer to her, attempting to grab her hands. "By then I had already fallen for you, and when I saw the fox necklace and you told me when you bought it… I realized that you knew what took me too long to realize."

"Do you know why I stab my lambs in the heart?"

She shakes her head. "No, but the media spectated it was your signature along with the rose."

I look around the room, chuckling to myself. "The media and cops got it wrong. So wrong. They think I'm a surgeon or artist, not some entrepreneur."

"Why do you do it then? What is the real meaning behind everything?"

I stare up at the ceiling, glancing back down to meet her curious eyes. "I stab them in the heart as a representation for the heart I don't have. The rose is the last gift they were given before the grim reaper came and took them."

She uncrosses her arms and looks at me, and when I go to grab her hand she lets me. "This heart," I say, jabbing at my chest, "has never beaten for anyone. I didn't know I was even capable of feeling until I met you." Her lips start to tremble, "You awakened things in me I thought died the night my parents were taken. A heart that never beat started pounding for you, little by little, and-"

"Everything was a lie!" she cries.

Grabbing her chin, I force her eyes to meet mine. "I may have been lying to you, but I was never pretending. Every minute, every fucking second spent with you, was real. It took me longer to figure out because I'm fucked up, but I finally did. I didn't understand the feelings you've awakened in me, but I finally do.

I love you, Serena." I lean down to give her a soft kiss on her forehead.

Tears stream down her face, and she leans into me, her head resting against my chest. I wrap my arms around her, unable to believe I finally told her I loved her, I don't expect her to say it back. We have time for her to acknowledge the depth of her own feelings.

I love Serena.

She starts to sniffle, and I rub her back. She presses her forehead into my chest before glancing up at me. "What are we going to do about Tyler? The police are still looking for him."

I kissed the top of her head, resting my cheek against her hair. "I already took care of it, they won't find his body, and they'll never know it was me."

"What did you do with him?"

I turn us towards the incinerator and her mouth drops open, laughing. "I'm damn good at what I do, my little vixen, I haven't gotten caught for a reason."

She just shakes her head and nuzzles into my chest.

Now that she knows who I really am, and has accepted it, I need to make sure she doesn't tell anyone. She keeps saying she never told Jessica her secret, but who is Jessica? She said she was with her the night we met, but when she introduced me to her, no one was behind her. I went along with it, nodding my head and played it off because I thought she was too drunk and her friend already left. *Maybe she thought the group of girls behind her was her friend?* I don't know, but I need to find out and make sure my secret won't be shared.

"You can't tell anyone, not even Jessica."

She looks at me with the most innocent eyes, her gaze telling me my secret is safe. "I won't, plus, you met her, remember? She would never guess you're the Morbid Monet."

I brush my fingers down her cheeks, concern written all over my face. "Serena, I never met Jessica."

She slaps my chest, rolling her eyes, stepping back from me.

"Yes, you did, silly, at the bar where we first met. She was sitting behind me, I even introduced you. You didn't say anything, just looked back and forth between us and ignored her, which I thought was weird because she is gorgeous and guys usually drop dead at her feet."

I grab her hands to stop her rambling. "Serena, no one was with you."

She tilts her head and looks at me. "What?"

"You were alone. There was a group of girls behind you, but no one else. I even tried to find her online, but there was no trace of her."

She backs away shaking her head. "No, no that's not true. She was there! I swear she was. Wait… why were you looking her up?"

"She was getting in the way, I needed her gone, but I couldn't find her anywhere."

She looks at me with confusion and fear, "But, I don't understand."

Her eyes pinch closed, and she falls to the floor, screaming in pain, crying uncontrollably. Panicked, I rush to her side, holding her in my arms and rocking her back and forth. "What's wrong, Serena? Talk to me."

One second she was fine, the next she's in pain. It's like my question caused her agony. *Fuck, what do I do? What can I do?* For once in my life, I'm scared, the woman I love is in pain, and there is nothing I can do to help her.

"Aster…" she whispers, gripping my shirt.

I rub her head, her shaking trapping the air in my lungs. "It's okay, I'm right here."

She's crying into my chest, mumbling, "I did it, I did it."

"Did what?" I ask.

She looks up, tears streaming down her face. "I killed her."

I stop rubbing her back, frozen. "Killed who?"

"Jessica." She whispers, slumping against me crying in my chest.

Holy fuck… she really is just like me. Jessica was real, and she killed her. She must have had a psychotic break and made her up in her mind to deal with what she did. Once she calms down, we will figure out what happened. Together. She isn't alone, and I need to make sure she knows that.

She rocks back and forth in my arms repeating "I killed her" over and over and over again. We sit like that for what seems like hours and she eventually cries herself asleep. I lay us down, cradling her in my arms and falling asleep with her. When I wake up Serena is gone.

TWENTY-FIVE

SERENA

"It can't be real," I whisper to myself, gripping the steering wheel and speeding back home. It doesn't make sense. *How can Jessica be dead? I was the one to end her life?* She's my best friend. The only person who was ever truly nice to me. I would know if she was no longer around.

But it *is* real. I saw that glimpse of a painful memory when I was at Aster's. I was standing over her body, bloody and breathless. Then my dad, of all people, was helping me. I think.

After Aster revealed who he was, I was shocked. Scared. Then pissed. Yet… something inside me accepted it. The honking from the person behind me has me shaking my head, and pressing my foot on the accelerator. *How long has the light been green?* I've been obsessed with the Morbid Monet for so long, and to learn I was falling for the man himself, made it easier to accept. Who in their right mind would be okay with their boyfriend being a serial killer who intended to make you their victim? This isn't *Beauty and The Beast*, I'm not fucking Belle with Stockholm syndrome. Granted… Aster never kidnapped me, he only tricked me into loving him.

Did he really though? Trick me? He said he may have been lying, but he never pretended. That has to count for something.

Right? I roll the windows down, I cover my mouth, feeling the nausea climb up my throat. Taking a deep breath, I push it back down, letting the cool night breeze hit my face and whip my hair around.

I need answers. That's why I snuck out. I need to drive to my dad's. Calling him will get me nowhere. He can't lie when I'm in his face.

My phone rings throughout the car, Aster's name lighting up the screen. Decline. I'm not ready to talk to him. Not until I have answers. *I'll send him a text when I get home so he isn't worried.* I switch on the radio and "Bad Feeling" by Jagwar Twin booms through the speakers. I turn it all the way up, drowning out the thoughts swarming in my head.

Rushing inside, I throw a bunch of clothes and my bathroom supplies in a bag. I have no idea how long I'll be gone, so I would rather over pack then underpack. I zip up the bag, grabbing my phone charger before sending Aster a text, not even bothering to read the ones he already sent me. I'm on a mission, and no one, not even a sexy as literal sin serial killer, can distract me.

SERENA

I'm okay, I'm going to get the answers I need. We will talk when I get back

THE DRIVE FROM SALEM TO NEW HAMPSHIRE ONLY TOOK ME TWO hours, since I had to stop for gas.

The sun is starting to peek over the horizon. The blended colors of orange and red are helping calm my frazzled nerves. I've never been to dad's new place, but he sent me his address to keep in my contacts. At first, I was pissed he assumed I'd want it, now I'm thankful he's self-centered enough to believe I'd want to see him again. This is going to be a surprise visit. I don't expect him, or his bride to be, to be up, but this is too important to wait.

I park behind one of the four vehicles in their driveway. *What two people own that many vehicles?* One for each person I understand, but four? That's a little ridiculous, but hey, the rich will spend when they want. Anything to one up their neighbor.

I was never flashy with my parents' money, they had a lot of it, giving me everything I could ever dream of, but I was happy with the simple things in life. Just like my mom, she didn't care about money either.

When I first started painting and got into my love for art, my mom bought me everything I needed to create. I wouldn't accept their money though, that's why my mom and I went to the flea market to sell my art. It gave me a sense of responsibility, confidence, being able to support myself. That's why, after Mom died, I was grateful I already had money saved up to move and create a life for myself. It took me longer to leave because I was consumed by my grief, but I needed to escape when dad moved to New Hampshire right away after her death. I was happy I found a place in Salem, where I was born and raised, able to stay close to my mom despite her passing.

Salem always felt like home, everything about it. From the tourists who come around October to celebrate Halloween to the cold winter months huddled by a fireplace reading a book. I could never leave, this is my home.

I throw a hoodie on before I exit the car and walk up the long steps to stand in front of their door bracing myself.

This is it. I'm going to get the answers I need. I don't know what happened, no matter how hard I try to remember, it just comes up blank. Like static when the tv goes out. A grating, buzzing noise. That's all I'm getting.

I knock on the front door and wait a couple minutes with no answer. My foot taps, while my hands stay placed in the pocket of my hoodie, impatience running through me. *They're definitely still asleep*, but I need them to wake up, I bang on the door, uncaring what their neighbors might think. I hear my dad running down the stairs shouting he's coming in an angry tone.

He swings open the door, ready to tear my head off, when he freezes in the doorway "What the fu- Serena?" His face morphs from anger to shock. "What are you doing here? And why are you here so early? Is everything okay?"

I just stand there, silent. Staring at him. I know he wasn't expecting to see me, especially since I've been ignoring him, but the urgency of the situation is more important than their sleep.

His hair disheveled, in a robe barely tied around his waist, with gray house slippers on, his eyes soften, and he places his hand on my shoulder. "Hey, Serena, what's wrong?"

"What happened to Jessica?" I blurt out.

His eyes bulge and, before he can answer, a woman with red hair tied in a bun comes racing down the stairs, tying her robe. My nails dig into my palms to lessen the anger I feel at seeing *her*. "Honey what's wrong? Who's this?"

He looks back at her, then to me. "It's Serena."

"Oh." Her eyes widen, and she rushes down the stairs, motioning for me to come inside. "Come on in dear, it's chilly outside." She smacks my dad in the chest, rolling her eyes with a huff. "Why haven't you invited her in? Poor thing looks like she's freezing."

He looks at his fiancé, and his eyes soften. "She wants to know what happened to Jesssica."

Her brows crease. "Jessica?" she asks.

"*The* Jessica," he says.

I stand there, arms crossed over my chest, watching the two of them interact. They both know something, and whatever it is I am going to find out.

Her mouth thins into a line. "Oh. Why don't you come inside Serena, and I'll make us coffee."

I look to my dad, my anger and desperation rising "I need answers."

He steps to the side. "Come inside and we can talk."

I nod my head and walk past both of them, stopping because I've never been here and I have no idea where the kitchen is. I don't dare look behind me, I can already tell both their faces wear looks of pity, and I don't need that.

"Follow me. I'll show you where the kitchen is," Dad's fiancé says. I know he told me her name once, but I didn't care to remember it.

Following her to the kitchen I sit at the table, and Dad sits on the other side of the it. His fiancé starts to make coffee for all of us.

"What happened to Jessica?" I ask again, impatience lacing my tone.

My dad cradles his head in his palm, looking down, stress radiating off him. "Give me a moment to wake up, Serena. Sharon is making us some coffee, I'll answer your questions then."

I bang my hand on the table, heat thrumming through my veins. "No! I didn't drive all night to wait for you to have your *coffee*. I need answers. Now!" I yell, my body starting to shake.

"Serena..." Before he can finish, Sharon walks over, placing coffee in front of us and taking a seat next to my father. She grabs his hand, her thumb rubbing some of his stress away. He gives her a small smile, and she returns it. The motion has me remembering how he was like this with Mom, and seeing him like this with *Sharon* has my hands balling into fists.

He takes a sip, stalling. "What do you remember?"

What do I remember? That's a stupid question. He knows I forgot. *Wait... does he know that my memory is all messed up?* My hands relax, and shoulders slump. *Has he been lying to me?*

I look at Sharon, my brow lifting in a silent question.

"It's okay, she knows everything."

Of course she does.

"All I remember is that..." I can't even say it, if I do, I feel like it will be true. *I'm not ready to accept that.* I start to tap my fingers on my coffee mug, nervous energy surrounding me.

My dad grabs my hands, silence filling the kitchen. "Tell me what you remember, Serena. I can't help you if you don't."

I take a deep breath, tears falling down my cheeks. I look at my fathers hand in Sharon's, both squeezing the other for support. "I. killed. her," I whisper.

I look up to meet my father's eyes, finding no shock on his or Sharon's face, just relief. "So you finally remember?" my dad asks.

Now I'm the one shocked, the tears falling harder. "No! I don't remember; that's the problem. All I remember is standing over her body, covered in blood, and you. That's it." My breathing becomes erratic, my vision going blurry at the edges. "Please, Dad, tell me what happened."

His eyes drop, his body seeming to collapse in on itself. "I can only tell you what happened afterwards, after I walked in. Only you know what happened. What caused it."

My head tilts to the side. "You don't know why I did it?" *How can they not know the reason if they helped me after I killed her?*

He shakes his head, his face paling. "No. I only helped you clean it up. After she was gone, it's like your brain flipped a switch, just like with your mom."

"With mom? What do you mean?

He takes a heavy breath, his eyes meeting mine without hesitation. "Serena, I never cheated on your mom."

I scoff, pulling out of his grip and crossing my arms over my chest. "Yes, you did. I saw you with another woman when mom was dying."

"Hunny, your mom was already dead."

A sharp pain pierces the back of my head, the same pain I felt at Aster's. *Do I even want to remember?* I cry even harder, between sobs I manage to choke out the word. "I. Killed. Mom?"

The words leave my lips, but I don't believe them. Yet... my memories don't lie. *I don't understand? Why would I kill my own mother?* She was my best friend. "Dad, please tell me that isn't true."

He lets go of Sharons hands and takes my hands in his, "You didn't kill her, Serena; you set her free."

I look up at him, swiping my nose with the sleeve of my hoodie. "What?"

"Your mother was dying. She asked to see you alone, so I left the room, but I stayed by the door. I had a bad feeling." I start to sniffle, shaking my head slowly. "I heard you and your mom talking, and she begged you to set her free. To let her go. You refused at first, but then she whispered something, I couldn't hear what. It was silent, and the next thing I heard was your mom's heart monitor go dead. I rushed in there, but it was too late. You were crying over her with the pillow covering her face."

My breathing evens out as I try to come to grips with every-thing he is telling me. Mom begged me to kill her. *And I did?* The pain lessens, but my head throbs and my body feels weak. *Why can't I remember that? How is this like Jessica?*

He starts to cry, but continues. "I was too late. You granted your mother's last wish and became a shell of yourself. You wouldn't speak. You stopped going to school. You even started avoiding that awful friend, Jessica.

"Awful?" I ask.

"Yes, *awful.* Truthfully, I wasn't surprised you killed her for everything she put you through." He sighed, pinching the bridge of his nose. "But a couple weeks went by, and I went to bring you food, and you weren't there. I looked all over the house, and I heard your voice coming from the room your mother died in. I walked in, and you were having a conversation with yourself. I brushed it off as your way of dealing with your grief, but then you started to act like your mom was still alive. It was like you completely forgot she died."

I bite my nails, not believing the words coming out of his mouth. *Why would I imagine my mother still being alive after I killed her? Why did I do the same thing I did with Jessica? I wish I could remember what happened.*

He looks at Sharon, and she grabs his hand, squeezing it. "I didn't want to put you back into your depression, so I let you believe Mom was still alive. Then, after Jessica died..." He swallows, like it's hard for him to continue. "You remembered Mom was gone, but forgot how she died. You hated me, claiming I was cheating on her, but before I could explain myself , you left. You said you were going to Jessica's. I was confused, I had just disposed of her, but I realized it was your brain's way of dealing with what you did. And... and I couldn't tell you. I wanted to, believe me I did, but I was so worried about what would happen. You already lost yourself with your mother; I knew I needed to wait for you to remember on your own."

I look away, unable to come to terms with what he is saying. *This is all too much, I'm crazy, I really am crazy.* I didn't kill just one person, I killed *two* and one was my own mother. I need to remember. *I need to understand why I snapped.* If I remember, I can only hope I don't forget something else.

None of it makes any sense, yesterday Jessica was still alive. Mine and Aster's secrets were still our own. While I am happy we were able to let those secrets spill, the mask I didn't even know I was wearing was slipping. The person who I truly am isn't the person I was yesterday. I can never go back to who I was, nothing will ever be the same. I'm glad I have Aster, I know he will understand. After all, he's a killer himself.

A killer, that's what I am now.

Every person, all the people who always looked at me funny when I was with Jessica... it all makes sense now. The guys at the club *both* were hitting on me. *She was never there.* I take out my phone, to go to her contact and notice for the first time an app I don't recognize. I open it up and see it's a text chain between me and Jessica. *I've been texting and answering myself this whole time.*

"I need to lay down." I get up from the table, and my dad

wraps his arm around my side, I let him as he walks me to a spare room.

He shuts the door, and I hear him and Sharon whispering before walking back to their room.

I start reading through every text, analyzing every message. I think back on all the conversations I had with myself. Every single interaction was a lie, one I wished to be true. The reason for her canceling going to the flea market was because if she came, my brain knew I would find out the truth too soon. The reason she ignored my panic text, because my brain knew I was getting closer to remembering. Since meeting Aster little by little things started to fall into place, and him revealing his secret and bringing her up was all it took for the pieces to start to fall together.

I lay down, staring at the ceiling fan going around and around for what seems like hours.

"You know what you did."

I spring up; it wasn't a dream, it was a memory!

My head vibrates with pain, encompassing every nerve ending in my skull. I scream, but nothing echoes around the room. Everything goes black, I fall backwards.

I remember it all.

TWENTY-SIX
SERENA

Stage four. That's what the doctor said. Only has a couple months, if that, left. My mom, the brightest, happiest person in the room, suddenly has a ticking clock, and it's moving too fast. Everywhere she went, there was light. Even the most miserable of people couldn't help but smile at her. She was, *is*, everything.

How could a person, who has so much love to give and who has helped so many people, be dying so quickly? When Mom first got diagnosed, it wasn't this bad. She was only stage two, and the doctor had high hopes for a full recovery. She even did clinical trials to slow down the cancer.

It was working at first. She didn't have to go through chemo anymore. That stuff only kills you faster anyway. Her color started to return, and her hair slowly started growing back. The doctor said the treatments were working with a fucking smile on his face.

So why now? Why after all this time? Why did it stop working, and how did it progress so fast? The doctors can't explain it, and they say she's deteriorating fast, from the inside out. I feel like my world is falling apart, that I'm dying right alongside her, and there is no one who can stop the pain from killing us both.

Dad screams at the doctors for their mistake, the veins in his neck throbbing. Mom is pulling on his arm, trying to calm him down and holding back the tears I know are threatening to fall.

Me? I want to cry and scream, but I feel numb. Broken. Empty. I sit, unable to comprehend the doctor's words, the chaos of the room flowing through me.

My mom comes over and touches my shoulder, my heart pounding with fear. "Honey, are you okay?"

I just stare at her, frozen. The words I want to say, the tears I want to cry, don't come. They're stuck. Refusing to come out. Dead. Just like she will be.

"Serena, everything is going to be okay. Doctors make mistakes all the time; it is a part of life. I'm here if you need to talk, hunny. You know I'll always be here."

I nod my head knowing it's what I should do but not hearing her words. The world around me stands still, I feel like I'm floating. I feel like I'm in a wave pool, and waves are trying to pull me back as I try to swim free.

Dad curses the doctors, as they leave, and he comes over and hugs Mom. She starts to sob in his arms, he rubs her head telling her they will figure this out, and Dad pulls me into their embrace.

We stay like that for a while, simply holding one another. Mom crying, dad holding back his tears, and me staring into the abyss.

It isn't until we get back home and I take a scalding hot shower that the tears finally fall. I have the music loud so my parents can't hear me fall apart. They don't need my pain added to theirs. They never have. Especially not now. We all need to be strong, and I need to be there for Mom for whatever time she has left. I hug myself crumpled on the shower floor, letting the water hit my back, and cry and cry and cry. It isn't until my fingers and toes start to prune, and the water runs cold, that I finally get out.

I head to my room, not bothering to get dressed or turn on the light. Laying in bed, wrapped in my towel, I watch the fan go around and around, until finally my eyes start to drift closed. I tumble into the abyss of my sweet nightmare knowing nothing could be worse than my current reality.

IT'S BEEN SIX MONTHS SINCE WE GOT THE NEWS FROM THE DOCTOR. Longer than anyone expected, and for that, we are grateful. But it hasn't been easy. Mom is dying. The light that once shined so brightly has been completely snuffed out. She is bedridden and can't even eat anymore. She has food bags, and hydration IVs. Her skin is pale, and she can barely speak. Dad only visits her at night to say goodnight, but every Saturday he sets up little dates in her room. Every Saturday they both look forward to it, and the light returns to Mom's eyes briefly, until sleep claims her.

I visit her every morning and every night, talking to her and telling her about my day. Most days it's to complain about Jessica and how she's being cruel or mean. I try not to complain too much, but Mom insists I tell her everything. She said after that incident in high school I needed to ditch her, and I did. For a while. Then I got lonely. I had no friends, and Jessica apologized. We were really good for a long time after that, she would only make rude remarks every once in a while. All I would need to do is give her a look and she'd shut up.

Lately though it feels like we are right back in high school, and I am getting fed up. With my mom being as sick as she is, Jess should understand I want to spend as much time with her as I can. I don't know how much time I have left. But she's always been a selfish narcissist and canceling on her every time she wants to go somewhere is making it all worse. The rude comments, the snide remarks, her commenting on my weight, or what I'm wearing. She's looped back into her old habits of bringing me down to make herself feel better. I can't handle being her personal punching bag anymore, so the best solution I've come up with to avoid the drama she brings is to just ignore her. Until I can erase her from my life for good.

It's time for me to go see Mom, I'm going to tell her how I've finally decided to follow her advice. To let Jessica go once and for all, and not fall back into old habits. I'm bouncing with each step I take, getting excited, knowing how happy the news will make Mom.

Walking in, I see Mom in her bed, IV's hooked up and her hair a mess. Dad is sitting next to her, holding her hand. They're talking in soft voices, both of their eyes closed. They don't notice I'm standing in the door, I freeze and just watch them. Soaking in a moment I don't know if I'll ever see again.

My parents are so in love. The look in my dad's eyes while he talks to her about his day is like how a couple looks at one another when they first fall in love, but there is also sadness shining in his eyes. An understanding. A begrudging acceptance.

Mom is the first to notice me as she looks past Dad and gives me a small smile. Dad turns around, following her gaze.

"Serena, is it time already for you to see mom?" he asks, a pitch of sadness in his tone. I nod my head, and Dad kisses Mom goodbye, Gripping my shoulder he looks at me and whispers, "She isn't doing too good today, don't stay long, she needs rest."

I tap his hand to let him know I heard him, something we've started doing when difficult news needs to be shared in front of Mom. He leaves the room but doesn't close the door all the way.

"Hey, Mom; how are you feeling today?"

Dad's right, Mom doesn't look good. She looks paler than usual, and her lips are so chapped the skin is flaking. Her arms and hands have become so boney, and her cheeks have sunken in more, she looks like a barely breathing skeleton.

"I'm okay, honey," she wheezes, unable to say anymore.

I take the glass of water on her nightstand and hold the straw to her lips so she can take a little sip. "How's that, Mom?"

She coughs a little, drinking too much, but nods her head. "I want to talk to you about something important, Serena."

My body tenses and I set the cup down, bracing myself for what's to come. She only uses my name when it is serious. "What is it?" I ask, wariness in my voice.

"I'm dying," she whispers.

We all know that, but we don't talk about it. We like to live in denial, yet Mom is flat out saying it now. Why?

"I know, mom." I say looking down.

"Not fast enough," she rasps.

My head shoots up, and my eyes go wide. *What does she mean by that?*

"I need you to help me go," she croaks.

I start shaking my head violently. "No. Mom, you can't be serious. I know things are bad, but they could," my voice breaks, tears filling my eyes. "No; they *will* get better. Don't say things like that. Please, Mom!" I cry.

She can't ask me to do this. She's my best friend. My rock. My *person*. Without her to guide me, I know I'll fall apart. She wants to leave me forever, and she wants *me* to be the one to do it? No. I can't. I won't. I refuse.

She motions for her water once more, and I place the straw in her mouth. Her hand shakes as she tries to wipe her mouth. My heart breaks, watching my mother get closer to death's door. I grab a tissue and dab it softly; she smiles, thanking me without words.

"Serena, I'm not getting better. I won't get better." I start crying harder, and she takes my hands in hers. "Please, I can't do this alone. I'm in so much pain. I hate the way you and your father look at me." She coughs, spit dripping down her chin and clearing her throat. "Don't think of this as me dying, think of it as setting me free. One day I'll see you again." She wipes the tears from my cheek. "This is my last wish. I need it to be you."

Her dying wish. She needs me to set her free. *I don't...* I stare down at my mother who already looks ghostly. She's begging me to let her go, telling me goodbye without ever saying the words. *She needs me to be strong.* The strong girl she's raised me to be.

I nod my head, letting the tears fall. She smiles, relief relaxing her muscles.

"Thank you."

I kiss her head, grab a pillow, cover her face while closing my eyes and set her free. "I'll see you again, Mom." Once her monitor goes off, I sit there with a pillow still over her face.

My dad rushes in, yelling at me, asking me what I did, why I did it.

"She asked me to," I whisper, staring at the pillow.

She's gone. She's really gone, and I am the reason why. She begged me, and I told her no. I couldn't do that. Then she looked at me with such hopelessness and resignation in her eyes, and something in me snapped and agreed. I set my mom free. I'll never see her in this life again. She's gone. Forever.

I walk numbly back to my room, shutting my door, falling to the ground, and cry. I hear the sirens of an ambulance outside my door, voices of my dad and strangers talking. I sit like that all night, numb and motionless.

The tears stopped. *My life is over.* My eyes ache as the sun streams in through my window. *How will I move on without my mom? How will I ever get over what I did?*

6 MONTHS LATER...

After work, I take a shower, change into my pajamas, and head to my mom's room to tell her about my day. Walking in, Mom is sitting up in bed, deep in a new book, a content smile on her face. When she sees me she beams and sets the books down, taking off her glasses and placing them on her night stand.

"How was work, honey?" she asks with the brightest smile on her face.

My mom is so beautiful with straight black hair, and eyes as blue as mine. *I hope to look as good as her when I'm her age.* She ages so gracefully; not a wrinkle in sight. The sickness she once had slowly faded away. The new clinical trial she was put on seems to be working, and it's like she never had cancer at all.

We're so lucky. I'll never let any of us forget that.

"Work is work; whatcha reading?" I ask, plopping down next to her on the bed. I'm the youngest person working at Salem's busiest art gallery at just twenty-three years old. I couldn't believe it when I got the call saying I was hired. The whole family celebrated; we went to our favorite Italian restaurant, then froyo after.

"Just a new romance book I found when I was browsing the bookstore." She says with a slight blush, embarrassment lacing her features. Mom loves her spicy books, I don't know why she feels so embarrassed to tell me about them. We all have our hobbies. Mine is art, and hers is book porn.

I lean on her shoulder and grab the book from her lap, placing the bookmark in it, before putting it next to her glasses. "Oh yeah? Tell me about it." She launches into her story, all earlier embarrassment about her book forgotten. This one is about monsters and has tentacles and things that shouldn't intrigue me but do.

Her words slur together, and she yawns, telling me she's tired. It's only four in the afternoon, but naps are the best for her continued improvement. So, I kiss her forehead and leave her room.

I start making dinner; Dad's working late tonight again. *I have a feeling he's cheating on Mom.* He's been working late every night for several months and he comes home, a smile on his face, smelling of a woman who isn't my mother. I will confront him one of these days, once I have the proof. He won't get away with hurting Mom like that. She deserves better; I thought he loved her, but I guess love fades away if it was never true to begin with.

There's a knock on the front door, making me stop chopping

the onion. *Who could be at the door? I'm not expecting anyone.* I leave work at work, and I don't have any friends. That night I told mom about kicking Jessica to the curb, that is exactly what I did. She hasn't been a part of my life since that night, and I couldn't be happier. Less drama, less stress.

I open the door, and freeze, my face morphing from shock to anger. Standing there is a face I haven't seen in months. Blonde hair shining, brown eyes, looking like the shit she is. *Jessica.* "What are you doing here?" I say, crossing my arms, disdain lacing my face.

She pushes past me, ignoring my question. "What's for dinner? Smells good."

I shut the door behind me and stomp back to the kitchen. "I'm going to ask again; what are you doing here?"

She turns around, fake sadness in her eyes, "That's no way to treat your best friend."

I scoff, "Best friend? We haven't been that in a long time."

She places her hand over her heart, and in a mocking tone, says, "That hurts, Serena, I would have thought after your Mom died-"

"What?" I ask, eyes squinted and brows pinched together.

"What?" she asks back.

"My mom isn't dead."

Now she looks confused. "Uh, yeah, she is; she died, like, six months ago and then you disappeared. I thought it's been long enough of this silent treatment, so I came over to tell you to knock this shit off. It's getting old."

I point to my mom's room. "She's not dead. I was just talking to her, telling her about work."

"Work? You haven't been to work since she died, Serena."

I shake my head. "No; that's not true. You're lying."

She grabs my arm and drags me to my mom's room, opens the door and points to her bed. "See? She's not there; hasn't been for six months. You're crazy." She walks back into the kitchen, and I just stand there looking at the dusty room.

My head begins to throb, and the longer I stare the more intense the throbbing becomes. Soon it becomes a pain so intense, my vision blurs and the room starts spinning. I close my eyes, clutching my head. I cry as I remember it all. Remembering I killed her.

I go back to the kitchen, my fists clenched, and teeth grinding. Jessica has her nasty little finger in my sauce tasting it. I take the knife from the counter and go back to chopping the onion.

How could I forget my own mother's death and that I was the cause of it? What is wrong with me?

Jessica snaps her fingers in front of me. "Earth to Serena. Believe me now?"

"What?" I ask, still chopping.

"That your mom is dead. That you're crazy and forgot. I don't know how you could forget or why you thought she was still alive, but I can't wait to tell everyone about it."

I glance at her, anger coursing through my veins. "Fuck!" I pull my finger up, sucking the blood off, from where I cut it when I wasn't paying attention.

"Are you dumb or something? Your blood is going to ruin dinner," Jessica sneers, pure disgust on her face.

I pull my finger out of my mouth and look at the blood seeping from it, then look at the knife. Grabbing it, I glare at Jessica, and say, "Actually, your blood is going to ruin dinner." I slice the knife across her arm. Blood pools out.

She screams, gripping her arm. "What the fuck is wrong with you?!"

I smile at her. "I'm crazy; isn't that what you said?" I ask, cocking my head and stabbing the knife into her thigh so she can't run. Jessica falls to the ground, grabbing her knee and crying uncontrollably. Her blood looks so pretty coated on my knife. My heart pounds, my own blood singing and begging for more. *I want to make her bleed. I want every last drop of her life.*

Snatching her hair, I drag her to my mom's old room and throw her on the hardwood floor. She kicks, and screams, desperate for me to stop, but I'm bigger than her. She always loved to point that out, and now it is to my advantage. I sit on top of her and start punching her face, blood spraying everywhere. I take the knife and slice it across her chest, watching as the blood drips down, soaking her shirt.

She tries to buck me off, so I wrap my hands around her dainty little throat and watch as the life leaves her. Her eyes close and head falls to the side. I'm breathing heavily and angry. Angry she opened my eyes to my mom being dead. Angry my mind was playing tricks on me. Angry I didn't get to torture her, if she died. I check her pulse. Still there, but barely. The anger starts to dissipate knowing I get to make the bitch, who made my life miserable for so long, scream.

I get up and walk to the kitchen, grab a chair, and slowly drag it down the hall. I go to the garage and grab some rope to tie her up with. Grateful my dad already has everything I need. I lift her body up, the rage inside me boiling over at how light the bitch is, and set her down. I tie her arms behind the chair and her feet to the legs, making sure it's tight enough to leave marks. I want her *perfect* skin to be ruined.

Going back to the kitchen, I grab a glass of water and the blow torch I was going to use for creme brulee, numb to everything except the task at hand.

Walking back to the room, I splash the water on her face, startling her awake.

"What the fuck?" she groans as she starts to open her eyes and she tries to move, but quickly realizes she is tied up. "Are you out of your mind? Untie me right fucking now!" she screams.

"Not gonna happen," I smirk, shaking my head. "Now be quiet, this may hurt." I shove a sock in her mouth and bend down to slice her achilles, making her scream. Though it is muffled, it's still loud enough for me to enjoy, a sinister smile, like the one Cheshire wears spreading across my face. I watch as her legs start to shake from the pain, and tears pool in her eyes.

She glares at me with such hatred, it makes me slice the other one.

That'll show you, bitch.

I trace the knife up to her face, placing the blade against her cheek. "You've always been so beautiful, Jessica. And you always loved to make me feel less than. I wonder how you would feel if I destroyed the one thing you love." Her eyes go wide, and she starts pleading through the sock. Her cries go unanswered. I feel so much joy. So much power. Making her be the one begging for once. I place my hand to my ear. "Huh, what's that? I can't hear you? You want me to slice your beautiful face?" She starts shaking her head, tears streaming down her cheeks. "I'll take that as a yes." I slowly drag the blade across her skin, watching as a red line forms behind my blade. The blood slowly drips down.

"You know, red never was your color. Maybe we should try something else. What do you say?" She doesn't answer, turning her head away from me and squeezing her eyes shut.

This fucking bitch thinks she can look away from me; I'm going to make her look me in the eyes as I take away her power.

I take the sock out of her mouth, wanting to hear her beg and she spits at me. A wicked laugh escapes me, echoing around the room. I wipe the spit away, my eyes going wild. "I'm going to fucking ruin you when I get out of here. I'm going to have you locked up forever. You're going to regret doing this to me. You're a coward. A loser. A-" I silence her by shoving the sock back in.

"What makes you think you're getting out of here?" I ask, head tilted and my hair falling over my shoulder. She cries, fear finally replacing the anger in her eyes.

I get in her face, gripping her chin with a bruising force and making her look me in the eye. "Some people are a poison, a weed that needs to be plucked." I stand and grab the torch, the anticipation heavy between us. "A leech that sucks the life out of you. You, Jessica, are both. You have bled me dry for the last time. I'm through being your personal punching bag. I'm done being the weak little girl you made feel small."

I turn the torch on and stare into the fire. "Do you know how to kill leeches?" I ask, not bothering to look at her.

Her cries get louder, and I know she's trying to scream. *Little help that will do her when no one can hear.* I look her dead in her terrified eyes, "You burn them." I take the torch and place it on her arm, watching as her skin starts to bubble. The room smells like torched flesh as I work my way up and down her body with the flame.

This is power. This is me taking back the confidence and control she stole from me. Too long have I let her slowly kill me, slowly take the light my mom tried to give me. I was too weak before, but calling me crazy? Saying she was going to tell everyone? I had to do something.

She has to die.

I don't think about the consequences, and I keep burning long after her screams have stopped. Watching her feel a semblance of the pain she caused me brought a sense of peace I'd been yearning for for years. This earth being rid of her is the greatest blessing I could have given anyone.

I untie her hands and start burning each fingerprint off. Even in my haze of retribution I remember all the murder documentaries I spent countless hours watching. Every little thing to do to make a person unidentifiable. Leaving no trace of who she once was, I walk back to the garage and grab pliers from my dads tool box, ready to start plucking every single tooth from her mouth.

Even if she is found, she will forever be a Jane Doe. Maybe I'll set her up and display her like the Morbid Monet would do. Maybe he'd come and find me to punish me for being a copycat. The idea makes me giddy. He tortures his victims in different ways, I'd just have to finish with his signature. The murder would be blamed on him, despite it not being his normal victim profile, and I would never get caught. I've been fascinated with him for so long, if he saw me now would he spare me? Help me kill her?

I don't hear the front door open or hear my dad call out my name. I'm too lost in the fantasy of being the accomplice to the Morbid Monet. It isn't until he walks into the room and starts shaking me that I'm pulled from my dream.

"Serena! Oh my god; what did you do?!" He looks at the burnt body before him. "Who is that, Serena?"

"Jessica," I say with a huge smile spreading across my face. I drop the pliers, finally done with my task, and my dad pulls me into him.

"Everything will be okay. I'll take care of it. Just go shower, and we will talk about this later."

I nod my head and leave the room. *He's a lot calmer than I thought he'd be.* Granted, maybe he's used to me being a killer now. First mom, now Jessica. *I really am a monster.* Got to hand it to him though, he gets the Best Dad in the World award for not turning me in.

Turning on the shower, I watch as the blood goes down the drain. Hypnotizing me as my sins wash away with it. I hear the door open to the bathroom and peek out to see my dad grabbing my bloody clothes. He shuts the door softly behind him, and I stare down at my hands. The hands of a killer. That's what I am now.

I leave the shower, heading straight to my room and completely forgetting about dinner. I close my eyes and wish to dream of my nightmares, to find comfort and acceptance in what I did.

I fall asleep, and that night I don't dream, not about anything.

The next morning, I wake up and go straight to the room my dad turned into my studio. A place where I can escape and perfect my art without any worries of the world.

Sitting down at my easel, I start to paint, each brush stroke starting to blur. I don't know what I'm painting until it's finished, and even then, I don't understand. The canvas is of a faceless woman with cuts and burns all over her body and her teeth missing.

Looking at it starts to hurt my head, so I grab the red paint with shaky hands, my chest heaving, and throw it over the image. It looks like blood dripping over the image, hiding it away.

"Serena?" My dad pokes his head through the door, looking haggard and worn. "Is everything-" He stops talking as he stares at my painting, throwing it to the ground. "Have you lost your mind?!" He screams, grabbing my shoulders and shaking me. "Why would you paint that?!"

Tears well in my eyes, my voice wobbly. "What do you mean? I just started painting."

"Do you have any idea what this could do? I *just* got rid of the evidence and you go and paint it?" He stops shaking at me, the vein in his neck throbbing.

"I don't understand what you're talking about. What evidence?"

He turns his head, sympathy coating his eyes. "You don't remember what happened last night?"

"No," I whisper,

"Oh, Serena." He pulls me into him, rubbing my back.

I pull out of his arms, confusion swirling through me. "What happened, Dad?"

"Nothing, baby; nothing happened." He lets me go and walks over to the painting. "I'm just going to take this." Then he leaves, leaving me there alone, wondering what he was talking about.

What happened last night? Why did he get so upset when he saw the painting? I put everything away with stilted movements. *I don't understand. What don't I remember?*

TWENTY-SEVEN

ASTER

It's only been a day, but I feel restless. I can't eat. I can't sleep. I don't even want to hunt. I haven't felt the desire for pain since the little lamb right after I met Serena. I just haven't had the urge, the need to kill, since she's walked into my life. Ever since I can remember, the impulse to end a life has always been in the forefront of my life. I have a system, a routine, one that I have never strayed from, until now. Serena has come into my life and created beautiful chaos, she is and always will be my equal and I would *never* go back to who I was before her.

I know she said we will talk when she gets back, but how long will that be? Will she be gone for a couple days? Weeks? I pace back and forth in my bedroom, staring at the last message she sent me. My head is sore from how much I've been pulling at my hair.

Patience. I need to be patient. She's getting the answers she needs. The answers I need as well. I need to understand what happened. I want to help her become who she was always meant to be. My partner. *She killed Jessica?* I thought she was like an imaginary friend or some shit, and my girl was just crazy. Turns out she's *crazy* crazy, but in a way that matches my own. I knew there was something about her from the moment I met her, a darkness swirling in her eyes. That's why I told her my secret. Her eyes; they look like the north sea. Dangerous, yet beautiful. She's truly a vixen.

My vixen.

My phone bounces on the bed, hitting the pillow and disappearing under the sheets. I collapse onto the edge of my bed, my arms on my knees and my legs vibrating. I take a deep breath, trying to calm my buzzing nerves.

Everything will be okay. She trusts me. I trust her.

Trust. That's a word I never thought I would use. Let alone truly, willingly, giving it to a single soul. But Serena is different; our souls are entwined with one another. Since I started killing and she started painting, we've been connected.

We have always been destined for one another. Her fucked up yin, to my just as fucked yang.

I lay down on the bed, my hands crossed over my eyes. The rain outside is getting heavier, the drops making a melody against the window. The colder days are coming as we inch closer to Thanksgiving. I never do anything for any holidays, aside from Halloween, but I only go to my haunted house and watch as people scream and flee.

The joy I feel watching the fear in their eyes, listening to the terror leaving their lips, makes me excited every year for it. People are strange, paying to be scared shitless. Sometimes, I get lucky and find my next victim at my haunted house, never taking them from there directly. That is rare, though, since I only visit on Halloween.

My birthday is coming up, but I don't feel like celebrating this year, which is odd especially since I finally have someone to celebrate it with. Every three to four years on my birthday, I pick a victim who doesn't look like my regular lambs. It isn't my usual preference, but around my birthday, since it was the day my parents were taken, I become greedy. The compulsion I have to take another life is so overwhelming I take any girl I deem worthy of my blade that night. I never display them. My birthday victims are for my eyes only. After the life leaves their eyes, I cut them into pieces and throw them into the incinerator. Watching as their skin bubbles and turns to ash fills me with peace. Once the last piece is disintegrated, I scrub the place clean, and even burn the outfit I was wearing, standing in nothing but my birthday suit.

Doing this never connects those missing girls to me. No body, no crime, simply a missing girl, every several years, on my birthday.

No one has connected those dots or even figured out that a girl goes missing every couple years on November thirteenth. If they did, they would probably think it was a different serial killer since the motives are different.

Staying here is doing nothing but driving me crazy. My foot taps incessantly as I make images out of nothing from the popcorn ceiling in my room. The only thing I want to do is go to the haunted house and watch people enjoy and fear my creations. It's only open for a couple more weeks, the event closes down at the end of November, giving me time to think and create new ideas. Maybe going there is the motivation I need to kill again, to spark what fizzled away with my vixen's rise.

I'm not liking this feeling to not kill, that isn't me. I'm a monster. A killer. A predator. I need to reignite that, and maybe, since my vixen is away, this fox can hunt.

Screams from the guests can be heard across the parking lot. I reverse in the spots designated for employees. Taking one of the spots reserved for the higher management.

The rain stopped on the way over, but even if it didn't, the attractions are open. Unless it is a bad thunderstorm, we stay open. I find running through the forest when it's raining can be even more frightening for the guests. It makes their adrenaline heightened, and they always come back for more. Plus watching some of them slip and fall is quite amusing.

The door is locked to the employee entrance, grumbling, I take out my keys trying to find the right one.

"Uhm, excuse me? You can't go in there; that's the employees only entrance." I look behind me, gritting my teeth, hands fisting at my sides, and see a petite redhead in zombie makeup, probably for the day of the dead house. Her hands are on her hips, and she nods to the sign above the door. "Can't you read? It says 'employees only'."

Of course I can read, and it's no surprise I know this entrance because *I'm* the one who put the sign there.

You can't kill your employees, Aster.

I take the pack of cigarettes from my pocket, placing one in my mouth and lighting it. Taking a long drag, letting the nicotine hit the back of my throat, I blow it into her face. She waves her hand in the air and has a coughing fit. *That'll show you, bitch.* "I know the owner," I say, taking another long drag.

"Ha! That's funny. No one knows the owner. How would a nobody like you know them?"

I lean down and whisper in her ear, "If I told you, I'd have to kill you." She shoves me away from her, her lip curling in disgust. "Like you said, it's a secret."

She pushes past me to unlock the door. "Well, I don't believe you, so get lost." She opens the door just enough for her to fit through and tries to shut it on me.

Big mistake.

I slam my hand on the top, forcing it open and watching in triumph as she falls to the ground. Cigarette still in my mouth, I take it out and tap the ash onto her foot, watching her legs retract into herself. I kneel in front of her and drop the cigarette to the floor and crush it with my boot, killing the flame. She watches in horror, and her breathing becomes labored.

"You know, my birthday's in a couple days, but I've had a really shitty couple of hours, so I was thinking about celebrating early."

Shock crosses her face, making her eyes bulge, "W-what?"

I stand up, offering her my hand, she hesitantly grabs it. "Do you want to celebrate my birthday with me?" I ask, putting on my fake smile, the one that makes pretentious girls like her swoon.

"Why? So, you can seduce me and I get you in for free? Ha! Nice try. Thanks, but no thanks." She rips her hand out of mine, "You need to leave before I call the manager."

Amused, I cross my arms over my chest and lean against the wall. "Go ahead."

She huffs out a breath and takes out her phone, tapping her foot while she waits for an answer. After the third ring a voice on the other end answers. His voice is muffled, but she tells him a customer is saying he knows the owner, is trying to get in for free and he needs to come here right away. She hangs up with a satisfied smile on her face.

"You're going to regret testing me."

I shrug. "We'll see."

A few minutes later, a familiar freckled face comes walking through the door, chest puffed out and face red. She runs into his arms and buries her face into his shoulder. He hasn't even looked at me yet, but I know he'll be sorry once he does.

"Baby, this guy," she motions towards me, lip jutting out, and clutching his shirt. "threatened me and won't leave." She nuzzles into his arms, he kisses her head and shushes her, mumbling something I can't hear. When he finally looks up, he sees me, the blood drains from his face, and the words about to leave his tongue evaporate.

Of course, this chick is dating one of the few people who actually know my identity.

He pushes her off of him. "Shit, Aster; I'm sorry. Please don't be mad at Sherry; she doesn't know any better. She's new. I got her the job, cause she loves to act, and I thought she would do great-"

I hold my hand up and step off the wall. *Her name is Sherry, and her hobby is acting?* I scoff, looping my thumbs into my belt loops. Of course it is; with her dyed red hair and stamped on freckles, she looks like she's always trying to be something she isn't. No wonder she wants to play a zombie. She wants to act like her true self: dead inside. *She's probably just using Sam to get in here free and experience what Graves truly is.* Plus, as a worker you get three free tickets to give to your family or friends as an added perk to the job.

He nudges her forward. "He knows the owner; I forgot to brief you since you missed orientation. I show all the employees a picture of Aster, letting them know he's a family friend of the owner and gets in for free. He usually only comes on Halloween, or lets me know when he's coming, and has keys, but I guess he forgot this time." He raises his eyebrow, making the last comment a subtle dig.

"She skipped orientation, and she's still working here?" I ask, annoyed one of my trusted employees is bending the rules for his plaything.

He looks away in shame. "Yeah, but I was going to brief her later. Then things happened, and I forgot. Totally on me; sorry." He elbows her in the side. "Say sorry."

She crosses her arms. "Why should I? It's *your* fault I didn't know about him, and you already apologized."

He drags his hand down his face. "Sherry, *please.*"

"Please what? I'm not doing it; I don't care if he knows the owner," she says with an attitude.

"Sherry-," he groans.

"Sherry was it?" I ask.

"You heard it several times; what are you, slow and stupid?"

"Sherry, shut the fuck up," Sam begs.

I light another cigarette, the flame illuminating my face. "You're fired."

"You can't fire me!" she bellows.

"Actually, I can; you want to know a little secret?"

She throws her hands in the air, "Do something, Sam! He can't fire me."

I give Sam a look and nod toward the door. He leaves without argument. *I'll deal with him later and fire his fling who has no respect working in my establishment.*

I walk around Sherry, my hands clasped behind my back. "Remember when I told you, if you knew the secret identity of the owner, I'd have to kill you?"

Her spine straightens, and I can see her forehead starting to sweat through her makeup. "Yeah, but you don't actually know, do you? It's just a ploy; Sam is just covering for you."

"You'll never know." she shrinks away, her body recognizing the danger before her mind does. "Now get your shit and leave. I was serious when I said you were fired."

She doesn't say anything, just stomps out the door, and slams it behind her.

Part of me really wants to kill her, but the need to slice and burn her just isn't there. I was so close to snapping her neck, but Sam knows who I am. I can't risk being questioned about her when I'm already being questioned about Tyler.

She ruined my night, and now I don't even want to watch people get scared. I was already agitated, but now I'm pissed. I punch the wall and let out a guttural roar. All the emotions I'm trying to understand are being ripped through me, as my fist punch holes in the wall. I miss Serena, but she told me to leave her alone. My fists rest above me on the wall, head hanging down, and my breathing ragged. *I really need to hear her voice.*

I walk back to my car, and my phone is ringing before I can stop myself. She probably won't answer, but I just need to make sure she's okay. Just as the phone rings the last time, I hear her sweet voice.

"Hello?" She asks, caution in her tone. *Is she nervous I'm call-ing, or does she not know it's me?* I hope it's the latter.

"I miss you."

"A-aster?" she asks hesitantly.

"My little vixen, who else would be missing you?"

"Sorry… I've just got a lot going on."

"You don't need to explain, it's okay; did you get your answers?

She's silent and, for a moment, I think she hung up, but I look at the screen and see the call is still going.

"Vixen?" I ask.

"Yes?" She sniffles.

Fuck, she's crying; they must not be the answers she was looking for.

"Everything is going to be okay, just take a couple days to process what you found out. I'll be here when you're ready."

Being ready after remembering something like that is going to take time. I don't know how long I can wait before I find out where her dad lives and drive to her. The tremor in her voice has me clutching my heart, and I just want to hold her. I know she needs her space. I know she needs this time away with her dad to cope and process, and I'm going to have to let her.

Even if it eats away at the very essence of my being.

"Thank you."

"Just… don't take too long. I don't know how much longer I can go without you." I light another cigarette. I haven't smoked in a long time, but all this stress is making me take puff after puff.

That makes her chuckle, my chest finally relaxing. "I'll be home soon."

Well, at least I know she can still laugh. "Good; talk soon?"

"Yeah."

"Good night, little vixen."

"Good night, Aster."

The line goes dead, and I drive home to my empty house, regretting not cashing in my birthday present early.

TWENTY-EIGHT
SERENA

It's been three days since I've been with my dad and my memories returned. I stayed in my room, only coming out when absolutely necessary. Sharon keeps leaving food by the door, but I can't bring myself to eat anything. I can't imagine being hungry. Not right now. Not for a while. I turned off my phone, not wanting to hear from Aster again. *I know he misses me and means well, but… I need time.*

Time is a funny thing. One minute you're a kid without a care in the world, living your best life, then you blink and you turn into a killer who forgot everything as a way to cope with what you did.

How can I accept what I've done? Last time I forgot it all, but this time, after three days, I still remember. What I did for my mom was mercy; she begged me, and I hated watching her wither away, so I granted her last wish. No matter how much it destroyed me.

Jessica on the other hand? That was revenge. Revenge for everything she made me endure. She was evil, someone who got off on making others miserable, and I was her favorite plaything. I had enough. I snapped. And I couldn't truly make myself feel sorry for what I did.

I went on her old Facebook page, and there were a couple posts, from fake people who didn't truly know her, saying they missed her and hoped she comes home safe. *Everyone thinks she ran away.* Then there's the mean messages blanketing her page, saying they hope she stays gone and pray she never comes back.

Little do they know, she never will.

The covers I'm snuggled under are keeping me warm, and the only sound is the ceiling fan going around and around.

I can't believe my dad knew what I did and didn't tell me or try to get me help. I chew on my nails, a habit I picked up recently, one I do when I'm anxious.I know we couldn't tell anyone I killed two people, but he could have done a better job helping me cope. *How did he just let me forget? Let me hate him for years?* He even disposed of Jessica's body and got rid of all the evidence. It's been five years, and we were never questioned about her disappearance. Which is weird, but I'm not looking a gift horse in the mouth.

A small knock sounds on the door, making my body curl up tighter under the covers.

"Serena?" Sharon asks on the other side. "Can I come in?"

Instead of answering, I just grunt and hope she takes that as a 'leave me alone' demand. She doesn't. Instead, she opens the door and walks over to me, sitting on the edge of the bed. She rubs my back, my body freezing at her touch. *Who does she think she is? My mom?* I move away from her touch, digging myself further into my blankets.

"Honey; it's been three days. Your father and I are worried," she whispers in the sweetest voice.

Her voice may be sweet, but I'm not ready to talk to her or anyone. I turn away from her, not wanting to even look at her, hoping she'll catch the hint and go away. "I know what you went through was traumatizing, and now reliving it feels earth shattering, but I wanted to let you know I'm here for you. When you're ready to talk." I feel the bed shift and hear the door click closed.

Finally. I squeeze my eyes shut, blocking out the chaos of my thoughts. *I'll talk when I'm ready, but it won't be to* her. Even though my dad didn't cheat on my mom, he fell for someone else too quickly after her death. *He didn't mourn her long enough.* There isn't a set time for it, but six months seems too fast especially with how long my parents were together.

They were made for one another. Their love story was my favorite, and when Mom got sick, their love never faltered, but I could see them both breaking inside.

They met when they were in college. Mom was working at the school library; her sanctuary, she claimed. She always loved reading, proclaiming it's the best escape. When she was reading, if she was really into a book, she said it played out like a movie in her head. Sometimes when she took a break from reading and would go do something else, she would think 'what was I just watching?' only for it to be a book she was reading. I didn't understand; I never found joy in reading, but after she died, I started reading her romance books. I became absorbed in the stories, like she was, and I finally understood what it meant to get lost in a book. It's a feeling like no other. A world you never want to escape. The slump and loss you feel after reading a really good book is soul sucking, but picking up the next one brings back that high feeling.

Dad was the playboy on campus. The baseball player with a different girl every week. Never settling down, never giving his heart to anyone. Until he saw Mom. He never went to the library, avoided it like the plague. Said 'books distract me from the game'. He needed to have better grades in order to play the game. Which meant he had to go get a book for class, but he couldn't fathom spending his beer money on a book. Luckily, the library had a copy. He went in and saw Mom sitting in one of the aisles eating a granola bar. She was on break, reading one of her romance novels, and when dad saw her he dropped the book he was holding, claiming 'it was love at first sight'.

They didn't get along right away. Mom knew exactly who he

was and wouldn't give him the time of day, which made Dad pursue her harder. They were a real life enemy to friends to lovers. It took a while, a lot longer than my dad was expecting, but he eventually secured her. The heart he never gave anyone, he finally gave it to my mom.

That's why I can't wrap my head around how he moved on so fast. I throw the covers off and shakily stumble into an upright position. My head is a little dizzy from lack of food and staying in bed for three days straight. I needed to talk to my dad, but first I needed food.

"That smells good; can you make me one, too?" Dad asks when he walks into the kitchen.

I dip my head, take out two more slices of bread and put together the grilled cheese. I slap another slab of butter into the pan watching and hearing it sizzle. My dad sits down at the kitchen table, and I can feel his eyes staring at the back of my head.

I turn off the burner and place our grilled cheeses on separate plates, grabbing a bag of cheddar Ruffles and the tub of cottage cheese in the fridge. Mine and Dad's favorite snack. I set every-thing down, placing my dad's plate in front of him .

"Thanks."

I don't acknowledge him. The cheese pull is so satisfying, and the crunch from the bread is exactly what I needed. Humming with delight, I do a little dance in my seat without thinking about it. I take a chip from the bag, dipping it in the cottage cheese. Dad does the same, and we smile at one another, a peace offering from me to get more information out of him. We sit in comfortable silence, enjoying our lunch.

The snack sounds gross, I know. Most people hate cottage cheese, but as a little girl wanting to eat everything her parents did, I love it. From the moment I first tried the cheddar flavor mixed with the cold curds of the cottage cheese, to when the smile spread on my dads face as my eyes lit up at the flavors, it has always been a favorite. Thinking back on the memory of how mom was disgusted by the combination and then dad chasing her around the kitchen trying to get her to try it makes this moment sitting across from him easier now. I grab a big chip from the bag and a huge dollop of cottage cheese, thinking about how Mom took her first bite and was pleasantly surprised with the taste. It became a staple snack in the Raven household from that day on.

"I'm ready to talk." I say, wiping my mouth with the sleeve of my hoodie, nervous energy surrounding us.

My dad closes the bag of chips and puts the cottage cheese back in the fridge. He's stalling, appearing to be as anxious about this conversation as I am.

"Let's talk."

"I don't understand how you could move on from Mom so fast."

His eyes widened, surprised that is what I chose to start with. "I didn't move on fast," he whispers, tracing invisible lines on the table. "I still love her. I will never stop loving her, but I love Sharon too."

"How could you still love Mom but love Sharon too?" I ask, anger lacing my tone. He isn't making any sense. *You can't love two people at once.* You stop loving one person to start loving the next. The heart isn't meant to love like that. Mom was his soulmate; Sharon is not. There is only one twin flame to each person's soul, and Mom was that for Dad.

"Serena, listen; please." Dad grabs my hands. "Your mom was my person; I will never stop loving her, and she will always be in my heart. Sharon knows that." He takes a deep breath, like he's having trouble saying his next words. "When your mom got sick, we both stayed strong for as long as we could, but when we got the news from her doctor, we had a talk that night." He starts to sniffle and looks away, squeezing my hands a little harder. "She told me she wasn't long for this world, and, in order for it to hurt less when she left, I needed to start to let her go." He lets out a pained laugh, tears collecting on his lashes. "I told her she was crazy, that there was no one else for me but her. Then she met Sharon, one of her nurses when things got really bad, and she had to stay at the hospital. She saw how kind her soul was and, even if it wasn't romantic, she wanted me to meet her." He looks at me, tears falling from his eyes. "When I met her, I was not kind, kind of how your mom was to me when we first met, but as your mom was worsening, Sharon was there for us both. We both started to love her for the person she was. Your mom…" He takes a shaky breath, his tears dripping onto the table. "She told us to be happy together after she passed. We both thought she was crazy, but after she died, we found solace in one another, and our friendship turned into love."

Now I'm crying, my tears matching my dad's. *Mom was the one who introduced them?* She pushed them to be together after she died. I can't believe my mom would do that. She loved my dad furiously, but she didn't want him to be alone and fall apart after she left us. It makes sense, and I guess Sharon put Dad back together after I ran away.

"How come I never saw her or even knew about her until after Mom died? Why would you hide that from me?"

"Mom wanted it that way; we made sure you were gone every time Sharon came over. She didn't want to confuse or hurt you with what she wanted for us."

It makes sense, but keeping it from me made me hate him, made me think he was betraying Mom and her memory. I snatch my hands from his, crossing my arms over my chest. "Why did you let me hate you?"

He smiles softly. "We do what's best for our kids, and letting you hate me, forgetting everything that happened, was what was best for you. When you have kids one day, you'll understand. You will do anything and everything to protect them."

"Sharon knows what happened?"

"Who do you think knew what to do with the body?"

I fall into my chair, mouth parted, eyes wide, and staring at my dad. *Holy fuck. Sharon was the one to help my dad get rid of the evidence? Why would she do that?* If we got caught, we would all go to jail. *She must really love my dad.* I still don't believe you can have more than one soulmate, but I'm glad Dad and Sharon found one another through mom. It's going to take me some time to get used to seeing them together, but if mom was the one who orchestrated the whole thing, then I can accept her. Especially since she was risking jail time for me.

"She did?"

Sharon walks into the room, startling me. "I did it for you, Serena, and your dad. I knew you were hurting. I heard stories from your mom about how Jessica treated you, and I don't blame you for snapping."

She stands behind my dad placing her hands on his shoulders. He squeezes her hand, resting his head back on her hip. "I know you don't know me, but I knew you through your parents. I loved you without ever meeting you; that's why I wanted to protect you." She walks over to me, a hesitant smile on her face. "May I?" She reaches her hands out, asking to hold mine. I hold my hands up for her to take. "I will never *ever* try to replace your mom. I will never be her or as amazing as she was, but I hope, one day, you will love me as I love you. I know you're not my daughter by blood, but, in my heart, you're my child. *I could never have any children of my own.* Your mom knew that, hoping we could be there for one another after she passed once you were ready. Then everything happened, and I knew your mind was playing tricks on you. I begged your father to tell you, but he was scared you'd snap again, so we decided, together, to let you hate us." She squeezes my hands tighter. "I hope now you know the truth, we can get through all of this together and form the relationship your father and I want with you. Be a real family. A new family."

I stand up, and she pulls me into her arms. Dad comes over and hugs both of us, tears shed between us.

"I'm sorry," I weep.

She runs her hand down the back of my head, the caress

welcomed this time. "Oh, sweetie, there is nothing to be sorry for. We've spent so much time being sorry for the what ifs, let's spend the rest of our time being happy."

I bob my head up and down on her chest. I look up and sniffle, "Thank you." Looking behind her at my dad, I give him a watery smile. "You, too." We stand like that, embraced in one another, as the sun starts to set.

"How did you know what to do with the body?" I ask, holding onto them both.

Sharon smiles down at me. "This isn't my first rodeo." My eyebrows shoot up, tilting my head, she laughs. "That's a story for another time."

Dad just smiles, staring at her with admiration. I look back and forth between the two, wondering what hidden secret is being shared. Dad pats and rubs my head. "I promise one day we will tell you everything."

Not wanting to unpack anything else, I eye them suspiciously, but agree.

Their secrets will be revealed all in good time.

"Can I help with anything?" I ask, rubbing the towel over the ends of my hair, now in pajamas. After three days I needed a shower. Staying stuck in that room was making me ripe. Once the hot water hit me, I felt the weight of everything lessen and wash down the drain. Sharon said she was going to make her famous baked ziti for dinner, but she used cottage cheese since none of us like ricotta. I've never had baked ziti before because it is always made with ricotta, but I can't wait to try it.

She pulls the pan from the oven, placing it on the stove. "If you can set the table, that would be great."

"I can do that." Keeping busy and being useful is actually

helping me heal. I've accepted what I did, but I haven't accepted what I am. I may be in love with a killer, but that doesn't make me one. I haven't said the L-word back to him yet, but I will when I return. I honestly can't wait to see Aster again; I'm going to pack up my things tonight and head home tomorrow. I'm starting to get withdrawals. Plus, I could use some cuddles. I snort, grabbing the dishes from the third cabinet I open. *Who am I kidding; I need a good dicking.*

I set the table, and Sharon brings the ziti over. We all gather around and load up our plates.

The moment the food hits my tongue, I'm sent to tastebud heaven, I close my eyes, letting out an appreciative moan. "Oh my God, Sharon, I'm going to need this recipe. Aster would love this."

She smirks and her eyebrows lift in success. "I'll be happy to give it to you *if* you tell me who Aster is."

Dad drops his fork and cocks an eyebrow. "Yes, Serena, do tell us who this Aster is."

I laugh. *These two are so funny.* "Aster's my boyfriend."

Sharon squeals, which startles me. "You have a boyfriend! Where did you meet? How old is he? How long have you two been seeing one another? What's his job?"

I raise my hands up, feeling overwhelmed with their reaction, but excited to talk about Aster to someone who isn't made up in my head. "Woah, woah, woah! Yes, I do. We met at a book bar. He's thirty-two. We've been seeing each other for three months, and he's an entrepreneur."

"Entrepreneur; so he doesn't have any money?" My dad scoffs. "Sounds like a winner."

Sharon smacks him, shooting him a scathing look. "As long as he treats her right, and they're happy, be nice."

Dad rubs his arm, a sheepish look crossing his face., "Sorry, I just don't want my daughter with a deadbeat."

"He isn't a deadbeat dad; he actually makes a lot of money, but I can't tell you what he does without his permission."

He points his fork in my direction. "I want to meet this Aster guy, see if he's good enough for my little girl."

"I'll talk to him; maybe on my next trip I'll bring him with me," I say as I take another bite. This really is in the top meals I've eaten; I'm absolutely adding this to my list of foods I will be making frequently. *I hope Aster likes it.*

The rest of the meal we talk about everything, how my painting is going, why Dad was so mean about my business and having to keep up a face of Mean Dad to make me hate him so I wouldn't remember. Which doesn't make sense to me, but whatever. I want to turn over a new leaf, let the past stay in the past. He said he is actually really proud of me and has bought a couple of my pieces under different names and sent them to his friends. He shows me his pieces, and I can't believe he has been secretly supporting me this whole time. *So weird.* Dad says business is booming, and Sharon says work has been going steady. She became a vet after Mom died, and couldn't be a nurse anymore. She said watching animals pass is hard, but easier than watching someone you love go. I didn't know that, which makes her even more lovable. She gets to help and see animals all day long, and she told me I could come to her clinic and hang out sometimes. Being around the animals really lowers stress levels. *I may take her up on that offer.* After Dad shows me my paintings, we all say goodnight.

"I really wish you would stay longer," Sharon says.

I give her a hug. "I know, but I need to get home and figure some things out with Aster."

She holds me at arms length, holding my arms, and searching my face. "Is everything okay?"

"Yes, it's just we both opened up to one another about some big things, then I left without warning, so we need to talk."

"Okay." She eyes me skeptically. "Promise me you'll be back soon, or we can come down there."

I give her one last hug, enjoying her embrace. "I promise." I shut the door to my room, stumbling over, and laying down in bed.

That was a lot of information to digest, but I'm glad they're giving me time to process everything. That talk was exactly what I needed, and I now have a newfound respect for them both, bandaging some, but not all wounds on my heart. It will take time to become a *real* family, but I know we will all put in the work to get to that point. I know they'll both love Aster. He is quite the charmer, and I can't wait to get back to him. I can't wait to talk about everything and grow with him. He may be a killer, but he's *my* killer, and I wouldn't have it any other way.

TWENTY-NINE

ASTER

Birthday kills always give me the best high. I feel like I'm soaring, covered in blood, watching the soul leave their eyes. There truly is nothing like it.

It wasn't my intention to cash in my birthday gift early, but my conversation with Serena had me on edge, and my hands were *itching* to get some blood on them. After I drove away, I turned the car around back to Graves; I had a feeling Sherry would still be there. My suspicion was right; as I pulled up, parking further away, I saw the dumb bitch trying to get back inside. At first I was pissed, wrapping my hands around the steering wheel at her audacity, watching as Sam opened the door. I couldn't see what was said, but I could tell they were fighting. Sam was about to join her for my birthday celebration, until she slapped him in the face, and he slammed the door shut as she stormed back to her car. *I knew I put my trust in him for a reason.*

Rain started to drizzle, and, lucky for me, she wasn't parked very far from where I waited. While she was in her purse digging around for her keys, I stepped out of my car and walked up behind her. My adrenaline racing, and hands twitching, wanting to be wrapped around her dainty little throat, sapping the breath from her lungs.

The rain started to pelt harder, my approach was drowned out. It wasn't until I was behind her, lighting a cigarette, that she saw me and spun around yelping.

"Hey," I say, blowing smoke into her face. She coughs and waves the smoke away.

She squints, unable to tell who is in front of her because of the downpour. She fumbles for her phone, turning on the flashlight. "What do you- Wait, you're the asshole who got me fired!" Turning around she opens her door, visibly shaking. *From the rain or from me?*

My hand shoves it closed. "Yeah, sorry about that." I say in a charismatic voice, leaning down, I push her back against the car. "I decided I wanted to celebrate my birthday early and thought you might want to join."

"Fuck off," she growls and her eyes harden, and reaching for the door handle once again. *Got to give it to her; she seems fearless.* A sadistic smile threatens to wrap my face. *I can't wait to bring that fear out of her eyes later.*

"That depends; are you fucking off with me?" I ask, giving her my signature panty wetting smirk.

She smiles right back. "You know, you're kind of cute for an asshole." She jabs her finger in my chest, her pupils dilating as she meets my gaze through her lashes. "I'll celebrate your birthday with you on one condition."

Here we go. I just know she's going to ask for her job back. I'll give it to her willingly. She'll be ecstatic, but she doesn't know she won't have a life after tonight. People will look for her, no doubt. Signs will go up. Posts will be made, but eventually, she will fade away along with her memory.

Grabbing her hand, I move it away from me. "Yeah, and what's that?"

She steps into me, her french whore house perfume invading

my senses. "You give me my job back; since you have so much power, it shouldn't be hard for you."

I grab her hand, making her drop her purse, her phone, and keys still in it, and pull her to my car.

"Hey! You didn't answer my question! Do we have a deal or not?" she whines, trying to plant her feet.

"Deal." I open the passenger side, looking around ensuring no one is in sight. Then go to my side and quickly shut the door.

She tries to get out, her handle jammed. "I dropped my phone; I'll be right back." Grabbing her hand, I pull her back, shutting the door and locking it. "That's not funny, asshole; let me out. Right now. I changed my mind; I don't want to celebrate with you anymore." I stare at her, the beast rising to the surface. "Seriously! Let me the fuck out!" she screams. She turns around and starts banging on the window. "Help! Someone, help me!" No one can hear her over the screams coming from the haunted house. Her screams melding with theirs, making a beautiful melody of fear. I take her distraction as my chance to reach in the glove box and grab the syringe already filled with ketamine. Her banging becomes louder as she finally realizes the trap she's snared in. "Please! He's crazy. Help me!" I stab the needle in her neck and release the liquid. She grabs her neck, looks at me wide eyed, and passes out. I place her seat belt around her and drive us back, excited to cash in my gift.

I've waited three years to cash in my birthday kill, although not intentional, and not on my birthday, I'm thrilled to get blood on my hand one more time before my vixen returns. I was hoping this year I could celebrate my birthday with my little vixen, especially after learning she truly is like me, but there is always next year. I have a feeling she will enjoy taking lives just as much as me. Her darkness matches mine, after all.

"Where am I?"

I turn around, already dressed in my work uniform, not even bothering to put on gloves since her body will be burned. She's strapped to the metal table, without a gag, because what fun would that be? I want to hear her screams. I want to revel in them. The only light I have on is the one above her, preventing her from seeing who is hovering over her. She looks around, trying to lift her arms and break free.

"What the fuck? Okay, asshole, this isn't funny anymore."

A Cheshire smile lifts my cheeks. "Actually, it is," she gasps, her body tense, as she squints where my voice traveled from. I walk into the light, so she can see exactly who her captor is. "Hello, Sherry."

Her face turns red, her eyebrows pinching down as her body freezes. "You?" she seethes, "Untie me right now, or so help me God."

I click my tongue, my frustration becoming evident. "God, or any deity for that matter, won't be helping you." She starts squirming even more, looking for a way out of her binds. She'll soon find when I want someone bound, they stay trapped until they're no longer of this earth.

Fear starts to enter her voice when she realizes she can't get out. "Why are you doing this?"

I groan, a shiver tracking down my spine. My favorite part. The *why*. The reason they're on my table; telling her is going to be a sweet, *sweet* treat.

Walking around behind her, I take a piece of her hair, lifting it, examining it, then dropping it like the nothing she is. "Remember our conversation from earlier? The one at Graves?"

"You mean when you fired me?!" She scoffs. "How could I forget?"

"Before that; think back, Sherry, it's very important. About the owner; what did I say?"

Her eyes crinkle as she remembers our conversation. Her eyes squint, jumping around, trying to remember exactly what I said. "You wanted to celebrate your birthday early, and that's why I'm here? Listen, I love to be tied up as much as the next girl, but ever hear of consent? Fucking asshole."

This bitch is dumber than a box of rocks. Granted, I did have to flirt to get her to come to my car. I hated having to do that. I felt guilty. A feeling I wasn't used to, a pang pounding in my chest because all I could think about was what Serena would think. It isn't just me anymore, it's my vixen too, but it's in my nature, and Sherry needed to be punished for her blatant disrespect.

"No. Think harder. Before we went into the house."

Her head turns away from me and her hand twitches, like if she could, she would bring it up to her lips to think harder. "You said if I knew the owner, then you'd have to…" she gulps "kill me."

I clap my hands together making her jump as much as one can when they're tied down.

"Ding, ding, ding! We have ourselves a winner; guess you aren't as dumb as you look."

Her voice trembles, her eyes unable to meet mine. "But… but you didn't tell me who the owner was." Hope reignited her voice. Hearing that spark is going to make it all the more delicious when her fate comes crashing down.

I place my hands behind my back. "You're right; I didn't. Shall I tell you?" Glee registering in my tone.

"N-no," she stutters, "I'm good."

I throw my hands to my side, a manic grin slashing my face. "Pity. I thought you wanted to celebrate my birthday with me early," I pout. "You are, after all, my present." Sherry's body freezes, her eyes snapping to meet mine, only to find the devil staring back at her.

She masks her emotions, putting back on that brave face. "Nope; totally good. Now untie me, and we can pretend none of this ever happened."

Funny, she thinks she's leaving here alive and believes I'm stupid enough to trust she wouldn't tell a soul.

My face hardens, my voice severe. "I'm the owner of Graves, and you, Sherry, made a big mistake crossing me when I was itching for a new victim."

The hope starting to burn through her snuffs out in an instant, and she starts to cry. I close my eyes, soaking in the fear being released with her tears. *She was alot weaker than I thought;* she put on a 'fuck off, I'm a badass bitch' vibe, but underneath her carefully crafted exterior was just a weak little girl.

Pity, I wanted to break her.

"Please, please," she begs, sobbing, snot starting to leak from her nose. "I'm sorry, okay! I shouldn't have been such a bitch. I know I was, and I'm sorry. Please, *please* don't kill me."

I turn around and open the drawer filled with my collection of knives. I select the one I use specifically for my birthday victims. A twelve inch, curved cimeter knife. *Perfect for carving.*

"Beg all you want." I turn around, holding up the knife and looking at her reflection in it. "But I'm still cashing in my gift early." I pin her arm down with one hand so she can't wiggle while I cut. When they wiggle, my slices aren't as clean as I want them to be. "You see-" the blade rests just above her skin, her eyes bugged out as whimpers fill the air. "Every year, on my birthday, I do something a little different with my victims."

"Victims?" She trembles, sweat starting to trickle down her face, her eyes never leaving the blade resting on her arm.

"Oh, how rude of me. I never introduced myself. You heard my name at Graves, but you don't know who I am." I bring the knife up, and I can see a little breath of relief escape her lips. Bringing it to my chest, I take a little bow. "I'm the Morbid Monet. Salem's most notorious serial killer." The panic in her eyes returns, and she starts sobbing. I pin her arm in place and bring the blade down as I start slicing. Her screams get louder. I groan, thinking of my vixen as I bathe in my victim's blood.

Music to my ears.

Her skin cuts like butter, hypnotized by how easily her skin opens for me, I trace her blood with my finger, painting a rose, leaving my mark, in a different way. Just for me. I make sure all my knives are sharp as my birthday nears. It's the only time I carve. I think of it as carving a pumpkin, but instead of seeds falling out, it's blood and guts.

As I slice and carve through her skin, walking over to the other side to slice more, her screams become louder. *I wonder what my vixen is up to.* Now she knows who I am, I can't help but wonder if she is going to accept it, and join me, or try to make me change. I swipe my forehead with the back of my hand, wiping the sweat away and leaving a splatter of blood. Cutting up a living human is strenuous work. You're hunched over, having to pin them down, enjoying them begging for mercy. It's hard, but the reward is worth it.

My vixen shares the same darkness as me. She has taken a life as well. She may not know how to cope with her truth, but one way or the other, I'm going to get her to accept who she is. A monster just like me, darkness consuming us, wrapped up in one another forever.

The screaming starts to die down, and I smell something foul. I stop cutting, looking up to see Sherry passed out, looking down, I see she shit herself. *Disgusting.* Don't get me wrong, it has happened before, but not as much as you'd think, and only with my little lambs.

How dare she pass out when I was enjoying myself? I grip the knife, my molars feeling like they could crack, the anger rolling off me in waves. My favorite part is the screams. I grip her leg, leaving bruises behind, and start carving her leg. Still, she doesn't wake. I throw my knife into the sink, stalking over to pick a new one. *Usually, my birthday presents stay awake while I cut.* She's the first to ever faint *and* shit herself. Grabbing the meat cleaver, I walk back to my ruined gift. Raising the blade above my head, I bring it down. *Still asleep.* I bring it back up, then down once more, and her leg completely separates, blood squirting out. She jolts awake. *Finally,* her body trying to come to as she lets out a banshee wail. I smile. *That is what I was looking for.*

Bringing the cleaver up, I do the same to her arm, watching the lower half of her arm separate. Blood squirts onto my face, and I bask in the feeling of her life force covering me. Her eyelids start to flutter, and before she can pass, I lift the cleaver one more time and bring it down across her stomach. She splits open easily, her organs falling out slowly like hot ramen spilling out of the bowl.

Dead. She is dead. It didn't last as long as I wanted, but I still enjoyed it. I cut up the rest of her body, her eyes still open and lifeless. I don't bother closing them, leaving them open makes me feel like she's watching me cut her to pieces. After ruining the night I had planned, she deserves to watch me dismember her from the afterlife.

Once all the pieces are small enough to fit in the incinerator, I take them one by one and throw them in. Shutting the door, I turn it on, singing happy birthday and watch the fire destroy her. My anger from a quick celebration dissipates as the flames lick her skin. Watching the fire burn, her body turning to ash, I feel she is truly gone from this plane, even her spirit. Nothing is left of the pathetic excuse of oxygen.

I have a feeling no one will miss her.

THIRTY
SERENA

After waking up the next morning and seeing what I saw in my dream, I now know what it means. I hugged and kissed my dad and Sharon goodbye, with promises of seeing them soon and got on the road. I threw on a concert hoodie over my pajamas to keep warm. I was heading straight to Aster's house for answers, why did he kill again? Who did he kill, they never have faces, his victims in my dreams, but this time his face is as clear as day.

The sun is just rising; it's early, but I was so anxious I couldn't wait any longer. I had to wake Dad up. The only reason I didn't leave in the middle of the night was because I didn't need them asking questions I couldn't give the answer to. They might be cool with me killing people, but I highly doubt they'd welcome my serial killer boyfriend with open arms.

Rolling down the window and turning up the radio, I rub my eyes and let out a big yawn. Although I need answers, and I know Aster is going to want the same, I need coffee. Our heavy conversation can wait until *after* I'm caffeinated.

The sky smells of rainwater since it rained last night. It's fresh and comforting. When I watched the drops fall from the window last night, I looked at it as if all my sins were washing away. Every awful thing I did, the lives I stole, gone, but not forgotten this time.I didn't want to go back to believing the one person who made my life a living hell was the only one I could rely on. It's much better to know she's burning there eternally. I smile at that thought, a peaceful calm settling over me.

Honestly, the reason I think I didn't forget is because of Aster. Since meeting him, he has awakened things in me I never want to put to sleep again. I felt a darkness growing inside me since he entered my life, a part of me realizing the dreams I had were memories. The pain he inflicted was pure ecstasy, and now I know everything I've been dreaming about is all true.

The truth isn't as scary as I thought it would be. At first, I was devastated, confused, and angry. For forgetting, mostly, but after I let those emotions process, I felt peace. A sense of serenity washed over me knowing the truth.

Once I get into Salem, I head straight to my favorite coffee shop, Sinister Beans. They are known for their horror themed coffees and milkshakes. They opened their location here a couple years ago and, being a town like Salem, the spooky Halloween place it is known to be, everyone flocked to them. I, too, was a part of the horde of people who waited outside the long line to try their themed drinks. The first, and my favorite, was their Pennywise drink for obvious reasons. It is made with two shots of espresso, white chocolate raspberry, topped with whipped cream, raspberry sauce drizzle, and a red balloon. The cup itself is a thirty two ounce glass, with Pennywise's face on it, *and* they spin it in the raspberry sauce at the top so it looks like blood is dripping down the sides. It's twenty-five dollars a drink, but you get to keep the cup and the balloon. I say that is a great deal, since their opening I have ordered every single theme iced coffee, and the best part is they always come up with more ideas and cup designs. My cupboard at home is full, and I still can't get enough.

Walking in, I'm hit with the smell of coffee beans and sweetness. I stop in the doorway taking in all the sounds and smells.

You can hear the can of whip cream being sprayed, and it is music to my ears. "Zombified" by Falling In Reverse is playing over the speakers, and I can't help but smile at the irony of this song playing after everything I just found out.

There's a new sign posted showing they have new drinks and horror characters I can't wait to try. The line is longer than usual, especially this early. I take out my phone and see they posted on their Instagram about their new drinks. *This is why it's so busy; everyone wants to try it before they're sold out.* While they do sell out, and pretty quickly I might add, they always restock, it just takes longer than one would expect. Everything from the cups to the whip cream, and even the ice cream, are all made in house, which is another reason I love coming here. Can't beat anything homemade, none of that processed shit.

"Serena! How are you?" Lena, one of the owners' daughters, greets me. I'm a regular here, and I've come to know the family pretty well.

"I'm good, Lena! How are you?" I ask, staring at the wall of the new drinks behind her.

She laughs, the crinkle in her brown eyes lighting them up. "I see you're here for a new drink; what will it be today?"

"Actually, I didn't even know about the new drinks. I was headed back home from my dad's." Her face falls, she knows all about my relationship with my father. While I don't consider us friends, coming here can be like going to a bar where the baristas become your counselor while you drink if they're not busy. With how often I've come here, they got to know my story pretty well, and I theirs. Lena is happily married to her husband, Jessie, for four years, and they have two beautiful boys and one little girl. She runs the coffee shop and is the brains behind the operation, making the designs for the cups.

"Things are better. I went up, and we had a long talk. Everything that happened between us is forgiven, but not forgotten, and I even got closer to his fiancé." Her face softens, but apprehension is still there. "I promise; I'll tell you about it another day, but things are better, and I'm happy."

She grabs my hands. "I believe you, but just be careful. From what you've told me, I worry."

I squeeze her hands back. Taking my hands away, I point to the Texas Massacre drink. "I would love to try that one."

She turns around, her strawberry blonde curls bouncing when she does, and says, "Oh! The Texas Chainsaw Massacre; that is one of my new favorites, and you're going to love the design." I smile, already knowing it's going to be a hit. "Hey, Theresa!" she yells at her sister. "Can you take over the front real quick?"

Her sister walks over, an annoyed look on her face. "Why? I thought I was on coffee duty today?" Theresa is younger than us, still in college, but spends her weekends here to earn extra cash and help the family. She has the same curls as her sister, but her hair is more orange than blonde. She looks like a true ginger with the freckles to match.

Lena touches her shoulder, an exasperated smile on her face. "You are, but I wanted to make Serena's drink."

She looks over and, for the first time, notices me. "Oh, Serena! I didn't recognize you; you look different."

I cock my head to the side, a small blush creeping up my neck. "Different good or different bad?"

She laughs, making the freckles on her cheeks look like they're bouncing as well. "You look like you're glowing." My brow furrows, not understanding what she means. "I don't know, just… happier, I guess. You used to look happy, but it never reached your eyes. I know why, but now it shows." She stares into my eyes, which makes me shiver. *I don't like it when people stare that hard at me.* She shakes her head and looks at her sister, pink staining her cheeks. "Anyway; Lena, I'll take over. It was nice to see you, Serena."

"Nice to see you, Theresa." I walk over to watch Lena make

my drink. An extra boost of confidence knowing that my truth has made me glow. A new love shining through my eyes,

"No, no, no; you go sit down. I want this to be a surprise when I bring it over."

I put my hands up, and a chuckle escapes me. "Okay, okay; I'm going."

As I sit and wait in my favorite spot by the window I stare at the passersby, the cars coming and going, listening to the bell chime every time someone leaves or enters the shop. The Massacre drink sounded interesting, combining some of my favorite flavors with toffee, mocha, two shots of espresso, and cinnamon.

Lena places the coffee down in front of me, the biggest smile on her face. "Ta-da! What do you think? And be honest."

The cup is Leatherface holding a chainsaw coming out of the Texas state symbol, making it look like he's coming right for you. The top is rolled in a red sauce, their signature blood dripping down the sides. It's finished off with whip cream sprinkled in cinnamon and more red sauce, giving it a dirty, bloody look, and a mini chainsaw also dripping in the dark red sauce. Where she got the mini chainsaw, I don't know, but I love it. I take a picture and quickly add it to my Instagram story, tagging the shop as I always do.

She watches, eagerly waiting for me to try it. I take a sip and instantly am hit with an array of flavors, being sent to coffee heaven. I can taste the mocha and toffee, but there is something else I don't recognize immediately. I lick the whip cream, my tastebuds singing, knowing exactly what the mystery red sauce is. "Is that caramel?"

She nods her head enthusiastically. "It is! I added red food coloring to give it a bloodier look; that's what's dripping down the sides too."

"You're a magician when it comes to flavor," I say, taking another bite of whip cream and washing it down with some coffee. The flavors mesh perfectly together, you would never guess caramel was the red sauce. "How did you come up with caramel instead of your usual red flavors?"

"Well, I did try raspberry, cherry, even the white mocha dyed red, and none tasted right. The fruit flavors mixed with the toffee made it taste like medicine, and the white mocha was too sweet with the other flavors, throwing everything off balance. I wracked my brain for days, and finally Jessie gave me the idea to do caramel."

"Jessie?" I ask, lifting one eyebrow.

She laughs. "Yes, Jessie; at first I thought it would be too thick and the color wouldn't work, but after a couple tries, I got the right consistency and voila!" She gestures to the cup, a huge smile on her face. "The Texas Massacre."

"I love it, especially the design. It's very creative; can't wait to come back and try the others."

"Lena, a little help please!" Theresa hollers.

Jumping when her name is called, Lena looks behind her and sees the line has grown nearly out the door.

"Shit; sorry, Serena. Duty calls." She rushes back behind the counter, and I go back to enjoying my drink. I take out my phone and open my reading app, eager to catch up on the book I was reading while I finish my drink.

Three taps hit the table, taking me out of the world I had disappeared to in my head. "Hey, Serena."

I look up, not recognizing the face in front of me, annoyed that someone is bothering me. *Who is this guy? Why is he interrupting me and how does he know my name?*

He places his hand on his chest. "We met at the flea market. I asked you out, but your boyfriend interrupted." He places his hand on the back of the chair, eyes darting around, fingers tapping, nervous energy radiating off of him. "Can I sit here?"

Oh yeah, Bradley. He was very touchy and didn't understand personal space. *I'm surprised he's asking to sit instead of just doing it.* I nod my head, and he takes the seat across from me.

"Funny running into you here. I didn't know you liked this shop." He chuckles nervously.

The way he won't look at me, and keeps tapping his fingers incessantly, tells me he's lying. *Why is he so nervous? Does he think Aster is here? Should I lie and tell him he's in the bathroom so he'll leave me alone?*

"Actually, that was a lie. I saw on your Instagram; I knew you were here."

My eyes narrow, anger and suspicion darkening my face. *Is he fucking stalking me?*

He holds his hands up defensively. "I'm not stalking you. Shit. Well, *I am*, but I needed to talk to you, and I had no idea when you'd do another showing at the market."

Oh, fuck this. I already have a serial killer in my life; I don't need a stalker, too. Granted, Aster is probably a stalker, but I love him. I don't even know this guy. I stand, but he grabs my hand, stopping me.

"Please hear me out," he begs, "It's about Tyler."

Tyler? The guy Aster killed? How does he know him, and why does he want to talk about him with me? His words have me freezing, turning around to look at him, and I examine his face this time. *Fuck.*

"He's my brother. Meeting you at the market wasn't an accident. I knew you'd be there, and I just wanted to know what happened to him. Or if you knew anything" He lets go of my arm after I sit back down, hanging his head and looking absolutely defeated. "I know Tyler went on a date with you the night he went missing. I told the cops. They showed me the footage of your boyfriend pushing him down, and, after meeting him myself, I have a feeling he has something to do with his disappearance."

My leg starts to shake, and I sip my drink watching him, listening to him. *He thinks Aster did something.* My leg stills. *He can't find out.* He led the police to me and Aster, and he found my

Instagram to find me and confront me. As much as I want to be mad, I can't. It's his family, and he just wants answers.

Answers he will never get.

"He texted me that night about what happened, saying he was going to his ex's house for comfort." He adds quotations and an eye roll at comfort.

"Okay, so he went and saw his ex, then she was the last person to see him, not me or my boyfriend." Since his ex was the last person to see him, the police probably questioned her as well. I can turn this around and get Aster out of this mess, making everyone think the crazy ex did it.

He tries to grab my hands, but I cradle my glass with both hands, restricting him from touching me. He clears his throat, and looks away. "Yes, but she would never hurt him. She loves him; she *always* comforts him."

I lean back and shrug my shoulders. "Sounds like she got jealous and reacted without thinking. You can do things you don't mean or remember."

His fist slam on the table, startling me. "You're not listening to me!"

Lena rushes over, concern and anger on her face. "Sir, I need to ask you to leave; you can't act like that here," she says in a stern voice.

He brushes her off, leveling his eyes with mine. "I know your boyfriend did something to him. Call it a brother's intuition or a sixth sense, but I'm going to find out. When I do, you'll be sorry."

"Sir!" Lena demands, "If you don't leave, I will call the police."

He stands up, eyes never leaving mine. "I'm going." He walks to the door and stops, refusing to look over his shoulder. "Mark my words, Serena, I will find out the truth."

A breath I didn't even realize I was holding breaks free when the door shuts behind him, and Lena wraps her arms around me. "Are you okay? What was that all about?"

"Nothing; I'm fine, I-" I start to panic, grabbing my phone and drink, as I get up. "I have to go."

I leave Lena standing there confused and worried. I feel bad, but I need to protect Aster. He's the most important person to me, and I won't let anyone ruin what we have.

I rush after Bradley, determination in my steps. "Bradley, wait!" I yell.

He stops and turns around, "What?" he snaps.

How did he get so far? After all that running, I'm out of breath, and I place my hands on my knees as I gasp. "I believe you."

His hardened face softens. "You do?"

"Yes, but we have to talk in private. Aster has eyes everywhere, and if he knows we're talking, he might hurt you." I lie, knowing full well Aster won't be the one hurting him.

"Okay, where should we talk?"

I look around, checking for cameras. *Can't leave any evidence, Can't let anyone know I was the last to see him.*

"I need you to go to a couple stores and talk to people." He eyes me suspiciously. I hold my hand up, glancing over my shoulder like I'm scared. "It's so Aster can't track you; he could be on his way at this very moment." His back straightens and he glances nervously around. "After an hour, once you're sure no one is watching or following you, meet me in the alley behind Louie's bookstore. You know where that is?" He nods, fear clouding his eyes. "Good. Don't tell a soul where you're going. He probably already has your phone bugged, so leave it in a store bathroom and I'll do the same with mine."

He gives me a hug and, to keep up the act, I hug him back, making sure everyone in the coffee shop and surrounding stores sees there is no bad blood. Can't have anyone assuming I had anything to do with his disappearance when the cops come asking questions later. "Thank you, Serena," he whispers in my ear, making me shiver, causing bile to crawl up my throat.

I pull apart. "Now go. Remember to ditch your phone and meet me in an hour; we will get justice for Tyler." He smiles and leaves. I watch him until he wanders into a store, hoping he listens to what I say and doesn't tell anyone; *if he does my plan would be ruined, and I'll be the cause of Aster's demise.* I won't let that happen.

THE SUN WE WERE PROMISED TODAY HAS TURNED OVERCAST. IT looks like a storm is headed our way, and if that is a premonition for how this is all about to go, I may change my plans. *What am I doing? I have no idea how to kill someone and actually get away with it.* Every cleanup has been done by someone else. Bradley needs to disappear, but I need help.

I text Aster what's happening. Right when my phone vibrates, I hear running. I don't bother reading his response, hoping he understood my coded message.

An out of breath Bradley comes running up to me. "Were you followed?" I ask, looking behind him nervously. The nerves I'm feeling are real, but not for the reason he thinks.

He shakes his head. "Where's your phone?" I ask.

"Left it back in a Target bathroom, hidden; I'll go back for it later."

"Good, Get in." He walks to the passenger side and gets in without hesitation.

I turn the car on, hesitating with my foot still on the brake. "Lean all the way down and cover your face; we can't have anyone see you with me. Stay covered until I say otherwise."

He quickly does what I say, putting on his hoodie and sliding on the sunglasses I hand him. If any cameras catch a glance of him on the way to Aster's they wouldn't be able to identify him. *I hope.* I start the drive to his house. I turn on the music to avoid conversation and take Bradley to get the answers he's craving.

Too bad it'll be at the expense of his life.

THIRTY-ONE

ASTER

Getting a text from Serena was unexpected, but what she said made my hair stand up.

SERENA

> On the way to your house with a surprise. It's my version of lamb. Meet me at your workplace. Can't wait to see you!

She's finally coming home, and I can't wait to see her. She knows my victims are little lambs. She said it's *her version*. I leave everything at the house, door unlocked, place on some boots, and run to the shed. I don't know how far she is from the house, so I don't have much time to prepare everything. The sky is over-cast, and it looks like a storm is coming. The weather is causing my stomach to knot; a premonition for what's to come.

ASTER

> Excited to see you, I can't wait for my surprise. I'll be ready.

I burst into my workshop and start to get the room ready. I lay new plastic down, and get my work clothes on, taking off my regular boots and replacing them with my rubber work boots.

The only thing I can think of is she needs me to kill someone. *But who?*

I will gladly take every life she asks me to, but I can't figure out who she's bringing me. I grab a needle and fill it with ketamine in case she doesn't knock out my newest victim.

Dirt on the road starts to crunch and my phone dings, alerting me Serena has arrived. Everytime an unwilling soul has been brought into my slaughterhouse, it has been on my terms. Nothing has ever gone wrong. The steps I take make sure I never get caught. Serena has never done this. *Will her taking this person be the reason for my demise?* I take a deep, calming breath, shaking away the nerves before walking out and seeing only her beautiful face, nervous and glancing toward her passenger seat. *The person in the car must be laying down.* I walk over and open the door, making the guy jump. He freaks out, trying to unbuckle his seatbelt, but before he can, I stab his neck and inject the drug, making him slump backward.

I unbuckle him, and I drag his body out of the car into my shed. Serena grabs his feet, helping me lug his body onto the table. I hold him up, take off his shirt, then lay him back down. Strapping him down, I take off his sunglasses, instantly recognizing him as the guy from the flea market.

I've been wanting to get my hands on this loser ever since he asked my girl out but had no information on him. To have my vixen bring him to me... a wicked smile spreads across my face. *This really is a gift.*

Serena paces back and forth, biting her nails. "I didn't know what else to do. He's Tyler's brother, and he is hellbent on the idea that you killed Tyler."

No wonder he wanted to go on a date with Serena.

"He said he knew who I was before the market, and he found me to find out what happened to his brother." She's rambling and messing with her hair, showing how nervous and anxious she is. *I hate seeing her like this.* I hate even more that this loser stalked my woman. Killing him is going to be his penance for that.

I grab Serena by both shoulders, halting her pacing and making her look at me. "You did the right thing coming here; it's okay." I walk over to my newest victim and search his hoodie and pants to check for a phone.

"What are you doing?" Serena asks, coming to stand behind me.

"Making sure he doesn't have a phone on him."

"Oh, I made sure he left it in the store. I told him you had eyes everywhere and we needed to be careful."

My naughty little vixen, I haven't even taught her anything, but she knew to make sure he couldn't be tracked.

"You did good," I whisper and kiss her forehead. "Now go wait in the car. You don't want to see what I'm going to do to him."

"Actually," she fidgets with her hands, looking down at her feet. "I was wondering if I could help?"

My eyes bug out of my head. *Was not expecting that.* "I don't know-"

"Before you make a decision, while we wait for him to wake up, I need to tell you what I found out."

Listening to Serena speak about what she's done, I was expecting tears, but none fell. *I can't believe she was the one to end her mom's life, and then forgot about it.* That trauma stays with you forever, but my vixen has never been like anyone else. I'm impressed she murdered two souls, but also worried she forgot all of that happened. *What if she forgets again?* What both her mom and dad told her, it was a mercy kill. She was miserable and in pain; she couldn't wait any longer. I would have done the same thing for my mother had she asked.

Now Jessica, the way Serena killed her and the things she said to her. I'm proud of her younger self for finally ridding the world of the leech she was. Her methods of torture are a lot more… creative, than mine. I stare at her bewildered with who *my* woman is, smiling as she tells me her past. That darkness inside her has been locked up for so long, and it's finally begging to be freed. We met, we've been connected for so long, because I'm supposed to unleash her beast. I'm supposed to train her. Hone her. Mold her.

She said she started to remember when we met, that she had dreams she didn't realize were memories, but every time she tried to dig deeper, she would get an intense pain. I can't even imagine the agony she went through to finally understand everything from her past. My face softens to one of concern, when she tells me that. She said she blacked out from all the pain, and when she woke up all of her memories returned.

Once she finished telling me everything, the reason for her animosity towards her dad and his new bride to be made more sense. I'm glad their relationship is slowly mending; a girl needs her dad.

Weird that her parents had an open relationship, I can only ever see myself being with one person, and that is this feisty girl in her pajamas standing before me. I never thought my heart would beat again, but it started beating for my little vixen, and belongs to her until, and after our dying breaths. Looking her up and down, makes me chuckle with how cute she is. Her tiny stature in red tie-dye shorts and a matching spaghetti strap tank top with two skeleton hands holding up the rockstar sign. *When did she take off her hoodie?* I look around the room and see it's discarded by the door. It is a little warm here, especially since I turned on the incinerator. She must have taken it off, and put her hair up in a messy bun with loose strands falling into her face, when I was strapping our newest victim down.

Distracted by that one piece of hair, I tuck it behind her ear, and she stops talking, eyes locking with mine, her breath frozen. It is just us in this moment, two souls finding and understanding one another. *God, she is beautiful.*

"You're just as fucked as your boyfriend," the man on the table coughs.

Serena yelps, and I turn around to glare down at him. "You're going to regret saying that to my vixen; speaking to her like that is signing your own death sentence."

"Fuck you both," he spits.

I turn back to Serena as she eyes us curiously. I place a hand on her shoulder, gauging her attention. "Are you sure you want to do this?" I stare hard into her eyes, trying to see any sense of hesitation.

She looks to our victim, then back at me, and bobs her head, determination in her eyes swirling like the dangerous sea. "Okay, but before we begin, you need to change."

I walk us over to the closet full of my work clothes and help her into the coveralls. Seeing her standing there, dressed the same as me, makes my cock twitch. *Not now.*

She opens the drawers, curiously picking up and setting down the tools she doesn't want to use. I've never killed with anyone before, so this is not only new for her, but for me. Mom and Dad were partners in crime, maybe I finally found mine.

"You're a lying bitch-"

Smack

"Don't call me a bitch, Bradley, or I'll never tell you what happened to your brother." She turns back around, still trying to find her weapon of choice. If Serena didn't slap him when he insulted her, I was going to punch him. *But my vixen can take care of herself it seems.* I lean on the door and watch as she wanders around the shed, looking for something that calls to her. Bradley is acting tough, but I know he's scared. I can see the sweat drip from his forehead. *Pathetic. Just like his brother.*

"Do you want to know what happened to Tyler?"

Bradley's head snaps in my direction, and I push off the wall. "He insulted my girl, so I followed him after I had my dessert." I look up to see Serena holding a hammer, her eyes meeting mine. She's wide eyed and blushing, and I smirk at her. She shakes her head and turns around to resume her search. "I drugged him, took him back here, laid him on this very table-" I tap it while walking around him "-Then I tortured and killed him for looking and *touching* what is *mine*." I tug on his restraints. "You? You are getting worse. See, my little vixen wants to play, and being the generous man I am, I'm going to let her."

"You're both sick; you're not going to get away with this!" He seethes.

I walk over to Serena, who is watching our interaction, placing my arms around her waist and laying my head on her shoulder. "We already did. Sure, they'll look for you for a while, but no body, no crime. You'll fade into ash, just like Tyler" I turn to look at the incinerator, flames burning bright.

"You're going to burn me alive?" he stutters, his body flexing against the table.

I kiss Serena's neck, "No, I'm not doing anything. Serena is going to decide your fate, and I promise it will be worse than death."

She smiles wickedly, leaving my arms, making me miss her touch already. "Bradley, you thought Aster was who you should be afraid of, but haven't you been told you should never trust a pretty face."

She turns around and whispers in my ear. A sinister smile spreads across my face, and I go get what my vixen asked for. I return with the chainsaw in my hand, her eyes lighting up like a kid on Christmas getting exactly what they asked for from Santa; it's cute.

She takes it gleefully, lovingly tracing her hand over the chain.

"Looks like she's chosen her weapon of choice."

"Please! Please, don't do this. I'm sorry; okay? I'm sorry I insulted you. I'll stop looking for my brother. I can even get the cops off of you and point them to his ex. *Please!*" he cries, "don't kill me."

Serena ignores his pleas, and starts talking, "You know, I didn't know how I wanted to kill you. Everything I picked up just didn't feel right. Then I thought back to how you ambushed me at the coffee shop, and it clicked. The drink I ordered had a chainsaw with it, and what better way to make you bleed than with one?"

Damn; the things this girl says turns me on so much. I reach down, adjusting myself. She sees from the corner of her eye and smiles.

I walk over while she's talking to Bradley and grab some goggles for both of us. *Things are about to get messy.* She pulls the starter cord, after a couple tugs, it pulses to life. I place the goggles over her eyes as she brings the chainsaw down, letting it hover over his dick. Bradley squeezes his eyes shut, waiting for a cut that hasn't come.

"You know," she hums, bringing it back up, "I wonder what is going to be louder; the chainsaw or your screams? Shall we find out?" With no warning she brings it down on his leg, cutting just below his knee. Blood shoots out with every inch she cuts, spraying us both. The screams ripped from his throat are much louder than the chainsaw, which makes Serena stop once again, her head tilts and a wide smile lifts her cheeks. "I guess it was your screams." I stay in the shadows behind her, watching her, with a raging hard on, shifting occasionally to readjust.

She cuts the next leg off and he passes out, probably from the pain, being unable to endure it. She turns off the chainsaw and places it down, turning a pouty face towards me. "Is he already dead? I was just beginning my fun." Her bottom lip pokes out, and I seize it between my teeth. Her mouth parts eagerly and I let out a guttural moan, pulling her flush against me.

I force us apart, breathing heavily. *Can't get too excited when there is still work to be done.* Her chest heaves, and her eyes are glassed over. I swipe the blood from her lips, smearing it across her chin. "He's still alive, for now. I can wake him back up, but you won't have long until he dies from blood loss."

She nods her head eagerly and retrieves two hooks from the drawer. I lift my brow in a question. She shrugs her shoulders. "Just sticking with the theme." I laugh, shaking my head.

She might be more twisted than me.

Grabbing a bucket to fill with water, I throw it over Bradley's face. He wakes up in a coughing fit, and Serena leans over him, hooks raised in her hands. His eyes widen, and he starts pleading again, barely above a whisper.

"Have you ever seen the movie *Texas Chainsaw Massacre*?" she asks, turning and looking at the hooks.

He slowly nods, his eyes glued to her hands.

"Do you know what Leatherface does with these?" He gulps. "I can't very well do the same thing; there's nowhere to hang you from, so I have to get creative." She scrapes one hook across the table, a piercing, screeching sound echoing around the room. He flinches from the noise, leaning away from her as much as he's able.

She bangs both hooks on either side of his head, making his body shake, hovering above him. She's in her element. She may have forgotten who she truly is, and I thought I would have to help navigate her back, but it's like riding a bike. Once you willingly take one life, the next is as easy as breathing. Sweeter. Watching the life leave their eyes is euphoric. That is where Serena is right now. *I don't think she remembers I'm in the room with her.* The way she's lost in torturing him is how she is when she paints. Completely absorbed in her work, her mind singularly focused.

I watch as her head cocks to the side, a small smile slipping from her face. "I don't want you to die yet, Bradley; that would end my fun." She places one hook down and holds the other above his face, his eyes crisscrossed watching. "Let's see if this kills you." She brings the hook down, stabbing it into his eye with a satisfying squelch. He bites his tongue so no screams are to be heard. Not reacting in the way Serena was hoping for, she brings the hook, and eye, out. She repeats with his other eye, and this time he screams, giving us both a satisfied smile. "Oh, you're still alive; goody! What shall we do next?" She drops the bloodied eyeball hooks to the ground and walks back to my workbench, ready to choose her next weapon.

He starts coughing up blood. I grimace, knowing he's close to meeting the grim reaper. I walk over to Serena, and whisper in her ear, making her jump, "He's close to death." She glances behind me and sees his eyelids fluttering, his breath stuttering in his chest. The last thing she grabs is the knife I use to end my little lamb's lives.

She looks at me and smiles, knowing exactly what it is because of her dreams. "Let's end him, together." I smile at her, resting the blade over his heart. Her hand wraps around mine, her eyes piercing my very soul. We slowly push into his chest, the skin giving under the sharp steel. I hear him start gurgling, but we never look. We stare at one another, blood covering her hair and face. I stood behind her a couple times, so I can only imagine how much blood is on me.

I cup her cheek with my free hand. She nuzzles into my touch, and I bring my lips to hers. The kiss tastes metallic, but it is sweet and she and I crave more. Our hands leave the blade, fingers dancing along one another's skin. I pick her up and set her on the table next to a lifeless Bradley, her legs wrapping around my waist, her lips never leaving mine.

Breaking away from the kiss, both breathless and desperate for more, I leave her sitting there and grab pieces of Bradley to chuck into the fire. I grab the saw and break away the other pieces to fit and burn nicely.

Almost all of him is burning now, and Serena comes up behind me with the hooks. She plucks the eyes off and throws each one in, watching them burst after hitting the flame.

We stand there, watching as he turns to ash. Our bodies glued to one another, her suit, that was always too big for her, starting to sag from the weight of the blood covering her. I take off mine, and she proceeds to do the same.

Throwing both into the fire, I take off my shirt next, her eyes widen and the other side of my vixen comes out to play. She bends down to take off her shorts, her panties slipping off with them.

My breathing accelerates, and my eyes roam over every inch of her succulent naked body. Her pussy, already glistening, begs for me to take it. My eyes reach hers, and I reach down removing the rest of my clothing, my cock springing free.

She looks down, a playful smile spreading across her face.

"Run," I growl, and she takes off into the woods, waiting for me to find her and fuck her.

THIRTY-TWO

SERENA

That was exhilarating.

The rush I felt taking Bradley's life, the rush I'm feeling now running from my fox while waiting for him to catch me, is unlike anything I've ever experienced. I can only imagine the naughty things he's going to do once he does.

I feel a chill hit my naked breasts as I'm running as fast as I can, hearing Aster not far behind.

"You can run from me, little vixen, but no matter where you hide, I *will* find you and when I do, you'll be the one screaming."

I pick up my pace, my heart pounding in anticipation. This is Aster's property; he knows this place better than I ever will. He grew up here. It isn't about *if* he'll find me, it's a matter of *when*. Last time we played this little game, I hid behind a tree, and he still snuck up on me. I need to find a place where I can be hidden, even if he looks there.

I stop to catch my breath, peering into the night sky, the clouds starting to roll in. My eyes have adjusted to the darkness now, but all I see are trees and bushes, places he could get me too easily. Slowly I walk around, looking everywhere around me. Then, up ahead, I see a grand oak tree, one I didn't notice before. One with branches thick and low enough I could climb. *Perfect.*

I sprint to the tree, stopping to look up at the massive trunk.

"I can hear your breaths quickening, my little vixen" Aster taunts.

My heart jumps to my throat. *I don't have much time.* I place one foot on the branch and wrap my hands around a taller one, pulling myself up. I struggle for a second, trying to lift myself, but eventually I haul my ass up. My adrenaline high, I don't even feel when the branches scrape across my skin.

Deciding it isn't high enough, knowing Aster would still be able to see me, I climb higher and higher, until I'm covered by the night and hidden by the branches. With winter approaching, most of the leaves have changed color and fallen, leaving me more exposed than I would like.

I see him before I hear him. *He really is quite stealthy.* "Come out, come out, wherever you are, little vixen. Your fox just wants to play."

I hold my breath, covering my mouth for fear he might hear me, my eyes tracking his every movement.

He stops, looking everywhere but up. "Don't you want to play with your fox?" he teases.

I smile beneath my hands. I do, but this game of hide and seek is too fun to end already.

"I can feel your eyes on me; where are you hiding?" He starts walking around the tree, then to the one next to it, checking behind the towering trunks. "You know I'm going to find you; the longer you hide, the longer you'll be punished."

His promise has me wanting to clench my thighs, but one movement could make my location known. So I ignore it, sucking my lips in to distract from the agony of not relieving some of the ache and desperation. I watch as Aster starts to walk away, proud of myself for staying hidden this long. He thought his threat would make me give myself away, but it didn't. *I'm stronger than he gives me credit for.*

When I can no longer see him, positive he walked somewhere else looking for me, I reach down and rub the sensitive bud that has been screaming at me since the moment we ended Bradley's life.

Something about doing it together made me so horny I could hardly see straight. When I saw his eyes darken, I knew we both wanted the same thing. To fuck, covered in the blood of *our* first victim.

I know it isn't the first victim for either of us, but it is the first we shared together. *The first of many.* He didn't help me torture him, he left all that for me. Which was awfully gentlemanly of him. I wanted to jump his bones right then and there, but I had a life to end first. The sex, no matter how agonizing it was, had to wait. I wanted to share ending his life. I wanted the intimacy of taking his soul with the same knife he ended all his lambs with. It was a special moment, life changing, and after feeling that... I never want to go back to who I once was. *Maybe I can be his partner in crime.* We'd have to change who we kill. No more lambs. No more innocent blood; only those who deserve it or those, like Bradley, that get in our way.

I think about the look in Aster's eyes when he watched me play with Bradley, and I start rubbing my clit faster. I let out a moan, without a care in the world. Completely forgetting about our little game. All I can think about is the sensation between my legs. How good it feels to finally release that ache. I stick a finger inside, coating it with my juices, and start to tease that spot just inside. I start rubbing in a circle, eyes closed, breaths coming faster and faster. *I'm so close.*

"What do you think you're doing?"

I gasp, freezing entirely and looking down at a hungry fox staring up at me. He starts to climb the tree which makes me panic. I quickly climb to the other side and down.

"You think touching what's mine, then running, is going to be beneficial?" I jump down, hearing a thud and knowing Aster has followed. "Your punishment is going to be far worse, little vixen, since you sampled dessert before I could even get a taste."

I steal a glance back, seeing he's right on my trail. Testing my luck, and seeing how far I can push Aster, I stick the finger I was fucking myself with in my mouth and lick my lips. "Delicious."

Darkness enters his eyes, making my heart beat so fast spots dance in my vision. I turn back and pick up speed, only to be tackled to the grass seconds later. He flips me to my back, taking that same finger and puts it in his mouth, sucking hard, moaning at the taste and making me wiggle underneath him. He takes my free hand and pins it above my head.

His erection is pressed to my stomach, as his tongue swirls around my finger. My finger pops out of his mouth, his eyes gleaming in the shrouded light. "Are you ready for your punishment?" he growls, coming down to inhale me.

I try to wriggle out from underneath him, but he presses himself further onto me, trapping me in place. "You thought hiding in a tree meant I wouldn't find you." He grabs my hair, looking at the blood mixed with the silky strands. "At first I didn't think you'd go up, that would be a bold choice for my little vixen, but when I heard your softs pants and moans echoing through the woods-" he grips my hair, making me wince. "-I followed that heavenly sound. When I saw your silhouette in the night sky, reaching down and playing with what's *mine*-." he places the hand that was in my hair around my throat, tightening with every word, a wicked smirk splitting his face. "-I felt possessive."

That was not what I was expecting to come out of his mouth; based on the tone of his voice I thought he would say pissed or betrayed. I am glad to hear that was his feeling, because I feel the same for him. I smile back, a daring look in my eyes.

"Oh yeah?" I taunt. "Show me then."

He smirks, his hand squeezing the life from me.. I thought the action would cause some pain, but all I feel is pleasure from his grip. Controlled. Cherished.

He leans down to whisper in my ear, "You'll regret asking me that."

He takes his hand away from my throat and I take a breath I

didn't realize I needed. He sinks down to my waiting pussy, his lips inches away. Breathing. Teasing. I take a deep breath, his tongue slipping between my lips. Stroking and tasting my clit, stars bursting across the night sky.

His tongue always finds the right spot, the right rhythm. He looks so beautiful feasting on me, his sandy blond hair covered in streaks of blood. I push one hand into his hair, pulling him further in.

"You taste like sin, little vixen."

He slips a finger inside. "Oh, fuck! Yes, just like that." His thrusts start to pick up, and his tongue flicks faster. My legs shake, my orgasm crests. My stomach tightens, my fingers going numb. "Yes! Yes, Aster. Fuck!" I cry out, and just as I'm about to enter bliss, he pulls away.

Just like that my orgasm is ripped away from me. *Bastard.* A devious smile lifts his glistening lips. "I promised you punishment for touching what's mine." His green eyes darken, the blue completely wiped away. "I'm going to bring you to the brink of bliss over and over, and right before you explode, every time, I'm going to stop."

His threat makes me want to be spiteful and touch myself again, I reach down, his eyes tracking the movement, my hand freezing, a cocky grin on his face. I desperately want to give myself what he refuses to give me. I know if I do that, he will just prolong my punishment. He's as petty as me. So I lay there, pretending to be the good girl I'm not, and take it.

He pinches my nipples, and my back arches off the ground, the pain combined with the restrained pleasure sends goose-bumps up and down my arms.

He moves back up my body and lines his cock to my entrance. Placing the tip slowly in, he hisses, "Fuck." He eases himself in, forcing my legs wider. He holds his dick and slowly pulls back out.

Coated in my juices, he places his cock over my clit and starts rubbing up and down. Bringing me right back to the high I was feeling moments ago when I was about to come.

I feel the pressure build back up, and my eyes start to close. "Eyes on me," he demands, and they snap open as he rubs faster. He presses his hand on my stomach, making the pressure climb more. I feel myself about to explode, and his hand and cock disappear once more.

Right when I think it's over, he slams into me making me scream, "Your screams are a sound I never want to stop hearing; your moans a melody I will never grow tired of."

He thrusts in and out, each one harder than the last. The sound of his balls slapping against me are echoing through the night, his pants and moans mixing with mine, disturbing the otherwise silent night.

He circles my clit, pumping faster and faster. I don't let myself hope, afraid my pleasure will be taken from me again. I fight against oblivion, my eyes pinching closed. "Don't hold back; I promise your punishment is over," he says, his thrusts never slowing.

I do as he commands and lightning flashes in the sky as thunder booms overhead. We both explode, and the euphoria I've been denied crashes through me. I feel his balls constricting and emptying inside me. My walls clench around him as rain starts to fall.

The crusted blood on us starts to drip down our head, the rain getting harder and harder. Aster stands up, offering me his hand. We stand hand in hand in the rain, staring at our naked bodies.

He looks like a scene right out of the movie *Carrie*, when pigs' blood is thrown on her. *If he looks like that, I can only imagine what I look like.* Probably the same, but more sinister like *The Grudge*. He brushes my hair out of my face, smashing his lips against mine.

Our tongues dance, and, for a moment, we are just two lovers, covered in blood, kissing in the pouring rain.

"I love you," he breathes against me.

My heart starts beating faster, my eyes start to water. This is the second time he's professed his feelings to me. I feel exactly the same, I wanted to say it back the first time, but with everything happening I couldn't. I look into his eyes and whisper back, "I love you too."

He smashes his lips against mine once more. "I've loved you since the moment I saw you at the bar sipping on your drink, and I love you even more after finishing our first kill together. You bring a different type of darkness into my life I didn't know I was missing. You made this dead heart beat a thousand times over, and it'll only ever beat for you."

Tears fall down my face. The rain mixes with my tears as Aster swipes away the bloody water. He holds his hand on my cheek and kisses me sweetly. Tenderly. A kiss filled with so much love, trust, and acceptance it makes my toes curl.

The rain starts to pelt harder, breaking our kiss.

I shout over the storm, "We should probably go back."

He grabs my hand and runs us back to the house, our feet splashing mud everywhere. Lightning strikes ahead, making me pick up my pace to keep up with him.

By the time we get back to his house, all the blood has washed away, but we're covered in mud and dead leaves.

"We need to shower," I giggle.

He braces his arm above the door, looking down at me, and pressing me against the worn wood. "I could go another round."

I push him away, laughing. "After all that teasing, I don't think I could take another round."

"Oh, you can take it."

I twist the knob, opening the door and dipping under his arm. I try to dash away, but he snatches my arm and freezes, his fingers gripping me with bruising force. I turn to see what he's looking at, spotting the painting of the fox I sold at the flea market sitting in his entryway. My heart feels like it's about to beat out of my chest.

He pushes me behind him, his body tense as all the fun and laughter drips to the floor. "Stay here."

Fuck that; I'm not staying here. Who left this here, how did they get in? Who did I sell this to? The shock of seeing it has blurred my memory of the girl who bought it.

I tiptoe behind Aster as we enter the kitchen. Sitting on the island, picking her nails with a knife, is the beautiful blonde I sold the painting to. Not a drop of jealousy flows through me when seeing her here. I'm more concerned with how she got in unnoticed, Aster has everything set up to notify him when anyone comes onto his property. There wasn't a car parked out front, so she must have walked. I take in her appearance, she's dressed in jeans and a black tank top, her nails matching her shirt with a red glint to them.

"Who the fuck are you, and how did you get into my house?" Aster seethes, teeth clenched.

"You're the girl from the flea market," I whisper, making Aster look between us, anger coursing through his eyes.

"You have five seconds to leave before I kill you," Aster threatens.

She stops picking her nails and looks up, raising a delicate brow in a severe arch. "Awe, is that anyway to speak to your baby sister?"

I stumble back, almost falling to the floor. *I thought Aster was an only child?* I look up at him, finding the same look on his face that's on mine. *Well, Fuck.*

THIRTY-THREE

ASTER

"I don't have a sister," I grit out.

"Yet here I am." She motions to herself.

Who is this girl claiming to be my sister? Mom and Dad were taken away, and, as far as I know, Mom wasn't pregnant at the time. She would have told me. That isn't something she would ever keep from me. My fists clench at my side, my eyes boring into hers.

I study her face, my thoughts nearly too chaotic to focus. Her hair is a light blonde, almost white, and she has brown eyes that kind of look like my dad's, but the shape of my mom's. *That's just coincidence; there's no way she's who she says she is.*

"I know you probably don't believe me, long lost sister and all, so." She reaches behind her, pulling out a piece of paper. "This should convince you." She jumps down off the counter, and I snatch the paper from her, instantly recognizing my mother's handwriting. My hand crushes the corner of the paper crumpling it, as anger, confusion, hurt, swirl through me.

My Little Fox,

I know you haven't heard from us in a long

time. Probably thought we were dead, me and your father. We are not, and I am so sorry for never writing. You see, after we were taken, I wrote you the letter I hope you were given. It was meant to be the last time you heard from me. That wasn't for no reason; you see, a couple weeks after I wrote that, I found out I was pregnant. I was in a state of shock. Your father was locked up. I was locked up. I knew they would never let me keep her; she'd be placed in the system like you. Never knowing who we are, or that she had a big brother. To deal with that, I had to become stronger for both my kids. Your father and I made connections everywhere we could, and when I gave birth, your sister was taken from my arms, I went into a fit of rage. One of our friends calmed me down and said he would find out where she goes and keep eyes on her for me. I asked him to find out where you were and what you were doing. He did, and as you both grew I heard everything from the inside and had him relay it to your father as well. When he found out your sister was snatched from my arms, he killed a guard. That got him sent underground for a while. He never could manage his impulsiveness well. But my companion told me who you became, that you were doing what you were destined for. I am so proud. Then, when your sister came of age, she started to have questions. I didn't want her to know where she came from yet, she was too young to start, but your sister is smarter than she looks. She found out my connection was watching her and almost killed him for it. The only thing that saved him was breaking my trust and telling her who we were. She demanded to know the truth, and he told her everything. She sought me out, and I had my first visitor after eighteen years. Seeing her in person took my breath away. She is so beautiful and looks just like you, with Dad's eyes. She would visit when she could, and my inside contacts let us have private time, where I finally taught her everything I know. The woman before you is your sister, Zephira; she's known as a man eater. She has much to tell you that I can't write, but heed her warning or there will be consequences. I love you so much my little fox.

Mom.

I crush the paper in my hand, throwing it to the ground, angry at my mother for never reaching out. She waited eighteen years to tell me. She should have told me the moment she found out or when I turned eighteen myself.

She didn't.

She waited for this moment. Mom has always been one to plan, to wait patiently; she wasn't spontaneous like Dad. She's methodical. Cunning. The only thing that has changed in my life is Serena. She couldn't possibly know about her though, I'm observant; I know when I'm being watched. I pace in front of

Serena, looking down at the floor, fingers running through my hair.

I didn't know I was being watched though. *Her connection is better than I thought.* When I find out who he is, he's going to pay.

My sister is a serial killer like me, and she happens to be one of the best. I never care to know about other killers since I like to work alone. As long as they don't get in my way, I don't get in theirs. With the Man Eater only going after men, and myself only going after women, I didn't look into them. Turns out, she's my own flesh and blood.

I've always wondered what it would have been like to have a sibling. What it would have been like to grow up, being molded into the person we are today. I was born to be a killer, but my sister; *how did she follow in our parents footsteps?*

I halt my pacing, looking at her once more. *She looks young. Maybe early twenties?* Her eyes show the tortured parts of her soul she tries to hide. *What has she been through to age her so?*

"Believe me now?" she asks, opening my fridge to grab a bottle of water.

"What do you need to tell me that Mom couldn't?"

"Oh, we'll get to that, but first I'd like to get to know my big brother and-" she looks behind me "-your little lamb."

I push Serena further behind me, but she steps around me and holds her hand out. "I'm Serena, but you already knew that. Which means you know I'm *not* his little lamb; I'm his vixen."

Instead of shaking her hand, Zephira pulls her in for a hug and smells her. I snatch her back instantly, putting myself between them once more. My hand tightens around Serena's arm, as jealousy of my sister sniffing her courses through me.

"Oh, I like you. You smell good, and you're spicy, Such a shame. I'm Zephira."

"What's a shame?" Serena asks, sticking her head out.

I wish she would just stay behind me, where she's safe. Zephira may be my sister, but there is something about her I don't trust. My little vixen is too trusting. She trusted me easily, and now she's trusting her. I don't like it.

She ignores Serena's question, a seductive smirk twisting her lips. "Serena, how did you become wrapped up with my brother? Wouldn't you like to sample something a little sweeter?"

"Mom said you're Salem's Man Eater-"

"You're the Man Eater?!" Serena gleefully steps beside me, closer to Zephira, excitement shining in her eyes. *My little vixen really has a thing for serial killers.*

Zephira smirks, stepping closer to Serena. "I am. Have you heard of me?" Zephira teases.

Serena's eyes widen. "Heard of you, try you're my second favorite serial killer. Next to your brother." She starts to fiddle with her hands, her eyes plastered to Zephira's face. "I have this fascination with serial killers, I've been collecting newspapers of The Morbid Monet's since-"

"You have newspapers of my kills?" I ask, looking down, bewilderment shining in my eyes.

She looks up at me, her little brow furrowed, annoyed that I interrupted her, but this is more important. Another way we are connected.

I cup her cheek, her eyes softening. "Serena, I collect those papers, too. A different reason-"

"Another way we're connected," she whispers.

"Hate to interrupt whatever moment you two are sharing, but I was just about to ask your little lamb if she wanted to have a one on one with the Man Eater?" Zephira's eyes darken as she bites her lip, her eyes raking up and down Serena's naked body.

My eye twitches, and teeth grind. *Is she asking what I think she is? Is she hitting on my girl right in front of me? Is my sister gay?*

"N-no thank you, I prefer men." Serena stutters, backing into me.

Zephira shrugs. "Can't hate a girl for trying; you, brother, have impeccable taste."

If she wasn't my sister, she would already be dead. Even looking at my girl has my hand twitching, begging me to choke the life out of her. But she is family, and as much as I hate how she keeps looking at Serena like she's a snack, I can't blame her. We share the same blood, so there is no surprise we share the same taste in women. But Serena is mine, and she needs to back off.

"Stop looking at Serena like you want to taste her and answer the question."

"Oh, but I *do* want to taste her."

My hand tightens around Serena's. My patience is wearing thin. *If this is how she is as an adult, I'm glad we didn't grow up together.*

"Zephira," I say through clenched teeth. It feels weird saying her name as a threat. Not because I haven't threatened women before, but I usually threaten to kill. Except with Serena. My threats to her always end with pleasure.

"You're no fun," Zephira pouts, crossing her arms. "Fine; Mom sent me here to tell you she put a hit on your little girlfriend." My hand falls from Serena's.

I hear Serena gasp behind me, and the anger I've been holding boils over. "She did what?"

"Don't shoot the messenger," she says, walking past us.

Mom put a hit on Serena? Why? How did she even find out about her? I have to protect her; no one, not even my mother, will come between us.

"She said she's been distracting you from who you are and needs to be put down."

"She's not a fucking dog." I feel the vein in my neck throb, and if I clench my jaw any harder, I know I'll break a tooth.

"Never said she was; those were Mom's words." She walks to the front door. "You have a month, then other serial killers from all over are going to come, and they'll keep coming until she's dead." With that she shuts the door and leaves.

They'll have to go through me first; they'll be the ones whose lives end if they even lay a finger on her. I hear Serena's breathing fluctuate, my heart fracturing from her fear.

"Aster…" She clutches her chest, eyes wild in a panic. "I'm scared. I don't want to die."

I grab her face in my hands and guide her eyes to mine, "Breathe Serena; nothing will happen. I won't let it. I will protect you."

"She said they'll keep coming until I'm" she whispers the last word "dead."

I should kill my sister for scaring her like this. I should kill my mother for putting a hit on my girl. She may be the woman who raised me, but she's no longer the most important person in my life. The day she got caught, and then never reaching out, is the day she died in my mind. She has no right to my life. *She will regret doing this to us; that, I promise.*

"We have a month; I will teach you everything I know. You'll move in here." Her eyes widen. *This isn't how I wanted to ask.* "I will train you to protect yourself. Those killers coming for you, will be coming for *us.* I've seen what you can do in your element." I squish her cheeks, making her have a fishy face. "They will be hunted, not the hunters."

She starts crying, but nods her head. Pulling her into me, I brush my hand down her hair. We stay like that until her breathing begins to even out. I lift her up bridal style and carry her to our room. Laying her under the covers, I hold her until she falls asleep.

She is mine, forever and into the next life. I will kill a hundred men, women, everyone to keep her safe. Nothing and no one will ever come between us. She is my vixen, and I am her fox. My mother will rue the day she ever threatened the woman I love.

That is a promise.

To Be Continued…

ACKNOWLEDGMENTS

First and foremost, I want to thank my amazing husband, Nick. He is the reason I get to pursue my dream of being an author. Thank you, my love, words can never express how grateful I am to have you and our son in my life. That you work so hard to support our family and everything I want to do. Thank you for listening to my crazy ideas, and indulging me in the fantasies I created. You said you would read my book one day, even though you don't like to read, and that means so much to me. I love you so much, thank you.

To my alpha readers, Brianna, Savannah, Angelica. Thank you, yall reading my book when it was just the first draft, before the bones really started to snap together, just thank you. Y'all gave me some amazing ideas, really made me think more about the story and where I wanted it to go. Thank you for letting me rattle off my crazy ideas and be excited for what my brain came up with.

My amazing editor Casey, lord where do I start. First, Thank you, I am so grateful the universe brought us together. Out of being my editor I feel I have made a lifelong friend along the way as well. Without your edits, suggestions, input, summary at the end, my book wouldn't be as thought out. Your words helped turn my story into a novel, and I can never thank you enough. The way you treated my book like it was your own book baby; the comments throughout with your reactions, everything you have done, thank you. You are stuck with me now, so until you decide you don't want to edit anymore, which I hope that day never comes; you will be my editor. I love and appreciate you so much!

To my Beta's Rebecca, Carlee, Alex, Ally, Rebecca, Brenna, Megan, and Abi, Thank you. Thank you for wanting to be my Beta's for being so amazing at being them and catching all the mistakes before releasing. Your comments throughout, have made me giggle and blush. The reviews you have left me have warmed my heart and made me cry happy tears. To hear how much you love the story I have created has made me so happy. Y'all are amazing, I am so lucky to have such amazing friends who want to be a part of this journey with me.

Shay, my amazing, kind, and patient cover artist/formatter. Not only did you give my book the cover I could've never dreamed of, that is absolutely perfect and so out of the box like me; You also made the inside just as perfect, choosing the best pictures that represent my characters. Thank you so much for putting up with me, my crazy ideas, and fixing the errors that needed to be corrected. You are amazing, and I hope you know you're stuck with me. Yes, you will be my artist for every book I write because your brain and energy matches mine. Can't wait to work on our next projects together.

Lastly, to all my readers. Wow, thank you for taking a chance on a baby indie author like me. For seeing my book and wanting to pick it up and read it. I always believed in dreams do come true, faith, trust, and pixie dust, and seeing y'all read my book just cements my beliefs. Thank you so much for supporting and following along my author journey. I hope you stay on this ride with me, to see what else madness my brain creates.

ABOUT THE AUTHOR

Katelynn is a stay at home mom, who spends her day playing with her son and six dogs. When she isn't working on her next book, she spends her time reading all things smut, watching tv with her family, and making the best memories. She has a small business making satin ribbon roses as well, and loves making them for customers. She loves all things spooky, especially Pennywise. She loves Disney, anime, and Elvis. She is an Aquarius, who was born and raised in sunny California, but has made a life with her family in North Carolina. She has always dreamed of being an author, but her passion died off long ago, but was reignited through trauma; and in the darkness beauty was created.

9 798991 652414